CLICKING HER HEELS

Lucy Hepburn, never one to pass a shoe shop without the briefest of glances, has aspirations to be as famous as her on-screen idol with whom she shares a surname. Initially this was to be achieved on the ballet stage but the rigours of training and a liking for getting down and diva-ish on the dance floor diverted her from that path.

Having written humorous short stories and character sketches to keep her friends amused at work, she decided it was time to put an end to the email distractions and wrote *Clicking Her Heels* to entertain them in the evenings instead.

Lucy loves nothing more than browsing a magazine for the shoe ads that promise a life a good six inches above one's normal expectations.

Visit www.AuthorTracker.co.uk for exclusive updates on Lucy Hepburn.

LUCY HEPBURN

Clicking Her Heels

AVON

AVON

A division of HarperCollins*Publishers*
77–85 Fulham Palace Road,
London W6 8JB

www.harpercollins.co.uk

A Paperback Original 2007

Copyright © Working Partners 2007

Lucy Hepburn asserts the moral right to
be identified as the author of this work

A catalogue record for this book is
available from the British Library

ISBN: 978-1-84756-036-0

Set in Minion by Palimpsest Book Production Limited,
Grangemouth, Stirlingshire

Printed and bound in Great Britain by
Clays Ltd, St Ives plc

Mixed Sources
Product group from well-managed
forests and other controlled sources
www.fsc.org   Cert no. SW-COC-1806
© 1996 Forest Stewardship Council
FSC

With special thanks to Erica Munro

The average person walks the equivalent of four and a half times round the earth in a lifetime.

They're going to need a lot of shoes.

PROLOGUE

Saturday, early morning, and twenty-four-year-old Amy Marsh was running through her checklist, trying to keep a lid on her mounting excitement.

OK – purse, phone, Oyster Card – check.

A–Z – check.

Bus and tube maps – check.

Morning sunshine peeked in and winked at her through the slats of the wooden blinds in the third-floor flat she shared with her boyfriend, Justin.

Lip gloss – check.

Bottle of water – check.

Justin was still asleep, exhausted after larging it into the small hours at some hip PR party he'd organised for one of his new bands. Amy was glad. Had he been up he'd only tease her about how she got more excited about these missions than she ever did about going out on dates with him.

'Huh, that's not true,' she'd murmured.

Sensible shoes – NO WAY!

She looked down at her feet and smiled.

'Or is it?'

The blue denim Gucci wedges she'd bought for a song off the Internet a couple of months before looked stunning, as well as adding three much-needed inches to her five-foot-two frame. If she paced herself, they would easily carry her round the streets for a day. Well, at least they would if she took a bus or two along the way.

Then she caught sight of her reflection in the mirror, studying the young woman who looked back at her with a quizzical shrug. Her dark brown hair swung glossily around her shoulders, her pale skin looked fresh and clear, and her hazel eyes glittered with anticipation.

Not bad, I guess.

Comb – check.

Eyeliner – check – no, forget that, I'm fine with just the touch I've got on already.

She wore a crisp, sleeveless white top and her favourite skinny jeans, the pale blue bottom-hugging ones that flattered her figure. Then, as a final thought before skipping out of the Victorian apartment building to catch the tube, she pulled off the chunky wooden bangle that was knocking annoyingly against her watch.

After all, she smiled to herself, when it comes to shoe shopping, there's no room for distractions . . .

Thirty minutes later she was standing in a gorgeous shoe shop in Covent Garden with Debbie and Jesminder, her best friends from aclickaway.com, the Internet travel company where they worked.

Amy dug Jesminder in the ribs. 'Over there,' she hissed. 'Green snakeskin mules third shelf down.'

Jesminder looked and frowned. 'Hmm, do you think? Aren't they a bit flimsy?'

'*Flimsy?*' Amy echoed in disgust. 'Outright drop-dead gorgeous, I think you mean.'

Jesminder tilted her head to one side, taking another long look. 'Do I? Well, they just don't look very easy to walk in, that's all.'

Debbie, tall and curvy, her long blonde hair freshly highlighted and styled in a shaggy knot at the nape of her neck, called over her shoulder, 'OK, where did you say you were off to tonight again?'

Amy coloured. 'Um, well, actually, I didn't . . .'

Now was the time to come clean, she guessed. It was bad enough keeping it a secret from Justin, but she should be able to tell her friends.

'Jes, *hello?* It's Amy we're talking about here!' said Debbie, not noticing Amy's unease. 'It's *flat* shoes you want to be worrying about her walking in . . . well, *hubba hubba*! Good morning, curiously alluring stranger!' She had a loud, carrying voice, the confident Geordie accent undiminished by her three years of working in London.

'Pardon?' Jesminder looked lost.

Debbie turned round, huge-eyed and grinning. 'Over there, by the window – top-totty alert.'

A tall, well-built man dressed in baggy jeans and a donkey jacket was checking out patent leather boots by the exit.

Amy sidled over to Debbie, stood on tiptoe and put

5

her mouth close to her friend's ear. 'Sorry, Debbie, but take another look. Top-totty girlfriend alert, moving in from stage right – funny how girlfriends can sense when their men are being ogled.' A frighteningly skinny blonde woman had just joined the man and threaded her arm through his. She glowered briefly at Debbie.

Debbie tutted in disgust and tossed her head. 'Ah, well – his loss! Onward and upwards. Plenty more where that came from.'

'Now, Debbie,' Amy said firmly, planting a hand on her friend's shoulder, 'will you please at least make *some* sort of pretence of being interested in today's mission? I need to find new shoes for tonight, remember?'

'No promises,' Debbie replied sulkily. 'But I'll try, if you insist.'

'That's my girl. I do insist. Men and shoe shopping simply don't mix, whichever way you look at it. Priorities!'

Debbie frowned, removing Amy's hand. 'You've been with the same man for too long, Amy Marsh. Some of us are still browsing.'

Amy quickly scanned Debbie's face to see whether her feelings were hurt. They clearly weren't. 'Fair point,' she said, 'but might I just suggest that if you're on the lookout for available straight men then there are better places to start your search than women's shoe shops?'

Debbie shrugged, acknowledging the point before returning her attention to the shoes.

'Men are very good in the field of sports shoe design,' Jesminder put in thoughtfully and irrelevantly.

Both Amy and Debbie turned and gave her blank looks.

'It's true. Ergonomics, aerodynamics, moulded arch support. The technological advances have been unbelievable over the last few years.'

Amy and Debbie continued gazing at their superfit friend, who ran triathlons for fun. Well, ran, swam and cycled, to be precise. Her lean, toned body was testament to a lifetime of fitness, yet she wore her athleticism lightly, referring to herself as 'scrawny' and 'gristly'.

Jesminder continued, 'You've no idea the foot-health benefits that can be obtained from a properly cushioned and supported sports shoe.'

'Well,' Amy said after a respectful moment, 'thanks, Jes. I'll certainly bear all that closely in mind. Right then, where were we? Ah, yes – *stilettos!*'

She never did get round to telling her friends where she was heading that night.

CHAPTER ONE

'Salmon?' Amy gasped, her heart plummeting at the sight that greeted her upon opening the washing-machine door later that day. 'Who on earth wears salmon?'

From rescuing the very first pink garment from what ought to have been the whites (delicate) programme, she realised that Justin had done a 'Spectacular'. Salmon pants, salmon gym socks, salmon bra, salmon satin slip, and, most heartbreakingly of all, the salmon Whistles blouse she had planned to wear that night. Snowy-white, it had been, just an hour before.

With a little wail, she delved deeper into the machine, eventually yanking out the culprit – Justin's brand-new, dark pink Marc Jacobs shirt. She held it aloft in disgust, gesturing at the havoc it had wrought upon her precious white delicates, as though expecting it somehow to shrug and apologise. Honestly, why did Justin have to pick today to have a go at being domesticated?

Amy sighed, gathering up the ruined blouse and

carrying it, along with the Marc Jacobs shirt, cere-moniously through to the sitting room.

Oblivious to her dramatic entrance, Justin stood with his back to her. He was facing the window with its views over Finchley and Muswell Hill, talking animatedly into his mobile and making emphatic, Italian-ish gestures with his free hand.

'Yup . . . no problem. Absolutely, bring them along; it'd be great to meet them. About eight? Yup . . . yup . . . gig starts around nine thirty, so once I've sorted the meet and greet, and distributed the press releases, the boys'll be good to go . . . yup, limo's arranged . . . yup . . .'

Despite her anger about his laundry malfunction, Amy couldn't stop the tiny smile that caught the side of her mouth at the sight of her boyfriend. Six years her senior, Justin Campbell, self-made rock-music PR whiz, was looking decidedly fit this evening. With his designer stubble, pretty-darned-perfect gym-toned body and short, dark brown hair, there was something of the Ashton Kutcher – or no, even better, something of the young George Clooney – about him. Impeccably dressed in his Armani shirt, Daks trousers and those sub-zero Moschino sneakers (the chocolate-brown, round-toed ones with the suede details that shrieked 'fantastic taste!' to anyone who knew the tiniest thing about footwear), he was obviously reeling in some new contact or other with his consummate communica-tion skills and charm. Amy liked that about him; his easy confidence was the perfect foil to her more reserved temperament. But she had also come to know his vulnerable side, his need to be needed, for constant reassurance . . .

Whatever, he wasn't going to Clooney his way out of this one. She cleared her throat, and Justin whipped round. When he saw her face, he put his hand over the mouthpiece and said under his breath, 'Just a minute, Abe . . .' He usually called her Abe, as an affectionate compromise between Amy and babe, and Amy had yet to decide whether or not it annoyed her. Right at this moment, it *totally* did. Cheeky git!

She responded by gesturing first to the salmon silk blouse, then to the Marc Jacobs shirt, slapping her palm against her forehead, tossing the garments onto the leather sofa and, finally, planting her hands on her hips. She knew Justin was unlikely to be unduly intimidated by the sight of his bathrobe-clad girlfriend in the early stages of a full-on strop but, still, he could consider himself warned.

'Yup . . . twenty-eight thousand sold so far for the whole tour . . . yup, six and a half tonight . . . venue's got a really good vibe . . .'

And on he went. He turned again to look at her, appraising the situation with brown eyes that were ever so slightly crinkly when he smiled. But then he ruined it all. He *winked*.

Despairing, Amy shook her head. Had she never told him that she didn't trust winkers? Was he being deliberately provocative?

However, she was at a distinct disadvantage right now, barefoot and tiny, enveloped in her white fluffy bathrobe. She supposed she could let it drop to the floor and get his full attention that way, but given that he didn't currently deserve that option (besides, there wasn't time), she decided just to tut loudly, go and find something else to wear, and give him hell as soon as he deigned to get off his mobile and come to find out what was up.

'Tomorrow,' she muttered to herself as she stomped down the hall, 'I shall show that prehistoric man how to sort a washing load. Honestly, what did Phyllis teach him when she was bringing him up?'

Just then their landline rang. Amy padded over to the hall table and picked it up.

'Hello?'

As though summoned by mere thought, it was Phyllis, Justin's mum. Of course, there was a good chance it'd be her as it must have been, oh, a full three hours since her last call.

'Amy, is that you?' came Phyllis's thin, clear voice. Phyllis always asked Amy if it was her. *Who else would it be?* But still, Amy loved her. Having lost both her parents – her father in a car accident twelve years ago and her mother barely two years ago to breast cancer – Amy found that she often craved the older woman's company, even though she could be a little exasperating at times. Amy glanced nervously at her watch. She really didn't have a lot of time, but neither did she have the heart to make her excuses and hang up. So, crossing her fingers that the call would be brief, she smiled down the line and confirmed that yes, it was indeed she.

'Can I come up, Amy dear?'

Phyllis lived in the lower-ground-floor flat in the same building, an arrangement that had come about when Phyllis announced out of the blue to Justin the year before that she was, to all intents and purposes, moving in. Amy could see why it would be lovely for her. Phyllis's house in Kent was too big for her now she was on her own, and a number of her friends had either died or moved away. Yet it had been a bit daunting for Amy to imagine her living in the same building. But then, after the initial surprise had worn off and Amy started to think of the benefits of having Phyllis so close by – a shopping companion, a friend to chat with when Justin was away on tour, a babysitter (OK, this was thinking far too far ahead!) – she warmed to the idea and, in fact, things had turned out just fine.

'Oh, Phyllis, I'm really sorry, but Justin and I are off out this evening,' Amy replied. 'Well, I mean, we're off out separately, but whatever, we won't be in. Can I maybe pop down and catch you tomorrow morning? Scrounge a coffee?'

Phyllis didn't seem to hear. 'Amy dear, you know those putty-coloured linen trousers I was telling you about a while ago?'

'Oh, yes,' Amy fibbed, furrowing her brow.

'The ones in Next.'

'Of course I do. You look great in them!' I'm definitely busking it now, Amy thought guiltily.

'What?' Phyllis queried. 'But I haven't bought them yet. Maybe I told you they were cream, not putty? Well, more a biscuity beige, veering into a kind of taupe?'

'Ri-ight?'

'I've hidden them!'

'You haven't!' Amy grimaced and rubbed her forehead. No, please – not another attempt to beat the retail system. Only last week Phyllis had scored a replacement sweater in Marks & Spencer after accidentally snipping a hole in the original one when she was cutting the label off, then distressing the hole so that it looked like it had unravelled of its own accord. 'Phyllis, you'll get caught one of these days!'

'I have! They've only got one size twelve left, so I've stashed it behind the eighteens! Smaller ladies never rake that far back in those long rails, trust me.'

'Too right they don't,' Amy agreed, recalling the times shop assistants had pointed her towards the petites in disdain when she dared to touch some gorgeous item of clothing in the *grown-up* section. 'But why didn't you just, well, *buy* them?' she queried. Phyllis was, after all, comfortably off, having run her own bookkeeping business for over twenty years before she retired.

'Because they'll be in the sale next week, of course. Don't tell me you'd forgotten? I thought the two of us could go and have a look on the first day when the shop opens at seven? Mmm? Before work? They'll be half price!' Then, in a lower, conspiratorial tone: 'You can borrow them for work sometimes, if you like – oh, but then I don't suppose we're the same size. Hmm, well, if you wear a belt and heels, maybe?'

Amy played with the end of her dressing gown cord and murmured, 'That's a lovely idea, thank you.'

Phyllis's world hadn't always been small. It caught Amy in a deep, melancholy way that now it consisted mainly of searching for bargains, searching for her wayward cat with its prodigious vagabonding habit, and searching for reasons to ring up her only son, four floors above. And Amy, with precious few links to anyone else of Phyllis's generation, didn't really mind.

Justin, in the sitting room, was at last wrapping up his call. A wave of 'yup . . . great . . . yup . . .' assailed Amy's subconscious as Phyllis talked on.

These days Phyllis wore sensible shoes. Comfortable shoes. Footgloves, nubuck loafers, Clarks easy-fit sandals, and flat pumps for her fortnightly trips to play bridge in a decaying hotel in Greenwich. Once, Amy mused, Phyllis might have worn scandalous shoes. Dancing shoes. But not now. Today, Phyllis's shoes took her round the shops, and home again. Amy's passion for mapping people's lives according to their shoes had a habit of being spookily accurate.

'Phyllis, you're a star,' she said. 'I'd love to come to the Next sale with you next week. Seven o'clock it is. Uh-oh, we'll need to be up before six.' Amy realised that she didn't even know which branch of Next Phyllis was talking about and, flushing with guilt, resolved to spend more time with her in future. 'Those trousers have obviously got your name on them, and we'll make sure you get them.'

More than anything, Amy silently wished that she were talking about shopping trips with her own mother right now, rather than dear, lonely Phyllis, as lovely as she was. But there wasn't time to get all emotional.

'Tell you what,' Amy chirped, after a longish interval, 'I'll borrow those trousers for work if you wear my turquoise Christian Louboutin wedges on Christmas Day. OK? Deal or no deal?'

Phyllis chuckled on the other end of the line, just as Justin emerged into the hall, pocketing his mobile. He sought Amy out, sliding his arms around her waist from behind and nuzzling his face into her collarbone.

'I've never known such a girl for shoes!' Phyllis laughed down the line. 'High heels? Do you want to send me to my grave?'

Both women felt the full force of the dreadful pause that followed. Unwelcome tears pricked Amy's eyes.

'I'm sorry, Amy,' Phyllis said after a few moments. 'How clumsy of me.'

'It's fine, really,' Amy gulped as Justin, listening in, hugged her tight.

'Anyway, you have a lovely night, all right?' Phyllis went on.

'I will,' Amy whispered. 'Thanks.'

'And tell that son of mine he must be working far too hard if he's leaving you to go out on your own rather than taking you somewhere nice.'

'I hear you, Ma,' Justin mumbled, from deep in the hollow above Amy's collarbone.

'Bye, Phyllis,' Amy said, not trusting herself to say more.

'Goodbye, dear.'

Replacing the receiver, Amy wriggled out of Justin's embrace and turned to face him. She clasped his shoulders, took a deep breath, and eased him into an upright position, fixing him with the sternest glower she could muster. Justin couldn't help giving a little snort of laughter, which he unsuccessfully tried to disguise as a coughing fit. He smelled nice, though. Luckily for him.

'I'm sorry,' he spluttered after a few moments, 'but you are even cuter when you're cross.'

Amy drew back further, narrowed her eyes and raised a single eyebrow. An old trick, to be sure, but an absolute killer when it came to all things Justin.

'I appear to be in the doghouse,' he ventured. 'Don't tell me the colour's run on the Marc Jacobs?'

Amy nodded.

'Sheez, I hope it hasn't faded out too much . . .' He stopped when Amy whacked him. 'Ooyah! OK, I apologise. I'm sorry I turned your shirt pink. I shall never go near the washing machine again.'

'That's not the solution I had in mind,' Amy replied primly, stroking the fabric of her newly salmoned blouse. His flippancy was beginning to grate. 'This blouse is ruined and I wanted to wear it this evening. Not to mention my knickers.'

'That's a shame,' Justin smirked. 'I *was* just about to mention those.'

'Could you please at least pretend you're concentrating on my crisis?' Amy complained, capturing Justin's wrists just as his hands began to travel down her body.

'Spoilsport. OK, well, the blouse, let me think. Maybe I could dunk it in some bleach?'

It was impossible to tell if he was serious or not.

'I'm sorry?' Amy exclaimed. 'Justin Campbell, did you just say the word "dunk" within twenty yards of my beautiful clothes? Would you ever *dunk* your precious threads in a bucket of Domestos?'

Bingo. An arrow to the heart. She may as well have asked: 'Would you please jump off the balcony onto the concrete thirty feet below?'

Finally, he looked abashed. He freed his hands from her grip and laid them on her shoulders. 'Come on, gorgeous, let me help you find something else to wear tonight. Tell you what, you can put on a fashion show, and I'll be Simon Cowell . . .'

Amy awarded him a filthy look.

'OK then, I'll be Simon Cowell without the rude comments and dodgy strides.' He led her through to the rumpled tranquillity of their bedroom, and flung open Amy's double wardrobe doors.

It concealed an impressive collection. Not that much of it was particularly flash – Amy's salary was definitely more High Street than Bond Street – but she'd made some impressive finds in Camden Market and Portobello Road over the past few years, and was secretly very proud of her bargain-hunting prowess. Justin, on the other hand, who could afford designer clothes a little more regularly than Amy's once-in-a-blue-moon splurges, owned an immaculate capsule collection of casual work wear, which, for a straight bloke, was scarily tasteful.

'Where is it you're off to tonight again?' he asked, stroking his stubble.

Amy turned and made a show of riffling through

the rail. 'Erm, just to the pub. With Jes. Shouldn't be too late back.' Slowly, guiltily, she risked a glance round. Thank goodness he wasn't scrutinising her face; wasn't aware of her lie.

Justin nodded. 'OK, so no fancy gear, then?'

Colouring further, Amy breathed, 'No, erm, I guess not. Nothing fancy.'

Before long she had tried on, and rejected, about seven different outfits. Silently she cursed her small frame. *Come on!* she snarled at the rail. *I need elegant! Womanly! A bit of a chest!* Nothing was right and Justin by now was lounging on the bed, unhelpful, mentally co-ordinating his own big night and paying little attention to her travails. Which should have been a blessing but, still, Amy found herself stung that he wasn't being a bit more contrite, having just wrecked an entire drumful of her clothing.

'Thanks, Justin, I'd never manage to get ready without you,' she muttered sarcastically, tossing an Indian silk scarf towards the pile of discarded clothing and 'missing', draping it over Justin's face instead.

'Sorry, Abe, I was miles away.' He leaped up and surged over to her clothing rail. 'OK, pub night, yeah?' He twisted his face. 'Well, that's a no-brainer, isn't it?' He plunged a hand into the wardrobe and pulled out her bootleg Miss Sixtys in triumph. 'These!' he beamed. Then he surged into the rail once more. 'With this!'

Amy was aghast. Now he was holding out her old black polo-neck jumper.

'And some trainers!' he went on. 'You've got some

19

reasonably clean trainers in that shoe emporium of yours, haven't you? Job done!'

'I . . .' Stumped, Amy did not know how to respond.

'Well, what else would you wear to the pub?' Justin went on. 'You don't want your fancy stuff coming back stinking of beer, do you?'

Amy had to concede his logic, even though she knew that his subtext was: 'You, Amy Marsh, will go out tonight in the equivalent of a burka, and nobody will hit on you . . .' however little he was prepared to admit it.

Still, in a last-minute save, she had her answer. 'Justin, don't be daft. I can't go out in jeans and a jumper in June! I'll melt into a puddle.'

'But—'

'Listen, you,' Amy went on, firmly. 'I am *not* Natasha, OK?' She eased him towards her. 'OK?' she repeated, pulling him closer still. She experienced a momentary twinge of guilt – but really she was doing nothing wrong, not really.

'I know,' he mumbled, stooping and burying his face in her shoulder again.

'I will not cheat on you, have you got that?'

'Goddit,' came from somewhere around her clavicle.

'I'm going to wear something nice and cool, and when I come home, you can help me to take it off, OK?'

She felt his body relax. 'Man, you make me do everything round here, don't you?' he growled, not unsexily.

Released, Amy swiftly slipped into her coral silk vest, and pulled the matching sheer chiffon blouse on top.

The only thing to team with that was the chocolate suede Zara pencil skirt – despite the heat outside – so on it went, leaving only one more decision to be made.

The shoes.

CHAPTER TWO

Shoes entailed a short trip to the walk-in closet in the hall, the one most normal people use for suitcases and vacuum cleaners and ironing boards.

But this one was, as Justin had said, an emporium, a grotto, a shrine, a veritable sanctuary, a private working museum of all things footwear. It was Amy's mother ship.

Amy collected shoes like other people collected photographs, or bundles of letters, or life lessons. Each pair had been chosen with care, with love, with reason, with style – and almost every pair could pinpoint something special in her past, her present, and maybe, just maybe, might hold out the promise of something in her future.

For these weren't just shoe boxes for Amy; they were little treasure chests. Thirty-four of them to be precise. Yes, they contained wonderful leather smells, intricate stitching, supple straps, glorious heels . . . but the real treasure was the emotions, the memories, the turning-points that had somehow attached themselves to these tangible objects, making them such a vital part of Amy's life.

Each box meticulously displayed either a digital printout picture or a glossy Polaroid photograph of its contents. There, look! There were the black Prada sling-backs – if only the suede skirt had been black, not brown, those would have been perfect for tonight! And there, the knee-length Gucci boots, bargain of the century from that nice Greek man in Portobello Road – briefly Amy longed for the evening to be cooler so that she could wear them . . .

A galaxy of beautiful colours and styles was show-cased on these pictures, *boasting* of the treasure within each box. From pale peppermint to Moroccan amber, there was no footwear emergency that couldn't be catered for by a visit to Amy's shoe closet – provided, of course, that the circumstances permitted the wearing of high heels.

Amy paused, allowing the closet door to half close with her inside, switched on the light and breathed deeply, seizing a moment of sanctuary to try to calm her jangled nerves.

Cautiously, almost timidly, she traced her hand down the tiers of shoe boxes, scanning the photographs. There were the little espadrilles she bought in Majorca on that last holiday with her mother. And there – the gorgeous bronze Gina mules, practically the only pair of shoes she'd ever paid full price for, but worth every hard-earned, beans-on-toast-for-weeks-after penny. Oh! The red pumps – her ruby slippers! The photo of these showed not just the shoes, but Amy, four years ago, spinning round at a party chanting 'There's no place like home' over and over; Justin would think it totally childish but she smiled at the memory.

And there – in the middle tier, halfway down, was the little blank box that would make her cry if she so much as touched it.

She stretched out her hand.

'You reached Narnia yet?' came Justin's voice from just outside the door, making her jump back to reality and jerking her into a decision. Those Michael Kors brown slingback sandals would be absolutely fine – balancing the heavy suede of the skirt and adding just a tiny sparkle with the diamanté buckles. The heels were less than three inches, which wasn't ideal, but they'd at least give some extra height without arousing Justin's suspicions. Sorted.

Briefly, regretfully, she glanced at the box containing the newest addition to her collection: today's purchase, the fabulous green snakeskin mules she'd spied when she'd walked into that first shoe shop with Debbie and Jesminder. Usually she couldn't wait to wear new shoes the moment she got them home, but tonight, alas, if Justin saw her teetering out of the apartment on four inches of green snakeskin sexiness, he'd smell a rat for sure.

She touched the lid of the box. *Not tonight, my pretties* . . .

'Will I do?' she asked a little nervously, twirling in front of Justin, who was shrugging on his jacket and getting ready to leave as well.

'You look great,' he answered, letting his eyes move

all the way down her body and back up again. 'Be careful out there. And . . . em . . . have a nice time. Shame we're going in opposite directions so we can't share a cab.'

'Mmm,' Amy replied, trying to sound as though she agreed.

'See you in bed,' he whispered as he passed.

'Yup. Hope it goes well for you tonight,' she replied over her shoulder.

'Always does, Abe, always does,' came, ever fainter, from the stairwell.

Once he was gone, Amy breathed deeply to try to dissipate the deep crimson colour in her cheeks. After a few moments her hands had stopped shaking enough to allow her to apply some Juicy Tube gloss in Marshmallow, and, after a last quick, guilty check in the mirror, she was done.

Hmm, not bad for a twenty-four-year-old fibber, she thought, as her mobile bleeped, signalling that her taxi was waiting downstairs.

The fact was that these evenings, these covert, deceitful evenings, were what had really put the spring back in Amy's step since the death of her mother, and as the taxi pulled away towards the West End Amy's guilt gave way to mounting anticipation. Life wasn't bad on the whole, but, Amy mused, as the city glided by outside, it was definitely a bit short on spark these days. She'd held the same job since leaving uni, and whilst she enjoyed it most of the time, well, surely the world of work held greater challenges?

Amy's nerves at the evening ahead grew as the taxi idled in a long queue at traffic lights.

And what of Justin – how could anyone not find Justin Campbell exciting? This handsome, clever man with the best taste in shoes of any man Amy had ever known, this man she'd met only a year and a half ago . . .

She'd been standing in the packed auditorium halfway through the warm-up band's set. Pushing her way through the gyrating crowd to the back doors, she felt as if her head was about to implode from the drilling sound of electric guitar. Crashing through the doors into the cool bar area, she collided with the most gorgeous guy she'd ever seen. And he smelled great too.

'Hey, steady on, missy! Is something the matter?'

'Oh, sorry, but it's so hot in there, and the band's so loud, I need to clear my head . . . oh . . .'

'Careful, now – here, let me help. You nearly fainted.'

'No, no, just stumbled. I'll be fine after some fresh . . .'

'Come on, you're coming with me . . . Excuse me, guys, got a bit of a damsel/distress/shining-armour situation brewing here. Mind if I abandon you to the hordes? Cheers. Right, let's go upstairs.'

'Upstairs?'

'Yup, VIP suite. Got air conditioning, lots of space, and some great big sofas.'

'Em . . . the VIP suite?'

'For you to recover. Oh, don't worry; I'll kick Bono off the sofa. That got you smiling! Must be a good sign.'

'You're being very kind, thank you . . . ?'

'Justin.'

'Thank you, Justin.'

'You're welcome. . . ?'

'Amy.'

Now, glancing at her watch, it was touch and go whether she'd make it on time. Amy closed her eyes as the taxi pushed its way towards Covent Garden. She hated lying to Justin.

At last, the taxi drew up outside the Royal Opera House. Amy searched the sea of beautiful faces, trying to pick him out, as a doorman bustled forwards to open the cab door for her.

Stepping out, Amy felt like a movie star. She forgot all about Justin.

The foyer was filled with flowers and chatter.

And there, there he was.

Sergei.

CHAPTER THREE

'Well, what do you think so far?' Sergei asked as he led her out of the auditorium during the interval. Americanised, his voice still carried the richness and depth of his beloved Russia. They hadn't had time to talk properly since dashing in to catch the first act.

'Oh, I can hardly speak!' Amy breathed. 'It's so perfect! Those costumes! The music, it's so full of joy, don't you think? And isn't Darcey Bussell just a genius? She makes it look as though she isn't really trying; she just *dances*, doesn't she?' Then, catching herself, she glanced up at Sergei. 'I mean, that's what it looks like to me – I forgot I was talking to a mega-genius world-famous choreographer for a moment. What's your verdict, Sergei? Thumbs up or down?' Finally she stopped and bit her lip. For someone who could hardly speak, she seemed to have just had something of a breakthrough.

Sergei waved away the compliment, then thrust his arms out and planted both thumbs firmly up.

'I think it is an extremely good production so far,'

he replied. 'Excellent, in fact. I am so glad you think so too. Shall we have a drink?'

The bar was already crowded, noisy, hot and swimming with a potent mix of expensive perfumes, and a heady theatrical buzz. Beautiful, confident people mingled with even more beautiful, even more confident people, and Amy shrank back a little as she moved towards the bar, clutching Sergei's arm. It felt firm and strong under her hand. When would she ever feel that she belonged at places like this, as these people obviously did? So sure of themselves – so 'solid in their shoes', as her mother used to say.

Sergei always seemed to cause a stir at the ballet, Amy mused, as all around them people nodded greetings in his direction and hustled out of their path. He was still very handsome, with his strong ex-dancer's body, and his dark hair only lightly flecked with silver, and more than once Amy had to stifle an immature giggle as the words 'Baron', 'Von' and 'Trapp' swam in and out of her brain when she looked up at him. She reckoned he was about forty-four, and he had gorgeous, twinkly eyes and a special brand of transatlantic exuberance that was hard to describe but delicious to experience.

And his effect on women was nothing short of remarkable. Most of the females in the place seemed to greet him with such full-on, kissy-kissy enthusiasm that in a strange way Amy quite enjoyed the cold looks they bestowed upon her moments later.

'Thank you,' she said, accepting the glass of cool white wine.

'So,' Sergei began, 'how have you been? I have missed you.'

'Great, thanks,' Amy replied. 'Bit of a nightmare getting out of the flat tonight . . .'

'Oh?'

'Well, it was nothing, really, just a bit of a disaster with the washing machine, nothing important.' She could have kicked herself. Here she was, standing in the Royal Opera House with the most distinguished-looking man in the place, whom she hadn't seen for ages, talking about her sodding washing machine! She shot a glance round the room. *Honestly, why am I such a moron?*

But Sergei, ever the gentleman, replied, 'Oh dear, how inconvenient for you. But I am so glad you are here.'

Amy felt the beginnings of a blush creeping around her hairline. 'So, how long are you in London for?' she asked quickly.

'Not so long, I am afraid,' he replied as they ascended the stairs. 'I go to China tomorrow. Just for a short while and then I return to the States in a few weeks.'

Amy nodded. 'Well, it's lovely of you to make time to see me,' she said, giving his arm a squeeze.

He gave her a strange look. 'How could I not?' he asked, his eyes flashing, before covering the look with a smile of heart-melting warmth.

A pause followed, and Amy took a large gulp from her wine glass. She was grateful for the extra height afforded by her shoes, knowing from past experience that flat shoes in a noisy crowded room, for a small

31

person, meant only two things: instant deafness, and a sore neck from craning upwards all the time. Plus, as ever, her beloved heels imparted an injection of confidence that just might get her through the evening without her making a *complete* idiot of herself.

'I'm off to the Isle of Wight Festival at the weekend,' she announced, suddenly inspired with the thought that she could ratchet up her self-esteem by nailing 'music' and 'travel' in a single sentence.

'Really?' Sergei replied. 'With whom?'

Is that a slight edge to his voice? Amy wondered, before immediately dismissing the thought.

'Oh, with my two best mates, Debbie and Jes – should be brilliant!'

'Any chance that I might know any of the bands that will be there?' he asked.

Amy bit her lip. 'Um, well, I'm not sure – how about Foo Fighters?'

Sergei shook his head.

'Coldplay?'

'Is that a name, or are you asking me a question?'

'The Kooks?'

'Kooks? With a K? As in, David Bowie?' He seemed chuffed to have made a connection.

Amy frowned. 'David Bowie? Not sure, could be – I think they named themselves after some song from years and years ago.'

'It has to be! David Bowie, *Hunky Dory* – "Kooks" is one of the best tracks on it! Nineteen seventy-one!' He punched the air, looking as though he was about to launch into the song, only to elbow a passing waiter, narrowly avoiding knocking the wine tray from his hands while upending his own wine glass all down his front in the process. Amy gasped.

'Oh, I am – what do you call it? – a klutz,' he muttered, shaking wine droplets from his trouser leg.

'Let me help,' Amy flustered, grabbing a bunch of paper napkins from a nearby tray and dabbing furiously at Sergei. 'Lucky it wasn't red!'

'Thank you, really, it's fine, there's no need . . .'

'No, really, I'll fix you in no time. Here, hold still.'

And he did. He stood stock-still, if a little embarrassedly, as she rubbed furiously at his sleeve, the front of his shirt, even his trouser leg, before the wine had a chance to sink in. She could feel his eyes on the top of her head, and given that she was in the process of rubbing his leg, she realised she *had* to find something else to say. Something *normal*.

Like, *now*.

'Actually, that's a Coldplay song title, did you know that?' she chirped, from somewhere around his knee level.

'What, "Hold Still"?'

'No! "Fix You" – have you heard it?'

'I'm afraid my pop music tastes date back to prehistoric times, Amy.'

'Oh? For example?' She straightened up and looked at him with interest.

'Kraftwerk? OMD? Erasure?'

Amy raised an eyebrow. He was grinning sheepishly. 'I'm not particularly proud of my electro-past,' he whispered, 'but that's what we all listened to in Russia.'

'Well, I'm sorry to hear that, Sergei, but there must be organisations that can offer help . . .'

Sergei hooted with laughter. 'That's just the sort of comment your mother would make!'

Amy looked up sharply. This was it. This was what she had been waiting for. Sergei was her link to the past – and a side of her mother she was hungry to know about. Her mother – Hannah Powell – the most perfect Odette in *Swan Lake* that this country had ever produced, or so the reviews of the time had exuberantly claimed.

'Do you know, once in my dancing days when I was about to go on stage, I spilled orange juice over my costume. Your mother did exactly as you have done tonight – she was always looking after me, like a mother hen.'

'I can imagine,' Amy said, clutching a clump of damp napkins in her hand, with nowhere to put them. 'She mothered everyone.' Glancing round the room, she couldn't spot a single woman who looked like she'd allow herself to get into this sort of predicament. They probably all could have summoned up a member of staff to help out with a click of their perfectly manicured fingers.

'I once dyed my hair orange to try and look like Bowie in his Aladdin Sane period, you know.' Sergei was like that. He could put a coiled spring at ease.

'Really?' Amy laughed, relieved.

Sergei nodded. 'I think that was just before I had it cut very short – it was just before my Yellow Magic Orchestra fixation. Oh, and there was the Sparks weekend . . .'

As Sergei launched into a somewhat baffling reverie

about his seventies and eighties musical journey, Amy tried, she really, really tried, to keep up with his encyclopaedic knowledge of synthesiser pop, but within minutes she felt herself drifting off into another place – a fantasy world, or a reality check, she couldn't decide which . . .

Sergei Mishkov. What on earth am I doing here yet again? And yet, how could I have stayed away?

It's because of Mum, that's why. This place, this is Mum's world, and Sergei was Mum's friend from another time – pre-me, pre-Dad, pre-retiring from ballet to bring me up . . . I owe Mum this, to live in her world now and again, to try and feel what she felt, with people she cared about. That way I guess she can live on in me as a whole person, rather than just as my mum . . .

'Ah, Ultravox, now that was a conundrum. Did they truly fit the genre . . . ?' Sergei was in full flow, waving his arms to emphasise the finer points of the *Vienna* album . . .

And they're not half bad, really, these evenings, even though I feel like a kid in a crowd of adults. Sergei's great, the dancing's great, the music's a bit iffy sometimes but I'm working on it. I just wish . . . oh, I wish I'd told Justin from the start. Why the heck didn't I?

She knew the answer perfectly well. When Justin had first met Sergei – what, a year ago? – he'd made his feelings perfectly clear. He didn't like him, didn't trust him.

'Amy? The bells?' Sergei had stooped to look directly at her.

'Pardon?'

'I think I lost you somewhere between The Human League and Fad Gadget, did I not? I apologise.'

'Oh! I'm sorry!' The theatre bells rang again.

'No need to be sorry!' He waved his arms energetically. 'But we must go back in: time for the second act!'

CHAPTER FOUR

Monday morning, over a week later, and Amy rolled over in the otherwise empty bed, pushed the duvet covers away and forced herself to get up and pad over to the bathroom.

I am never going to go to the Isle of Wight Festival ever again as long as I live. I am never going out with Debbie and Jesminder ever again as long as I live.

Amy had just caught sight of her bleary, hungover face in her bathroom mirror.

Well, not until next year, anyway.

She shook her head painfully at the sorry reflection, and forced a dry-lipped smile. Thank goodness Justin had left yesterday to catch up with one of his bands in Manchester. Besides, he'd been a bit moody and preoccupied for most of the past week – the break from routine was bound to do him good. Now, all she had to do was drink lots of water, swallow some aspirin and get ready for work.

It was scorching outside, so after choosing the H&M wrap dress in shades of turquoise and lime green that looked, from a decent distance, not unlike a Pucci original – a sure-fire hangover-buster if ever there was one – Amy walked slowly and carefully to her shoe closet to pull out the Christian Louboutin wedges. They'd be perfect.

Thank goodness for my impeccable filing system, she thought to herself, pinpointing the Louboutin box immediately, thanks to the jazzy Polaroid on the outside.

But the box was empty.

Amy frowned. Had she kicked them under the bed one drunken evening? No, Amy was never, ever untidy where her shoes were concerned. Then, she remembered: perhaps Phyllis borrowed them after all. Still, she didn't have time to ring her now. The white canvas mules from Russell & Bromley's autumn sale would have to do instead.

But that box was empty as well. Crying out in dismay, Amy picked out box after box after box.

They were all empty.

Her shoes were gone.

For a few moments Amy couldn't process the information her hands and eyes were relaying to her brain.

Now she was fighting for breath. She felt as though she might be sick, and she turned dizzily towards the bathroom. But the sensation passed and she swayed instead into the sitting room, where she sank onto the sofa and gave out a little wail. Then panic lent wings to her bleary feet and she shot up and raced back to the closet.

Take 2: My Hangover is Causing Hallucinations and My Shoes Will Be Here This Time.

They weren't.

She had been robbed. It was the only explanation. Terrified, she lunged for the phone.

'Justin?' she sobbed into the receiver. 'We've been burgled.'

There was silence on the other end of the line. Shock, probably.

'Justin, are you there? Can you hear me?'

Then, at last, 'I can hear you.'

'My shoes are gone. Somebody's taken them. Every single pair . . .'

'I know.'

'I've looked everywhere, but the boxes are all empty, and I've checked all round the flat and your stuff's OK and it doesn't seem like anything else has gone but I can't be certain— What do you mean, you know?'

'Abe, did you really think I wouldn't find out?'

'Pardon?'

'I know everything.'

'Wh . . . what do you mean?'

'About your affair.'

'My *what*?'

The phone reception wasn't particularly brilliant. She must be hearing things. Amy pressed the receiver so close to her ear it hurt.

'Remember Steve Roberts, my friend the arts journalist?'

'Who?'

'No, well, of course you wouldn't, otherwise you might have been more careful last weekend at the Royal Opera House, mightn't you? He saw everything, Abe.'

Now Amy really did feel that she was about to be sick.

'You made quite a spectacle of yourself, by the sound of things.'

'Oh, Justin, I—'

'Don't bother. Christ, you were seen *groping the guy's leg*!'

'What? Oh!' With horror, Amy recalled her vigorous rubbing of Sergei's thigh to get the wine off . . . 'Yes, but no, but listen, that's ridic—'

'Save it, Abe. I rang Jesminder.'

Panic-stricken, Amy sank back onto the sofa. She may have told Justin that she was going to the pub with Jes that night, but she would never have dreamed of asking her friend to lie for her. Jes would have been baffled by a call from Justin, out of the blue.

'She wasn't half surprised to hear from me, given that she'd been out speed-dating that night, and not in the pub with you at all.'

'I'm—'

'Don't worry, I covered for you. Made up some stupid story about a friend who was interested in going along and hung up. Then I went online and read all your emails.'

'You did *what*?'

Now his anger was fizzing down the line. Amy didn't know whether to be glad or sorry that they weren't doing this face to face. Glad, probably.

'How?'

Then she heard him sigh. 'Took me, oh, a whole minute and a half to guess your password. Maybe two?

40

I started with "Manolo" and worked my way through every flaming shoe designer you'd ever mentioned until I hit on "Gina". Bingo.'

'Oh. Very good.'

'Sergei, huh? I really should have known after that evening he came round for dinner that there was more to it than *friendship*.' He spat the last word as though it tasted unpleasant.

'Yes, but—'

'I thought *I* was a bit on the old side for you but obviously that's the way you like 'em.'

Amy began to cry. 'Justin, will you stop? I am *not* having an affair!'

'Sure, Abe, sure,' Justin sneered. 'Your emails to Sergei really show that, don't they?' He launched into an impersonation of a Russian accent: '*Oh, my dear, I cannot wait until Saturday . . . meet me in the usual place . . . I've been thinking about you . . .* For heaven's sake!'

'Justin, stop!'

'I want you out, Amy.'

'Listen to me!'

'No!'

'Justin, please!'

'Just get out of my life, Amy. I want you out of the apartment by tonight, is that clear? And I never want to see you again.'

'Justin, are you going to let me explain?' Amy sobbed.

'Those emails are all the explanation I need. And to think, I sat at the table and ate dinner with you two! Honestly, Amy, was it all a lie? All that "Oh, I'll never cheat on you, I'm not Natasha" bull?'

'No!' Amy wailed.

'I don't believe you.'

'You have to, it's true!'

'I'm going now; I've got a gig to sort out. Don't call back.'

'Justin, wait!'

'Goodbye, Amy.'

She thought he'd gone. She held her breath, waiting for the click on the other end of the line.

Instead, this:

'Oh, and, Amy, your shoes?'

She had temporarily forgotten all about her shoes.

'Y . . . yes?'

'I sold them.'

What? It may have been a dodgy phone line, but had she just heard that correctly?

'I sold the lot on eBay while you were away in the Isle of Wight. Or, come to think of it, while you were away who-knows-where. Could've been the Isle of Wight, could've been Moscow, for all I—'

'YOU SOLD MY SHOES?' Amy had never shrieked so loudly in her entire life.

'Yup,' came the calm reply. 'You didn't even notice that I'd been beavering away on my computer most of last week, did you?'

'But—'

'Huh, you were probably too busy dreaming about *Sergei*. Sheez, what a name! But yes, the bidding went on all last week. It was very decent of you to have stored a photo of each pair on your hard drive – made my job a whole lot easier.'

'You *utter—*'

'And thanks, as well, for going away at the weekend, to wherever it was you actually went to – and giving me peace to parcel them all up and get them posted out.' Then, after a pause, 'And to arrange to get the locks changed later this morning.'

'You know how much they meant to me,' Amy breathed, not knowing or caring if her words were audible or not.

There was the merest pause at the other end of the line. Then Justin replied, 'It hurts, doesn't it?'

Now, at last, Amy was beaten. Robbed of words, of responses, even of anger. She closed her eyes and let the hot tears course down her cheeks.

'They've all gone, Amy, to the four corners of the earth.'

'No,' she whispered.

'Goodbye, Amy. Have a nice life.'

CHAPTER FIVE

'Isle of Wight wellies again, Amy?' Jesminder said, raising an elegant eyebrow as she glanced beneath Amy's desk later that morning.

Amy was on autopilot. She'd almost not come in to work at all – not having any shoes to wear playing only a small part of that decision. But then in a pocket-sized flash of defiance she'd pulled on the wellies she'd worn all weekend at the sodden festival and trudged in to the office. Besides, the four walls of the lonely apartment were suffocating her.

And work would be a distraction. She could immerse herself in the cyberworld of Internet travel – and life at aclickaway.com was always busy – then before she knew it the horrible, horrible day would be over. Plus, she'd be able to talk to Jesminder and Debbie. Hopefully get some advice.

Then, when she got back to the apartment, it would all have been a horrible mistake. Justin would give her time to explain everything, and he would apologise, and so would she, and her shoes would be safely back in her cupboard where they belonged, not on their way all around the world, as though blasted from a scattergun.

Jesminder drifted away, frowning, as Amy remained silent. She worked in finance on the floor above Amy, not far from Debbie, who was in the sales section.

It was impossible to concentrate. Amy found herself veering between wanting to howl with anguish, or else leap to her feet in fury, go to track Justin down, in her wellies, and force him to see sense.

But putting aside her wounded feelings about Justin, she was full of a kind of bewildered wonder at how badly the loss of her shoes was affecting her. They were only *shoes*, for heaven's sake – she could easily put in an insurance claim and buy more! But somehow that missed the point. Rightly or wrongly, Amy loved her shoe collection; *depended* on it, even. No longer having her shoe collection was like losing a personal diary that one had been keeping faithfully year after year, recording the events, the people, the emotions of the time. They were her private history, the blocks on which her memories were built. Remove them and she was in danger of collapse.

Worse had been to follow. It hadn't dawned on Amy until an hour or so after her discovery of the missing shoes that Justin had even gone so far as to get rid of her most precious possession of all – her mother's ballet shoes. The only pair Amy owned, stored in that plain little box, the one without a photo on the outside. And Justin, the snake, wasn't answering his phone now, so she couldn't find out where he'd sent them. But anyway, who would bid for an old pair of dancing shoes? Then Amy's heart sank as the answer thumped right back out at her. The Internet was crawling with souvenir hunters. There would be ballet aficionados all over the world who would *jeté* at the chance to pick up a small piece of Royal Ballet history – the shoes once worn by Hannah Powell, Britain's most beautiful Odette.

And meanwhile, as the shoes winged their way to some nameless, faceless, thoughtless, tactless, *blameless* buyer, there was a young woman, wearing yellow wellington boots that smelled faintly of beer-soaked mud, sitting distraught behind a desk at aclickaway.com, trying to make sense of her monthly target sheet, who had just been robbed of her most precious link to her dead mother.

Just then, on her screen, her Instant Messenger sprang into life. It was Jesminder, from upstairs:

Jes: U ok, Amy?

Then, from the other end of the building:

Debs: Jes tells me ur wearing ur wellies to work. Have u finally flipped?

Amy forced half a grin, and tapped her response:

Amy: How long have u got?
Debs: How long is the so-called 'working' day?
Jes: Only tell us if u want to, Amy, we don't want to pry.
Debs: Speak for urself, matey.

Amy took a deep breath, and began to type.

Amy: Justin has accused me of having an affair. He wants me out of the flat and he's changed the locks. And he's sold all my shoes on eBay when I was away with you guys at the weekend. He's up north and won't answer the phone. It's over.
Debs: Ur having a laugh.
Jes: Unbelievable!
Amy: I know.
Debs: What a total creep.
Jes: Are u going to go?
Amy: I don't know.
Debs: So is it true?
Jes: Debs, leave it.
Amy: Is what true?
Debs: R u having an affair?
Jes: Foot in mouth again, Deb.
Amy: Course not.
Jes: See?
Amy: Well, not like u think anyway.
Deb: Here we go.
Jes: Anyone free for lunch?
Amy: Not hungry.
Debs: All your shoes? Every last pair?
Amy: Xept the wellies. I had them on, remember?
Debs: That is almost funny, sorry, my pet.
Jes: Debs, will u leave it?
Amy: He sold my mother's dancing shoes.

There was a pause.

Jes: Oh.
Debs: Ah.
Amy: I don't know what to do.

Jes: Well, first you need to eat. Shall we see you at 12?
Debs: And then we need to get the girl some shoes. Our treat, right?
Jes: Right. ☺
Amy: Thanks, you guys.

Shortly after twelve Debbie and Jesminder ducked off to the cashpoint and left Amy to have a preliminary browse around Shooz, the little Camden shoe shop that lay just around the corner from their office. It wasn't Amy's normal shoe haven, but desperate times called for desperate measures and there was absolutely no way she was going to grace any high street stores in Day-Glo yellow wellington boots, despite Debbie insisting that all she needed was to put on a bit of an attitude and soon every style-conscious girl in Camden would be heading for the outdoor shops to get a pair of her own.

It wasn't really *enough* of a shoe shop to lift Amy's mood. No leathery smell, no edgy lighting, just Dullsville shoes on racks. Still, something inside Amy told her that this sort of shop was no more than she deserved, not today. As if she could face a designer shop – or even one of her favourite market stalls – in wellies, with puffy eyes and a faintly deranged expression. No, what she needed was to be taken in hand by a nice, matronly shoe retailer who would sit her down and bring tissue-filled boxes full of unchallenging shoes for her to ease her feet into, backed up with some nice chat, some gentle encouragement to try different pairs in different colours, and lots of use of the word 'comfortable' . . .

There were three shop assistants standing right at the back behind the counter, chewing gum. Each looked no more than about sixteen, and not one was displaying any eagerness to come near her. Amy sighed, left them to their chat, and began to browse the racks.

It wasn't until she dislodged a shoddily displayed rack of sandals that one of the girls finally rolled her eyes and looked in her direction. She jolted visibly when she caught sight of what Amy was wearing on her feet.

'Look!' the girl squeaked at her companions, gesturing at the wellies.

The ensuing splutter of laughter sounded like they had all just exploded. Amy, scrabbling on the floor trying to pick up the fallen sandals, wanted to cry.

'Didn't realise it was milking time!' the largest of the girls stage-whispered to her companions.

'I'd have thought knowing when it was milking time would be second nature to you three,' came a loud, Geordie voice from the door.

Big, blonde, fabulous Debbie stood at the shop entrance, glaring at the three girls. She had heard every word. Behind her, Jesminder clapped a hand to her forehead but couldn't resist a smile.

'I used to giggle like an idiot when I was twelve as well,' Debbie went on, 'but you three are employed for a reason so I suggest you do what shop assistants are meant to do and get over here and assist.'

Put simply, Debbie didn't take any nonsense from anybody. Her self-confidence when it came to standing up for what was right belied her twenty-four years. Amy couldn't imagine having a more loyal, or a more fun friend. Crammed with big-hearted sexiness, everyone loved Debbie – apart, perhaps, from the grumbling ringleader of the shop assistants, who was making her way sullenly towards Amy and mumbling something that may very well have been 'Can I help you?' but could just as easily have been 'Fnerganelpoo?'

Jesminder, still by the door, was trying not to giggle. She was cut from altogether different cloth. Calm, caring, you could trust her with your life. While Debbie was a gale that swept away all in her path, Jes was more a steady breeze, caressing and warm, but still with a strength of her own. She, above everyone, had spent most time with Amy since the death of her mother, and it was she, on their way to the shoe shop, who had offered Amy a place to stay until she sorted herself out.

Amy could feel their stares of incredulity when, after trying on only two pairs of shoes, she settled for the flat, beige canvas pumps.

'I'll take these,' she said, not even looking up. 'And, if you don't mind, I'll keep them on.'

'That doesn't surprise me,' smirked the assistant.

'Careful,' Debbie warned.

'They're lovely,' Jesminder lied. Amy glanced up at her and giggled for the first time that day.

'No they're not, they're Guilty Conscience shoes,' Debbie decided, as she and Jesminder paid for the shoes. 'Right, you, we're going to the sandwich bar and you're going to do some explaining.'

Amy trudged beside her friends to Squishy's on the corner, loathing the practical, silent footfalls made by her new shoes. Now, on top of 'miserable' and 'furious', she could safely add 'frumpy' to her portfolio for the afternoon. Maybe 'invisible' as well. It's not only height that you get from high heels, she remembered.

Ten minutes later, she was staring down the thick end of a tuna mayo baguette and wondering if she'd ever feel like eating again.

'OK, shoot,' Debbie mumbled through a mouthful of chicken tikka wrap.

'Debbie!' Jesminder scolded. 'Give Amy time!'

Debbie gave Jesminder a withering look. 'It's for her own good, Jes. She said herself there was another bloke . . .'

'OK!' Amy held up her hand. 'Listen, I appreciate you being here for me and you're both wonderful, but I have just been dumped – at least, I think I've been dumped . . .'

'You *think* you've been dumped?' Jesminder queried. 'Was there some scope for doubt in what Justin said?'

'"Get out by tonight" doesn't sound like a playful warning shot to me,' Debbie concurred.

'I know,' Amy nodded. 'But he just wouldn't listen to me! He'd got himself worked up into a real state. He literally did not give me a moment to tell him the truth. Look, once he gets back I'll be able to sit him down and explain everything, and he'll be . . . fine.' Amy knew this was unlikely even before she'd finished the sentence. After all, he hadn't answered her calls all morning.

'Well, if you say so,' said Jesminder, doubtfully. 'It's worth a try.'

'Worth a try?' Debbie spluttered, slamming her Diet Coke down on the table. 'Why should he get away with being a one-man judge and jury, and *evil seller of shoes*, without hearing Amy's side of the story?' Debbie sat back and folded her arms indignantly. Then, her face softened and she leaned towards Amy, wrinkling her brow. 'Amy, what exactly *is* your side of the story?'

CHAPTER SIX

'OK,' Amy began, 'here goes. I've been seeing a man for about a year now.'

'You're a dark horse,' Debbie breathed.

'But it's not like that at all!' Amy protested. 'He's just a friend!'

'I take it you didn't tell Justin?' Jesminder asked gently.

Amy shook her head.

'Why not? Does he know him?'

'His name is Sergei Mishkov, he's maybe forty-four, he used to be a dancer, and he was one of my mother's best friends. I think I may have even mentioned him a while back . . .'

'Ah,' said Jesminder and Debbie simultaneously.

'Now he's a choreographer – he's very famous in the ballet world, lives in the States, mainly, but he tours a lot, and often visits the UK. He's wonderful.'

'Fit?' Debbie asked playfully. Jesminder dug her in the ribs.

Amy ignored her. 'He got in touch a year ago, about

a year after Mum died – they'd been dancing partners for a while, though Mum was quite a bit older than him – and I invited him round for dinner.'

'As you would,' affirmed Jesminder. 'Quite right too.'

'Well, I thought so, but Justin didn't take to him at all, which upset me at the time.'

'*Pig*,' Debbie spat. 'Sorry. That slipped out.'

'Well, Justin said he didn't like the way Sergei looked at me, and he said he felt excluded from the conversation all evening, like Sergei and I had made some sort of connection, so . . .' Amy tailed off, and shrugged.

'Did you like him?' Jesminder asked, her sandwich halfway to her mouth.

'Oh, yes, I really enjoy his company, he's so different, so grown-up and charming, but he's funny too,' Amy said fervently. Maybe Justin's jealousy *was* understandable after all.

'Anyhow, after Sergei left, Justin and I had this huge row. I was mad at him for behaving so stroppily in front of my friend, and he accused me of flirting with him the whole night.'

'I don't like the sound of that possessive streak of Justin's,' Debbie mused.

'It's not possessive, as such,' Amy said defensively, groping for the right words. 'He's, well, he *is* afraid of being cheated on, though. I must have told you that his last girlfriend, Natasha, cheated on him with his best friend?'

'You did,' Jesminder affirmed quietly. 'So it's not surprising he's wary.'

'Hmm.' Debbie wasn't convinced.

'Anyway, not long after that Sergei rang up and asked me to go to the ballet with him.'

'And you didn't tell Justin?' Jesminder guessed.

Amy nodded. 'It seemed easier. Justin's not interested in ballet. Oh, he'd go with me if I begged him, but there was something really, really nice about going with Sergei. He's so passionate about it, and he's such lovely company, and he knew my mother . . .'

'Was it only once?' Jesminder pressed.

'No. That's the trouble. Last week was the fourth time. I'm afraid I used you as an alibi, Jes. I'm sorry.'

Understanding spread over Jesminder's face. 'Aha, that would explain why Justin rang me up last week to find out how my evening had gone.'

'I told him I was going to the pub with you,' Amy mumbled, touching Jesminder's arm. 'I'm really, really sorry for involving you. What a mess! No wonder he's changing the locks.'

'Outstanding. He was checking up on you,' Debbie growled.

'He had good reason, don't you think?' Amy replied.

'So you do fancy this Sergei, then?' said Debbie.

'No! I don't! It's just . . . well . . . he's a link to my mother – to both of my parents, really – and we have the same things in common, and he's charming, and interesting, and fun . . .'

'Can I have him, then, if you don't want him?' Debbie teased. 'I'm coming over a bit Anna Karenina all of a sudden . . .'

'Have you tried calling Justin today?' diverted Jesminder, rolling her eyes in Debbie's direction.

57

Amy nodded her head, and tears began to well up for the umpteenth time. 'He won't answer his mobile. I've tried about twenty times.'

'Did he really sell *all* of your shoes?' Jesminder asked, unwrapping a chocolate chip muffin and cutting it neatly into four. Without asking, Debbie helped herself to a quarter.

'He did. At least, I think he did. He says he did, and there's no sign of them, and I really loved them, and he knew that and . . . do you know what?'

'What?' came in chocolatey chorus.

'I don't think he could have done anything more hurtful if he'd planned it for a thousand years. Mum's ballet slippers . . . they were the only pair of her shoes that I had.'

'We'll need to get them back,' said Jesminder.

'Some people keep diaries or photographs to remind them of special times . . .' A tear ran down Amy's cheek and plopped onto the paper plate in front of her.

'Too right we will,' agreed Debbie, thrusting her paper napkin under Amy's nose.

'Most people my age can talk about old times with their parents, but I can't . . .' Amy wasn't really aware of the other two any more as she sank deeper into moroseness.

'And I think I know how we can do it.' Jesminder was smiling conspiratorially at Debbie.

'I can tell you ten, twenty stories about each pair . . .'

'I'm all ears,' smirked Debbie.

'. . . where I was, what I did, who was there – it's mad, I know, but . . . sorry, what did you say?'

'I said,' Jesminder repeated patiently, 'that I know how to get the shoes back.'

'How?'

'Go and retrieve them from the buyers, of course.'

'Road trip!' Debbie yelled, to the alarm of the old lady at the table in front of them who dropped her umbrella on the floor, triggering the automatic opening mechanism so that the brolly exploded into a fan of pink and white roses with a loud pop.

'Yeah, right. How will we even track them down? Besides, I can't even get into the apartment without Justin's mother's say-so. That'll really work. But thanks, guys.'

Jesminder's beautiful, almond-shaped black-brown eyes had narrowed. 'We'll see, Amy, we'll see.'

It was almost half-past eight that evening by the time Amy plucked up the courage to ring her own doorbell.

Phyllis's thin voice answered. 'Yes?'

'It's Amy. May I come in?'

There was a pause and then a buzzing sound. Amy's knees felt decidedly wobbly as she mounted the stairs. Phyllis was standing at the open doorway to meet her. Her face was filled with pained disappointment.

'Phyllis,' Amy began, 'this is all a terrible misunder-standing—'

'I've already put most of your things into boxes,' Phyllis cut in, although there was no anger in her voice. 'You can get the rest some other time.'

'Truly, Phyllis, I haven't—'

'I'm sorry, Amy, I really am, but Justin is so hurt,

and so am I.' Amy walked past Phyllis, into the flat, as though drugged. Why wasn't she being believed? It all seemed so surreal. And so unfair.

But nothing prepared her for the sight that greeted her in the sitting room. A neat stack of large cardboard boxes stood in the centre of the room, immaculately labelled 'Clothes', 'Books', 'Bags', 'Toiletries', 'Paperwork', 'Kitchen Equipment', 'Miscellaneous' and, as a final insult, 'Shoe Boxes'. It must have taken Phyllis all day.

Phyllis followed her into the room and handed her an envelope.

'What's that?' Amy asked, her voice utterly flat.

'It's a cheque. From Justin,' Phyllis replied. 'The proceeds of the sale of the shoes. I don't necessarily approve of my son's action, but I know one thing: he is not a thief.'

Amy took the envelope. She didn't know what else to do. But just as her mouth was about to form the heartfelt 'Oh, yes he is,' a piercing, deafening noise made both women jump.

'The fire alarm!' Phyllis shouted, as they covered their ears. 'It's probably another false alarm, but you can never be too careful. Quick, can you smell smoke?'

Amy couldn't, but she followed the older lady to the door. The fire alarm had gone off twice in the last month and both times had been false alarms. Amy knew for a fact that the Turkish couple in the apartment opposite were fond of smoking shisha.

'Oh, no! Mrs Tompkiss!' Phyllis exclaimed.

'Be careful!' Amy shouted above the din, as the older

woman hurried downstairs to find Mrs Tompkiss, her precious cat. There were still no signs of smoke or flames. People were beginning to emerge onto the staircase above and below, and clatter downstairs to the fire assembly point.

But not Amy. Seizing her chance, she glanced from side to side and slipped back into the now empty flat, sitting down in front of Justin's home computer. Loud voices told her that the landing was busy, and she shook all over as she waited for the machine to boot up. It seemed to take for ever – Phyllis could return at any moment – but at last it sprang into life and Amy began to navigate her way to Justin's eBay account. She was dizzy with anticipation: two more minutes, and she'd have all of the buyers' details . . .

Only he had changed his password. Amy typed in the familiar 'moshpit' password four times before forcing herself to accept the obvious – he'd won.

Stunned, Amy sat back, wanting to wail with anguish. So close! How was she going to get the information now? Justin sure as heck wasn't going to email the details to her, however nicely she asked. She knew he wouldn't back down. He was such a stickler for seeing a job through, doing things thoroughly . . .

Aha – light-bulb moment! At once, Amy had her solution. Justin *was* such a stickler, wasn't he? He was bound to have done proper printed address labels on his computer, wasn't he? There was no way he would do anything as time-consuming as writing on the parcels with a pen if there was a technological and cunning

61

way of doing it! Excitedly, and ignoring the panicked voices outside, Amy opened Justin's Word documents.

There it was. A file carefully titled 'Shoe Labels'.

Quickly, Amy printed it off, shut down the computer and was about to run downstairs when she remembered the letter.

The night before, unable to sleep, she had taken out her writing pad and poured everything out in a letter: all about Sergei, and why she hadn't told Justin about their meetings. She hadn't been sure whether she would ever let Justin read it, as it ended up tear-stained and far, far too emotional, but now, with all her senses jangling, she thought, oh, what the heck, and laid it down beside the computer for Justin to read – or not – when he eventually came home.

She made it downstairs to the fire assembly point just a minute before Phyllis, who arrived clutching Mrs Tompkiss, relief spread all over her face. Neighbours were milling around chatting. Since the fire alarm had started malfunctioning, the neighbours had actually got round to knowing each other by name rather than just flat number.

'Looked everywhere for her. Finally found her hiding in the laundry basket.' Phyllis beamed at Amy, before obviously remembering that they were no longer supposed to be close, and sidling awkwardly off to talk to someone else.

It cut Amy to the core.

A moment later, Jesminder crept up and stood by Amy's side.

'My goodness, someone really needs to see to that

smoke alarm. Anyone could wander in off the street and set it off, oh, say, by waving a lighter underneath it.' Jesminder winked.

'Thanks, Jes. I owe you. Did you have any troubles?' Amy hissed out of the corner of her mouth.

'None at all. It was scarily easy – I could get used to the criminal life,' came the euphoric reply. 'Success?'

Amy frowned. 'Kind of. I think I've got all the addresses, but no phone numbers, unfortunately.'

'Worth doing, though?'

'Definitely!'

They basked in a momentary enjoyment of an illicit job well done before Amy sighed and turned to her friend. 'Well, guess we'd better start loading our cars with all my surviving worldly goods. Thanks again for letting me use your spare room.'

Jesminder nodded and gave her a hug, and Amy walked sadly over to Phyllis, to seek her permission to return, briefly, to clear her things out of the apartment.

Two hours later, after the girls had done lugging all Amy's stuff out of their cars and into Jesminder's tiny South London basement flat, the thrill of their successful mission had thoroughly worn off. Instead Amy felt the beginnings of a numbing blankness. *It had actually happened* – Justin had kicked her out. And Phyllis had helped. Oh, Phyllis's sadness over the situation had been as plain as day, but it had been obvious where her loyalties lay.

'Poor Phyllis,' Amy sighed as at last she sank down

on the carpet in front of Jesminder's gas fire. 'This must be awful for her.'

'Pardon?' Jesminder poked her head round the kitchen door. 'Poor *Phyllis*?'

Amy nodded. 'Yes, it can't be nice for her, thinking her son's girlfriend is a cheap shagabout, can it?'

'She knows you're not that!' exclaimed Jesminder. 'Don't be ridiculous!'

'Does she, though?' Amy pressed. 'Why shouldn't she believe her own son? *He* obviously believes I'm a cheap shagabout, doesn't he?'

'Stop it!' Jesminder made a show of covering her ears. 'Stop using that word! And you're not! In fact, you deserve a medal for feeling sorry for anyone other than yourself right now. Glass of wine? Beer?'

Amy gazed at the photo of Jes with her beaming parents on graduation day. She was very, very tired. 'Please may I just have a great big mug of tea?'

'Of course you can, sweetheart. Then you and I must begin plotting.' Jesminder ducked back into the kitchen and Amy heard the splishing sound of the kettle being filled. 'Stick some music on, why don't you?'

'Sure.' Amy crawled on all fours over to Jesminder's CD collection – with its Punjabi MCs, Rishi Rich and, horror of horrors, Justin Timberlake – which was housed in an unsteady wicker tower beside her stereo and portable TV in the corner of the room. 'Got any new stuff from the festival? I could do with something cheerful.'

''Fraid not. I downloaded all the festival stuff last night. Put on Justin Timberlake, there's a pal.'

'Must I?' Amy whined. 'I've had about all I can take of Justins for today.'

'Ah – sorry. You choose, then. Want a biscuit?'

'No, thanks. Actually, Jes, do you mind if we don't listen to anything?'

'Sure.'

Amy sat back and closed her eyes. She felt too flat for tears – that would have involved dramatic emotion and she'd had enough of that for one day. But nor did she want to go to bed. She knew with certainty that sleep would be in short supply. Her brain was repeatedly turning over the events of the day.

Where was Justin? *He could even be in the apartment right now . . . reading my letter . . . reaching for the phone, racked with guilt . . .*

'. . . just the way you like it, not too strong, just a touch of milk.'

'Jes, you are an angel. I'm so grateful.'

Jesminder sat on the sofa and curled her long legs underneath her. She shook her head. 'It's fine, Amy, truly. I know you'd do it for me.'

'Course I would,' Amy replied.

'But we need to make a plan, don't we? You're going to have to hit the road and get your shoes back. You *have* to.'

Amy sniggered.

'What's so funny?' Jesminder asked.

'Sorry, but I notice you're not kicking off with a plan for getting my *man* back. Priorities, huh? You been listening to Debs all afternoon?' She grinned as she spoke.

'No!' Jesminder aimed a cushion at her. 'But you've got to see this through, right? Besides, this'll be good for you. It'll keep your mind occupied and, most importantly, get you your mum's dancing slippers back. Now, where's that list of addresses?'

Amy stretched towards her Karen Millen bag and pulled out the list, checking her phone as she did so for the umpteenth time to see if Justin had sent her a text.

'OK.' Jesminder gently prised the list from her hand and scanned the details. 'Ah. Quite an itinerary for you. Wow, Japan!' She read further. 'And the USA! Ireland! Newcastle!'

'But I can't go all round the world knocking on doors asking for my shoes back,' Amy moaned.

'Why not?' Jesminder actually looked serious.

'Oh, come on. I've been thinking about it. Hacking into Justin's computer to find out where they've all gone to is one thing, but setting off round the world to ask for them back? People will think I'm a bizarre shoe fetishist if I turn up on their doorsteps and start asking about their shoes.'

'*Your* shoes, Amy,' Jesminder corrected. 'And you *are* a bizarre shoe fetishist. Get over it, as Debs would undoubtedly say if she were here. Right, how long can you take off work?'

'Two weeks max,' Amy replied instantly before checking herself. 'I mean, no. I didn't mean that. No time off work. Drop everything and circle the globe, not knowing if the people will even be there or what I will find? It's bonkers. Who on earth would do a thing like that?'

'Someone with nothing to lose?' Jesminder said quietly.

Amy opened her mouth to reply, but no words came. Instead she turned her head and gazed out the basement window to the shoes of pedestrians passing by on the street outside.

Is Jes right? Do I really have nothing to lose? She shook her head, panicked by the notion, and rounded on her friend.

'Since when was I defined by my boyfriend and my shoes?' she said, far more sharply than she meant. 'I'm me! I've got a life! And a job! And friends! And . . . and . . .'

Jesminder slid down from the sofa and sat silently by her side. Now both of them gazed outside with glittery, tear-filled eyes. The only sounds were the faint hum of traffic outside and occasional slurps as they gulped their tea.

'Do you know something?' Amy said, after a long, long time.

'Not yet,' Jesminder replied.

'I miss them. I miss my shoes. But I don't miss Justin – not yet. I'm too angry with him to miss him and that's not going to change until he believes my "side of the story", as Debs put it – huh, cheek! That makes it sound like there are *two* sides, doesn't it? But there aren't. There never were. I'm not cheating on him – there is no so-called *other* side. And if he won't believe me, well – y'know, I'm starting to think that even if he does believe me now, I can't imagine just jumping back into his bed tomorrow as though all this never happened. I didn't know he had such a vindictive streak in him, Jes, I really didn't.'

Jesminder nodded. 'Sounds like it's going to take time, sorting that lot out in your head. You know you're welcome here for as long as it takes.'

Amy reached over and hugged her friend. When she drew back, her eyes were like saucers. She'd made it. Out of the blue, she had made a decision.

'That's the key, isn't it?' she cried, leaping to her feet. 'Time!'

'Erm . . .'

'Time. It's like, time is showing me the way.'

'Is that a song?' Plainly Jesminder thought Amy had flipped.

'No. Well, probably, but anyhow, listen, Jes. Justin needs time to read my letter, calm down and come to his senses, correct?'

'Definitely.'

'And I need time to work out how I feel about him not being prepared to face me like a man and hear me out. Correct?'

'Correct.'

'But on the other hand – or at least, on the other foot – with the shoes, there's no time to lose, is there? I need to get them back in as short a time as possible so that their owners don't become too attached to them and wear them to death and forget where they bought them from.'

'Bingo,' Jesminder agreed.

'And if I don't go and find them, then in time I'll forget them and that would be horrible.'

'Bingo again.'

'And even if it's impossible to find them I'll be getting away and giving *myself* time to think things over.'

'Bingo times three.'

'And I'm due some holiday, having finished that big Morocco contract last Thursday *ahead of time*, so work might just about manage to stay afloat without me if I took off now.'

'Uh-huh, we'll muddle through somehow,' Jesminder nodded, her voice full of mock-doubt. 'Debbie and I will pull every string in the business and get you some disgustingly cheap flights, have no fear.'

Amy was circling the room, her hands fidgety. 'The time is right!'

'Is that really a decision?' Jesminder asked. 'You're going to get your shoes back?'

'I am. It's show time!' Amy gulped, flinging her arms out wide and feeling better than she had done in hours.

'Don't you mean *shoe* time?'

Laughing, Jesminder ducked to avoid the cushion that flew in her direction.

CHAPTER SEVEN

For the most part Amy was grateful to have Debbie, a Newcastle native, in the passenger seat of the crumbling 2CV as they negotiated their way into the city centre on a stuffy Friday evening. Debbie had swiftly arranged a weekend trip north to see her family, so that she could keep Amy company on the first of her shoe-finding missions, brushing off Amy's gratitude with a gruff, 'No, no, if it wasn't for you I'd never get off my arse and come to see the old folks at all.' Which was untrue, but deeply touching all the same.

The car hadn't enjoyed the long journey all the way to the north-east of England, and the girls had had to make three unscheduled stops to give it rest time and allow it to cool down. Now, though, on the final stretch of the journey, stopping and starting at traffic lights, it wasn't just the car that was overheating.

They were trying to find Delsey's Gym, the first address on the hit list, and Debbie had spent a lot of motorway time bragging about her thorough knowledge of Newcastle city centre. Amy, her eyes and head aching from concentrating on the road for hours, was growing irritated at Debbie, whose skills as a navigator seemed to depend entirely upon the existence of familiar shops and nightclubs in the immediate vicinity.

'Gottit!' she exclaimed at last. 'Go that way! There! Past the building that used to be TK Maxx!'

'*Used to be?*' Amy echoed, indicating right and turning the car into a bothersomely narrow side street. 'Since when was that a help?'

'You know my orange cashmere tank top? Fourteen quid? That was from in there – you had to go on a Tuesday, that's when all the new stuff – Careful! You've gone too far. That was the next turning back there; you should have hung left into the lane that's got Harley's nightclub at the end! Look, there's a garage with its door open. You can turn there.'

'Oh, goody,' Amy deadpanned, jamming the brakes on far too hard. The 2CV coughed its disgust.

'There, look, on the left – Delsey's Gym. Told you I'd find it. There's an underground car park round the corner. We made it, kiddo.'

'Thank goodness,' Amy breathed, as the 2CV bumped down the ramp into the underlit car park. 'My will to live was seeping away.'

'You're welcome,' Debbie teased.

'Sorry.'

Yawning and stretching, they sat still for a few minutes, summoning the strength to heave themselves out and make a start on their mission.

Amy's brain was buzzing. 'Do you know what's really weird about this whole trip, Debs?'

'Um, the fact that neither of us have discussed this year's *Big Brother* yet?'

'No, not that . . .'

'No? What about my unusual good manners in not using the words "Justin" and "bastard" in the same sentence since, oh, first thing this morning?'

Amy smiled. 'I hadn't thought of that one – yes, but the other weird thing about this trip is having no idea which pair of shoes went to which address.'

'What? I hadn't realised that!' Debbie exclaimed.

'All I've got are the buyers' addresses, but no information on what they actually bought, so in here, for instance, could be my Jimmy Choos, or my walking boots, who knows?'

Debbie frowned. 'Or could it be an old tin of toy soldiers Justin decided to sell while he was busy flogging stuff on eBay anyway?'

'No way!' Amy's heart lurched. Was this a flaw in the plan? Swiftly she tried to push the notion away. 'If Justin was selling toy soldiers on eBay he'd have a label file on his computer titled "Toy Soldier Addresses". I'm certain of it.'

'What a bundle of laughs life with that man must be,' Debbie said – in such a low voice Amy wasn't sure she picked her up properly.

'Come on, we've got work to do.'

They clambered stiffly up a bright yellow-painted stairwell, four steep flights to the door marked 'Reception'.

'I feel fitter already,' Debbie panted. 'Come on, let's do it.'

Amy, bracing herself, pushed open the swing door and the girls entered the gym.

Here goes: Operation 'Best Foot Forward' commences right now . . .

The dark-haired receptionist, who was talking on the phone in a language Amy didn't recognise, briefly pressed the receiver to her chest and glanced at them. 'Ah, hello! So nice to see you back again!'

Achingly tall. Beautiful. Foreign. Insincere. She lobbed them a toothy smile, omitting to involve her eyes in the gesture, before returning to the telephone conversation from which they had so thoughtlessly deflected her.

Behind the reception desk, a frosted glass door decreed 'Private – Staff Only', and to the left a sign pointed to the saunas and steam room. On the right a corridor led to the male and female changing rooms and the ladies' and gents' toilets, then beyond those the gym. Amy could hear the thrum of running machines from behind the double doors and, briefly, she thought of Justin. He loved his four-times-a-week workouts.

Huh, if the staff at his gym look like this specimen here, then no wonder – just look at that girl! You just can't compete with Eastern European bone structure, and no mistake . . .

'Aha!' said Debbie, gesturing down the corridor. 'Bathroom break! I'm bursting – won't be a tick.' And she bounded off towards the ladies' room.

Amy stood and chewed her lip, feeling awkward, wishing Debbie hadn't gone, trying to conjure up the mantra used by Jesminder in situations like this: 'No one can make you feel inferior without your consent!' But this receptionist was so glacial, her cheekbones so sharp and her disregard of Amy so total that it was hard not to just apologise and run out.

Oh, for heaven's sake – have a word with yourself, Marsh!

Amy was wondering where in Eastern Europe the ice-queen receptionist was from – could she even be Marta Kowalski, the very woman she was looking for? – when her eye fell upon a gigantic poster that took up the whole of the staff pinboard behind the desk.

NEWCASTLE POLISH SOCIETY
ANNUAL BALL
AT THE MARBURY HOTEL
THIS SATURDAY
FORMAL DRESS
CARRIAGES 3 A.M.
DANCING TO THE ALFONS ALEKSANDER
SWING BAND
TICKETS FROM POLISH CENTRE
OR MARTA OR IWONA KOWALSKI,
DELSEY'S GYM, LOMBARD LANE, NEWCASTLE

She was close then. Excited, Amy took a step forward, only for the door to open behind her, and for Adonis to walk in. At least, if you asked a hundred women to describe their version of Adonis, then pooled all the images into a single big, blond, beefy hunk of love, it's highly likely this is what you'd end up with. Amy gawped. She'd never seen such a ludicrously perfect specimen of muscly manhood and for some reason had to stifle an urge to bark with laughter.

Not my type at all, but if ever I need a wall built . . .

On seeing the man's arrival, though, the receptionist hurled the phone down as though it had caught fire, and rushed across to fawn over him, practically knocking Amy over in her flight. They triple-kissed enthusiastically, left cheek, right cheek, left cheek, exchanging greetings in Polish, but then, drawing apart, Adonis somehow found a moment to flick a brief, appraising glance in Amy's direction.

'So, then, beautiful, have you had a busy day?' he asked the receptionist in heavily accented English. Then brazenly, he shot another, longer look at Amy before once again returning his full attention to the woman under his nose.

Amy's skin prickled uncomfortably.

Huh, I know when I've been mentally undressed. And I bet he's only speaking English to keep his options open.

'As always,' oozed the reply. 'There is never time to . . . *relax* in this place; you know what I'm saying?'

She flicked her ponytail with her fingertips, then lasciviously licked her lips, laid a hand on her hip and *bang!* The right side of her body dropped until she stood in a provocative, thrusting pose that owed nothing to subtlety and absolutely everything to Marilyn Monroe.

Amy watched, anxiously chewing her fingernail, yet

entranced by the display. *I am receiving an award-winning lesson in shameless flirting – even Debbie would struggle to match this pair. Outstanding!*

Just when Amy thought the heat couldn't rise any higher, the staffroom door flew open, and an Amazonian blonde shot out and hurled herself over to where the other two stood. Practically pulling the receptionist off the man, she rubbed her hand provocatively down his arm and purred, in the same foreign accent, 'Well, *hallo*, stranger!'

Adonis was loving it, Amy could tell. Both women had fit, athletic builds – it was clear that any spare time they had left after flirting was taken up working out in the gym.

'So, what can I be doing for you this evening?' the blonde woman lisped, her mouth about two inches from the man's ear. 'Come to arrange a little *personal training*, hmm?'

'Hey!' the receptionist barked. 'It is me who is in charge tonight!' She wriggled between the blonde and Adonis. 'So! How can I help?'

Adonis took a moment, probably to savour the hedonistic delight of having two women squabble over him so blatantly. He looked first at the blonde, then at the brunette, and sighed, 'Ah, ladies, I need to buy two tickets for the ball, naturally. I can get them here, yes?'

Immediately the women fell away from him, trying to disguise looks of crushed disappointment.

'Oh?' The receptionist's striking face snapped back into an impassive mask. 'Well, you must wait. I must see if there are any tickets left.'

'Who is lucky lady?' the blonde hissed, trying to appear uninterested when her eyes shrieked the opposite.

Adonis shrugged his massive shoulders, and treated the two to a smouldering look. 'I have not decided yet . . .'

The receptionist whipped round. 'Plenty of tickets! I have just remembered!' Amy, by now fully blended into the background, was slightly annoyed at being ignored, although another part of her was quite enjoying the pantomime being played out before her.

Debs, hurry back – you'd love this.

'Hmm. Excellent.' He was still appraising the women, like a tiger who'd accidentally caught two gazelles at once. 'I would not want to come between sisters, however. Catch you, as they say, later.'

And with that, he tore himself away, swaggering down the corridor towards the gym.

You could crack nuts with those, Amy thought, inwardly giggling at his pert departure.

The receptionist and her blonde sister were standing bickering in the same spot where Adonis had stood between them.

Amy spoke up. 'Erm, excuse me?' It was now or never.

The women turned to glare at her. Amy raised a hand in a self-conscious little wave.

'Yes? Oh, it is you – you are still there.'

Taking a deep breath, Amy said, as confidently as she could, 'Yes, I am still here. I'm sorry to bother you,

I can see you're very busy, but I believe you have a Marta Kowalski working here?'

The sisters exchanged looks. Then the receptionist, narrowing her eyes, replied, 'And you are?'

'My name is Amy Marsh, but Marta doesn't know me. I need to speak to her about a mix-up over a pair of shoes she bought on eBay.'

There was a silence. Amy was certain she felt a crackle of recognition pass between the two, though their faces remained impassive.

'Oh, yes?'

'Yes. I . . . I sold them by mistake, and I was wondering whether I could possibly get them back. *Buy* them back, I mean, obviously . . .'

'We don't know what you are meaning. Do we, Iwona?'

Iwona? This must mean that the receptionist is Marta.

The receptionist glowered at her sister, then hissed something to her in Polish. Iwona responded sharply, her sister snapped back, and soon, gesturing and glowering, they were on course for another quarrel.

Stumped, Amy let them get on with it for a few minutes, wondering what to do.

Come on, this is mad! Debbie would have joined in by now, Jesminder would have us all sitting round a table discussing things rationally and here I am, standing like a lemon in the middle. That is just, like, totally . . . pants!

She took a step forward and held up her hands. 'Excuse me!' How she longed for a bit more gravitas, some higher heels, a deeper voice, a pair of cymbals, *anything*! But somehow it worked – sort of. Gradually the row simmered down, and the dark-haired receptionist turned to face her.

'OK. I am Marta.'

Hurrah! At last, she was getting somewhere, although could they have been any more difficult?

I may regret tempting fate with that thought – these two are dynamite . . .

Iwona, the blonde, cut in, 'You want to know about shoes? *eBay* shoes?' She stormed over to the side of the reception area where a row of lockers sat beneath an array of heavily laden coat hooks. Pulling a set of keys from her belt, she stabbed one of them into the lock as though trying to kill it, pulled open the door and yanked out a pair of shoes. '*These* shoes?'

Amy caught her breath.

There, being slapped onto the reception desk like a pair of wet fish, were her black patent Ferragamo court shoes, the ones with the three-inch pale wooden heels, tiny heart-shaped peep-toe and wide, grosgrain ribbon ankle tie; the ones she'd bartered as though her life depended on it from the man on the stall in Spitalfields two years ago: the ones that meant the world to her.

Just looking at them, Amy was assailed by a raft of nostalgic memories. Now she realised that her shoe quest wasn't only worthwhile, it was *essential*. But seeing them was one thing, getting them back from this pair was going to be entirely another.

'Thank you for nothing,' Marta snapped, grabbing the shoes. Iwona growled something earthy in Polish, as her sister made a face.

'Hey!' Amy cried.

'You been making friends here?' To Amy's relief, Debbie had finally returned from the ladies.

'*You* tell her,' Marta mumbled, jabbing the heel of one of the shoes at her sister and turning her back.

CHAPTER EIGHT

'You know,' Debbie growled in Amy's ear fifteen minutes later, 'there's a version of Cinderella that has one of the Ugly Sisters chopping her big toe off so that she can fit into the glass slipper.'

'You what?' Amy was only half listening, transfixed in horrified fascination by the sisters who sat before them, trying, as though their lives depended on it, to fit into her precious shoes.

'Straight up,' Debbie went on. 'She saws her big toe off, then crams the shoe onto what's left of her foot, and then the quite frankly not-all-there Prince sweeps her away on the back of his horse. It's only when he spots the blood flowing from the shoe as they gallop off into the sunset that he realises he's been suckered.'

'Cinderella never was like that!' Amy cried, elbowing her in the ribs.

'Was where I come from! We like our fairy tales hardcore up north.'

'Sicko. Oh, careful!' Amy made to lunge forward as one of her shoes flew to the ground, hurled by an increasingly desperate Iwona. Meanwhile Marta was sitting with her back to them, dusting her feet with talcum powder in readiness for another attempt to get the other one onto her wide, resistant foot.

'It's no use!' she snarled. 'It will not fit!'

'Hacksaw, anyone?' Debbie chirped.

Earlier, interspersed with gesticulations and corrections from Marta, Iwona had explained why the sisters were at war over the shoes. They had spotted them on eBay when they were surfing the Net together, couldn't agree who would bid for them, so agreed to share if their upper price limit of thirty-five pounds was accepted.

But Marta had upped her bid to forty at the last moment, thus securing the shoes for herself. This infuriated Iwona who, on seeing the parcel containing the shoes arrive at the gym, stashed it in her locker before Marta could get her hands on it, and had been holding the shoes hostage since.

Now, as Amy and Debbie looked nervously on, they were trying the shoes on for the first time, peeling off their trainers to reveal feet as wide as planks.

'Didn't they check the size before bidding?' Debbie hissed with a frown.

'They'll need a fairy godmother with a wand to stand a hope in hell of getting 'em on, surely?'

'It is because of the sweat,' Marta wheezed.

'What?' Amy cried.

'The feet in the trainers all day, they sweat, they get bigger.'

'No way!' Iwona retorted. 'Your feet have always been half a size bigger than mine.'

'Wait . . . one moment . . . oh!' Marta, with one final tug, slid off the bench and clattered onto the floor, panting and defeated, as the shoe rolled to one side. Amy stifled an urge to yell, 'Come to Mama!' and launch herself towards it.

'Ten out of ten for effort, over there,' Debbie whispered. 'You've got to hand it to her.'

'Shh!'

Now it was just Iwona. Surreptitiously kneading at the patent leather to try to soften it, she bent down for a final, valiant attempt to get the shoe on her foot. But it was clearly useless. Even from where Amy stood a few feet away, she could see that no more than her toes and the bridge of her foot had made it into the shoe.

Iwona sat up, folding her arms on her lap. Then, exhaling deeply, she cast a longing look in the direction of the poster advertising the Polish Ball.

Amy made a lightning-fast deduction.

She must be hoping to wear them to the ball – with that big beefy bloke!

'To be honest,' she began, tentatively, 'the shoes are murder to dance in.'

Iwona's gaze dropped to the shoe in front of her. Then she held it aloft, examining the heel and sole.

'I only wore them the once,' Amy went on, 'and they nearly killed me. Those wooden heels are very unforgiving. I was limping for days afterwards.'

'So why you want them back?' Iwona shot back.

Good point, Sherlock. What on earth do I say now? Well, I guess when all else fails, how about the truth?

'Because they have very special memories for me. I love them.'

'She really does,' Debbie put in. 'She's a funny one, is our Amy.'

A silence followed, the first since Amy had pushed open the door of the gym, approximately three lifetimes ago.

'So,' Marta said eventually, not meeting Amy's eyes, 'you want them back, these shoes that do not fit you either?'

Amy nodded slowly. 'Would you mind? I'm so sorry to have caused all this trouble.'

Then, after a few more moments of indecision, Marta finally heaved herself to her feet and placed the left shoe on the reception desk. And after still more agonising moments, a scowling Iwona followed suit with the right.

'I will need my forty pounds back, of course,' Marta said in a low voice.

'Forty!' Iwona spat. 'You should only get thirty-five! The traitor must pay!'

'Thief!'

'Ladies! Still looking hot hot *hot* tonight, I see.' Adonis swaggered by, heading for the saunas, winking suggestively.

It was as though the sight of him wiped the previous fifteen minutes entirely out of their consciousness. Marta and Iwona shot off after him, Iwona pausing only to grab what looked like two ball tickets from under the reception desk.

Once again the reception area became spookily calm. The black shoes sat on the reception desk. Amy stared at them. Then, without a word, she fished forty pounds out of her handbag and slapped the money behind the desk. Debbie grabbed the shoes.

'Come on, Buttons, let's leg it,' Amy giggled, 'before the car turns into a pumpkin!'

'Right behind ya, Cinders,' Debbie called back as they made a dash for the stairs.

It took several minutes for the girls to compose themselves enough so that Amy could start the engine and persuade the grumbling 2CV to leave the underground car park.

'Take a left at the end,' Debbie ordered.

Amy obeyed. 'Wow, what a palaver for a pair of shoes I'll never wear again!' she giggled. 'They nearly crippled me the one time I wore them.'

'I thought you were making that bit up. Oh, turn right here, then left again at the lights.'

'First gig I ever went to with Justin. I didn't want him to know straight away what a midget I am, and I'd just got them, and you know how, whenever you get new shoes, you just have to wear them straight away? Like, that very night?'

Debbie nodded. 'Or else the Shoe Goblin comes and casts an evil spell on you? Left again at Millets.'

'That's the one. So, the gig was brilliant, and we were dancing, and I knew after only about half an hour that if I didn't take the shoes off I'd have to saw my legs off to get some relief from the excruciating pain and I didn't fancy doing that . . .'

'Right after Accessorize, which is round the corner!'

'So I took them off.'

'Your legs?'

'The shoes, you muppet. And danced barefoot, staring at his chest. Y'know, he can rest his chin on the top of my head – it's kind of nice.' *Or, at least, it used to be kind of nice.*

'And nobody stood on you? Straight on here, but look out for an opticians on the left, then go right.'

'He's got a really smooth chest, Debs. And that night it smelled of cocoa butter . . .'

'Amy, pet, I think you're over-sharing a bit now. Since when did a bloke smell of cocoa butter?'

'It was nice! And he carried me out of the tent – did I say, the gig was in a marquee in the grounds of this fantastic stately home?'

'No, you – Left at the Vodaphone shop, no, wait – did I say left? I meant right at the Vodaphone shop. Oops! *Orange* shop! Since when did the Vodaphone shop become the Orange shop? Or maybe it was always the Orange shop and I just forgot . . .'

'Whatever, so there's me, barefoot, being carried across this lush wet grass towards Justin's car, dangling the shoes from my fingers – I thought he was going to drive me back to the flat I lived in at the time but he asked me if I wanted to go back to his place instead . . .'

'And, oh, let me take a wild guess. You said, "Certainly not, sire. I'm a good girl, I am. Take me home this instant, or my governess will be most anxious!" Yup, straight along here, past the Good Luck Chinese – fantastic foo yung in there, by the way.'

Amy grinned. 'Something like that. Anyway, I moved in with him the very next day.'

Debbie was silent for a few moments. Amy sensed that she was wrestling with herself, probably dying to unleash a pithy 'That was your first mistake' type of comment but, for once, veered away from the killer one-liner. 'Ah. Nice,' was all she said in the end.

'So where are we going now? This isn't the way we came in, is it?' Amy asked.

'I thought you'd never ask!' Debbie smirked. 'Here, yes, left here, into the car park.'

Amy indicated to the left. 'Wow, this looks like some size of a shopping mall!'

Debbie nodded. 'And tonight it's open till eight, as well.'

'Oh?' Amy pulled a ticket from the machine and the barrier lifted. 'What is it you need to buy? Something to take to your folks?'

'Don't be daft,' Debbie snorted. 'They'd think I was either pregnant or wanting to tap them for cash if I arrived home with presents. No, I, er, need to buy a dress, actually. And while we're at it, you could probably do with buying a couple of pairs of shoes for your trip. Those torture shoes aren't going to get you very far.'

'Fair point, but why tonight? What's the rush? And what's the mystery item?'

Debbie coloured. 'A ball dress.'

Amy blinked. 'Pardon? You're going to a . . . *Debbie*! Not the Polish Ball?'

'Yep, tomorrow night! Shame you won't still be

around to drive me there in this old pumpkin,' she giggled, patting the 2CV's dashboard.

It was just as well the car park was nearly empty, as Amy couldn't concentrate on manoeuvring the car into one of the spaces, and ended up straddling two. 'But how on earth . . . ? *Debbie!* I let you out of my sight for five, count them, *five* minutes back in that place and you manage to pull?'

'Correct. Don't look so surprised, kiddo. I can work fast when I have to.' Debbie pulled out her handbag mirror and licked her lips provocatively.

'So tell me all about this brave – sorry, I mean *lucky*, obviously – bloke, then? Was he hiding in the ladies?'

'Don't you remember him?' Debbie looked surprised. 'Big feller, fair hair, foreign, Rambo pecs – and the rest . . .'

'The *Polish* guy?' Amy shrieked. 'Mr Nutcracker-Butt?'

'Oh, Polish, is he? Yes, that would sort of make sense, wouldn't it, considering it's a Polish Society Ball – yes, that's him.'

'*How*, for Pete's sake?'

'Got talking to him at the water cooler just inside the gym – I peeked in to eye up the talent and what do you know? Talent appeared.'

'So how did you move from introducing yourself to blagging an invitation to a ball in less than five minutes?'

Debbie was reapplying gloss to her mouth, pouting into her metallic pink handbag mirror. 'I just asked him where a girl has to go to have a good time around here, that's all, and he invited me there and then – It was like taking candy off a kid. Don't you think he's just . . . *edible*?'

Amy couldn't imagine ever being *that* hungry. But she nodded all the same. 'Tell you one thing, though, Debs, you'd better keep out of Iwona and Marta's way. I think they thought they had him all wrapped up for themselves.'

Debbie spread her palm out and gestured at her face. 'See this face? Does it look bovvered?'

Amy laughed. 'Come on then, you big hussy – you *shall* go to the ball. And I'm picking the shoes!'

CHAPTER NINE

It had been twelve years since Amy had last been in Berkshire, even though the county lay only a short distance to the west of London. It had been in winter; her parents took her to Windsor Castle as a Christmas holiday treat. She had been thrilled to be told she was going to see the Queen's 'real' home and, according to her mother (although she couldn't remember this), had spent the entire trip trying to peer through windows to see if she could spot Her Majesty watching telly. She'd even asked if the Queen would be wearing slippers, and when she got home that evening, had made an elaborate drawing of what Royal Slippers might look like. Tassels and diamonds had featured heavily.

Now, the day after her success at Delsey's Gym, Amy was once again in Berkshire, only this time, alone. She'd said goodbye to Debbie in Newcastle that morning, wishing her luck for the Polish Ball before setting off early to track down the second address on the shoe list.

As the 2CV roared past Windsor, Amy tried not to glance at the castle looming on the horizon: pangs of nostalgia were making it hard enough to concentrate on the unfamiliar road as it was. She had had so few family outings – not many that she could remember, anyhow. But the Windsor Castle trip had been a truly golden day.

She remembered the strawberry ice cream her dad had bought her, which melted all the way down the front of her navy-blue duffel coat and onto her fur-lined silver plastic boots – her Spice Girls boots. Remembering these brought a smile to her lips for the first time that day. She'd worn them until they fell to bits, and had been heartbroken when her mother finally threw them out.

And only a few weeks after the Windsor Castle trip, her father was dead: killed in a car accident driving home from work late one icy night.

She shook her head violently, trying physically to wrench the sad thoughts from her mind. Her mission was hard enough without inviting in more painful memories.

Thatcham, Winterbourne, Chieveley, Peasemore. Amy drove past signs to towns and villages that sounded impossibly pretty, wishing she had Debbie or Jesminder with her to keep her company. Or Justin. Where the heck was Justin?

At last, after two stops to check her road map, she arrived at the village on the list – Brightwalton. Her heart quickened as she navigated her way past the church, over the canal, and finally pulled up outside a pretty, red-brick terraced cottage. Number three. She was there.

Putting off the moment, she pulled her mobile phone out of her bag and punched Justin's number on speed-dial.

She jumped when an automated voice announced: 'The number you have called has not been recognised. Please check the number and try again.'

He had disconnected his phone. He. Had. Disconnected. His. Phone.

On autopilot, Amy hung up and looked around her, the phone falling from her hands into the footwell. She had never felt so alone in her life.

Dully, she checked her reflection in her handbag mirror. Dark shadows circled her eyes and her forehead sported twin vertical frown lines just above her nose. They hadn't been there a week ago.

I look like shit.

With a sigh, she locked the car, made her way up the cobbled path to the green-painted front door, and rang the bell. Now her heart began to dance a brutal tango in her chest.

'I'll get it!' came a small voice from inside.

'Oh!' Amy exclaimed, as a little girl of around eight or nine greeted her, wearing a pale pink ballet tutu, complete with net skirt and ribboned ballet shoes. 'Hello!'

Immediately, the tango in her heart upped its tempo. *I don't believe it! This has to be where Mum's dancing slippers are! It just* has *to be!*

'You look pretty!' Amy twittered. 'Is your mummy at home, please?'

'Who is it, Miranda?' came a woman's voice from the kitchen.

Without waiting for a reply, the girl's mother appeared. Short, flustered, barefoot, pretty in a dishevelled sort of way and very, very pregnant. 'Hello, you're early, aren't you?'

Her voice was friendly enough, but Amy could tell straight away that the woman was exhausted. It showed in every move she made, in every trying-to-be-polite word she spoke, the dark circles under her eyes even more impressive than Amy's. Amy opened her mouth to speak.

'Sophie?' A man's voice called through from the back of the house, 'any chance I could get that kettle *now*, please? Bit of an emergency out back . . .'

The woman rolled her eyes. 'Coming.' She grimaced apologetically at Amy. 'Come in, please. My husband's doing something completely vital to the onion plants – won't be a sec.'

She bustled back towards the kitchen and Amy, unsure of the correct course of action, followed.

The kitchen was a sea of family clutter: ironing, toys, crockery and a paint-laden child's easel filled every available space. It had a warm, homely feel yet still Amy's heart went out to the woman who was yanking the kettle from its socket and handing it to the lanky, apologetic-looking man standing in the back doorway.

'And Tim? Don't get mud on it,' she sighed, rubbing her forehead.

'I won't, darling,' he replied. His voice was soft and patient. He too looked exhausted.

Something's not quite right here . . .

'Thanks.' Amy heard the faintly contrite tone in

Sophie's voice, but her husband was already gone, shoulders slightly stooped, back towards the canes and nets of a vegetable patch that lay beyond the child's swing set.

'Sorry about that,' the woman said, smiling weakly at Amy. 'So, you must be the lady who rang up about needing volunteers for the Community Council?'

Eh? Yikes . . .

'Me?' Amy pointed at herself with her thumb. 'No, not exactly. I'm sorry to trouble you, but well, my name's Amy Marsh and there's been a mix-up over some shoes I sold on eBay and I thought I'd better come in person to try and sort it out.'

Sophie's eyebrows shot up. 'Shoes? You're here about *shoes*? Oh, silly me! Well, that's much more fun than discussing bric-a-brac committees for the Autumn Bazaar! I love shoes!' Then immediately her face darkened again. 'Most of the time, anyhow.' She turned her head and shot a malevolent look towards the garden. 'Look, I'm sure if there's been a mix-up we can sort it out. Miranda!'

The little girl skipped through from the sitting room.

'Put this on your bed, then go and finish your practice outside. Take Peter with you. Daddy can look after him for a while – for once. *Please.*' She handed her daughter a freshly ironed summer frock. Miranda took it and danced upstairs.

'It's stupid, really,' Amy mumbled, 'but, well, I didn't mean to sell this particular pair, and I was passing, so I just thought I'd pop in . . .' she tailed off, feeling wretched, hating the half-truth. It seemed so out of place in the safe, family environment into which she had been invited.

'Don't worry,' Sophie replied, 'I do that sort of thing all the time.' Then she frowned. 'No, actually I don't – but I have got some new eBay shoes upstairs. Why don't you come up and take a look?'

'Are you sure?' Amy glanced guiltily at Sophie's impressive bump, the sheen of perspiration on her forehead. 'You're not too tired?'

'Course not.' Sophie smiled. 'Come on.'

They met Miranda again on the upstairs landing. She was pulling her small brother, who was engrossed by his Game Boy, out of his bedroom. 'Come on, Petey, Mummy said NOW! And Mummy's very tired, and Daddy says we've got to do what Mummy says until she has the baby!'

Sophie smiled at this. 'And every day after that for the rest of your lives, darlings,' she reminded them as they descended the stairs and went out the back.

'At least that's one thing he's got right lately,' she muttered. 'Oh, I'm so sorry, my name's Sophie – you're Amy, isn't that what you said?' She walked into her bedroom and crossed to where a huge antique pine double wardrobe stood against the far wall.

'That's right. And I'm really sorry . . .'

'No more apologies! Right, you want shoes? *Ta-da! Shoes!*'

As Sophie flung open the double doors, Amy gasped. Dozens upon dozens of pairs of beautiful shoes – a collection to rival her own, easily.

'Can't you just smell the leather?' Sophie inhaled,

her eyes closed. An expression of pure bliss flashed over her face, just for a moment.

Amy grinned. 'Are you my long-lost sister, by any chance? That's what I feel like when I open my shoe cupboard!'

Sophie smiled back. 'Do you sometimes touch them, you know, just to feel their shape – not like you're going to wear them or anything . . . ? Oh, my Lord, you must think you've been kidnapped by a shoe-psycho.'

'Nope,' Amy assured her, 'I'm right with you on that one. What a fabulous collection!' She was scanning the racks of perfectly stacked shoes, unboxed, though each pair was neatly pigeonholed in a contraption that resembled an oversized wine rack. But although the shoes were lovely, and just her style, Amy saw straight away that not one single pair was familiar. And there definitely weren't any ballet slippers. 'I could look at them all day.'

Sophie snorted. 'Huh, that's all I'm managing to do these days, *look* at them. It's doing my head in. See these?' She gestured down to her feet.

Amy peered politely down below the loose cotton shift dress Sophie was wearing. 'Oh, you poor thing!'

Sophie's ankles were terribly swollen and her bare feet looked so puffy that Amy couldn't help thinking that her toes resembled fat little sausages. She couldn't think of anything to say.

'Hideous, aren't they?' Sophie said. 'I haven't been able to wear any of my shoes for weeks; been flapping around in flip-flops half the time.' She shook her head.

'Don't you think flip-flops are the worst invention known to man? They're the black sheep of the shoe family, aren't they?'

Amy agreed. 'Mmm – and such a horrible name! *Flip-flops!*'

'I always used to think that life as I knew it would be officially over the day I started wearing flip-flops anywhere other than on the beach. And here I am! Flipping and flopping like an old walrus!'

'You're not an old walrus, don't be daft,' Amy soothed. 'But, well, you do have my sympathy.'

'Thanks.' Sophie turned and walked over to the window. She gazed down onto the back garden where rasping spade sounds mixed with Miranda's singing and the tinny music from Peter's Game Boy.

'See that man out there?' Sophie jerked her head towards her husband, who was trying to get Peter to turn the Game Boy off and kick a football. 'Do you know what he did?'

'Um, no?'

Sophie sank down onto her bed and sighed, rubbing the small of her back. 'Two weeks ago,' she began, 'was our wedding anniversary. Eleven years.'

'Congratulations.' Amy faltered, sensing that the next part wasn't going to be pretty.

'Huh, thanks. Anyway, Tim said he'd got a surprise for me – great, huh?'

'Usually . . .'

'Precisely. *Usually* we'd go for dinner, or on a mini-break, or to the theatre, or somewhere. I knew he had something special planned because he'd arranged for

Miranda and Peter to go to his parents' for the night. You know what?'

'Tell me.' Amy held her breath.

'I was hoping for a spa. A *spa*! I'm knackered, swollen up like a whale, nothing fits, everything hurts and my knickers make Bridget Jones's look indecently tiny.'

'Nice image, thank you.' Amy smiled.

'You're welcome. I've got loads more where that one came from. But anyhow, I would have sold my soul for a facial, bit of a hairdo, or just a good pedicure – why didn't he understand that?'

Erm, because he's male? Amy said nothing, tensing for what was to come.

'So, I put on the only nice garment that still ties at the back – my Ischiko wrap dress – and came downstairs. Turned out he was going to make my supper.'

'That's . . . nice, isn't it?' There was no correct response to be had, Amy was certain of that.

'I asked him if he didn't want to be seen out in public with a wife who looks like two side-by-side double-decker buses, and he got a bit huffy.'

'Perhaps he just wanted a quiet night in before the baby comes, with you all to himself?'

Sophie sighed. 'That's what he said. Anyhow, the apple juice was on ice, the candles were lit and suddenly he said he couldn't contain himself any more and he was going to get my present. So he told me to shut my eyes and dashed upstairs.'

'I'm not going to like this, am I?' Amy whispered through clenched teeth.

'Last year, he got me a pair of tickets to Vienna. Year

before it was a Mulberry tote bag – the dark green one, remember it?'

'Sorry, I'm a shoe girl. Bags are a foreign country.'

'So down he comes, clutching a shoe box tied with a big red ribbon – fantastic!'

'Yay, result!' Amy ventured, then held her breath again.

'That's what I thought. I thought he'd remembered me slobbering over a pair of black Manolo Blahniks the last time we were in London. He'd had to prise me away from the shop window . . .'

'Not the Riviera wedge with the gunmetal heel?' Amy just couldn't resist.

Sophie stared at her for a moment, then nodded, dumbly.

'Sorry,' Amy shrugged. 'Call it intuition. Go on, please!'

'OK, I thought he'd have thought I'd like some fab shoes to look forward to wearing after the baby comes.'

'I would have thought so too.'

'I just thought he'd *think*, Amy.'

'Yes, well, you'd think so. Um, what was in the box, Sophie?' Amy couldn't bear it a moment longer.

Sophie closed her eyes, forcing out the answer. 'Orthopaedic shoes.'

CHAPTER TEN

'*What?*'

Sophie scrunched her eyes tightly shut. 'Yes, you heard correctly. *Orthopaedic* shoes. Slip-on, navy-blue shoes with an adjustable buckle for an extra-comfy fit.'

'No!'

'Width fitting? Treble G.'

'Treble *what?*'

'Treble G. G for Gross. From a specialist orthopaedic shoe and brace company, the absolute comfiest of their ultra-comfy "Bunty" range. "No foot too wide", that's their motto.'

'Can I see them?' As soon as she asked the question, Amy was ashamed of it, shocked that her first reaction was to want to see just exactly *how* hideous they were. The mental image, as painted by Sophie, was bad enough – only now she longed for proof.

Sophie shook her head. 'Sent them back. The very next day.'

'Ah. Quite right.'

'And I didn't speak to Tim for two days.'

This was bad. Amy looked at the woman, swollen and miserable, slumped on her bed. Frantically, she searched her brain for something positive to say.

'I guess he did think, though, didn't he? I mean, he must hate seeing you so uncomfortable, and so he tried to do something about it?'

Sophie nodded. 'That's what he kept saying. He thinks I overreacted. He says he knew the shoes weren't exactly sexy, but it'd only be for a short time.'

'Which is true, isn't it? When's the baby due?'

'Another five weeks. Ages.'

'Not really, though, is it?'

'But I've got so much to do! And Tim's been spending every spare moment out in the garden – he's avoiding me, I know it. He's angry too. What was it he said yesterday? "Why don't you buy your own presents from now on since I'm so crap at it?" Oh, I don't know. Orthopaedic shoes, Amy! Can you believe a husband would actually seek these out for his wife *as a present*?'

Amy chewed her lip. This wasn't exactly a winnable situation. 'Poor you,' was all she replied.

Sophie heaved herself to her feet and slowly, painfully, reached under her bed and pulled out a polythene bag.

'See these, though – now *these* are a present!' Reaching into the bag, she pulled out . . .

Amy's shoes.

Amy's tummy lurched. There, being flung onto the bed with a flourish, like fresh evidence in a murder trial, were her funky espadrilles, the burnt-orange canvas ones she'd bought in Spain one summer, on holiday with her mum. Woven cord straps with little wooden beads on the ends, and tiny gold threads running through the canvas, which made them perfect for day or night. Great with shorts, lovely with a sarong . . . and just right, Amy realised, to cheer up a pregnant lady who couldn't fit into anything else.

'These yours?'

Amy nodded.

'So there's been some sort of mix-up?'

Slowly, Amy nodded a second time. 'Well, more of a mistake, really—'

'They're wonderful,' Sophie interrupted. 'Miranda and Petey went online at Tim's parents' house and bought them to cheer me up. I never knew they had such good taste! I think their granny helped – she loves her shoes as well. Shame she didn't pass on some of her passion to her son, don't you think? But there you go, that's men for you.'

'I guess.' Completely deflated, Amy flopped down onto Sophie's bed.

Sophie, mid-rant, didn't notice. 'Computer spares? He buys the best in the business. Ties? He's got a real knack for choosing fantastic ties for work, but *shoes*? I'm telling you, Amy, hell would freeze over before . . . em, Amy? Are you all right?'

Sophie's hand reached out and covered Amy's, and Amy, to her mortification, burst into tears.

'I'm sorry!' she gulped, scrubbing her face with her sleeve. 'It's so silly!'

'Oh, Amy, what's the matter?' Sophie's voice was full of concern. She pulled a tissue from the box on her bedside table and handed it to Amy. 'Is it the shoes? Oh, silly me, of course it's the shoes.'

'No, no . . .'

'Why on earth did you sell them?' Sophie's fingers trailed across the rich orange canvas of one of the espadrilles.

'I didn't, that's the thing,' Amy gulped. 'My boyfriend sold them. He sold all my shoes, two weeks ago, without telling me.'

'He *what*?'

'He thinks I cheated on him – which I didn't – and so he did the one thing he knew would hurt me more than anything else. Then he threw me out.'

'Oh, Amy, that's awful!'

Amy took a couple of deep breaths. 'It hardly seems real just now. He won't listen – won't answer the phone or anything. So I'm . . . well, I'm taking some time out to get my head together and . . .'

'And get your shoes back?' Sophie's voice was tender. 'I don't blame you.'

'Well . . .'

'Tell me about them. You didn't buy them in the UK, did you? I've never seen a pair like them in the shops – they just *scream* Euro-boho-chic, don't they?'

She placed the shoes in Amy's lap. Amy picked up the end of one of the cords and played with the little bead.

'Spain,' she sniffed, blowing her nose on the tissue Sophie had given her. 'I bought them in Spain. On the last holiday I went on with my mum – she died two years ago.'

'Oh, no! It gets worse! I'm so sorry.' Sophie handed Amy another tissue.

'Thanks. We were in Seville, looking round on one of those hot evenings when the shops are open late and people are drifting about and there's music coming from all the bars, and the squares are filled with cafés, and it's so relaxed, and Mum was in such good form. I wanted the evening to last for ever.' Amy smiled thinly at the memory. 'But nothing does, does it? Everything has to change . . .'

'Go on,' Sophie urged.

'Well, just about every second shop was a shoe shop and we were in heaven, peering in all the windows, fantasising about how many pairs we'd buy if we had unlimited money and our own jumbo jet to take them all back home with us.'

'I've had shopping trips like that too,' Sophie said dreamily.

'So I spotted these espadrilles, just a fraction of a second before Mum, and nipped in to try them on.'

'Don't tell me – you knew you were going to buy them whether they fitted or not?'

Amy nodded. 'Pretty much. But they fitted perfectly. I was chuffed. And I didn't notice Mum at all, until just as I was paying for them I heard her ask the assistant if they had another pair in *her* size—' Amy broke off and took some huge gulps of air. She wanted to hurl herself face-down on Sophie's bed and give in to huge, guilty sobs.

'What happened?'

'I just about had a fit. I told Mum she was far too

old for funky espadrilles – that she'd look ridiculous in them.'

Sophie grimaced, and Amy nodded ruefully.

'She wouldn't have, though. She was a dancer, and she was so pretty, and graceful, but I was just so stung that she wanted my shoes, so I lashed out. I was such a cow!'

'We all have things we wish we could have done differently, Amy. I'm sure your mother would have understood.'

'Well, she didn't tell me off or anything, just sort of went a bit quiet. In a way I would have preferred it if she'd totally gone off on one, then it would have blown over, but she didn't. We just wandered back to our hotel in silence.'

'Ah.'

'But do you know what happened later on?'

'Tell me.'

'There was a dance on in the hotel that night, a local band was playing some fantastic Spanish music, and I was dancing with a group of girls I'd made friends with . . .'

'Wearing the new shoes?' Sophie asked. 'I bet you were. Everyone wears new shoes the same day they buy them, don't you find?'

'Are you *absolutely* sure you're not my long-lost sister?' Amy cried. 'I was just saying *exactly* that to my friend Debbie a couple of days ago. Of *course* I was wearing the shoes! Anyway, we stopped for a drink, and we were just beginning to eye up the talent behind the bar when this clapping started on the dance floor.

A crowd had formed a semicircle and the band was playing this really sexy Spanish dance.'

'And?' Sophie prompted.

'I knew before I went over, to be honest, that it would be her. Mum was in the middle of the crowd, dancing, with her eyes closed, just moving to the music, twirling slowly, in total control and yet abandoned, somehow, her arms above her head, shoulders swaying. She looked . . . *electrifying*. She was very beautiful, you see.'

'I can imagine. You're a very pretty girl too, Amy.'

'Oh, but I wish you'd seen her,' Amy cut in. 'Nobody could take their eyes off her. I wanted the music to go on for ever, and when it eventually stopped and everyone was clapping and cheering, she was laughing and came over and gave me this huge hug, and suddenly all I could think was: this is the woman I said was too old for a pair of shoes. This woman who had just, well, *rocked* the joint!'

'Way to go!' Sophie cried, clapping her hands. 'What a woman!'

'You know, it didn't really register at the time, but every single man in the place was practically standing in a puddle of drool, watching her. It's hard to think of your mum as sexy, but my goodness, she totally was that night!'

'Well, let's hear it for sexy mamas,' Sophie replied. 'Sometimes motherhood feels like the unsexiest thing in the world.' She put her hands on her belly, and sighed.

Amy wanted to reassure Sophie that she looked perfectly sexy to her, but stopped herself. *Bit weird, sitting on a stranger's bed, saying stuff like that.*

'Come on,' Sophie said at last. 'How about some peppermint tea? It's about all I can stomach at the moment.'

Back downstairs in the kitchen, Amy was relieved on Tim's behalf to see that he had dutifully returned the kettle. Somehow she knew he'd be made to suffer if he'd forgotten. Sophie refilled it, switched it on and closed the back door.

Outside, Tim had abandoned his digging and was multi-tasking with the children, standing in goal for Peter whilst throwing a Frisbee for Miranda to catch. Amy pictured herself in a scene like this in years to come, lovingly baking for hordes of sweet-faced children . . . until reality hit her and Justin came crowding to the front of her mind.

I've got nobody. Justin doesn't want me – what gives me the right to think anyone else ever will?

'Biscuit?' Sophie asked. 'I'm seeing off two packets of Rich Tea a day at the moment.'

'Thanks. Um, Sophie, can I say something potentially dodgy?'

Sophie sat down beside her and poured hot peppermint tea into two bone-china mugs. 'Go on, I can take it.' She smiled as she pushed one of the mugs in Amy's direction.

'I've just realised something. I think it would be lovely to have a doofus-brained man buy me orthopaedic shoes.'

Sophie froze.

'I'm sorry,' Amy rushed, 'and I *was* listening when you were telling me about him, and I completely understand how you must have felt, but now I've had a chance to think about it, well, it was thoughtful, wasn't it?'

'I know!' Sophie burst out. 'But I didn't need thoughtful – not in that way, anyhow. I didn't need my husband reminding me I'm too huge for nice things!'

'But that's not what he would have been thinking. He probably just wanted to help you feel better! Look, we can all be insensitive sometimes, can't we? I mean, I was pretty insensitive in Spain, telling my mum she was too old for espadrilles, wasn't I?'

'Well, I'd have to say yes to that one.'

'But I didn't see it like that. I just thought about myself, and thought: I can't buy the same sort of shoes my *mum* likes – but then she showed me that it's all about *who* you are, not how old you are, and she was the one who kicked butt on the dance floor that night, not me, so I guess I got what I deserved.'

'So,' Sophie pointed out, 'going by your own rules, don't you think Tim deserves to suffer a bit for buying duff shoes?'

A silence ensued as Amy tried to follow Sophie's logic. She sat, inhaling the comforting steam from her mug, the quiet broken only by excitable noises from the children outside. Sophie lifted her head and stared out at her little family. Amy groped for words, for something to say that might help, or at least comfort the other woman, but nothing came.

'I suppose I've been a horrible old witch, haven't I?' Sophie said, at last.

Amy looked up, tilting her head to one side. 'Well,

perhaps a tiny bit, if you want an honest opinion – but I would have been exactly the same.' She added the final part quickly. The last thing she wanted to do was upset Sophie even more. 'I guess it's a bit like being bought deodorant after asking whether you smell nice, or something like that.'

Sophie laughed. 'Or a wig if you say you're having a bad hair day.'

'Big pants if you mention your thong's a bit tight,' Amy spluttered.

'Thongs!' Sophie scrunched her eyes. 'Ah, *thongs*. I used to wear them.' She dabbed her eyes with a tea towel. 'Tim definitely approves of them – not that he wears them himself, of course, the love.'

'Sure?' Amy giggled. She liked this new, vibrant Sophie. Her eyes were alight when she mentioned Tim's name now, unlike mere minutes ago when they had been clouded with exhaustion and hurt.

'Mums don't wear thongs,' Sophie declared. 'Thongs are for chickadees like you, Amy.'

'Don't be daft!' Amy retorted. 'Anyhow, if Tim likes to see you in thongs, why deny him the pleasure? Well – after the baby's born, I guess . . .' She glanced, embarrassed, at Sophie's bump.

'*Way* after the baby, perhaps,' Sophie conceded. 'After it's born I'll have the sleepless nights and aching boobs to contend with. And all the rest.'

'Well, what about now? Why don't you make the most of the last few weeks before Junior arrives?'

Exasperated, Sophie rubbed her forehead. 'Because there's so much to do! Tim's got to get the garden sorted out, and I need to make sure everything's organised in the house because I'm not going to get a minute to myself with a new baby, as well as Miranda and Petey.'

'Hmm, tricky,' Amy agreed.

'Anyhow, I don't *feel* like a woman, as Shania Twain nearly sang – not these days. I just feel like a big, round, pregnant mama.'

Sophie gazed out the window again and caught Tim's eye. Amy held her breath. A flash of affection crossed Tim's face and he half raised his hand before the expression vanished and he kicked the ball away and reached for his spade again.

'I've got an idea,' Amy said in a low voice.

'You have? I'm listening,' Sophie replied.

Forty-five minutes and another mug of mint tea later, the plan was in place, the phone calls made. Sophie mixed a jug of iced lemonade, and called Tim and the children inside. Tim greeted Amy warmly, nodding in polite bafflement as Sophie outlined the reason for her visit.

'My goodness, the power of shoes,' he said, shaking his head. 'Sounds like you're having a bit of a tough time, though. I'm sorry.'

For some reason his response made tears prick the back of Amy's eyes. Then, all in a rush, she knew why.

He sounds like my dad used to . . .

Kind, dependable, caring – somehow Amy just knew that Tim shared lots of her father's precious qualities. It was all there, in those gentle eyes, the easy demeanour. For a moment Amy felt a familiar stab of regret as she tried to conjure up a clear image of her father, but it was hopeless. He'd already faded in her mind's eyes and there was nothing she could do about it.

Sophie made Tim sit down. Amy could tell she was nervous. Miranda and Peter sat too, looking from adult to adult expectantly, and at once Amy realised she was surplus to requirements.

'Oh, my goodness, is that the time?' she exclaimed, taking them all by surprise by leaping to her feet and flailing her arms in mock panic. 'I really have to be going!'

'Amy, that was terrible,' Sophie laughed. 'Don't feel you have to go. In fact, why don't you stay and have dinner with us?'

Amy shook her head. 'No, really, it's kind of you, but I must think about getting back to London. I've got lots of packing still to do for the rest of my trip.'

'Sure?' Sophie heaved herself to her feet.

'Quite sure, thank you.' She moved towards the front door, and Sophie and Tim followed her.

'Oh! The shoes! I must get them for you. Wait here.' Sophie turned towards the stairs.

'No!' Amy caught her arm. 'I don't want them any more – you keep them. They . . . they'll suit you far more than they ever suited me, with your lovely olive skin tone.'

'Amy, don't tell me you've come all this way and now you've just realised you don't want your shoes back after all? Come on, I'm not buying that one.'

'This is getting weirder by the minute,' Tim murmured, putting his hand on his wife's shoulder.

114

'Well, it's pretty clear you've got more need of them than me at the moment, and it'd make me feel happy knowing they've gone to a good home so . . . please, Sophie. Hang on to them. But keep in touch, OK? Let me know how . . . you get on?' She jerked her head in Tim's direction, and Sophie giggled.

Tim planted his hands on his hips, not the tiniest bit menacingly. 'OK, you two, spit it out.'

They were interrupted by a tooting horn, and a dark green mini-van pulled up behind Amy's car.

'Wow, that was quick – he's here!' Amy exclaimed.

'That's a good start,' Sophie replied.

'*Who's* here?' Tim demanded. 'What's going on? Anyone?'

'Darling, there's a bit of a clue on the side of the van,' Sophie said, pointing towards the road.

Tim frowned. '"Trevor Smith Gardening Services"? But we didn't order a gardener.'

Sophie nodded. '*We* didn't, but *I* did.'

'But . . . why?'

She threaded her arm through his. 'I've just realised that I need you more than the onion patch needs you at the moment, my love. Besides, haven't Miranda and Petey been going on and on about that new movie at the Multiplex? Why don't we all go, right now?'

Amy began to walk down the path, fishing in her bag for her car keys. Behind her, she could hear Sophie explaining herself to Tim.

'I never got you an anniversary present, did I? So here it is. I've bought you some time off for good behaviour – *family* time.

'Goodbye, Amy, and thanks for everything,' Sophie called.

'You're welcome,' Amy replied, sidling past the gardener, who was making his way up the path to discuss his new assignment. 'All the best with the new baby.'

She started the engine and pointed the car back towards London.

Now, why can't I sort out my own life so neatly?

CHAPTER ELEVEN

'You know what I think about airports?' Jesminder announced as she and Amy joined the end of a queue that seemed to lap Gatwick Airport's check-in area about four times. Amy had driven back to London late Saturday afternoon and spent the night at Jesminder's, and then her friend had sweetly volunteered to drive her to Terminal 1 and wait with her.

'Um, you think they're designed by mad scientists to test how humans behave under extreme stress?' Amy ventured, fumbling for her passport for the umpteenth time that morning.

'No.'

'You think the Almighty made them like this to have a big, cosmic laugh at our expense?'

'No. I just think they're dull.'

Amy gazed round at the clamour, the noise, the chaos of hundreds of people parked behind trolley-loads of luggage, the coffee stands, the tie shops, the stewardesses towing wheeled cases and clipping by on regulation airline-issue heels, the billboards and the flashing information screens. 'Dull?' she echoed. 'How can you call all this pandemonium *dull*?'

Jesminder frowned. 'Dunno, but there's a dullness in the air, as though everyone's excitement about their trip is being sucked out of them, somehow. Maybe it's the security precautions. How can you relax if you're about to be searched and probed for suspicious devices? Where's the trust, where's the camaraderie, the sense of all being in this great big adventure together?'

'You don't like flying, do you, Jes?' Amy smiled, touching her friend on the shoulder.

'Hate it,' Jesminder admitted.

'That'll be why you work in travel, I suppose.'

'Absolutely. I'm facing my fears. The more I know, the braver I get. And the duller it is. Look around you!' She jabbed a finger randomly round the huge building. 'Dull, dull, dull!'

'Well, mate, thanks again for the lift, but all this cheering-up you're doing is making me giddy . . .'

'Sorry.' Jesminder clapped a hand over her mouth. 'This is no way to see you off on the international phase of your big adventure, is it? So how do you feel now you're actually here?' She nudged Amy's suitcase a few inches forwards.

'Truthfully?' Amy replied.

'Of course.'

'I feel a little dull, as though all the excitement of the trip is being sucked out of me.' Amy looked directly into Jesminder's eyes. Jesminder half smiled, but was silent. 'But I'm nervous too, and I'm still questioning the whole idea – you know, whether I'm doing the right thing or not.'

They shuffled forwards another few feet.

'Nobody's going to force you on to the plane, Amy.'

Amy tugged at the canvas handle of her shoulder bag. A burly man in a Newcastle United football top pushed past her, towing a massive, wheeled set of golf clubs. 'Sorry darlin',' he breezed, as Amy clutched at Jesminder to maintain her balance.

'It's OK,' Amy whispered, though he was gone. The queue picked up speed and before long the girls found themselves within squinting distance of the actual check-in desk.

'Amy?' Jesminder pressed. 'Do you want to step out of the queue and grab some more time to think?'

'No,' Amy replied firmly. 'I'm going. I might as flaming well, mightn't I?'

'Oh, Amy!' Jesminder's face was a picture of anguish. 'You can't set off in this frame of mind. This is a huge trip – first Ireland, then all the way to the States all on your own. It'd be one thing if you were excited, but if you're just trying to prove a point, to Justin, or to us—'

'Or to myself,' Amy cut in. 'Sorry, Jes, I didn't mean to upset you.' She forced a grin. 'Hey, I'm so grateful to you for getting such dirt-cheap fares for me – did I say that?'

'You did, but it's nice to hear it again.' Jesminder smiled.

'Listen, Jes, I'd be fibbing if I said I was over the moon about the way life's going right now, but at least this way I'm showing Justin that I'm not going to suffer his cruelty lying down, and I'm taking my mind off the whole situation, and seeing a bit of the world. Mum would be proud of me, I know that much.'

'I'm sure she would,' her friend nodded.

'She travelled all over the world with her dancing. She always used to say that travel was a privilege, not a chore. So I'm trying to remember that.' Amy was slipping into a reverie, and Jesminder kept nudging her suitcase forward, ever closer to the front of the queue.

'Plus, you'll be getting your shoes back.'

'Well, obviously.' Amy brightened. 'Say, Jes, Sanjay plays football with Justin on Saturdays, doesn't he?'

Jesminder nodded. 'Oh, yes, without fail. He is a bit of a creature of habit, that brother of mine, I'm afraid.'

'Erm, well, Jes?'

'Ye-es?'

'You don't think you could . . . ?'

'Ask him to talk some sense into Justin for you? Don't worry, Amy, I'm way ahead of you on that one. He's practically got a script to read from! And remember, Amy, Debbie and I will be with you in spirit, every step of the way.'

Jesminder accompanied Amy all the way to the security desk, and both girls fought back tears as they hugged their goodbyes. And as Amy watched her friend melt away into the crowds, her mobile phone bleeped. It was a text from Debbie.

Bon Voyage Slagheap. Bring me back Colin
Farrell ☺ Dbs xxx

The departure lounge was heaving with travellers of all shapes and sizes. Amy bought a magazine and found a seat tucked away in a corner. She had just settled down and was turning to the horoscopes page, her habitual jump-off point for all magazines, when her phone rang. It was Sergei, calling from Malaysia, where he was touring with his ballet company.

'*What?*' Sergei spluttered, when Amy told him where she was.

'I'm at Gatwick, heading for New York after a stopover at Shannon Airport in Ireland to, er, attend to a small matter there.'

'Amy, you're going to have to explain.' And so, patiently, because there was over an hour to wait before her flight was due to be called, and because she needed to rationalise her plan once again to herself, Amy told Sergei everything.

He listened, mostly in silence, punctured now and then with sighs, and small exclamations, and mutterings under his breath of things like 'the blockhead!' or 'my poor dear', until Amy had brought him fully up to speed with all that had happened. She didn't see any need to conceal anything from Sergei – after all, none of this was his fault – and the more Amy told him, the more she found she wanted to tell him: it felt good, having a real, proper grown-up to confide in.

'Amy, my dear,' Sergei said in a low voice after she was done, 'I will be travelling with you in spirit, every step of the way.'

She felt a glow of happiness. Jesminder had said the same thing. 'Thanks, Sergei, that means a lot.'

'And I insist that you make full use of my house in the Hamptons when you are in the States – you will do that, will you not?'

'Oh, Sergei, that's terribly kind . . .'

'No, no, it would be kind of you to accept! I will feel much easier in my mind if I know that you have a – oh, what would be the better word? – a sanctuary to escape to, or to return to, should you find you need it. So, that is settled, yes? In fact, you will go there as soon as you get to the States, to get to know the place? It will be empty, but I have a housekeeper who lives nearby who can give you some keys.'

Almost speechless with gratitude, Amy whispered, 'Thank you so much. I accept.'

Glancing up at the boarding information, Amy yelped in alarm to see that her flight to Shannon had been called. She had been talking to Sergei for over an hour. She shot to her feet. 'I'm going to miss the flight if I don't go now. Goodbye, Sergei, and thank you again. You will keep in touch, won't you?'

'Of course I will. I will email you all the information you need. Godspeed, little one.'

CHAPTER TWELVE

The scrap of paper lay spread out on the passenger seat beside her: 'Mrs Nuala McCarthy, Burren Lodge, Ballyvaughan, Co. Clare, Ireland.'

What a lovely address, Amy mused, as the little silver hire car nosed its way northwards from Shannon Airport, through the rugged landscape of County Clare in western Ireland. The sky was dark and brooding, casting dramatic shadows across the uninhabited hillsides, which seemed to envelop her as she travelled on increasingly narrow roads. How could such a short distance take such a long time? The road twisted and turned, as though the road builders had considered it a matter of pride not to disturb a single rock or hillock of the landscape, but rather to hug and caress it, laying the road upon the earth, like placing a ribbon on a piece of crumpled cloth.

After what seemed like hours of driving, Amy slowed the car to a halt in front of a signpost that claimed Ballyvaughan lay in two opposing directions. Turning off the ignition, she glowered at the treacherous signpost.

Now what?

Reaching for the tourist map, which the hire company had thoughtfully stashed in the glove compartment, she tried to make sense of the complex web of little roads, but they all looked the same. Despite gazing at it until her head began to ache, Amy still couldn't be absolutely certain where she was.

I am in the wilds of Ireland, I'm lost, and I'm lonely. Whose idea was this, again?

And there was nobody to ask for help. Spirits plummeting, she restarted the engine, muttered, 'Sod it!' and screamed off to the left, only because that way had a smattering of whitewashed houses dotting the hills, whereas taking the bleak road to the right would have felt like setting a course for the end of the world.

After another twenty minutes or so of snaking through the countryside, Amy was relieved to find herself entering a small town that was positively buzzing with human activity. Cars, Jeeps and tractors were parked on either side of the street, and yellow and green bunting festooned the lampposts, zigzagging down what looked like the main street all the way to a pretty town square in the centre. The sight of so many human beings had a distinct cheering effect. Crawling through the narrow streets, stopping occasionally when the crowds on either pavement spilled onto the road in front of her, Amy responded chirpily whenever anyone peered in and gave her a friendly wave.

But amidst all the unexpected gaiety she forgot to look out for signposts and before she knew it she was completely enmeshed in the throng, heading at a snail's pace towards the centre of the town.

Yikes, she thought. What on earth's going on here?

The hats and scarves provided a clue. Some wore red and white, others plain blue, and everyone was moving in the same direction. Amy realised, at last, that there was some kind of sporting event in the offing and if she didn't want to be held up for the rest of time she'd have to somehow take herself off in the opposite direction.

But there was no way of turning the car without the aid of a helicopter and a winch. The car behind, crammed with burly sports fans, was disconcertingly close and Amy simply knew that they would honk their horn at her, or worse, if she tried to indicate that she needed to turn round.

Sure enough, after she'd hesitated once too often, a horn blared angrily from behind. Flustered, Amy tried to look behind and wave, whilst pressing the accelerator and checking the map at the same time. The hire car stalled.

'No!' She shouted at nobody. 'Come on, car!'

A sharp, rapping knock on her window nearly made her pass out with fright, and Amy whipped her head round, to see a tall, dark and rather handsome policeman peering in at her. Oh, thank goodness – the cavalry. Or at least, the garda, because her little tourist map had helpfully provided details of various emergency services, even if it hadn't managed to tell her the right direction in which to travel.

Rolling down her window, it was all Amy could do

to stop herself grabbing him by the back of the neck and pulling him towards her for a big, grateful kiss.

'Everything all right there with you, miss?' he asked, grinning in a slightly crooked way that might have been considered inappropriately sexy.

Amy blushed a little. 'Well, not really. I'm trying to find Ballyvaughan and now I'm holding up the traffic. Please could you tell me what I should be doing?' She smiled apologetically.

From behind, the car hooted again and the garda cast a leisurely look over his shoulder before calling out, 'All right there, lads, there's an hour before the start and I seem to have a wee visitor who's lost her way in here, so just give us a minute, why don't you?'

Amy poked her head out of the side window and cast an apologetic glance at the car behind, mouthing 'sorry' to the driver. The driver looked first to her, then towards the garda, rolled his eyes, and settled back in his seat, smiling and shaking his head.

'Now then,' the garda went on, resting his elbows on the window frame, 'if I were to be telling you that you're not too far at all from Ballyvaughan, would that cheer you up a bit?'

'Really? Am I? That's a stroke of luck – I seem to have been driving for ever.'

'You here for the hurling, then?' he asked, smiling down at her.

'I *beg* your pardon?' Amy had no idea what he was on about, but it didn't sound particularly pleasant.

'The hurling – you know – Irish ball game? Lots of

big fellers in shorts knocking seven bells out of each other with long sticks and a wee white ball?'

Amy flushed scarlet. 'Oh! No, I'm sorry, I've never heard of . . . hurling.' Now she felt more of a ditzy London chick than ever. 'I've led a sheltered life, obviously.'

The garda smiled again, and waved her apology away. 'No worries, miss. There's plenty of people who can lead long and really quite fulfilling lives without ever involving themselves in our beautiful game.'

Amy giggled. 'Well, that's a relief!'

There was a pause. He was keeping his eyes on her just a fraction too long. Amy blushed some more. Eventually he spoke again. 'Ballyvaughan, then? Let me help you get your car turned.' He gestured towards a side street that lay slightly behind her car. 'See that wee road back there? That's the one you want. Stay on it, you'll be in Ballyvaughan in no time.'

'Thank you,' she replied. 'My hero!'

The garda tipped a hand to his hat, a gesture Amy couldn't ever remember being made to her before. She was rolling up her window when he tapped on the glass again. Raising an eyebrow, she rolled the window down once more.

'Yes?'

'Well, I don't suppose you'll be coming back this way any time soon?'

Really, Amy thought, I must be beetroot red by now. His eyes were the greenest she'd seen for a long time. Green as Irish shamrocks. Amy hadn't ever seen shamrocks, but she'd seen plenty of clover and reckoned that shamrocks were probably in the same ballpark.

'Only, it'd be my pleasure to be taking you out some-time – show you around, you know?'

Her mind was racing as the implications of the invitation filtered through.

Is he asking me out?

But then, taking her by surprise, Justin's familiar, hurt face flashed before her eyes and she turned apologetically to face the garda. 'Oh, em, thank you, but, well, what a shame! I'm only here for a brief visit, then I fly to the States tomorrow, and then I'm needed back in London for work.'

As soon as the words were out of her mouth she could have kicked herself. The garda shrank back immediately, looking embarrassed.

Why on earth have I just made out that I'm Donald flaming Trump's more successful girl cousin? What exactly was nice about giving that charming, uniformed boy the impression that I'm some sort of big shot, rather than lonely old Amy Marsh who could really do with spending a little time with a nice man to remind me that the entire species doesn't comprise untrusting, shoe-selling hotheads like Justin Campbell?

'Ah, right you are then – sorry to have presumed, miss.'

'No . . .' Flustered, Amy tried to protest but the garda had straightened up and was surveying the throng. He soon cleared a path through the cars and the sports fans so that she could turn the car round without squashing anyone. He beckoned her through with another brief touch to his hat, avoiding her eyes. Amy waved her thanks, but he wasn't looking. He studiously kept controlling the traffic and the crowds as she passed. She couldn't have had more assiduous treatment if she'd been a world leader in a cavalcade of limousines. But she'd lost whatever connection there had been.

She drove contemplatively the final ten-minute stretch to the coastal town of Ballyvaughan, scarcely noticing the striking beauty of the landscape, known as The Burren, according to her intermittently helpful map, which unfolded around her. Smooth, lunar limestone hills, grey amidst the green of the heathland, rose gently on all sides. She could have been on Jupiter, but her mind was contending with mounting nerves about the reception she was, hopefully, about to receive from an unsuspecting Mrs Nuala McCarthy, and faint regrets that she hadn't been a bit friendlier towards the cute garda. What harm would it have done, spending a little time with him?

Nah. There's not enough space in my head for that sort of stuff right now. Debbie would've been all over him like a rash, though, that's for sure . . .

Nervously she tore open a packet of crisps and gobbled them, realising that she hadn't had a thing to eat for hours, and then, dusting crumbs from her tight black jumper and grey skirt, she entered Ballyvaughan at last.

Winding down her window to get a gasp of air, the sharp tang of the ocean caught her breath immediately as she pulled up on the sea front and tried to get to grips with her new surroundings. A gigantic seagull, surely far too large to fly, screamed furiously at her before stabbing its beak at a discarded bag of chips beside her car, and taking off in a steep, chip-encumbered trajectory over the bay. There were very few people about. A couple of old men sat, smoking roll-up cigarettes and putting the world to rights, on a paint-spattered municipal bench in the shadow of the memorial that looked mournfully out to sea.

What now?

Fishing out the map, Amy scanned its selective contents for clues. Nothing. A dark pit of hopelessness threatened to rise up from deep within her – that urge again, to abandon the trip, ring Jes, and scurry home. She sighed and gazed around, wondering who'd be kindest to her if she got out and asked for help.

But then the seagull returned looking for more chips. Screaming at her, louder and more angrily this time, he perched upon a little wooden sign nailed to a bollard, which, judging by the dried droppings and nibbled paint, he had made very much his own.

The sign pointed towards a little road that led south, away from the harbour, up a green knobbly hill and on towards the horizon. And it was quite hard to make out the writing on it: 'Burre L dge I mil . . .'

Smiling, Amy restarted her engine. 'Thanks, birdie, I owe you one. Did Jesminder send you, by any chance?'

CHAPTER THIRTEEN

The entrance driveway to Burren Lodge had been almost obscured by cars – twenty or thirty of them parked all round a large, stone house with an old-fashioned, painted front porch and some tumbledown wooden outhouses to one side. Already jumpy, Amy's heart lurched at the sight.

Great. I'm gatecrashing a party.

She sighed. Still, there was no turning back now, and at least she could get the job done quickly and get out of there; Mrs McCarthy would have enough to do without entertaining strangers as well as her bona fide guests. Amy found a parking space in the adjoining field, approached the house and knocked firmly on the door.

A low buzz of conversation could be heard from within as the door was opened by – a *butler*? Amy couldn't contain a small gasp of surprise as the man, aged around fifty and dressed head to toe in an elderly-looking black suit, inclined his head slightly and held the door open solemnly, for her to enter.

What would a woman with her own butler be doing buying shoes on eBay?

He inclined his head towards the entrance hall as Amy, too confused to say any more, dumbly walked inside. She moved towards the buzz of conversation, relaxing a little in the warm, wood-panelled interior, even allowing a little smile to creep across her face.

Things are grander than I thought here – a butler! Memo to self: do not prejudge people just because they happen to live in the sticks. Hey, maybe I'll get my Prada slingbacks back here.

Biting her lip, she entered the drawing room, which was crowded with guests, all standing around with glasses of what looked like whiskey in their hands and . . . ah.

They were all dressed in black. Amy didn't even need to look further into the room, to the open coffin that stood in the centre, to tumble to what was actually taking place.

Oh, OK. So that wasn't a butler, then . . .

'Maureen! And here's us thinking you wouldn't make it.' A man who seemed to be as old as the hills of The Burren surged towards her, more nimbly than his appearance suggested he might, thrust a glass of whiskey into her left hand, and clasped her right.

Amy gave an embarrassed little laugh. 'Oh, sorry, but I'm not Maureen!' she protested, though she accepted the whiskey gratefully.

'Very good, very good! Wonderful to see you again, Maureen!' The man appeared to be deaf, as well as a little bit tipsy.

'Um . . .' Searching for something pertinent to say, she wanted to ask the only question she couldn't ask: So, who's dead, then? She tailed off and said nothing, taking a sip from the glass instead. The fiery liquid burned all the way down and, immediately, a wonderful warm surge washed over her.

'So how's Dublin treatin' ya, then, Maureen?'

'I'm afraid I'm not Maureen . . .'

'Terrible business about Nuala, wasn't it?'

Nuala! Oh, no!

'Of course it's not that we weren't expecting it, what with the bad turn she took and everything, but it's always a shock to the system, don't you find? You know, Nuala and I were just having a cup o' tea together the other week. I called round to tell her how I was getting on after the surgery, you know? Your Auntie Clodagh would have told you about my surgery, wouldn't she, now?' He jerked his head downwards, towards his nether regions, and Amy coughed politely and looked away, wondering what on earth to do next.

'Ladies and gentlemen, may I have your attention just the one more time, please?' An elegantly dressed woman in her thirties raised a slim arm in the air and addressed the crowd. Her black shift dress fitted her to perfection, and Amy couldn't help thinking that her own beloved Prada slingbacks would have been far better teamed with it than the low-heeled court shoes she had chosen to wear. 'Now I won't detain you for much longer, but I just wondered if anyone else would like to say a few words about Mother, before I make my own tribute?'

A low buzz started up around the room as people

looked at each other and murmured about whether or not to say anything. Amy's brain was in overdrive. Obviously, poor old Mrs Nuala McCarthy had died very recently – that had to be her lying in the coffin in the middle of the room.

Yikes.

The sight of a coffin inevitably brought to Amy's mind the funerals of her parents, and feelings of grief could still catch her unawares in such moments. She glanced towards it but couldn't bear to step closer to peer in. She knew she had no right to do so, anyhow. But what a shame, to have bought new shoes so recently, and then to pass away without having a chance to enjoy them. She wondered whether Mrs McCarthy had managed to get any wear out of her new shoes before she died, then pondered, briefly, whether that might be the most unworthy thought in the room that day – the most unworthy thought *ever*, even. Or, hang on, perhaps it had been her walking boots that she'd bought. It was strangely cheering to think of her trusty Brasher boots tramping over The Burren on the feet of their new owner, within sight of the rolling ocean . . .

'Here! Over here!' The old man who had given Amy the whiskey now caught her elbow and pulled her, gently yet firmly, forward. 'Our wee latecomer hasn't had her chance to say a word, Breda!'

'No,' Amy protested under her breath, but to no avail. The crowd was already beginning to shrink back to form a semicircle around her, and she found herself propelled towards the centre of the room until she stood, sharing the limelight with the open coffin.

'That's it, lass, better late than never. She'd be proud to see you come all this way, so she would.' The old man grinned, before draining his glass and looking at her, smiling expectantly. Amy, realising that she still held her whiskey glass in her hand, raised it to her lips and took a huge gulp, draining it in one go.

'That's it, girl, you wet your whistle.' The old man nodded approvingly, walking up to her and removing the empty glass from her hand. Amy's only other alternative would have been to balance it on the edge of the coffin, so, grateful for small mercies, she smiled her thanks.

What on earth do I say?

Catching Breda McCarthy's eye, she smiled nervously. The dead woman's daughter was clearly trying to place her, but she smiled back thinly and said nothing. Then from nowhere, Amy thought of her own mother and, fired by the whiskey, emotion threatened to overcome her.

My mother was a performer. Come on. Marsh!

Her head began to spin. Whiskey on an empty stomach: bad idea.

Mum would rise to an occasion like this. Do it! Say something!

She knew she would never see these people again.

'Well,' she began, 'I'm sorry I'm late. It's a long way to get here, from England.'

No reaction. Emboldened, Amy plunged on, kicking off with a stroke of genius.

'There probably aren't very many of you who'll know that my dear mother and Mrs McCarthy – Nuala – were

135

great friends.' *Excellent. What now?* 'One or two of you who came to my mother's funeral two years ago will remember me saying that Mum's time in Ireland was the most special part of her whole life, roaming the beautiful hills with Nuala.'

Still the crowd remained silent. She was getting away with it. Closing her eyes for a second or two, she mouthed, 'Sorry, Mum,' and continued.

'Mum thought Ireland was the most beautiful place on earth. And I know for certain that one of the reasons that led to her thinking this was the warmth of her friendship with Nuala. Of course, the landscape is magical, but what is beauty without friendship? That's one of the things Mum said to me, not long before she died. I know she was thinking of her old friend Nuala as she spoke.'

More silence. Somebody cleared their throat.

OK, wind it up now, girl – bring it home . . .

'Mum and Nuala's days out together, roaming the hills in all weathers, shaped the woman that she became. And now, now that Nuala too has sadly passed away, I felt I had to come here and pay my respects to such a vibrant force of nature. If you like, I'm trying to walk in my mother's shoes, the way she walked with Nuala over those beautiful hills, forging their friendship that meant such a lot to Mum. Thank you.'

A sprinkling of applause tickled the corners of the room as Amy stepped back to her place.

The old man thrust another tumbler of whiskey into her hands. 'Good on yer, Maureen, you've done County Clare proud, so you have.' He clearly hadn't heard a word she'd said. Shrugging inwardly, Amy sipped the whiskey, and began plotting her escape.

'Thank you for coming all this way,' came a woman's voice from beside her. Breda McCarthy was looking at her with a puzzled, though not unfriendly face. 'I'm sorry about the loss of your mother.'

'No, no! I'm sorry about the loss of yours!' Amy blurted out, before grasping a measure of composure and adding, 'Well, yes, thank you, but it was two years ago, and I still miss her dreadfully, but poor you, it's all come so suddenly for you, hasn't it? You must be so shocked.'

Breda McCarthy frowned thoughtfully. 'Shocked? Well, perhaps there is an element of shock but as she'd been in the hospice for all those months before she died, we have had a little time to come to terms with it.'

'Ah. Quite. Of course.' The urge to run like the wind out of the room was almost overwhelming.

Breda touched her on the arm. 'Mothers are strange creatures, aren't they? Who could have known all those things from her past if you, a *total* stranger, had not just walked in?'

Amy had never felt so uncomfortable in her life. She almost kissed the older lady who came over to them and whispered to Breda that perhaps she might like to begin her tribute as old John O'Donnell was needing to be going for his train.

'My dear friends, old and new . . .' Breda McCarthy began to speak, whilst Amy thought furiously about what she was going to do next. She had become so flustered, firstly by the stress of the journey, then the shock of walking into the funeral of the very person she had come to speak to, and then by the mortification of weaving a colossal pack of whiskey-fuelled fibs in a spectacular and clearly failed attempt at drawing attention away from her outsider status, that she was only jolted back into remembering the purpose of her visit when she dimly heard Breda McCarthy move on to a subject dear to her heart.

'. . . shoes of her dreams . . .'

Pardon? Amy's head shot up and she began to pay attention.

'My mother, as you all know, was a great one for her shoes. She always used to say that if ever she won the lottery, she'd buy only three things for herself: a front-row ticket to watch Michael Flatley in *Riverdance*, a lifetime's supply of Marks & Spencer Florentine biscuits, and a pair of shoes made by Christian Dior.'

There was a ripple of subdued laughter.

'I think she believed that Mr Christian Dior himself would sit down in a workshop and hand-stich a pair of gorgeous shoes, just for her.'

Amy smiled. She thought along those lines as well, sometimes. It was all falling into place.

'And so,' Breda went on, 'I was happy and proud to be able to make one of Mummy's dreams come true – no, Michael Flatley's not here this afternoon, thank you, Uncle Robert, but I was able to find a pair of Christian Dior shoes for her to wear, as you will have seen.' Her head nodded towards the open casket.

But Amy hadn't seen. The crowd had pressed forward

a little as Breda made her speech. Amy was only a step or two away from being able to peep inside.

Warm applause started up as Breda thanked everyone one final time and stepped back. There was a light commotion as people moved forward to embrace her. Amy moved too, until she found herself standing right beside the open coffin. Taking a deep breath, she looked inside.

The dead woman looked unreal, like a waxwork. Amy hoped she would look 'peaceful', or 'serene' or one of those reassuring words she'd heard so often relating to dead people, but no. How could she look 'serene' to Amy when Amy had no idea what she'd looked like when she was alive? The curious, sculptural form in the coffin seemed devoid of every trace of once having been alive, and Amy was instantly relieved that she wasn't going to have to fight her way through too many anguished flashbacks to her own mother's funeral, where letting go of the woman in the coffin had been the hardest thing she had ever had to do. But Amy had never seen poor Mrs Nuala McCarthy vibrant and well; the person who had once been there – whoever she had been – was no longer, and as such, Amy was more able to hold it together. She cast a furtive glance round the room, head half-bowed, lashes lowered, to make sure nobody was paying her any attention. They weren't. Everyone apart from herself was forming into an orderly queue to embrace the dead woman's daughter. Breda McCarthy's composed demeanour was beginning to slip at last, and Amy watched, full of sympathy, as the woman reached for a lace-edged handkerchief from her bag.

Come on, Marsh, stay on mission!

She took a small step towards the other end of the coffin, and, steeling herself, looked down at the shoes on the dead woman's feet.

Ah.

There they were. The black Christian Dior shoes with the tiny diamanté detail on the buckle of the little ankle strap. The shoes she had worn on one of her first proper dates with Justin. When they'd gone to that underground bar in Mayfair that served cocktails made with fruit purée that were so delicious Amy had drunk four in a row in under an hour. To this day Amy didn't know how she'd managed to stay upright, let alone make witty conversation to impress Justin, but she had always credited the fantastic construction of those Christian Diors for enabling her to walk from the bar to her taxi home, without falling flat on her face in a puddle. Justin used to joke that he'd finally found the woman of his dreams: one who could drink him under the table and still stay awake long enough to curl up and share cheese on toast with him at three in the morning. Huh. Those were, indeed, the days.

Stepping away from the coffin, Amy found a quiet corner of the room in which to do some hard thinking. Leaning against the reassuring oak of a sturdy door-frame, she observed the scene as though removed from her body, hovering unseen over the spectacle, as though shoulder to shoulder with the spirit of Nuala McCarthy.

She had several options open to her. She could sit in her car until after the burial then return at midnight with a spade, exhume the body and grab the shoes. She could take advantage of the fact that the coffin was temporarily free of surrounding mourners, whip the shoes off the dead lady now and make a break for it via the window, the nearest escape route to her car. She felt Debbie nodding enthusiastically in spirit. Or she could take poor, grieving Breda McCarthy to one side, tell her the truth and ask, very, very nicely if she'd be good enough to remove the shoes from her darling mother's dead feet and hand them over to her, a stranger, thus thwarting an unseen, vengeful ex-boyfriend, the existence of whom Breda McCarthy was going to have to take on trust – and why precisely would she do that, given Amy's Oscar-standard pack of lies so far?

Or she could do nothing. Gather up all the remaining dignity she could muster, apologise inwardly to the people in the room (for going up to explain everything to Breda McCarthy suddenly felt like an intrusion too far), and, well, leg it.

Amy knew she was in trouble when she realised she was deliberating over a straight choice between the final option and the midnight churchyard with the spade.

She laid her whiskey glass down on top of the upright piano beside which she was cowering, trying with all her might to be invisible, insignificant.

Her course of action was clear. Looking over at the coffin one last time, she bent her head and offered a silent farewell, then turned and walked away.

But her departure didn't go wholly unnoticed. Wordlessly, and almost noiselessly, the man who had opened the door to her on her arrival appeared at her shoulder to show her out.

141

'Going already?' he asked, not unkindly, as he eased in front of her to open the door.

'Y-yes, I'm afraid I have to. I'm catching a plane to the States.' This, at least, was the truth.

'So, your mother and Nuala were friends, you say? What did you say your name was?'

Amy froze, convinced that she must have the words BIG, FAT and LIAR spelled out in flashing neon lights on her forehead.

'Um, I didn't say, actually! Silly me! It's Amy. Well, anyhow, goodness, that can't be the time already, can it? I really must be going. I just wanted to pay my respects, and I don't want to intrude any further, so, well . . .'

The man was half-smiling at her. 'Your mother must have known Nuala an awful long time ago, by my reckoning.'

Amy forced out a thoughtful nod, petrified at what was coming next. She inched towards the door, ducking under the man's arm as he held it open for her.

'I mean,' he said thoughtfully, 'if you think that Nuala was in her wheelchair since that accident when she was sixteen, oh, let's see now . . .'

'Would you excuse me?' Amy gushed, her cheeks aflame with whiskey and shame. 'Aeroplane.' She started walking as fast as she could towards her car.

The man nodded again. 'And now, let's see, if the accident was sixty years ago, that would make . . . Amy? Hello? That really is quite an extraordinarily unusual friendship, wouldn't you say?'

It couldn't, just couldn't get any worse. Reaching the

sanctuary of her car, Amy jumped in and waved at the man who still stood, motionless, by the door. A silly, guilty, childish wave. She had been comprehensively rumbled and there was nothing she could do about it. Starting the engine, she turned the car and pointed it back towards Ballyvaughan, back towards the name-less, ribbony roads, back towards the airport where Debs had blagged her a cheap hotel room before her flight to New York the next morning.

It was going to take the rest of the journey for the heat in her face to subside. She couldn't even stop in the busy hurling town to track down the garda because he'd be bound to smell whiskey on her breath, and even though she didn't think she'd had all that much, none the less the prospect of being breathalysed and hurled into a cell for the night appealed even less than skulking alone into a soulless hotel room on the edge of an Irish runway.

By tomorrow, I'll have put a whole ocean between me and this place, thank goodness, she thought, as in her rear-view mirror Burren Lodge curled out of sight behind the brooding, knobbly hill.

CHAPTER FOURTEEN

After a night and day twiddling her thumbs on standby in Shannon, and a bumpy, sleepless flight across the Atlantic, Amy finally landed in the US of A on the Fourth of July. Well, I am truly asserting my independence with this unconventional trip, she thought.

Following Sergei's careful instructions, which she had picked up at an Internet café back in Shannon, she had travelled from the airport into the heart of Manhattan. She'd been looking forward to this – New York! How had it happened in the space of less than a week that she'd switched from her comfortable routine in London – work, Justin, and occasional shoe splurges at the shops – to being a (presumably) single girl riding alone into the very core of the Big Apple?

Despite her jet lag and an increasing sensation of dazed, nervous exhaustion, the skyline took her breath away as the yellow cab drove up the New Jersey Turnpike, turned for the Lincoln Tunnel and on into New York.

Arriving in Manhattan, Amy asked her driver to take her the scenic route. It was all so breathtaking, and she didn't want to miss a thing.

She could hardly believe she was actually there. Nothing – no photograph, no TV show, no movie – had prepared her for the sheer scale of it. Sure, she'd seen skyscrapers before, but here, she could scarcely contain a whoop as she caught a quick glimpse of the Statue of Liberty, so solid and splendid, standing tall and iconic in the bay. There was the majestic Chrysler Building spearing into the clouds and the Empire State Building, so stately and imposing.

But it was in the shopping districts where her heart skipped a beat. She stared open-mouthed at the Jimmy Choo flagship store, not to mention Manolo Blahnik's season must-haves flaunting themselves in a fabulously exotic window display. Amy wished Debs and Jes were here to see this.

She pictured them all strutting along, laden down with rope-handled bags, straight out of some scene from *Sex and the City*. Everywhere she looked was reminiscent of a scene from film or television. Looking down one street, she was reminded of the grittiness of *CSI: New York*; down another and the glamour of *The Devil Wears Prada*; another and the cut-throat world of *Wall Street*.

Stepping out at Penn Station, after a whistlestop tour of Manhattan, she was greeted with an explosion of sounds: car horns, helicopters hovering overhead, thick-accented New York voices, and swathes of tourists babbling excitedly in their native tongues. It was like being on a movie set with its vast, brooding buildings, lively characters, and men and women in sharp dark suits beetling along the sidewalk. The whole city was teeming with life, and the promise of adventure.

Awesome! Thank goodness I'm coming back here later. Now, where's the bus stop . . . ?

The coach that would take her on the three-hour journey north to Sergei's summer residence in the coastal town of East Hampton was known as the 'Hampton Jitney' and was, according to Sergei, famous for ferrying rich New Yorkers out of the city for their weekend fun. Amy flopped down into her seat and settled down to enjoy the ride, but, to her annoyance later on, fatigue finally overwhelmed her and she crashed out, sleeping for most of the trip and having to be woken at her destination by the driver.

East Hampton lay on the eastern tip of Long Island, in Suffolk County, New York State, and Amy knew, both from Sergei and from a bit of cursory research before her arrival, that she would find glorious sandy beaches, lighthouses, windmills and tourist-friendly shops practically on her doorstep if she only cared to step outdoors and explore.

But today, all she wanted to do was catch up on some sleep and gear up to meet the North American stage of her quest head-on the following day.

She was met at the bus stop by Sergei's brisk and jolly housekeeper, a tiny woman aged around sixty, with dyed jet-black hair, olive skin and a wide, friendly smile.

'Miss Marsh?' she called, waving furiously from the pavement.

Amy rushed over and clasped the woman's hands. 'Amy – please call me Amy. You must be Maria? Sergei told me that he was going to ask you to come and meet me. It's so nice of you – you've gone to so much trouble!' Realising she was babbling, Amy paused to catch her breath. But it just felt so lovely to be met by a human being who knew her name – particularly after the anonymous mortification that had been Ireland.

'It is my pleasure,' the older woman replied, in a soft South American accent.

Still clutching Amy's hands, Maria stepped back and regarded her closely, a smile lighting her features. Yet there was a definite expression of puzzlement as well.

Amy hesitated. *Yikes. What have I done?*

'Em, is something wrong?' Amy asked. 'Oh, no! I don't have a blueberry moustache, do I?' Instinctively, she scrubbed at her top lip with her thumb and forefinger. 'Only I was drinking berry juice on the coach, and I haven't got a mirror . . .'

Maria smiled and shook her head. 'No, Amy, you look fine. Just a little tired, and no wonder. You must be longing to get some rest. Now, you go to the car – it's over there – and I'll take your bag.' She indicated Amy's giant suitcase. 'Is that it?'

'No, I'll take it. Really, I'm fine. It's terribly kind of you, though.'

One polite scuffle later and Amy and her luggage

were in Maria's station wagon, being driven the short distance to Sergei's home.

Amy gazed at the landscape outside, green and sun-kissed. She was roasting; the air conditioning in Maria's car did little to compensate for the fact that she was still dressed for brisk Irish coastal weather rather than a Long Island heatwave. Fanning herself with her baseball cap, she tried, through tired eyes, to take in her surroundings.

And at last, there it was, the ocean with sailboats drifting through the waves.

Soon Maria was indicating left and turned the car into a wide, tree-lined road. 'Look – we're here.'

'Wow!' Amy caught her breath.

Sergei's home was beautiful. Amy had known it would be. It was a big, traditional-style wooden house, painted a gentle shade of blue, with white windows and doors, and an elegant veranda that skirted the entire building and shaded its occupants from the worst of the summer heat, which, according to Maria, was scorching the entire state with record-breaking ferocity.

A paved driveway led up a small slope to a gigantic double garage, and on either side thick herbaceous borders overflowed with flowers.

'The flowers are all white!' Amy exclaimed. 'Oh! Those lilies are spectacular – and the roses, and is that white lilac?' Instantly she was transported back to the tiny, chaotic London garden of her childhood. Her mother had loved flowers.

Maria nodded proudly. 'Special request of Mr Sergei – only white blooms. Antonio, my husband, he is the gardener here. In Brazil, where Antonio and I come from, the flowers are so much more wild, so colourful, but the white, it works here somehow. You like?'

Amy could only nod.

Just like the garden Mum dreamed of creating one day . . . white flowers only.

The white theme continued indoors: open-plan, with wooden floors, neutral rugs and massive, sprawling pale sofas. Amy floated round, her tired senses brought alive by the airy tranquillity of Sergei's family home. And the photographs! Framed photographs were everywhere, on every wall, the stairwell, clustered on side tables and on top of the baby grand piano that stood at the far end of the entrance hall. Maria had picked armfuls of white lilies and roses and arranged them artlessly all around the house, so that their scent reached every corner.

'I could stay here for ever,' Amy breathed.

Sergei had married late in life, to a beautiful Californian woman named Lisa, who was fifteen years his junior and whom Amy had seen only in photographs. They had two little daughters, Katya and Anna, and their laughing faces were everywhere, making Amy happy and sad in equal measure as she moved from one to another, gazing with a strange mixture of anguish and delight at the picture-perfect family scenes. Somehow she felt that she knew them all already, such was the effect that Sergei's kindness and hospitality had on her.

Look, Justin, hardly a threat to you, were they?

Lisa had taken the children to her parents' home in Anaheim for the holiday period, and was due to return in five days' time – the same day as Sergei's scheduled return from his tour of Asia.

'Amy?' Maria, who had left Amy alone to have a look around, now called softly to her from the doorway.

'Yes?' Amy whipped round. She'd been lost in the study of a big ensemble photograph of Sergei on stage during a curtain call for some ballet or other, the entire company clustered around him and clearly giving him an ovation at the end of a performance. But – and she had checked very, very carefully – her mother was not in the picture.

'You can't spend the evening here alone. Come and have dinner with Antonio and me. It would be our pleasure.'

Despite being overwhelmed by her kindness, Amy hesitated. She was totally, utterly wiped out. 'Oh, Maria, thank you so much, but, well, do you mind very much if I don't? You've been so kind to me, and I don't want to appear ungrateful, but . . .'

Amy didn't need to say any more. Maria nodded and pressed a set of keys into Amy's hand. 'Take these. They are yours. My phone number is written on the pad over there. You must promise to ring me if you need anything, no matter how small, is that OK? You will do it?'

'I will, Maria.'

'And, Amy?'

'Yes?'

'You must make yourself at home here; help yourself to whatever you need. Mr Sergei insisted that I made this clear to you.'

'I . . . I will. Thank you.'

Alone, Amy drifted round the house. She began to feel some of the tension lift from her shoulders as the effect of the flowers, the serenity, of just having her own space for a short time worked its way into her system. Out in the back yard a large, tree-shaded swimming pool beckoned her invitingly, but even though she was already beginning to feel brighter than she had done since the start of this whole adventure, stripping off and plunging in was definitely a leap too far.

Sergei had made it abundantly clear that she must treat the house as her home, even to the extent of insisting that she use his office, a wood-panelled room leading off from behind the dining room, to catch up with messages from home.

Huh, not that there'll be any.

Still Amy felt like a guilty interloper as she tiptoed in and hovered above his laptop, which lay upon an enormous oak desk. Sergei had mentioned that the house had wireless Internet connection so, rather than stay within his private inner sanctum, she picked up the machine and crept back through to the living area.

Something about handling someone else's computer gave her unwelcome flashbacks to her sleuthing mission in her – or should that be Justin's? – apartment.

She could feel her heart thumping as she waited for the laptop to boot up. Although rationally she knew that the chances of Justin making contact to apologise via email were remote, none the less she felt better nursing the small hope that he might, than give up on the idea completely.

But, of course, there were no messages from Justin. Amy sighed and rubbed her forehead, trying to quash her disappointment before it blossomed into a full-blown wail of misery. There would have been no one to hear her, after all. One by one, other messages popped up. Several kind offers of low-interest loans, stock market opportunities and penis extensions, and notification of mind-blowing reductions in the upcoming Topshop sale. Cut-price airline offers. SPAM alerts. But then, to her delight, up popped one that she really could enjoy: Debbie.

'Yippee!' she cried aloud. 'Debs, you trouper!' Amy hugged the machine close, then, tucking her legs underneath her on the sofa, settled in to do justice to the message.

From: Debs
To: Amy Marsh
Subject: Polish Balls!!!
Hi there, little Miss Wandering Star, how's it going?

Hope you are behaving yourself (not), and that your luggage is bulging with reclaimed shoes – go, babe! Haven't seen anything of J-you-know-who but that's a good thing as I'd only lamp him one if I did. Did you keep Colin Farrell to yourself in Ireland, then? And hey, now you've got a whole new continent to choose from! Start with Leonardo DiCaprio then move on to Josh Lucas – steer clear of Kevin Federline, though, and who knows where you'll end up!!! ☺

Just had to fill you in on all the happenings at the Polish Ball – I wish you'd been there, Amy, you'd have loved it!!!

The email was several pages long, so Amy snuggled into a corner of one of Sergei's fabulous squashy cream sofas and balanced the laptop on her knees.

OK, here goes. First things first, my dress was amazing. I felt incredible in it – whatever made you persuade me to choose the gold one rather than the black was a stroke of sheer genius, I felt like the only girl there with a bit of personality among all the little black numbers that were all over the place – wowser, did it get me noticed! Gabriel's eyes nearly popped out of his head when he saw me! (Did I tell you his name was Gabriel – how mad is that! But he was no angel, as you'll find out . . .)

Where was I, oh yes, the dress – maybe I should've gone for the bigger size like you said but hey, I was still able to dance in it, and though I say it myself, my cleavage was quite, well, arresting, if you get my drift!

Anyhow, the ball was held in this enormous country house hotel on the edge of the city. I told Gabriel I'd see him in the bar rather than have him showing up at Mum and Dad's house to collect me – how weird would that have been! Dad grilling him on whether his intentions were honourable (duh! course they weren't) and Mum offering him a nice cup of tea – nightmare!

I left that scene far behind me years ago when I moved to London.

So I arrived fashionably late and tottered into the hotel bar in those gold T-bar Ginas you talked me into getting (another good move – I SO owe you one), and I'm wearing a plain black wrap that I borrowed off Mum, oh, and I put my hair up – you know that French knot Jes taught us how to do a year or so back? Well, I did that and put this feather thing in at the back and then a touch of hair glitter – just a tiny spritz, I didn't want to run the risk of looking like a giant Christmas decoration, but no, it looked wicked. So I walk in and he's at the bar and he's in this black tuxedo with a white tie and he looked incredible – dead sexy but sort of – HUGE, you know? Like he'd got a whole other person welded to his body underneath his shirt!!! His neck disappeared under all that collar and tie and shoulders, and his thighs were straining to get out of his trousers . . . still, I got used to it quite quickly (ahem*, cough*) if you know what I mean, because he sort of grabbed me and kissed me THREE TIMES, left cheek, right cheek, left cheek and my wrap fell off my shoulders and he looked down and – oh, Amy, you should have seen his face! The shock! I mean, I could tell he was impressed (how could he not be? har har) because he sort of hesitated and stared like he wanted to bury his face in my chest and then he pulled himself back and said, 'Debbeee, where I come from our women do not often dress like so. It is not being modest, you know?' and I said, 'Gabriel, sweetie, where I come from our men remember their manners and if there isn't a vodka and Coke in my hands in the next FIFTEEN seconds you will find THIS woman, in THIS dress, making for THAT door over there and you'll need to find yourself ANOTHER woman to talk down to for the evening.' And, Amy, do you know what? He was a puppy dog after that!!! Haven't I always said that the tougher the man, the more they enjoy being put in their place?

So, he's drinking vodka too, but straight shots, down in one, and I think he'd necked a few before I'd got there (is there such a thing as Polish Courage, or does it always have to be Dutch?) because he starts telling me I'm beautiful and how I should come to his gym – hey, I've just thought, d'you think he was having a go at me for not being a scary size six? Whatever, by the time we left the bar I was comprehensively clued up about his fitness regime, his diet, his daily moisturising routine, what brought him over from Poland (he works on a building site – arrrrr!!!!) and all he asked me was did I think I might get cold dressed like that? Men . . . Still, it's not like I'm planning to marry him and have hundreds of half-Polish babies with killer cheekbones or anything, but a bit of interest in Debbie-above-the-neck wouldn't have gone amiss. Ah, well. I didn't agree to go out with him for his impeccable manners, I guess.

So, by the time we move through to the ballroom he's pretty chilled out and we're getting on well and he's managing, most of the time, to address my face rather than my boobs but he keeps his arm round me like the WHOLE time in a really 'this is my property' kind of way, and I'm not sure about that, especially as it seems to be such a nice crowd of people there except for – yeah, you guessed it – your twin nightmares! I'd managed to forget that they were likely to be there – eeek!!! You should have seen their faces when Gabriel and I walked in. It was like they'd just been force-fed sour grapes soaked in lemon juice. They were standing with two random blokes on either side of them like bookends who looked like they'd been phoned in from Planet Geek so I'm ashamed to say (not) that I had a bit of a private gloat about that!

There was a real mix of people there, all different ages, which made a nice change from the usual parties full of beautiful people we trawl our way round in London, and I knew it was going to be a cracking night. Gabriel finally let go of my arm to head for the bar at the far end of the room so I grabbed a nifty-looking man who didn't have a woman in the immediate vicinity and hit the dance floor. Gabriel just stood at the bar like a sulky toddler. He was obviously talking about me because he kept flicking these looks in my direction but hey, bit of jealousy's good for a guy, wouldn't you agree? Oops, well, perhaps not too much in your case but, um, shall I move on?

Amy smiled ruefully at the screen. 'Jealousy?' she said aloud. 'Oh, yes indeedy – fine if you've done something for him to be jealous about; not so great when he's got the wrong end of the stick and dumps you without listening.'

Pretty soon I'd whipped up a whole crowd onto the floor and we were giving it some licks, I can tell you! One man who looked like he was about a hundred was actually breakdancing! He breakdanced (or should that be brokedanced?) up to my ear and shouted, 'Michael Jackson very very hot stuff, no?' and I nearly died laughing!!! There might as well have been a handbag in the middle of the floor, we formed this huge circle, and the music was brilliant, a mix of disco, funk and Polish folk music (quite sexy – I'll play you some when you get back) and some weirdy-beardy international stuff – fantastic!!!

I took a break and got talking to a big group of people who were standing around watching the dancing. They were telling me all about the Warsaw nightlife (wild!) – it definitely made me want to visit sometime. What do you say, Amy? Big trip east once you get back from your big trip west? Find you a Gabriel of your very own?

'Hmm, think I'll hold fire on that one for now,' Amy decided. 'One adventure at a time, Debs, one adventure at a time . . .'

So then I thought I'd better go and see how old Grumpy-pants is doing and he tells me he's used to being in charge of things where 'his' women are concerned. – that's actually the phrase he used – 'MY women!' So I explained to him that as far as I'm concerned I'm his date for the night, but if he's going to ask me to a ball where I'm not going to know anyone and there's going to be dancing, then being 'his woman' involves being introduced to his friends and included in his conversations and even – steady now, Gabe – being asked for the occasional dance!

'Attagirl, Debs,' Amy whispered at the screen. 'Show us all how it's done.'

Well, he was much better after that, much more fun. He introduced me to a couple of his mates, and they were a real laugh, and he made sure I had a drink, and it was all going well until the meal . . .

Hang in there, Amy love, it gets better!!!

Well, the meal was a bit disappointing, to be honest. We trooped through in couples to sit down and they served us up this sausage stew with dumplings – can't remember the name – but it was 'very famous Polish delicacy' according to Gabe (oh, and he hated it when I called him Gabe!!!) so I felt a bit rude not managing mine but y'know when you're expecting maybe a bit of salmon, or some rare roast beef or something at a gaff like that and someone puts a sausage casserole in front of you? Somehow I know you're with me on that one, Amy! Gabriel wolfed his and then polished most of mine off as well, but I was getting a bit worried about him because he was really gunning the vodkas by this time and I thought he'd be too plastered to dance later on but, fair play to the lad, he seemed to hold it together, he just got louder and louder when he was talking to his mates. I think the meal helped soak up the alcohol a bit. Plus he's a big bloke, as I think you noticed, so I guess he could take it – har, har!!!! Then he tried to feed me my pudding. I think he thought there was something seductive about spooning super-sweet jelly down my throat but, well, y'know, I'm not very good at that sort of thing so I pretended to be too full. How he fell for it I don't know as he'd eaten my main course but, hey, enough about the food!!!

It was lovely for Amy, losing herself in Debbie's story, laughing about sausage casseroles and jelly, forgetting for a while that she was all alone in a huge house on a new continent. Not for the first time, she felt a rush of affection for her friends back home.

Oh, I can't believe I haven't told you yet – we were sitting at the same table as the Terrible Twins! Marta was wearing a black dress and Iwona was wearing . . . oh! Quelle surprise! A black dress! Yaaaaawnn!!! They were both still trying it on a bit with Gabriel and paying no attention whatsoever to their partners, which was a bit of a giggle, and they didn't say a single word to me all night! Mind you, I did open with, 'I see you managed to find some shoes to fit you for this evening, ladies!' which, if I'm being honest, wasn't the friend-liest conversation-starter!

Oh, and it's important to point out that it wasn't an actual ball in the Cinderella tradition I'd been expecting. It was an evening known as a 'Sobotka', which, as one of the girls I got talking to explained, is a traditional annual event in Poland to celebrate the summer solstice and St John's night (pay atten-tion, now, Amy my love – I shall be asking questions later), so there were lots of traditions to be observed. For instance, after the meal there was an interval where these Polish girls came in dressed in white and sang love songs – they were dead sweet and virginal-looking (Gabriel approved, obviously), but I loved it too, it was kind of touching. Anyway, appar-ently there are meant to be bonfires as well, but that was out of the question given that we were in a posh country house hotel that wouldn't have looked too kindly upon fire-raising in the gracious spacious grounds, but the men are meant to jump over the flames – how symbolic is that, then? Gabriel told me that it was always him who jumped the highest and the furthest at these things so I humoured him and said, 'Of course it is, my pet,' and he seemed happy enough with that. There were gorgeous floral wreaths draped everywhere, and huge bunches of herbs that smelled wonderful – basil, tarragon, dill, sage, mint, lemon balm. I nicked a few sprigs to stash in my clutch bag, thinking I'd put them under my pillow, or something romantic like that, but never got round to it. They must still be in the bag, come to think of it! I'll smell like a giant human bouquet garni next time I'm out on the town!!!

While she was loving her friend's story, Amy couldn't quite stifle a yawn as she stretched. It had been a long day, and she was beginning to grow nostalgic. Her mother had always had lots of herbs in their kitchen window box when she was a child. She used to crush a leaf or two between her fingers and tell Amy to smell the crisp fragrances. Amy decided that, come what may and wherever she ended up after her adventure was over, her next home would have a beautiful window box, full of herbs.

Anyhow, finally I get him to hit the dance floor with me and, my goodness, he was a handful! He flailed his arms around so much that he created a ten-foot exclusion zone around himself, there was a real danger of losing an eye, or a couple of teeth, if you'd got in the way of that man in full flow. Hey, you know how it's said that if you want to know what someone's like in bed you just have to look at how they dance? Well, on that evidence nobody would come out alive after a night in the sack with Gabriel!!!

And the slow dances — sheez, I could hardly breathe, he gripped me so tightly! Do you think he was using me as a human piece of exercise equipment? Work on those upper arms whilst romancing the English chick?

'You had your hands full there, missus,' Amy said.

He finally began to flag after a bit — think the vodka was hitting home. So he sort of hooked himself on to me and didn't let go — head on shoulder, arms round my waist, y'know. His hands kept sliding up and down my back and I had to keep removing them from my bottom until eventually I said, 'Gabriel, in my country if a woman tells you to keep your hands off her arse she generally means it,' and he took the hint, but he still kept getting amorous, telling me I was 'so verrrry verrry beootiful' and all that sort of stuff . . .
Then . . .

Drat, gotta go, Jes is dragging me out. Fire alarm test. So engrossed didn't even hear it. Wondered why so many people were filing past my . . .

From: Amy
To: Debs
Subject: Polish Balls
Debs, you legend! Well, things my end have been pretty tame, in comparison. So nothing new there ☺
Can boast a mystery element to the next leg of my tap-tastic adventure though. I wasn't even planning on tracking this next pair down because all I had to go on was a post box number in a town called Patchogue and the name Alice Hewitt — no actual address — but when Sergei made his kind offer, I saw

that the town of Patchogue wasn't too far away.
Serendipity, I guess, huh?

  Amy xxx

Shutting down the computer, Amy slowly made her
way upstairs. Exhausted, and not a little lonesome, she
wondered what lay ahead of her tomorrow. Trauma or
triumph?

CHAPTER FIFTEEN

Twelve hours' sleep later in the biggest bed she had ever occupied, and Amy was a new woman. Filled with freshness and optimism, she wolfed all three blueberry muffins Maria had kindly left out for her, sank four cups of amazing coffee, and dressed in pale blue shorts and a white halter-neck T-shirt, prepared to pick up her quest.

Out back, the pool glinted in the late morning sun. Amy stepped into the sunshine and gazed at it for a few wistful moments, wondering whether a quick dip might be just the thing to pep her up for the day ahead, then swiftly shook the thought away.

No more delaying tactics. I could happily spend all day pottering around here, but how exactly would that get me my shoes back?

'Catch you later,' she called out to the lapping water, before swinging inside to search for her bag.

She strolled downtown in the welcome sunshine towards the car rental place, through leafy suburban lanes, towards the beachfront. It was lovely to smell the ocean – balmy and calm, quite unlike the sharp, bracing tang back at Ballyvaughan, just three hundred or so days' swim away.

A dozen insurance forms later – she was in America, after all – she was on the open road. Pretty quickly she discovered that driving the cute little silver hire car, with its automatic gearbox, on the 'wrong' side of the road was going to take all her concentration: she kept snatching at the door handle, groping for a gear stick which, even if it had existed, would have been located on her other side.

Her destination – the coastal town of Patchogue – was about an hour's drive away. Most of the route lay back along the way she had travelled, asleep, the day before, and she was looking forward to actually being able to see it this time.

It wasn't a disappointment. The dazzling ocean winked at her and followed her, on the left-hand side of the car, for most of the journey, and the route took her past mellow rolling fields, dense green woodland, and through a succession of towns comprising clap-board houses, tree-lined streets, small shopping malls and sun-kissed parks. It was all so friendly, Amy found she couldn't stop a smile playing around her mouth for most of the way. Spirits soaring, she tuned the radio to a country-and-western station and sang along to every song, making up the words as she went.

> I'm goin' to get my shoes (oh, yeah)
> I got the missing shoes blues
> I'm goin' to pay my dues (yes, sir)
> There's just no way I'll lose . . .

The miles shot by as she sang, windows open, hair streaming in the wind.

> I'm gonna get my man to pay
> For sellin' my shoes on old eBay . . .

Finding words to rhyme with 'Justin' was tricky, but in a flash of inspiration she had just gleefully settled on 'dustbin' when she found that she was approaching her destination. Patchogue.

Amy scratched her head. *So, how do you pronounce that, then? Patch-oag? Patch-oagy? Maybe it's a silent 'g'? Patcho?*

She drove right in to what appeared to be the centre of town, ending up at the bustling harbour front, where she parked the car, stepped out into the heat and walked across the road to consult an information board that stood with its back to the bay. The only address she had to go on was the post office box number, so she scanned the map on the board for clues to the where-abouts of the post office. She was in luck: it was just round the corner. Serendipity indeed!

Around her a smattering of local people strolled and jogged and rollerbladed, enjoying the fresh air. Over on a patch of recreation ground by the water, a man was throwing a stick for an exuberant Labrador, and near him, about ten people were playing volleyball over a rickety net that was jammed haphazardly into the ground. Further to Amy's left, a handful of teenagers lounged on a bandstand; and the sunny calm was only faintly disturbed by banging noises from what looked to be a major housing renovation project nearby. There was a pleasant, positive vibe.

The town was quite large, big enough to support a downtown area crammed with interesting-looking shops, a theatre and a museum. All around lay an assortment of predominantly clapboard housing, just like the towns she'd driven through to get here, spread over a wide area hugging the waterfront and also, from what Amy had been able to make out, extending in towards the agricultural hinterland. But there was modern development too: apartment blocks, brand-new family housing and what seemed to be a street regeneration programme. Peering down one of the streets Amy saw that some workmen were in the process of replacing streetlights and signposts with quaint period replicas, but it wasn't in the least bit twee. Somehow it worked.

It all worked. Amy was experiencing a curious feeling of warmth about the place – not of *belonging*, as such, but a definite tug of yearning to find out more about Patchogue, to stick around for a while, see the sights . . .

Not for the first time, the feeling of having the entire day – the entire world – at her disposal came crashing in on her. Her life had been so *orderly* these past few years: turning up for work, being with Justin, always reliable, always in control, building up a future within a known universe, never questioning that it was the right thing – the thing she *ought* to be doing.

And now? Now it was as though life had stepped

forward, kneeled at her shoeless feet and pulled the Rug of Ordinariness out from under her. Putting her best foot forward, she marched along the hot pavement.

Entering the post office, she observed that the place was empty, save for a child sitting on one of the benches, reading a comic. When he saw her, he immediately lowered the pages and bounded over to her. His face had a scattering of freckles and his brown eyes shone with warmth.

'Hey, I'm Harry. You need some help?'

Amy smiled. 'I was hoping to speak with someone in charge . . .'

'That's me,' he replied. 'Mom's out back. Bathroom break. I'm looking after the place.' A huge grin spread across his face, displaying dazzling teeth in various stages of development.

'Um, well, maybe you can help me,' Amy replied. 'I'm new in Patchoagy, and wanting to track down the owner of this box. I'm Amy.'

She showed him the scrap of paper with Alice's name and box office number, which she'd scribbled down that morning at the breakfast table.

'You mean Patchog?' The boy corrected her kindly.

Amy coloured. 'Em, I think I probably do. Sorry – that was the first time I've tried to pronounce Patchogue out loud.'

The boy's grin widened. 'Not a problem, happens all the time. Hey, are you from England?' He didn't wait for an answer before hurtling on. 'Cool. My grandma and grandpa went to England last year, to search for their roots. Grandpa joked that if Grandma had stopped dyeing her hair they wouldn't have had to go so far. He got a slap for that one.'

Amy smiled at the boy.

'They stayed in a town called Stratford-upon-Avon. You know it?'

'I do,' Amy smiled as she managed to get a word in edgewise, 'but I've never been.'

'Really? Why not?'

She shrugged. 'Haven't had the chance. England's a big country . . .'

The boy's disbelieving face was a picture. 'So anyhow, what you doing here?'

He was staring at her with a directness she found as invigorating as the brisk sea breeze outside.

'Well, kind of the same reasons that took your grandparents to England, I suppose,' she replied. 'A search.'

He nodded, then gestured towards the wall of post office boxes. 'Well, the box is there but I can tell you exactly where you'll find old Mrs Hewitt in two days' time.'

Two days!

'Harry,' a voice boomed, 'what did I tell you?'

'Never talk to strangers.'

'Nope, the other one. The number one Post Office rule.'

'Never give out customers' personal information.'

Ten minutes later, and Amy was getting nowhere with Harry's mom.

'I'm sorry, honey, but that box only gets emptied on Thursdays.'

It was Wednesday.

Donna Baker, standing squarely behind the counter, was heavily built, with dark, wiry hair that curled to her shoulders, generous lips and a soft, unmade-up face. She wore a mannish postal officer shirt, with navy-blue elasticised trousers pulled high over the top, the waistband resting just underneath her gargantuan bust. She spoke in a matter-of-fact way – not unfriendly, but not to be messed with either.

'Are you sure?' Amy asked uselessly.

She was treated to a mock-withering look and a raised eyebrow.

'I don't suppose you'd let me have a quick look inside?' Amy pressed.

'Honey, these are secure post office boxes, not candy jars. Only person gets to look in there is the guy that's hired the key, and he only comes in Thursdays. Period. I'm sorry I'm not able to help you today.'

'Guy?' Amy repeated. She fished out the address on the scrap of paper, which she'd stuffed into her shorts pocket: Alice Hewitt, PO Box 8373, Patchogue, New York.'

'Er, excuse me?'

Donna had turned away to get back to her paper-work. 'Yes, honey?' she called over her shoulder.

'Can Alice be a boy's name in America?'

Donna snorted a little laugh, and turned round. 'Well, I guess anything's possible in the Land of the Free. There's Alice Cooper, isn't there? I once knew a guy named Ford Pickup, but hey, that's a *whole* other story.'

Amy folded her arms on the counter and let her head slump forwards. There was nothing else to be done. She would have to come back tomorrow.

'So, em . . .'

'Donna.'

'Donna – nice to meet you. By the way, my name's Amy.'

'Yes, Amy?'

'Do you mind telling me what time Alice – or whatever his name is – comes in to empty the box? Please?'

Donna shrugged. 'Comes in all different times. Could be eight in the morning, could be two in the afternoon – he sure keeps us guessin', if we were interested enough to guess, which we're not. So if you wanna catch him, best come back first thing tomorrow and bring a good book.'

Deflated, Amy trudged back outside. There was nothing else to do. She'd have to return the following day and stake out the post office, keeping her eyes glued to box 8373, until someone came in to open it. So much for serendipity! She'd been filled with such high hopes earlier on.

So what to do now? She looked all around. The town still looked lovely. The bay bobbed with boats, the beach looked inviting and for a moment she was tempted to explore some of the downtown speciality shops that the Information Board had advertised.

She sighed. Perhaps she still had a touch of jet lag. So much to do here – museums, those shops, the beach – a smorgasbord of possibility for the inquisitive tourist . . . but her energy suddenly failed her and, wearily, she rummaged in her bag for her keys and turned back towards her hire car.

With the prospect of a long day ahead of her tomorrow, all she wanted to do was head back to Sergei's for some R and R. It had been the most eventful and draining week of her life.

Patchogue looks great . . . but presumably it'll still look great tomorrow . . .

A couple of hours later, blissfully lounging by the pool, Amy propped the laptop up against her knees, and logged on. Hurrah! There was a message from Debbie. Thank goodness for friends.

From: Debs
To: Amy Marsh
Subject: Like a Virgin!
Actually, Amy, realised on reading over that last email that I'm making Gabriel out to be a bit of a creep, aren't I? Well, he had moments of being really quite sweet as well. For instance, he noticed a tiny scratch on my finger that I'd got taking the label off the Gina shoes and he took my hand, stroked it, and then kissed it better! That gave me a shiver, that did. Plus, he really was quite gorgeous to look at, once I'd got past the hugeness . . .

'I'm going to have to take your word for that one,' Amy grinned.

Anyhow, when it got to midnight, they suddenly threw open the big sets of floor-length glass doors that led out to the garden and everyone gathered round to watch. I asked Gabriel what was going on and he just said, 'You will see, Debbee, you will see!' with this – how can I describe it? – hungry expression on his face. I was mystified, but then some of the younger women stepped forward, and everyone started applauding. I thought they were going to give us a song or something, but they went over and each picked up one of the flower wreaths. Then they were joined by their partners, and began to walk outside. We all followed, and still Gabriel wouldn't tell me what the heck was going on!

Amy pulled herself upright on the sofa, intrigued, and read on.

Well, there was this little stream on the edge of the lawn, a short walk away. You know how you have to walk on tiptoes on grass when you've got heels on? Duh, silly me, I'm talking to the High Priestess of the High Heel here – of course you do, pet. But it was hard going, as you can imagine, and I had to grab Gabriel's arm for help. He loved that! So we form this big semicircle around the couples, and one by one, the girls kneeled by the stream and laid their wreaths on the water, then stood up and stood beside their partners, watching as they floated away on the current.

So I turned to Gabriel and said, 'Wasn't that sweet?' and d'you know what he told me? He said that the wreaths were symbols of virginity (or, in his words 'the being the virgin'), and in sending the wreath down-stream, they are giving up 'the being the virgin' to their boyfriends!

'No!' Amy barked at the screen. 'Don't let that have happened!'

And then he really knocked himself out. All of a sudden he turned to face me and produced from behind his back – ONE OF THE WREATHS!!! He'd been holding it in his other hand all along! Then he just handed it to me – he didn't say anything, but his eyes said it all – they were all soppy, and droopy, and pleading – and he kissed me again, three sodding times, left cheek, right cheek, left cheek, and jerked his head towards the stream!

I must confess I took a moment to work out how to react. Poor Gabriel must have thought I was over-whelmed with emotion, because he kept smiling at me with those lusty eyes (can eyes be lusty, Amy? Actually, Gabriel's already answered that one for me. Yes, they flaming well can), and waited for me to go over to the stream.

So after I'd got to grips with the situation I pulled Gabriel towards me and kissed him three times, left cheek, right cheek, left cheek, and carefully placed the wreath round the place where most ordinary people have necks, but in Gabriel's case, I put it over his head and rested it on those gargantuan shoulders of his. Then I whispered in his ear, 'You know something, my pet? My wreath floated downstream a long, long time ago – in fact, it's probably halfway to America by now!' and he just stood there, dumbstruck! It was, quite possibly, the most bizarre conversation I shall ever hold in my entire lifetime!!!

So I should be grateful to him for that, I guess . . . oh, and I genuinely WAS grateful to him for taking me to the ball. I mean, most of it was wicked, and I met

175

some brilliant people I'd never have got to know other-wise, which was a real bonus. And hey, that's not all I learned! I've learned that it is possible to be served sausage stew in a country house ball situation, which was enlightening, and I also know never to wear a little black dress if I want to pull breakdancing hundred-year-old blokes – and face it, Amy, who wouldn't?

Take care, kiddo, and stay in touch. Good luck with your sole-searching (do you see what I did there? Fnar fnar!)

Debs xxxxxx

Laughing, Amy fired off an instant response.

From: Amy
To: Debs
Subject: Re: Like a Virgin!
So, dare I ask, are you going to see him again? Shame on you for not telling me!

Amy xxx

She didn't have to wait long for Debbie's response. No sooner had she wandered through to the gleaming oak and granite kitchen (which looked as though it was kept strictly for magazine shoots) to get herself a glass of water, than Deb's reply came beeping into the inbox.

From: Debs
To: Amy Marsh
Subject: Polish your own balls, madam!
Will I see him again? D'y'know, I probably would – if only to get to meet his mates again and get another

feel of those pecs ☺ – but I'll be checking the Polish calendar before heading his way again! Wouldn't want to be getting in the way of any more Sobotka wreath-flinging shenanigans!

Take care, pet,

D. xxxxx

CHAPTER SIXTEEN

The following day, Alice Hewitt (who by now had taken on strange, mythical proportions in Amy's mind) was making Amy wait. Amy's bottom was getting progressively more numb as she sat on the wooden bench that ran along the side wall of the post office. She had been there since eight o'clock on the dot, having breakfasted two hours before that in Sergei's sparkling kitchen, and now she was beginning to get hungry. Her tummy growled loudly. She forced an exaggerated coughing fit to drown out the noise.

Donna had tried to hide her evident amusement at the sight of her, saying that as far as she was concerned she could sit there for a week, just as long as she didn't start whistling, or drawing on the walls, or shouting abuse at the customers.

Ten o'clock, eleven o'clock . . .

The opposite wall was entirely taken up with postal boxes, like little lockers in a gym. A steady trickle of people came in and out to send and retrieve their mail. Not one of them went to box 8373. At around eleven fifteen, Amy had to physically restrain herself from going up to interrogate the hairy biker who had the temerity to open box 8375. Soon she was concentrating so hard on box 8373 that her eyesight was going woozy. And she had the beginnings of a headache.

Over at the counter, most of the people knew Donna by name, and she them. Amy was struck by the easy courtesy, the 'pleases' and 'thank yous', the pleasantries about the weather and the neighbourhood that came so naturally and sounded so sincere. It soon became apparent to Amy that Donna was something of a town treasure. 'So, Arthur, how's your mom's leg?' 'Your grandma get that ointment, Cyril?' 'How's your little girl doin' with the new pup, then, Avril?' 'You like some help with that? Looks heavy, I can put it in the trunk of my car if you want and drop it off on my way out of town later?' And so on, all through the morning.

'Slow day today,' she called over to Amy during a lull.

'Really? But you haven't stopped!' Amy smiled. 'I'm amazed by how many people you know!'

'Oh, I don't know about that,' Donna replied. 'Patchogue's a big place these days – we got people moving in and out all the time. There's a pretty big population all along this coast. And because we're not so far from New York City we get a lot of people just come here on weekends, a lot of commuters, that sort of thing. But yeah, it's still a friendly place. There's a real good community spirit here.'

Thanks to people like you, Amy thought, but was too shy to say aloud. London life could be lonely sometimes, never seeing the same face twice on the tube or at the Tesco Express checkout.

'Do you know where the town gets its name from?'

'Indians!' Donna replied. 'Reckon there was a big settlement of Indians called the Paushag, or Pochaug, round these parts a long time before the white man got here.'

'It's, um, quite hard to pronounce, for a newcomer.'

Donna nodded. 'Used to be nicknamed Milltown, because of all the mills up and down the waterways – that a bit easier for ya? You should get out and explore, young lady, can't spend your whole vacation cluttering up my building!'

'Oh, I will!' Amy smiled. 'What sort of mills? Cotton?'

'Oh, all sorts. Cotton, wool, paper, sawmills – anything that could make a guy a nickel. You want some coffee?'

'Oh, No, thanks, you've been too kind already . . .'

'What, by letting you breathe Post Office air? Come on, honey. You want a cup, or not?'

'I'd love one. Thank you.'

Donna handed her a big mug of black coffee, just as a fresh stream of customers began to arrive. Amy watched them, wondering whether one could hold the magical key to box 8373. She tried not to think that maybe they'd already been and gone, and that she'd been focusing so hard she'd missed them, like listening intently to the radio when the weather forecast is about to come up only to find that you didn't hear it at all when it came on. Or – perish the thought – that they wouldn't be coming today at all.

The day crept by. Customers came and went. Donna

chatted when they were there, and was quiet when they were not, getting on with her paperwork. Nothing flustered her. And during the silences, Amy found her thoughts drifting back to Justin.

I shouldn't have made up those songs in the car. It was a cheap and juvenile attempt to cheer myself up and it's just left me feeling worse. But he did a really shitty thing. Why am I the one feeling bad? I wish I could be more like Debbie sometimes. She doesn't take any crap from anyone – if she can sort Gabriel out she should be working for the United Nations right now. I must remember to call her Condoleezza Rice next time we speak. If she were me she'd have tracked Justin down long ago, got him in a head-lock and forced him to listen to the truth! Why on earth didn't I?

A lorry had pulled up outside and the uniformed driver loaded up sacks of mail for distribution whoknew-where.

But I tried! He didn't give me a chance – I would at least have heard him out if the tables had been turned! Wouldn't I?

Donna had gone to the bathroom through the back. A young woman with a baby in a pushchair came in and walked up to the counter, awaiting her return. The woman was followed a moment or so later by a tall man in shorts, who was fishing in his pocket for his locker key.

It really, really sucks, not being believed. Knowing that Justin's out there somewhere, with this horrible opinion of me. It'll knock all the good times we had right out of his head. And it makes me feel dirty.

The baby was cute, giggling and gurgling, with a cloud of dark curly hair and laughing eyes.

And that's unfair! Our time together was worth more than that! Why am I thinking in the past tense? Surely I'm not giving up on the two of us as easily as he seems to have?

The train of thought was too hard to process, and it was doing nothing for her headache. She wriggled her shoulders and gently tilted her head from side to side, trying to physically wrench Justin from her mind. Then she pulled a funny face at the baby and it laughed aloud. The mother smiled at her.

'What a cutie-pie!' Amy exclaimed. 'What's her name?'

'Johnny,' the woman replied, just a touch curtly. 'She's a he.'

'Oh, no! I'm so sorry! It's . . . the lovely curly hair!'

'It's fine, really,' the mother replied, in a tone of voice that Amy knew owed more to good manners than anything else. 'I'm not going to cut his hair until he's old enough to give me his consent. He may be little, but he does have rights!'

'Ah,' Amy mumbled. 'Quite right!' She shrank back on her bench, robbed of follow-up conversation thanks to a cartoon image at the front of her brain of a boy with lustrous curly hair trailing along the ground, heading off to college.

The man in shorts had emptied his postal box, relocked it, and was leaving. Amy, realising that her conversation with the young mother was at a sticky end, groped for her book and tried to make herself look studious and engrossed.

A moment or two later she was relieved to hear footsteps from through the back. Tucking her shirt into her trousers, Donna was returning from the bathroom but then, squinting out of the door towards the car park, her eyes grew suddenly huge.

'That's him!' she yelled, pointing at the man who had just left. 'That's your man! Has he already been in?'

Amy leaped to her feet. 'Are you sure?' she asked, panicked.

'Sure I'm sure! Get after him, girl!'

The baby, alarmed by the sudden commotion, began to cry. Amy shoved her book back into her handbag and dashed for the door.

'Sorry!' she shouted at the young mother, who was lifting her wailing baby out of the pushchair to comfort him, and then to Donna, 'Oh, and thank you!'

The man was striding across the parking lot, heading towards a big dark blue Jeep. Tall and broad-shouldered, he was wearing a thick charcoal-grey windcheater and long shorts. And his legs were moving far too quickly for Amy, even at a run. *I can't believe I missed him in the post office!*

'Excuse me!' she called out. 'Hello! Could you wait, please?'

But the wind had picked up, and the man's Jeep was parked on the edge of the car park, next to a busy road, so he didn't hear – didn't even look over his shoulder. If he had, he would have seen a very flustered, slightly built brunette careening in his direction, waving her arms in the air in an attempt to get him to stop.

But hey, hang on – what exactly was that parcel

under his arm? Was it, or was it not, exactly the right size and shape as . . . a shoe box? Amy squinted as best she could. It was!

The man climbed into the driver's seat, and started the engine.

Amy didn't pause to think. Her hire car was just fifty yards away. She switched direction and made for it at top speed, losing precious seconds by almost climbing into the passenger's seat by mistake, then flooring the accelerator and screaming off after him.

He had pulled out of the car park. Amy wailed in panic as his Jeep passed her by on the highway, whilst she slammed on her brakes at the car park exit. She saw a gap in the traffic and went for it. A lorry blared its horn at her as she pulled out just in front, waving a silly apology before swerving out into the fast lane in hot pursuit of her quarry.

And then, there he was! Not too far in front, heading out of town.

There were all sorts of possibilities that made Amy's pursuit of a strange man in a strange country potentially hazardous. She could get mugged. Arrested for stalking. She could crash her car in panic, discover that the insurance Debbie had arranged for her wasn't valid, and spend the rest of her life working to pay off colossal hospital bills from an office specially adapted for her wheelchair. Or she could be just plain dead.

But she put all such thoughts to the back of her mind. She was driving an unfamiliar car at high speed on an unfamiliar highway, every nerve ending jangling with terrified excitement, tailing a stranger who'd made good his escape from Patchogue post office with a shoebox under his arm.

It felt fabulous.

The Jeep was heading east along the coast. Amy, who had watched her fair share of cop shows, tucked in two cars back so as not to arouse the man's suspicion. Besides, the whole scenario was faintly embarrassing, so she did her utmost to hang back.

She slipped on her sunglasses, for the merciless glare from the sun and the heat haze on the highway were aggravating her headache and making it difficult to see without squinting. Jesminder firmly believed that squinting against the sun's rays caused premature crow's-feet, and was always badgering Amy about wearing her shades, even in winter. Plus, the heat and her exertions had caused a sheen of sweat to form under her eyes – quickly, she snapped down the sun visor . . .

Yikes!

The Jeep was indicating to the right and was about to turn off into a side road. Amy followed suit, her heart thundering in her chest.

Now they were driving through the suburbs, very close to the coast. The Jeep turned left along yet another wide, leafy street, and then immediately right again, into an elegant driveway with a big painted sign on the wall: 'PLEASANT SHORES RESIDENTIAL HOME FOR THE ELDERLY'.

Amy drove right on past the entrance, then parked by the roadside a little further down. Her mind was racing. Did the man work there? Or was he visiting somebody – the mysterious Alice, perhaps?

She couldn't possibly follow him, not into a residential home for the elderly. That would be too rude, too disruptive. No, she would just have to sit exactly where she was and wait for him to come out again, then tail him to, hopefully, his home. That might take ages. And she'd already been sitting around waiting all day. But then she noticed there were security cameras, intercoms – the works. What if there were burly security guards? Whether they'd be there to keep the residents in or riffraff out she couldn't be sure, but in any event, the possibilities for making an utter fool of herself didn't bear thinking about.

Two, maybe three minutes passed.

Amy was glowering at her shiny reflection in the sun visor mirror.

Come to think of it, I'm getting pretty damn good at making a fool of myself these days – why on earth should today be any different?

She glanced furtively at the security camera.

It's not as if I'm going to harm anyone, is it? Just my dignity, and that's no great loss any more, is it?

She checked her watch. She would run out of day soon.

Where would the harm be in just going in to try and grab the guy for a minute or two? I've already gatecrashed a wake, for goodness' sake! This is a step back from that, surely?

For all she knew, he might work and live there, and not be scheduled to drive out again until the next post office collection day, in a week's time. He could be a recluse, or, hey (and this one really made her tummy flip), there could be another exit! He might have dropped off the parcel, and have headed back out on the highway by now!

That clinched it. Amy jumped out of the car and took off down the driveway at a run.

CHAPTER SEVENTEEN

The man Amy had tailed along the freeway was sitting
on a wooden bench in the rose garden in the back of
Pleasant Shores. At no more than twenty feet from her,
she recognised his tall, lean form, the baggy charcoal-
coloured windcheater. Not to mention the tanned,
muscular legs beneath those khaki shorts, the broad
shoulders . . . *Enough, Marsh. Focus.*

He was not alone. Sitting next to him was a white-
haired lady in a wheelchair. Alice Hewitt. And on her
lap, the package. Edging her bottom along the stone
wall that ran the length of the wide veranda and faced
out on to the rose garden, Amy moved in closer to
eavesdrop on their conversation.

'I wish you'd open it now, Grandma.'

'Jack, dear, my birthday's not until tomorrow.
Besides, I love keeping you in suspense. *You* never could
bear people not opening presents right away.'

Holding her breath, Amy discovered she couldn't
bear it either . . .

* * *

It hadn't been easy finding the two of them. On entering the large, airy, stone-built entrance hall, Amy had been impressed by the lavish decoration of rosy wallpaper, rugs, watercolour landscapes, framed photographs, vases of flowers and large bowl of fruit on the large mahogany reception desk. A heady scent of pot pourri hung in the air.

A nurse had appeared from a side room, making Amy jump. She was heavily built; her light blue gingham uniform had no room left whatsoever, and her wedding band cut tightly into her ring finger.

'Oh! Hello! I'm sorry, you startled me! Erm, I'm looking for Alice . . . Alice Hewitt? I'm afraid I haven't been here before.'

The nurse's face softened. 'Ah, Alice, of course! My my, she is quite the popular one today! Her grandson Jack's here already!'

'Jack?' Amy echoed. 'Oh! Jack! Excellent!'

The nurse frowned. 'You're not a relative, are you?'

'No!' Amy shot back, forcing out a little giggle. 'I'm a friend, that's all. From London, actually.'

'Is that so?' It was clear from her flat tone that the nurse wasn't particularly interested in her origins. She nodded towards the long corridor.

'Room one-oh-three. Straight down. Take first left, then second right, another right and it's the fourth room down on the left.'

Eyebrows raised, Amy tried to digest all those directions before trotting off down the corridor, consciously not breaking into a run so as to avert any suspicion. Music drifted into the hallway: big band stuff, an old recording by the sound of it, as though the band was sitting at the far end of a long tunnel. Still, it really did swing, and it nearly – nearly – brought a smile to her lips.

After about the hundredth wrong turn down yet another dead end, though, Amy's good cheer was all used up. She could have sworn the nurse had said left, right, right, right, but here she was lost. In fact, she, seemed to have come full circle.

Gingerly, she risked a glance through the doorway that led into the residents' lounge on the right, the source of the music. She caught her breath at the sight that greeted her.

About a dozen old people sat in armchairs, which were arranged in a circle around the room. And there, in the centre, were two old ladies, each wearing a floral tea dress, dancing a slow foxtrot. Oh, they were a little unsteady, to be sure, but they knew their steps and moved, straight-backed, heads up, in time to the music in a manner that seemed to come from another time. Both wore expressions of sheer happiness – there were no signs of having to concentrate, or avoid stepping on each other's toes – the sort of klutzy dancing at which Amy usually excelled.

The flowery dresses could almost have come from this season's Cath Kidston summer range, a collection that Amy, in her nostalgic moments, had had her eye on for some time – Peter Pan collars, covered buttons and those gorgeous cotton lawn prints. One of the ladies even wore a silk rose corsage in her hair. *And would you just take a look at her shoes!* Tan suede tango shoes, with thin laces and a scandalous retro heel that wouldn't have looked out of place in any Covent Garden shoe shop window. *Like, right now.*

The other lady, however, wore slippers.

Amy watched, pricked with a flurry of hitherto dormant emotions. She didn't know any old people, not really. She had no grandparents, no great-aunts or -uncles, not even any old folks from other parts of her neighbourhood – old people she could shop for, or visit at Christmastime, buy treats for their cats, that sort of thing. Well, there was Phyllis, but she was only in her sixties – that wasn't old, not these days. And anyhow, it looked like Amy didn't even have her any more, not since Justin . . . *Oh, enough.*

Justin Campbell, I despise you for removing Phyllis from my life.

The dance ended and the ladies returned to their seats to scattered applause. Immediately, the television was switched on, and a state of stillness fell upon the room. The lady in slippers picked up a piece of embroidery, but the one in tango shoes sat back in her chair and closed her eyes, a smile playing at the corners of her mouth.

I wonder who was in her mind as she danced, Amy thought. Because he's still there, I can tell . . .

'Good afternoon, may I help you?'

'Um, yes. I'm looking for room one-oh-three.'

'Oh, that's straight down. Take first left, then second right, another right and it's the fourth room down on the left.'

Oh, no. Amy didn't know if she could face that maze again.

'But if you're looking for Alice, which I imagine you are, I saw her with Jack, passing by the window, heading outside, about, oh, two minutes ago.'

The lady winked at a grateful Amy.

Graceful French doors stood open, their cream muslin drapes billowing in the slight breeze, giving out on to a lush garden. Wide, colourful flowerbeds skirted a bowling-green-smooth lawn, which seemed to slope to infinity, appearing to stop where the ocean began, at the crown of the gentle hill. Wrought-iron garden furniture, topped with frilled umbrellas, dotted the scene, and all around, white-haired residents strolled, or sat and read, or talked to visitors . . .

. . . And that's where Amy was now – in the rose garden with its raised beds of blowsy rose bushes, protected from the coastal winds by low stone walls, dipping and swaying in time with the ocean breeze – eavesdropping on a private conversation.

'Go on, please, you're almost there – just lift the lid! Hey, I'm sure I can still remember how to throw tantrums if I don't get my own way.'

Jack's voice was deep and steady. He had light brown hair, and an open, honest face with a strong, lightly stubbled chin, teeth that were a tiny bit crooked, and expressive, strong-looking hands. Not that Amy was looking too closely.

Alice laughed. 'And, oh my, did you throw some humdingers in your time! Oh, all right then, if it's going to stop you making a scene.'

Touching the lid of the box, she paused once and

turned her face towards her grandson. Her eyes were misting over. 'I just cannot believe you managed to get them, Jack. So kind!'

Her grandson smiled a nervous smile, full of anticipation, and Amy's heart gave a little lurch.

'Open the box, Grandma,' he urged again.

Alice lifted the lid. Then, a soft rustle of ivory-coloured tissue paper as she put a pale hand inside.

'Oh!' The old lady's face lit up for an instant, then clouded, as she rustled some more in the box.

'What the . . . ?' Jack murmured, reaching over and taking the box from her.

Amy almost fell off her perch, and then swayed back in stunned surprise at the next words out of the Alice's lips. '*What the . . . ?*' indeed.

'Only one?' the lady looked up at her grandson with an inquisitive smile. 'How very unusual!'

'No!' Jack exclaimed. 'There should be two! There's been a mistake!' He rummaged around in the tissue paper, then stopped, spreading his palms upwards, and turned to his grandmother in despair.

'Oh dear, you poor boy!' His grandmother patted his knee. 'Well, now, never you mind. It was a lovely thought anyhow. I mean, when you told me you were going to try to get me a pair of Margot Fonteyn's ballet shoes, well, I didn't think it was possible.'

WHAT DID SHE SAY? They've got one of Dame Margot Fonteyn's dancing slippers in that box? But . . . how on earth . . . ? What's happening here? Are these people shoe fetishists? If those are Margot Fonteyn's slippers, then where the hell is the shoe box containing my *shoes?*

Jack, leaning back, was rubbing his forehead in exasperation. 'No! I should've known not to trust eBay. How can there only be one in the box? Oh, Grandma, I'm sorry, I should have checked first, but I was so anxious to get over here to give them to you!'

'Oh, come on now,' his grandmother soothed, 'what would I have done with two of them anyhow – *danced* in them?' She gave a little laugh. 'Hey, I knew how to make them, but I sure never learned to dance in them! Just having *one* is a big enough treat for me, Jack dear. Thank you, thank you so much for going to all that trouble.'

She leaned across and kissed her grandson on the forehead, ruffling his hair. Jack still didn't look convinced, but he smiled at her anyway, shaking his head slowly.

'I'll look into it later, Grandma.'

'No need, dear.' His grandmother reached into the box. Then, with another soft rustle of tissue, she drew out the ballet slipper. 'It's perfect.'

'Oh, my!'

This, unfortunately, burst from Amy's lips. On seeing her mother's precious ballet slipper in the old lady's hands, she simply couldn't keep quiet. She felt as though every bone in her body had been temporarily removed, and wanted to slide to the floor in a little puddle, as Jack and his grandmother, startled, looked over in her direction. Two feet away.

CHAPTER EIGHTEEN

There was a heavily pregnant pause. Looking down, Amy wondered whether there was still a chance she'd get away with it; perhaps they'd get back to their conversation, forget she was there . . .

But what the hell's going on here? Why has that man, cute or not – which is, obviously, neither here nor there right now – got hold of my mother's dancing shoes on the Web? To give to his grandmother? Pretending that they belonged to Dame Margot Fonteyn?

'May we help you?' The old lady spoke directly to Amy, her voice louder than before, though not unkind. Amy looked up. Jack, meanwhile, was staring right at her with those sky-blue eyes, staring right *into* her.

'I . . . I'm sorry . . .' she faltered eventually.

'Are you looking for someone?' the old lady went on, leaning forward slightly.

Yes! Yes! Yes!

Still Jack was looking at her. Amy realised she'd have to invent something – fast – in order to keep herself there, close to the precious shoe.

'Mr Smith,' came out from some random place far inside her head. 'I'm looking for Mr Smith.'

The old lady looked around the rose-clad clearing, at the few others. 'Well, there's no one here of that name, I'm afraid.'

'No . . . I . . . erm . . .' *Think!* 'Well, I'm not looking for him as such, I'm just waiting for him, kind of. I'm over from England, visiting a friend.' *Well, I might see Sergei before I go back, so that isn't necessarily a fib.* 'Wendy. She's just dropping her father off here today – Wendy Smith? Her father, Mr Smith, is moving in here today. I'm just waiting while she settles him in.'

Lord, talk about verbal diarrhoea!

'Is that so?' Alice smiled indulgently.

Amy was beginning to realise that if she didn't move the conversation towards the dancing shoes, like, *immediately*, she may well miss her chance for good.

'Yes, but then I happened to see that dancing shoe and it gave me a bit of a start.'

'Oh?'

'I'm sorry if I gave you a fright, but, well, my mother was a ballerina . . .'

The old lady's face lit up. 'She was? Oh, but that's so exciting. I used to make ballet shoes when I was younger. Look – come over here and see this one. It's exquisite. Move up, Jack, make room for my new friend.'

Amy leaped at the chance. Sliding off the wall, she walked over to the pair. Jack stood up. He really was tall – over six feet. Amy was suddenly acutely aware of her short shorts and tight T-shirt. She could feel his eyes on her.

'I'm Alice Hewitt,' the old lady went on – Amy fought down the urge to reply, 'I know!' – 'and this is my wonderful, thoughtful grandson Jack.'

'It's nice to meet you. I'm Amy Marsh.'

They shook hands. Alice's hand was bony, the skin papery, contrasting totally with Jack's firm, warm grip.

'Sit down, Amy Marsh – is there room?' Alice indicated the little bench Jack had been sitting on.

So they sat side by side, and no, there wasn't really room.

'Sorry,' Jack mumbled, as his thigh pressed against hers.

Hmm, you smell fan-flaming-tastic, Jack. Incidentally.

'Sorry,' Amy mumbled back as she found her arm moulding to his.

What a shame you appear to be in the process of deceiving your lovely granny.

'Here, take a look at this.' Alice handed Amy the shoe.

Amy took it, her hand trembling.

It was nearly her undoing. There was absolutely no doubt; this was her mum's shoe. Those shoes had been such a source of comfort to her over the past two years. She used to clutch them to herself and cry her heart out, trace the contours of her mother's foot with her fingertips, picture her wearing them, twirling and dancing on stage, in her element.

Close to tears, Amy just gazed at it.

'What's your mother's name?' Alice asked.

Amy lifted her head and replied, 'My mother was Hannah Powell. She died two years ago.' Her voice was cracking. Pressed close beside her, she was sure Jack could feel her trembling. 'I'm sorry to make a spectacle of myself, but well, Mum thought the world of Margot Fonteyn, and it's so strange to be holding one of her shoes . . .' Tailing off, Amy felt that she was growing tired of tall stories. Enough, already. She shot Jack a quick, pointed, sidelong look without Alice noticing.

Alice patted her knee. 'You poor dear. Of course I've heard of Hannah Powell – that lovely English dancer. Such a tragedy. And what a happy coincidence that you've shown up here, to see one of Dame Margot's shoes.'

'You said you used to make ballet shoes?' Amy asked, steering the conversation into calmer waters. Her nerves were shot from the emotion of holding the shoe to the emotion of being pressed up against Alice Hewitt's big, handsome, not-entirely-honest grandson.

'I did,' Alice replied. 'I worked in New York City for twenty-seven years, for a company that made ballet slippers for dancers all over the world.'

'You were the best in the business, Grandma,' Jack put in. 'Or so you keep telling us!'

'Thank you, dear,' Alice laughed, mock-swiping his arm. 'But, though I do say it myself, I was something of an expert – you get to be, after all those years.'

Their easy familiarity reminded Amy sharply of Justin and Phyllis, and she tried to brush aside another unwelcome pang of loss.

'Mum always used to say that a dancer's career can succeed or fail according to the stability of her pointe shoes – amazing really, they seemed so flimsy. Her shoes sometimes lasted only a single performance.' Amy traced the satin with her fingertips.

Alice nodded. 'It's all in the smoothness of the construction.' Gently, she removed the shoe from Amy's hands. 'See this?' She turned it over, running her finger along the satin pleats tucked under the toe. 'These are perfect, but any irregularities in those tiny pleats can ruin a shoe, and consequently, a performance.' Turning the shoe upright again, she went on, 'Same with the toe – too much wadding can ruin the feel. The dancing shoe is . . .'

'. . . an extension of the body,' Amy murmured. 'Mum said that too.'

'And she was quite right!' Alice cried, thoroughly involved with her subject now, eyes aflame. 'See this?' She ran her hand along the sole.

'I see it,' Amy replied.

'Cardboard. Fibreboard, sometimes, but anyhow, these shoes are held together with nothing more than glue, clever sewing and a few tiny nails. No wonder they only last one show, at most. And the toes – my, but it's a small miracle these things held the ballerinas up. Just paper and burlap, soaked in glue.'

'Come on!' Jack exclaimed. 'Surely they must use more modern materials now?'

Alice shook her head. 'Nope. Pointe shoes have got to be ethereal. They are designed to give an impression of effortless grace, so they're moulded to the foot, used and then discarded.'

'Mum sometimes used to use old shoes for practice,' Amy pointed out.

'Yes, sometimes that happened, but there's such a small window between breaking a shoe in so the dancer can feel all five toes yet still be supported, and the toe box becoming too soft to be effective for bracing... You're nodding, Amy. Do you dance too?'

Amy sighed. 'Oh, I wish. But I was never any good. Poor Mum – she took me to lessons for years before accepting the inevitable. I inherited my dad's left feet, unfortunately!'

Alice smiled. 'That's a shame. It's a wonderful life, that of a ballerina, but I guess you know that?'

Amy's shoulders had begun to sag. She was loving the conversation, but she still felt terribly sad. 'I wish I'd had more conversations with Mum about her life as a ballerina, before she died. You know, adult to adult ...'

'Grandma, I think we're upsetting Amy. Shall we change the subject?'

Amy looked sideways at Jack. Could he sense her sadness?

She tried to shake the thought free. *Huh, he's a crafty one, and no mistake. A real smoothie. Of course he wants to change the subject! Palming his grandmother off with the wrong shoes, then trying to bluff his way through! Well, that does it – I am going to get that man on his own and give him a piece of my mind!*

'I'm fine, really,' she said, addressing Alice. 'Yes, Mum loved being a dancer. She used to say it was as much about receiving as giving.'

'What a wise woman!' Alice clapped her hands. 'All that hard work, the aches, the pains, the exhaustion and yet, to dance on stage, alone or with the biggest company in the world, is the greatest of gifts!'

Alice settled back in her wheelchair and closed her eyes, as though in a state of bliss. Jack, still pressed against Amy, was motionless.

Meanwhile Amy was in weary turmoil. Her headache had never gone away and there was just too much new stuff going on for her to let her guard down.

How can I tell the truth now? Flipping heck, I've done it again. 'Sorry, Alice, but there is no Mr Smith and you're holding Mum's shoe because your grandson is clearly not telling you the truth and, in addition to that bombshell, please would you give me it back?' Yeah, that'll really work. No, I'm going to have to somehow get Jack on his own and tackle him about it. But how? Hide out on the road and tail his Jeep again when he leaves?

'I've just remembered something!' Alice exclaimed, sitting bolt upright in her wheelchair again. 'Jack, dear, would you be kind enough to go to my room and bring down the red photograph album from my shelf beside the closet? I think there might just be a photograph with Amy's mother in it, from twenty years ago!'

'Sure, my pleasure,' he replied, leaping to his feet.

An earthy internal voice called to Amy as he rose. *Stop right there, large handsome man! Don't get up! I haven't felt bare skin on my body for such a long time!* She silenced the voice primly.

But still she watched him bounding off. *Debs would follow you, and jump you under a rose bush, for sure . . .*

Alice talked on in his absence. 'I never met your

mother, Amy, but she was very highly spoken of, that much I know.'

'Thank you,' Amy whispered. 'You are kind.' She groped for something with which to change the subject, a measure of self-preservation against the threat of more tears. 'Did you ever meet Dame Margot Fonteyn?'

'Did I *meet* her?' Alice echoed. 'I stitched her shoes for nearly ten years! She was my very favourite dancer, and such a wonderful woman, as well! She used to call me the Pleat Queen. She said nobody sewed such perfect toe pleats as me! Of course she was flattering me, but that's the sort of lady she was, so generous!' Then, in a lower voice, 'Actually, nobody *did* sew such perfect pleats as me, but it was nice of her to notice!'

Amy smiled, looking up to see Jack jogging back across the lawn towards the rose clearing, his easy running motion telling of a life lived in the great outdoors. A battered red leather photograph album was tucked under his arm.

'That's why it was so good of Jack to go to all that effort for my eightieth birthday. I only mentioned in passing that my good friend Ida-May in Iowa said in a letter that a pair of Margot's slippers were for sale on eBay, and Jack did the rest! He absolutely insisted – said it would be the perfect gift . . .'

Amy fumed. *Huh, well, it would have been if he'd got the right pair . . .*

'And it was.'

'What are you two talking about?' Jack asked breathlessly, squeezing himself back into the spot beside Amy on the bench and handing the album to his grandmother.

Amy looked directly at him. 'Shoes. And we've got a lot to talk about.'

She felt him jolt. It was satisfying.

'Aha! Here we are!' Alice turned the album round so Amy could see the large colour photograph, carefully placed under Cellophane and taking up an entire page.

It wasn't a staged group of dancers, as Amy had been expecting. Rather, it was an informal photograph of a celebration, some kind of party, taken from above, looking down on a sea of beautiful people, mostly dancers, by the looks of their naturally graceful stances, their effortless elegance.

Then, standing in a corner, Amy saw her mother.

She froze.

'There she is. That's her, isn't it? What a lovely woman,' Alice murmured.

There was a date in the corner. I would have been five then, Amy thought.

'It was a party to celebrate Margot's contribution to ballet – and what a party it was!'

Amy nodded, listening and not listening, staring at the picture. The rest of the world had faded away.

Alice pointed to the man who was standing beside Amy's mother. 'Say, isn't that—'

'Sergei Mishkov,' Amy whispered. 'That's Sergei Mishkov.'

Sergei Mishkov and Hannah Powell; their heads bowed towards one another, as they spoke intensely.

'Of course!' Alice cried. 'Dear Sergei . . .'

Amy froze. The sight of her mother in her prime

brought tears to her eyes. *Please, no, don't let me break down here.* Instinctively, she thrust the photograph back into Alice's hands, and shot to her feet.

'I really must go. Mandy will be wondering where I am.'

'I thought you said your friend's name was Wendy?' Jack said, as he too stood up.

Amy ignored him. 'Alice, I'm sorry, but I have to dash. It was lovely meeting you.' She turned to leave. She felt her whole body begin to tremble.

'Amy?' Alice called after her as she began to walk quickly back towards the house.

Amy waved over her shoulder. She didn't trust herself to look back.

'Jack?' Amy heard Alice address her grandson. 'Go after her. Make sure she's all right.'

CHAPTER NINETEEN

Now it was Jack's turn to tail Amy, back along the freeway towards the centre of Patchogue. Amy could see his Jeep in her rear-view mirror as she drove, occasionally flashing his headlights at her to try to get her to stop.

Why had the picture upset her so much? It was just so hard seeing her mother so alive. It brought home to her even more how alone she was now. It was madness to keep on driving in her current state of mind. Besides, she needed to talk to Jack about the shoes, otherwise the entire purpose of the whole, unsettling episode would be lost. So, indicating left, she turned back into the harbour front car park, pulled up, and got out, taking a few deep breaths of the warm, sultry air, trying to grab some composure from anywhere she could get it.

Jack pulled up and parked alongside.

'Thanks for stopping,' he said, coming round to join her.

'Why are you lying to your grandmother?' Amy asked, looking straight ahead and making for the harbour at a brisk pace.

'Excuse me?'

She rounded on him. 'Those shoes! Or should I say, that shoe! Honestly, Dame Margot Fonteyn, my foot!'

Jack gave her a sidelong, amused glance, as he caught up with her and matched his pace to hers.

'If you'll pardon the foot pun,' she added sulkily.

'Foot pun pardoned.'

'And another thing – do you know how dangerous it is to flash people when they're driving?'

'I apologise for flashing you.'

Now Amy, despite herself, responded with a half-smile, rolling her eyes.

'If you'll pardon the sense-of-humour-testing double meaning.' He was looking straight ahead, trying not to smirk.

'Hmm, OK then, sense-of-humour-testing double meaning pardoned. But only just.'

'Thank you.'

'You're welcome.'

Amy was beginning to feel inconveniently warm. *Are we flirting? Oh, for heaven's sake, this is not how this conversation was intended to go.*

. . . although Debbie would have approved.

'So,' Jack began, as they arrived at the waterfront and looked out over the rows and rows of assorted moored boats, 'are you OK? You left in a hurry back there.'

'I'm fine. Thank you.'

'And can I take it that there's no Wendy?'

'Pardon?'

He gave her a clue. 'The friend you said you were waiting for?'

'I know perfectly well who Wendy is, thank you very much!'

A subconscious mental flip of the coin saw Amy opting for attack as the best form of defence as she met his smiling glance with a steady glare of her own, although for a moment it could have gone either way.

If he'd only keep that touch of amusement out of his voice, the smug, bare-faced, granny-swindling . . . oh, what's a good word to come after granny-swindling? Maybe there isn't one. After all, what could be worse than being a granny-swindler?

So she shot back, 'Well, it's a bit rich of you to be mentioning Wendies at a time like this. That ballet slipper didn't belong to Dame Margot Fonteyn, and I'm pretty sure you know it.'

He opened his mouth to retort, then looked away, far out to sea, as though longing to be out there rather than here on dry land, defending himself to a stroppy English girl.

'You *do* know it, don't you?' Amy pressed, irritated by the distant look in his eyes.

He held his hands up, and shrugged ruefully. 'Yes, Amy – oh, excuse me, but your name *is* Amy, isn't it?' She responded with her most withering look. 'Yes, Amy. I'm sorry to admit it, but I *did* realise that it wasn't Dame Margot Fonteyn's actual dancing shoe. And I'm ashamed of myself, truly.'

Amy narrowed her eyes. Was he being flippant? She couldn't be sure. 'So why on earth are you pretending to your lovely grandmother that it was one of hers?'

He smiled broadly at this, turning to look at her again. 'You think she's lovely? She is, isn't she?'

'Of course I do – who wouldn't? But keep to the point!'

'That is the point!' He spread his arms, palms upwards. 'She's so special to me that I couldn't let her down! I tried to bid for the real things as soon as she told me they were on eBay, but I was too late, they'd just been sold. Then I tried everything else – emailing the seller to beg him to sell them to me, telling him to name his price, but he wouldn't go back on the deal he'd made with the successful bidder . . .'

'That's a little-known virtue called integrity,' Amy snapped, then immediately wished she hadn't. A flash of hurt passed over Jack's face, and his demeanour hardened a little.

'I do know what integrity is, Amy, thank you.'

'Sorry . . .' Jack had moved away from her side.

'Anyhow,' he went on, 'I researched Margot Fonteyn on the Internet for hours, trying to find out if there was any other way of getting hold of a pair of her dancing shoes, and I drew a blank there, so then I did a little research on ballet shoe manufacturing techniques, and once I'd established that they've been making them by pretty much the same method for decades . . .'

'You realised you could just pick up any old pair and pass them off as hers?'

Once again, Amy hadn't intended her voice to sound so condemnatory.

Jack shrugged, as though in defeat. 'Truthfully? Yes, Amy, I guess I did. And am I proud of myself? Not particularly. But I was really happy when I saw that the ones I bought were from not very much later than the Dame Margot ones – the early eighties. I *promised* her, Amy. I promised my grandmother that I'd get her the shoes. She's been there for me my whole life – it was the very least I could do after getting her hopes up. You see?'

Amy saw. She even felt a flash of envy that he had someone in his life he cared about enough to go through so many hoops to please. She took a step towards him, then stopped herself. And words failed her.

He didn't owe me that explanation. After all, I'm just a stranger with an imaginary friend . . .

'They're your mother's shoes, aren't they?' His voice was impossibly gentle.

She nodded.

Now he turned so that he was standing directly in front of her.

'Amy?'

'Yes?'

'Why did you put only one in the box? I bought and paid for two.'

'What? I didn't!' Amy planted her hands on her hips. 'Huh! Why should that matter? Nice to see you're thinking of yourself first.'

'Well, it's a fair question, isn't it? I'd have to ask some time. And actually, I'm not quite sure which of us has the stronger claim to the moral high ground this afternoon, do you, Amy? Wendy? Mandy?'

Amy sighed. It was impossible to *really* dislike this man.

'You're not letting me get away with much, are you, Jack?'

211

'Well, I have to say that the circumstances under which we find ourselves together are somewhat unusual, wouldn't you agree?'

'I guess . . .'

'I mean, I can't imagine the sequence of events that led you to be sitting on that wall at the precise moment Grandma opened the box, but I'm pretty sure you weren't just passing.'

There was only one option left: the whole sorry story.

'You see,' she faltered, 'there was this huge . . . misunderstanding . . .'

But then her voice tailed off. She just didn't have the strength. Besides, she had no idea how to begin.

'It was a mistake, Jack. Selling Mum's shoes was a big mistake. And it wasn't even me who did it. It was . . . someone else.'

A pause. For Amy, it was a great, big, Justin-shaped pause. The conversation was becoming overcrowded.

Jack looked down at her for a long while, as though waiting for her to elaborate, but Amy had fallen silent. She knew she owed Jack more. Something was compelling her to tell him everything, but then a louder, more cautious voice shouted at her from within to keep quiet.

'I'm sorry to hear that.'

'Thank you. It's not your fault.'

'Please don't tell me you've come all the way out here from London to ask for them back?'

'No!' She mock-giggled at the notion, waving her hands at the preposterousness of it all. 'What a thing to say!'

212

Jack moved closer. They were practically touching. 'Are you sure?'

'Jack?'

'Mmm?'

'Please may I not answer that?'

He smiled, and touched her on the arm, lightly, but still, it jolted her. 'Sure, Amy, you may not answer that.'

'Thank you.'

'How about I show you around the harbour instead?'

They began to stroll along the harbour front, dodging gulls that wheeled in their path, past walkers, joggers and rollerbladers, past the rows of boats that were moored on pontoons close by.

'Do you sail?' Amy asked. He just seemed so at home amongst the boats; it was the obvious question to ask.

Jack nodded. 'All I've ever wanted to do – build boats, then sail in 'em. My dad was a boatbuilder.'

'Alice's son?'

He shook his head. 'No, Alice is my mom's mom. My last name's Devlin, not Hewitt. Dad and Mom have known each other since they were kids. He ran a boat-building company for twenty years before he got bought out by one of the bigger boys.' His voice hardened as he spoke.

'I take it that wasn't a good thing?' Amy asked carefully.

'Well, who knows? Dad's health wasn't too great, he just got made an offer he couldn't turn down; thought it'd buy us all some security, which I guess it did, but he's never really been the same since.'

'I'm sorry,' Amy murmured.

'Thank you. Anyhow, now I'm busting my ass working for another of the big boatbuilders, trying to save enough to break out and open a yard of my own one day.'

Amy eyed him. 'Sounds good. You didn't look like an office man to me.'

'Thanks,' he replied, colouring a little. 'I'll take that as a compliment.'

Amy said nothing.

'That's because I spend every spare moment I have on the water, or in a friend's yard mending boats. See that ketch over there? I helped to build that!' He indicated the cluster of assorted boats that lay before them in the harbour.

Amy squinted. 'What, that great big white one with the two tall masts?'

'No, that's a schooner – it's a beauty as well, though. Just in front of it, there, the one with the long mast at the front and the shorter one behind?'

'Ah, yes, I see it – what a nice shape it is!' She glanced nervously at him. 'Or is there a nautical term for that? Nice clean lines, or something?'

He laughed. 'Absolutely, we're pretty strict in the sailing world! Ropes are called sheets, wires are called shrouds, we luff, we tack, we flake anchors . . .'

'Stop!' Amy covered her ears. 'La la la I'm not listening! It's like a foreign language!'

'It's not that hard, really,' he replied. 'It doesn't take long to get to grips with the technical terms – and they're easy to look up in the manuals. The clouds, for instance . . .'

'Clouds?' Amy echoed. 'You have technical terms for clouds? How very *prosaic* of you.'

'Prosaic?' He repeated the word uncertainly.

'Technical term,' Amy giggled. 'Look it up. Anyhow, you were saying?'

'Yes, as I was saying, the clouds. Look up, you see those wispy ones? They're cirrus. That means there could be a weather front moving in.'

'Is that so?' Amy was nodding, searching her head for an intelligent question to follow up her mini-victory with prosaic, but nautically, she was so far out of her depth she may as well have been actually treading water in the ocean.

How can I swing this round to a conversation about something I know something about – shoes, for instance?

'Say, do you want me to take you for a spin round the harbour?' His eyes were shining. 'I've got a cute little dinghy over there, all rigged up and ready to go, and it's slack water.'

'It's what?'

'Slack water, you know, it's just the other side of high tide, which is perfect for launching. Come on, it'd be fun.'

Amy glanced longingly in the direction Jack was pointing, wondering what this man was really like. He seemed to inhabit such a different world from the one she was used to. Trusting him with her life in what looked like a rather small dinghy was surely not sensible. Anyway, did she have the right shoes?

CHAPTER TWENTY

'Are you sure you won't come?'

'Yes. I'm afraid so. Sorry.'

'That's a pity. Sailing conditions are perfect right now.' He had raised his head and turned towards the slight breeze that lifted off the water.

Yes, they are, aren't they . . . ?

But then his face brightened a tiny bit, as he murmured, 'You know, you've been a good omen for me, Amy.'

Amy was puzzled. 'Omen? What on earth do you mean?'

'Well, OK, maybe omen's not the right word, but you've certainly reminded me about what's important about my relationship with Grandma. You've made me realise that I have to go back and tell her the truth.'

'Ah.' Amy saw that, technically, he was right but now, for some reason, it felt wrong. Which, considering she'd just been giving him a hard time for deceiving Alice, was confusing, to say the least. 'Really?'

He nodded. 'Yes, I think so. Maybe the single shoe was the omen – you know, showing me that something was wrong with what I did. Say, Amy, that was a smart move of yours, packing only one.'

'I told you, I didn't do it!' she practically shouted, before spotting the glint of mischief in Jack's eyes and whacking him indignantly on the arm. 'But, Jack, just leave it – perhaps you shouldn't tell her. You've gone so far down the line now, don't you think it might be best to leave things the way they are?'

'But then you won't get your shoe back! I take it you do want it back? It's why you're here, isn't it?'

Amy's insides had gone funny again. In persuading Jack to do nothing she would be missing out on getting her mother's shoe back.

I am an idiot. It's official.

She nodded.

'OK, then, that's settled. I'll go back and tell her tonight.'

'No . . .' Amy began, before stopping herself.

'Come on, Amy, I need to sort this out, don't I? For you and for my conscience!'

Amy chewed her lip, not knowing whether to trust the way she was feeling. Of course she wanted the shoe – it was her mother's! And yet . . .

'Yes, maybe, Jack, but well, your grandmother was so kind to me back there, and the way I see it, you've made a lovely old lady terribly happy, and you weren't to know that the shoes – or rather the *shoe* – you bought had such . . . emotional *stuff* attached. And well, it'd be a pretty hollow victory now, grabbing it back. I'd feel terrible . . .'

Jack was smiling gently at her. 'Don't worry about Grandma. I'll explain, tell her I'll trawl the Web every day for a proper pair of Dame Margot's shoes. Hey, I may even get two in the box next time!'

Amy smiled back. 'Yes, but she won't feel the same about another pair, after all this upheaval, will she? And she'll be disappointed in you too.'

'Sure, that's a risk, but I'll have done the right thing – and that's important, isn't it?'

'Of course!' Amy cried. 'But . . . oh, I don't know. My head hurts.' She turned away and rubbed her temples. 'Tell you what,' she went on, turning back towards him, 'just don't tell her tonight, Jack, please. Leave it for a while; sleep on it, OK?'

Amy was about to say 'Perhaps I can ring you tomorrow and we can talk about it again,' when a tiny, grey-haired woman, carrying several shopping bags, nudged her way past, pausing to greet Jack.

'Hi there, Jack. Looks like preparations are going well for your grandma's party!'

'Yes, thank you, Miss Hallyburton! Are you going to be coming along?'

'Sure!' The woman spun round, nodding. 'I'm on food duty. Just about the whole town's coming, from what I've heard. The world needs more Alice Hewitts, that's what we all say. You're doing a good job for her, Jack, honey.'

Jack inclined his head, modestly. 'Thanks. Can I give you some help with those bags?'

'I'm fine, thank you!' she called over her shoulder. 'See you tomorrow. You'd better save a dance for me, do you hear?'

'It'd be my pleasure!' Jack called, before turning back to a very thoughtful Amy. 'Listen,' he said, 'I'm throwing a big surprise party for Grandma tomorrow night – she doesn't actually turn eighty until tomorrow. Why don't you come? She'd love it!' Then, in a lower voice, 'And so would I.'

'Tomorrow?' Amy echoed. She'd planned to head off the following day, back to New York, before catching a plane to Miami. 'Tomorrow, as in Friday?'

'That's right. I'm going to be spending most of the day getting stuff ready for it. In fact, I could use some extra help if you're not busy?' He indicated down towards the beach, where, on a flat area of shingle, the beginnings of a temporary dance floor had been laid. 'We're putting a marquee up first thing, then rigging up some lanterns, a barbecue area, flowers, a stage for the band – should be fun!'

'Does your grandmother like surprise parties?' Amy asked, playing for time.

Jack smiled. 'We'll find out tomorrow night, won't we?'

Amy shivered. The sun had finally ducked below the horizon yet the ocean breeze hadn't quite let up.

'Jack, it's very kind of you, but I can't. I have to, em, keep to my itinerary or else I, erm, won't get it all . . . done.' *And I'm exhausted. And frazzled.*

'Pity. I could really have used the help. Hey, you're shivering!'

220

'I'm fine, really.'

Jack, in one swift, straight-out-of-an-aftershave-ad movement, had peeled off his windcheater, revealing a grey T-shirt (and a nice, firm torso), and thrown it around her shoulders. It felt indescribably good.

'Thank you.' She smiled at him, a jumbled mixture of tiredness and gratitude, pulling the sleeves of the windcheater close around her. Hesitating, she added, 'Jack, I have to go now. But thank you for inviting me, and I would love to have been able to help get things ready. Please give your grandmother my very best wishes. I'm sure it'll be a wonderful party.'

Jack's face was taut. 'What about your mother's dancing shoe?'

Amy turned away, tears pricking her eyes. 'I know your grandmother will look after it – it's fine, really!'

'I still think I should speak to Grandma, Amy – don't go!'

'Please don't, Jack.' She began to walk, saying the words over her shoulder. 'I'm sure my mum would be happy knowing it will be so treasured by . . . by someone else. It's enough for me to have found out that its new owner is someone so decent.'

That is not true but if I work really, really hard on it, I could begin to believe it in, oh, ten years from now . . .

She headed back across the road, which had grown busy with the early evening commuter traffic, towards her little rental car, pausing to dab her eyes with the sleeve of Jack's windcheater.

'Will you be OK getting home?' Jack called after her, from the other side of the road.

Home? Just what, exactly, does that mean right now?

But she nodded. 'I'll be fine. I hope your grandmother has a wonderful party.'

He smiled gently. 'I know, you said that. I wish you'd come.'

'I'm sorry. Well, goodbye, Jack. It was . . . nice.'

He stood on the pavement and watched as she drove away, raising his right hand in a subdued wave. Amy waved back. She couldn't summon up the will to roll down the window and wave properly, enthusiastically, could barely even muster up a smile. She just drove, back towards Sergei's house, her thoughts full of photographs, of dancing shoes she'd never touch again, of kind, handsome strangers who, in another time, another place, with another girl who wasn't such a screw-up, might have been a whole lot of fun to get to know. The country music radio station obligingly played its most mournful selection as she drove into the gathering dusk, snuggling into the comforting depths of the windcheater, tunnelling for solace against a miserable world.

A few hours later, back at Sergei's house, the phone rang, piercing the furious silence in the sitting room and making Amy jump.

'Yes?' she snapped.

'Whoah, tiger, keep your knickers on!'

'Debbie!' Amy was thrilled to hear her voice. 'How

are you, gorgeous? Hey, you idiot, what time is it over there?'

'Who knows? The hours are wee and small, that's for sure, but sleep's overrated, that's what I always say. And I'm on better form than you, by the sound of things, pet. What's up?'

Amy sighed. 'Oh, nothing much. Just had a bit of a long day. It's so nice to hear from you.' Hearing her friend's voice was exactly what she needed.

'You too,' Debbie said. 'Have you managed to get hold of any shoes yet?'

'Well, kind of. I found one of Mum's ballet slippers – Justin put only one of them in the box before sending it off, for some reason. But anyway, I had to leave it with the little old lady who'd been given it by her grandson, who was trying to pass it off as one of Margot Fonteyn's, only I saw through him and now he's asked me to her eightieth birthday party and he builds boats.'

There was a thick silence on the other end of the line.

'Debbie? Are you still there?'

It was a further few moments before Debbie spoke. 'Well, I think so, although for a moment I seemed to enter a parallel universe full of little old ladies who build boats. Amy, what the heck are you on about? Are you drunk?'

'No!' she giggled, before hurling herself onto the sofa and launching into a more detailed explanation of the happenings of the day.

'OK,' said Debbie slowly, after she'd finished, 'so you've lost a shoe and found a man? Sounds like a pretty good exchange to me. Is he fit?'

'I haven't found a man!' Amy retorted with far too much vigour. 'Yes, he's great-looking, although that's neither here nor there. Deck shoes, square toes, 'nuff said.'

'Listen, Miss Prim, why on earth don't you go to this party? You could kidnap the old lady and demand the shoe back.'

'Debbie, stop it! She's lovely, and I'll do no such thing.'

'And you could snog whatsisname – Jack?'

'*Stop it!*' Amy squealed, squirming at the notion. 'You're outrageous!'

'*Moi?*' Debbie drawled. 'What's wrong with having a bit of fun?'

'No, Debbie, I have to get going, first thing tomorrow. Gotta move on. Another day, another pair of shoes.'

'Amy, do you have any idea just how unsexy that sounded?'

'Hmm, well, I do now.' Somehow the words fell flat as soon as Amy spoke them. But it *was* true, she had to move on. Her schedule would be messed up, and she'd struggle to fit in the other shoe venues if she didn't up sticks soon.

'Oh, well, this Jack person can't be all that great, then.'

'He is so!' The words were out before Amy could stop them.

'Hah! Gotcha! Can you hear my feet? I'm dancing! Woo-woo!'

'Debbie! Leave it! I'm not going to the party – what's the point? I'm moving on tomorrow, remember?'

'Listen, Dumbo, not every man needs to come with a long-life label! Grab Jack while he's fridge-fresh! Plans are made to be changed – enjoy, then move on!' Then, in a softer voice, Debbie continued, 'Have some fun, Amy. Goodness knows, you could do with some! You're a free agent now.'

'Am I?' Amy spoke the words as much to herself as to Debbie. 'I suppose I am . . .'

There was a gentle knock at the front door. Startled, Amy looked over to see Maria waving apologetically in at the window.

'Debbie, I've got to dash – someone's at the door.' Amy waved back at Maria and stood up.

'Is it Jack?'

'Don't be daft.'

'Listen, Amy, just go for it, OK? Whatever "it" is, just tell me you'll go for it?'

'Sure, Debs, I'll let you know. Speak soon.'

Maria was flustered and visibly distressed. Amy ushered her indoors, indicating the sofas, but Maria remained standing near the doorway, wringing her hands.

'What's wrong, Maria?'

'Oh, Miss Amy . . .'

Amy laid her hand on Maria's arm. 'Please, could you drop the "Miss" thing? It makes me nervous . . .'

'Amy, it is my husband's mother, she has had an operation, to have a new hip, and she is to be let out of hospital in the morning, and it is too soon!

We thought they would keep her until next week at least!'

'Oh! I'm sorry about that. What can I do to help?'

'Well, she lives in New York City, and Antonio and I would like to go down there for a day or two so that we can help her to settle back into her house, organise some help for her, that sort of thing . . .'

'Of course you must!' Amy cried. 'And if there's anything I can do to help . . .' The offer was out before Amy had a chance to process its feasibility, but still, she knew without a moment's doubt that it was just the sort of thing Maria would do for her.

'Well, the thing is we just need to be sure that you will be staying here for the next day or two, as there are one or two small things, you know, with the housekeeping – the sprinklers, the pool pump, the mail, the security lights, that sort of thing . . . will you be here?'

Will I be here?

Unconsciously, Amy stroked the sleeve of Jack's windcheater.

A fresh sandalwood smell, with just a hint of saltiness.

She was meant to be going back to New York to catch her plane. She had to get on with her mission. She just *had* to. Didn't she?

But I'll need to return Jack's windcheater too . . .

Leaning over, she gave Maria an impulsive hug. A germ of excitement had begun to flutter inside her. 'Two days, you think?'

Maria nodded. 'It will not be more, I am sure of it. The operation went well, and we can have the nurses and the home care people arranged by the day after tomorrow . . .'

'You just give me a list, Maria,' Amy said firmly. 'Just leave it with me.'

CHAPTER TWENTY-ONE

'So, explain to me again the difference between a ketch and a yawl?'

'*Amy!*' Jack, halfway up a ladder stringing a row of lights between two temporary pillars, whipped round. A huge grin spread over his face when he saw Amy strolling over to him, still wrapped in his windcheater, but he swiftly stifled it. His eyes, however, still betrayed his delight. 'I thought you were leaving?'

Amy grinned. 'Well, I forgot to return this, didn't I?' Folding her arms across her chest, she rubbed her upper arms, revelling in the cosiness. 'Plus, I felt sorry for you, saying you needed help with the party but, for heaven's sake, just how much help do you need? This place is mobbed.'

There were indeed people everywhere, putting the finishing touches to the marquee, setting up tables, arranging flowers and pegging out parking areas, all the while laughing and chatting – it was one of the most delightful scenes Amy had ever witnessed.

Jack nodded. 'Well, a lot of us have been here since

six getting this tent up. We've made a lot of progress already – should be done in a couple of hours. What do you think?'

Amy twirled round and spread her arms out. 'It looks great. Alice is obviously a popular lady,' she replied, watching the happy, smiling faces wholeheartedly going about the preparations. It gave her a strange pang of melancholy too, which she fought down with a cough.

'I'll say,' Jack agreed. 'She's a good friend to so many people. In some ways I wish I could have brought her out here this morning, so she could be in the thick of all of this; this is just the kind of thing she loved doing when she was younger, organising celebrations for special occasions. She was always cooking for some party or another. Nothing was too much trouble. That's what I'm trying to recreate for her this evening, and practically the whole town's showed up to lend a hand.' He looked at Amy, his face filled with pride. 'And now, so have you!'

'So what are we waiting for? Give me a job!' Amy laughed.

'You sure?'

'Sure I'm sure!'

The dazzlingly white marquee was three-sided, with the side facing the harbour left open to give views over the boats and the water. Circular tables laid with crisp white cloths ringed a central dance floor, with a raised stage at one end. On the opposite side, about half a dozen people were carrying in covered trays of food and laying them on a long row of trestle tables, behind which a gigantic barbecue was being loaded up with charcoal. And accompanying the scene was the tang of salty sea air and the incessant buzz of chatter, liberally peppered with laughter.

'Hey, Mom, you need an extra pair of hands over there?' Jack called out. A petite woman, with a short blonde bob and a lively face wreathed in laughter lines, looked up from the task she was working on while sitting cross-legged on the floor.

'Everyone, this is Amy Marsh from London, a new friend of Grandma's and, erm, of mine.'

Straight away Amy was aware of the undisguised interest the people behind the trestle table took in her as they greeted her warmly, shaking her by the hand and introducing themselves.

Jack's mother unfurled herself, stood up and strolled over, hand outstretched. 'Hi there, Amy, I'm Sarah. Welcome.' She had a warm, firm grip. 'Over there, up on the ladder, that's Frank, Jack's dad.' She pointed at a salty-haired man waving down at her in a friendly fashion. 'I've kind of got things in hand over here but perhaps Helen could use your help.'

Amy turn to see Sarah gesturing towards the grey-haired woman with the shopping bags Jack had been talking to the previous day, who was unpacking fat loaves of crusty bread from a wicker basket on the ground behind the trestle tables.

'Hello again, dear. I'm Helen Hallyburton. We didn't get a chance to be introduced yesterday.'

Pretty soon, everyone was wandering over to introduce themselves.

'Hi there, I'm Doris Willoughby, Alice's neighbour from twenty years back . . .'

'James Downey, Alice's bridge partner . . .'

'Julie Kryzanowski. Alice taught me to sew . . .'

'Celia Harvey. It's a pleasure, dear. Me and Alice go *way* back – ask me about the Scandal Years some time!'

'Marcus Underwood from Patchogue book group, still waiting for Alice and me to approve of the same book . . .'

'Winifred Mendoza. I bought an old car from Alice thirty years ago, we've been friends ever since . . .'

'Katie Brown. Alice lived across the street from my mom before she went into Pleasant Shores. Mom sure misses the company . . .'

'Is your mom going to make it this evening?' Jack asked Katie.

'Is she ever! I never saw a woman get over a cold so fast. She even bought a new dress.'

'It's lovely to meet you all,' said Amy quietly, amazed at the tide of affection for Alice Hewitt. 'And it's great to gatecrash a party for such a wonderful person.'

'Who said anything about gatecrashing – you're here to work, right?' said Jack, playfully. 'So, Miss Hallyburton, you seem to be in charge here . . .'

'That's right, and don't you people forget it,' she responded with a mock-stern look around the others.

'Yes, ma'am,' Marcus called out, saluting.

'Good work!' Jack laughed. 'So, is there anything Amy can do to help?'

Helen Hallyburton was eyeing them slyly. She turned to the others. 'Do you know, Jack, I think that right at this moment we've got everything just about covered over here on my watch, wouldn't you agree, people?'

She winked at her friends. 'But say, Jack, when are you going to make a start on stringing the lights up on those masts out there? Won't you need someone young and limber to help you with that?'

Jack turned to Amy. 'That sound OK to you? How's your head for heights?'

Amy grimaced. 'I think I'm about to find out.'

The day flew by. Amy and Jack went from little boat to little boat, stringing rows of coloured lights from mast to mast, talking and laughing the whole time. Jack's knowledge of boats was mind-blowing, though he took care to explain all the new terms to Amy, occasionally checking himself when he began to go overboard about the merits of winches and cleats, or going into too much depth on clinker-build processes. Amy listened, concentrating as hard as she could, fascinated and irritated in turn at the wall of knowledge, wondering just how much she'd be able to quote back to him if he began asking questions.

None, probably. Maybe even less than that . . . barge-boards, spinnakers, telltales . . . blimey . . .

He was trying to impress her, she could tell. And it *was* impressive, just a little mind-boggling at times.

Later, skirting round the whole issue about the dancing slipper and Justin, Amy told Jack about herself, her job, about Debbie and Jesminder, even telling him a little about her mother, about how hard she had found it to adjust to not having her around. She didn't mention the shoe quest at all, though.

If I do that, you'll definitely ask your grandmother for

the slipper back, and I'm not sure that's what I want any more. Or is it? Oh, I don't know . . .

Then, from her shorts pocket, her mobile phone beeped, making her jump. She fished it out and flipped open the lid. It was a text from Jes:

Sorry, Amy, Justin called off football 2moro.
Hope u r ok. Take care, Jes xxxxx

'Everything OK?' Jack asked.

'Fine,' Amy answered far too quickly, while stabbing a response quickly into her phone:

Hi, Do u no why? I am gr8. A xxx

She hit 'send' and turned back to Jack. 'So, all these boats you build, do you race them, or just pootle around in them?'

Jack, busy with a dud lightbulb, grinned. 'Pootle? That's a new one. Can I make the assumption that the verb "to pootle" has got very little to do with breakneck speed and getting to your destination any time soon? And everything to do with just bobbin' around?'

Amy smiled primly. 'You can, yes. Excellent definition, Mr Devlin. Help yourself to ten points.'

'Why, thank you. Well, some days I pootle, certainly. Sometimes I pootle when I don't want to pootle, you know, when the wind's not right, or my sailing savvy stays in port. Then I can pootle with the best of 'em because pootling's all that's going to be on offer that day.'

'Glad to hear it,' Amy giggled.

'People should always make time in their lives for a bit of a pootle.' He grinned. 'But mostly I race. Have you heard of the America's Cup?'

Amy thought. She had, definitely. What was it again? 'Isn't that a golf thing?' she ventured, after a few moments.

Jack slapped his forehead. 'No! Oh, well, there goes my only chance to impress you today.'

'Ah. I take it the America's Cup is a sailing thing?'

'It is, yes.'

'A famous one?'

'It's only one of the biggest events in the sailing calendar, in the whole world. Nothing much, really.'

'And you've sailed in it? Or for it? Or, or, round it, or whatever?'

'Kind of. Twice.'

'Really? But that's amazing!'

'Thank you. Although I'm embarrassed now, because I had to tell you, instead of you knowing already.' Amy couldn't see his face, but she knew he was smiling.

She squirmed. It was coming back to her. The America's Cup was competed for every couple of years by countries around the world. It was, not to put too fine a point on it, *mega*.

Her phone beeped a second time and Jack waved away her apology as she retrieved it from her shorts.

Said he was 2 busy. Sorry, Amy. Jes xxxx

Huh, 2 busy doing what? Jumping to conclusions? That won't keep him fit . . . oh, well. Be honest with yourself.

Marsh — you weren't holding out much hope that Jes's brother would be the answer to your problems anyhow. And at least now I know Justin's still alive. OK, where was I? Ah, yes, making a fool of myself about my lack of sailing knowledge — onwards!

'I had heard of the America's Cup, and I only thought it was golf for a tiny moment, but that's the Ryder Cup, isn't it? I can't think what came over me. No, the America's Cup *is* a pretty huge event, right?'

Excellent. Now I'm gushing again. Why is it that with this guy I just can't seem to find a comfortable middle ground?

'It is if you're a sailor. But hey, don't worry about it! Let's move on — hold this.' He handed her a screwdriver, and went back to winding a coil of lights round another mast.

Then it came to her.

It's because we're both trying too hard. OK, say something nice and friendly and straightforward and not too dumb this instant.

'You didn't need to say anything to impress me, Jack. I'm impressed already.'

Yikes, did that sound a bit much? A bit trying too hard?

Jack, ten feet above her, glanced down and smiled cheekily. 'Were you looking at my ass when you said that?'

'What?' She squared up to him in mock outrage. 'Careful what you say up there, Jack Devlin! I'm the one on the ground with a screwdriver in my hand!'

* * *

'Don't like the look of that westerly,' Jack said later, as they sat on the shingle, in front of the marquee, sorting the final string of lights. Behind them, the preparations were almost complete; the marquee looked stunning. The band had arrived; instruments and equipment were being wheeled in from a truck parked round the side.

Amy looked out to sea. 'Hmm, yes, it's a bit of a stiff breeze. Do you think it'll get worse?'

'Probably.' Jack screwed up his face. 'Forecast's for it to get stronger tomorrow, but it looks like it's making an early appearance. It happens sometimes . . .'

'Disaster alert!' A voice from inside the marquee made Jack and Amy jump to their feet. Inside, two of the people who had introduced themselves to Amy earlier were stumbling to the front of the marquee, coughing their way through a cloud of smoke.

'What's up?' Jack called.

'Barbecue,' one of the women coughed. 'We've just tried to get it primed up but that wind's making the smoke blow right into our faces.'

'Should be an interesting night,' the other one said, smiling ruefully. 'We didn't take the wind into account when we ordered an open-sided marquee, did we, Katie?'

''Fraid not.'

'Any chance of moving it out of the path of the wind? To the other side, maybe?' Jack asked.

They looked around the marquee. It was full. 'Not without lifting the floor, switching the electrics and rearranging the whole place, and we don't have time for that, do we?'

'Well, Marcus, I guess we'll have to make do with cold finger food, won't we? There should be plenty to go round if we're careful. We can't risk suffocating everyone in the place now, can we?'

'Unless . . .' Jack was stroking his chin, staring up at the top of the marquee, where the cross-beams supported the roof and the canvas side walls. 'Yup, that oughta do it. Amy, Marcus, can you help? I've got an idea . . .'

'Jack Devlin, you're a genius.' Helen Hallyburton grabbed Jack by the shoulders and planted a kiss on his cheek. 'I swear it looks better than it did before the crisis began.'

Amy, Jack, Helen Hallyburton, Katie and Marcus were standing in a line, admiring the results of ninety minutes' dogged but inspired improvisation, following Jack's instructions.

A huge, curved sail swept out and over the shingle, pegged securely to the ground and then attached to the roof of the marquee by way of ropes and metal pins. Somehow the effect was to make the inside of the marquee look like an ocean liner, and apart from the gentle flapping of the sail, there wasn't a breath of wind to harm the workings of the barbecue.

'Should hold even when it turns into a north-north-westerly later on,' Jack murmured, with only his eyes betraying his pride in the construction that he'd master-minded. 'So, what do we still need to do?'

'I have to get back,' Amy said to Jack, as the others wandered off to find drinks.

'Get back? Where?'

'To the house I'm staying in. I've got a list of things to attend to while Ser— while the owner is away. Turn off the sprinklers, programme the burglar alarm, water the houseplants . . .'

'But you will be coming back for the party?' Jack cut in.

'. . . put a dress on for the party – of course I will! That is, if you're absolutely sure you and Alice won't mind me being there?'

'We'd mind if you weren't, Amy.'

'I still feel a bit of an interloper – we only met yesterday.' *Was it only yesterday? Sometimes I feel like I've known this man – and these people – for ever.*

Jack had a mysterious look in his eyes. 'You're no interloper, Amy,' he replied.

There was a pause. Amy, embarrassed, looked around the marquee, out over the boats, which were bobbing on the harbour in the wind, which had died a little but was still blowing strongly enough to have caused problems if Jack hadn't rigged up that sail. It was calm, like the calm before a storm. She felt strange, an unaccustomed mix of warmth mixed with anxiety; a sense of nearing the end of something, in a place that she would remember for a very long time.

Then she smiled. 'Here, I bet you thought I was planning to hang on to it for ever.' At last, she peeled off the windcheater, aware of Jack watching her, yet trying not to watch at the same time.

Reluctantly, she handed it to him. Reluctantly, he took it.

'You will be here later, won't you?' Jack asked, a note of urgency in his voice.

'Yes, Jack, I'll be there,' Amy whispered. 'I can't miss out on seeing what those lights look like all lit up against the dark now, can I?'

'And you won't be late? I need everyone to be here by the time I get here with Grandma at seven thirty, all right?'

'I'll be here. I hope the shock won't be too much for her!'

'You think?' His eyes widened. 'You think I should warn her in advance?'

'Course not. I was kidding – she'll love it!' Then, catching herself, Amy added, 'Erm, not that I'm presuming to know your grandmother better than you. It's just a girl thing. Girls love surprises. Don't worry, Jack, it's going to be wonderful. Catch you later.'

'Bye, Amy,' Jack called after her, hugging his windcheater to his body, before turning slowly back towards the marquee.

CHAPTER TWENTY-TWO

'Amy, you made it!' Helen Hallyburton cried, surging over as Amy shyly approached the marquee at a little after seven that evening. 'And you look adorable. Is that dress from London?'

Even though it wasn't quite dark by the time Amy returned, she could see that the fairy lights she and Jack had spent so long rigging up were going to be the highlight of the evening. The stiff breeze was determined to keep blowing, making the boats bob and dance in the harbour, and the hundreds of coloured lights swayed to and fro from mast-top to mast-top, looking like they were hanging unsupported in the sky like a huge, rainbow constellation.

She blushed, and smoothed the skirt of the one dress she had brought with her, a tight, Audrey Hepburn-style shift dress, sleeveless, in a soft floral print that stopped just above her knee. Bare-legged, she had craftily applied fake tan in a light golden shade and, though she said so herself, it made her legs look nice when set against the soft white of the strappy wedge sandals she'd picked up just three hours previously in an out-of-town shopping mall on her way back to Sergei's. Old habits died hard and she hadn't done a great job in getting any of her shoes back so far.

'Oh, this old thing, yes, it is. I only took it because it rolls up to almost nothing in a suitcase – wow, what a crowd!'

The marquee was already full. A wall of noise assailed her like a physical blow, and she swayed slightly on the cork heels of the sandals. She waved at Sarah and Frank, who were on the far side of the marquee, still in the thick of organising. They smiled back cheerfully.

She knew it was going to be a good party from her very first inspection of what everyone had decided would pass for 'party shoes'. All shoe life was there. Sandals, flip-flops (a lot of flip-flops), stilettos, sensible pumps, deck shoes, prim courts, slave-girl thongs, sneakers, loafers, mules and even, over in the corner with a beer, a large pair of wellington boots.

I'm going to enjoy this . . .

'Evening, miss!' A man who was, quite simply, enormous, passed by, tipping his fingertips to an imaginary hat.

'Oh . . . hi!'

'That's John Muldoon, the town fire chief,' Helen Hallyburton hissed. 'He's a good guy – wife died, left with seven kids . . . Oh, Marlene! Over here!'

A tall lady of about forty with expensively striped blonde hair returned Helen's greeting and walked over, bringing four others with her.

'My, Helen, who have we here, a new recruit for the Historical Society?'

'Sure, if you can persuade her to stick around! Marlene, this is Amy, all the way from London – says she's a friend of Alice's but she's been hangin' out with Jack all day so make of that what you will.'

'He's a friend!' Amy retorted, wondering if her cheeks could get any hotter. 'Oh, um, I'm pleased to meet you, Marlene.'

'A pleasure, dear.' Marlene smiled. 'And here we have Louise, Anya, Mary-Beth and Susie, otherwise known as the heart and soul of the Patchogue Historical Society – are you interested in history?'

'Well, erm, I can recite all of the Kings and Queens of England, if that's any good?'

Marlene laughed. 'Hey, perhaps that can be your party piece for later on!'

'Come on, let's find you somewhere to sit down,' Helen said, taking Amy by the arm and plunging into the crowd. It was warm in the marquee, even though it only had three sides; Jack's carefully rigged sail ensured no annoying draughts made it anywhere near the dance floor. The ladies from the Historical Society seated themselves at one of the few remaining free tables, close to the barbecue area. To the side, the trestle tables groaned with food, bowls of salads, bread, pastries, hams, cheeses, pickles and countless home-made apple pies. The aromas from the barbecue were delicious, and Amy realised she hadn't eaten anything since lunch.

But the best bits were hanging on the canvas walls.

The marquee had been hung with black-and-white, poster-sized photographs of Alice through the ages, starting with an adorable baby wearing a knitted hood and clutching a wooden rattle, moving through her gingham-pinafored childhood and (Amy had to fight for glimpses of each one as the guests milled around the floor) her beautiful, 1950s youth, her wedding, progressing gracefully to her serene old age. It was a beautiful tribute: a life in pictures. A surge of emotion overtook Amy.

If I did that for my mum, the walls would be half empty . . .

Marcus, on bar duty, waved in greeting. 'Want a beer?' he yelled above the noise, thrusting a bottle towards her without waiting for her reply. She raised it to him in gratitude and drank, closing her eyes for a moment.

Better make this my only one – got to drive back to Sergei's tonight.

She put the bottle down on the table and looked around for Jack. He didn't seem to be anywhere, but then the crowd was so thick . . . *Aha! Over there. Oh. False alarm. Blast!* So she plastered a smile onto her crestfallen face and turned to listen to the chatter around her table. These were good people. Nice, friendly, straightforward people who had accepted her into their company simply because she was a friend of their friend.

From time to time, she found herself looking up expectantly – and it wasn't just in hope of seeing the birthday girl.

Over on the other side of the marquee the band finished tuning up and, without fanfare or announcement, launched into a spirited jig. Whoops and cheers flew round the room as the people who had been cluttering the dance floor, standing around talking, cleared off it, grabbed partners and returned, beginning a set dance that Amy didn't recognise, but which looked fun. Conversation became almost impossible over the music, the thumping footfalls and the whooping, and Amy gave the dance her full attention, clapping and tapping her feet like an old lady, thrilled and excited. And she tried her hardest not to scan the crowds that lined the dance floor for Jack to return.

Enthusiastic applause greeted the end of the dance, and the band immediately launched into another, and another. The steps had a similarity about them but still Amy was grateful to be just an onlooker. There was no way she'd keep up with any of those – her mother's dancing gene was definitely lacking in her.

'Been watchin' you, honey. He's just coming back now.'

'What?' Amy whipped round. A large woman, beautifully made-up, with dark hair swept up on the top of her head, was whispering in her ear. Amy stared at her, blankly.

'That's two days runnin' you've been lookin' out for that man, honey – he better be worth it!'

'*Donna!*' Amy shrieked. 'I'm sorry! You look so different when you're not in uniform. Those shoes are gorgeous.' She grabbed Donna by the neck and gave her a hug, before pulling back and hissing, 'Erm, did you say he was on his way in?'

'I sure did,' Donna grinned. 'With the star attraction. He's been picking up his grandma from Pleasant Shores . . . look, here they are!'

As though by telepathy, the band finished the tune it was playing and the dancers cleared the floor like salt blown from a table.

And there they were. Jack, beaming shyly, was wheeling his grandmother into the marquee. Alice, beautiful in a moss-green dress with a matching cashmere shawl, wore an expression of pure shock as her hands travelled to her face. Her snow-white hair was wound into a loose bun, a peach silk orchid hovered on her bosom. She looked up at her grandson and pretended to shake her fist at him, pulling his head down so she could kiss him on the cheek. Cheers and wild applause broke out all around the marquee and the band launched into 'Happy Birthday'.

Alice reached into her bag and drew out a tissue, and as everyone sang, she dabbed her eyes. Glancing around, she saw she wasn't the only one. It was perfect, a triumph, and Amy's joy was as much for Jack as for Alice. How happy he would be that all his planning had paid off so beautifully! The crowds, the dancing, his grandmother so thrilled – it was wonderful.

'Why, what a surprise!' Alice Hewitt cried into the microphone that had been thrust into her hand by the band leader. 'You dear, dear, wonderful people! Why didn't any of you tell me this was going to happen?' She turned and wagged a finger at her grandson. 'I guess this was your doing, Jack?'

Jack pretended to shrug in bafflement as the guests gave him a spontaneous cheer.

'Oh, my, what a surprise – did I say that already? Thank you. Thank you all. What an extraordinary way to celebrate a birthday. I thought Jack was taking me out to dinner. Now, why did y'all stop dancing? Please, please continue.'

More cheers and whoops greeted her as, with a shaking hand, she handed the microphone back, then clutched Jack's hand tightly. The band struck up another dance and the floor swiftly filled up all over again.

Amy finished clapping and sat down, staring at Jack, wondering why her mouth was so dry. She was aching inside for him to notice her, to come over, yet at the same time she felt preposterously nervous that he might do just that. She kept watching as he was swallowed up by the crowd, by people shaking his hand, women embracing him, embracing Alice, and all the time he kept a hand on her wheelchair, making sure she was all right.

And then she couldn't see him any more. There were too many dancers, too many people. She knew he was over there somewhere, yet she was glued to her chair. There was no way she was going to take the initiative and go and speak to him, nope, not even if someone put a stick of dynamite under her, pointed it in his direction, and lit the fuse. This was a special occasion for Jack, for Alice and for their real, true friends, not the likes of her who had just shown up out of the blue the day before.

Instead, she smoothed her hair and adjusted the

straps of her dress. Licked her lips and leaned in closer to the conversation around the table, suddenly acutely aware of every little move she made, tossing her head, laughing at the jokes, trying not to scan the room too blatantly . . .

Funny, I didn't feel this jumpy yesterday . . . What's happening here? I'm a mess!

A faint commotion had started up at the entrance to the marquee as a minibus, with 'Pleasant Shores Residential Home for the Elderly' emblazoned in red lettering along the side, pulled up outside. Amy caught a tiny glimpse of Alice calling names out in delight as, one by one, around fifteen elderly people were escorted down the steps and into the marquee, some leaning on walking frames, others upright and spry, all of them, without exception, smart and comely in flat, comfortable shoes. Aha, correction – one exception. To Amy's delight, the final person to climb off the bus wore tan suede tango shoes with thin laces and retro heels – it was the dancing lady.

I bet she's got a tale or two to tell. Memo to self: when I am old I shall wear fabulous shoes . . .

'May I?'

'Pardon?'

Amy whipped round to see Harry from the post office, dressed in a smart checked shirt and a red bow tie, standing straight as an arrow in front of her, clear eyes looking at her intently. He held out his hand, waiting for her reply.

Delightedly, Amy reached out her hand and the boy solemnly shook it.

'So, you dancing or not, then?'

'Oh!' Amy hadn't registered that he had asked her to dance. 'I'm sorry, but I'm afraid I don't know how to do any of these dances. I might be safer just watching, wouldn't you think?'

'Go on,' Marlene urged, nudging her husband, who nodded enthusiastically.

'This is an easy one,' Mary-Beth chimed in. 'And Harry here will go easy on ya, won't you, Harry?'

'Sure.' The boy beamed at Amy. 'We learned this one at school – it's easy. At least, I think it's easy, I haven't done it with a real person yet.'

The weight of expectation, both from the boy and from the women seated around the table, was suddenly impossible to resist. 'Well . . .'

'Go on, Amy,' Mary-Beth urged. 'What doesn't kill you makes you stronger!'

'A new experience to take back to London,' Susie chimed in, raising her beer bottle and clinking it with Mary-Beth's.

Amy didn't want to think about London. Harry's freckled face was beginning to colour and his smile was showing signs of flickering. He was growing nervous in the face of her hesitation. She reached her hand out to him and stood up.

'I'd love to, sir, thank you for asking me – but I hope I don't tread on your toes.'

Harry gave a nervous little grimace and led her into the middle of the floor. Fortunately, Amy had been watching this dance earlier, and could at least pick up some of the steps. Harry, despite his apprehension, was a natural, his hand placed carefully in the centre of her back, the other holding hers. They skipped forward, turned towards each other, did a little jig step, promenaded around the floor, then Harry twirled Amy round (which entailed Amy crouching quite a way, despite her own lack of stature) and finally, a quick waltz step and back to the start where they did the whole thing all over again.

'This is fun,' she shouted in Harry's ear as her confidence grew. 'You're a fantastic teacher.'

'Thanks.' He beamed, concentrating hard. Amy could see, looking down at him, that the bow tie was fixed round his neck with a length of white elastic, and her heart warmed to him even more. Laughing, they skipped and twirled, promenaded and galloped round the floor. Amy forgot everything, the heat of the dancing bodies around her, the throb of the music and the sheer joy of dancing with a young boy who trusted her yet knew nothing about her; it was all so liberating, so simple, and so welcome.

'May I, please, Harry?'

From nowhere, Jack Devlin cut in and, whispering something in Harry's ear about the first of the hot dogs being served up over at the barbecue, swept Amy into his arms and twirled her around.

'You look beautiful,' he said with fervour. 'Like Audrey Hepburn – no . . . better!'

Amy was too surprised by the turn of events to respond. Her mouth opened and closed again; there was no breath in her body. She dropped her eyes, tried to think about the next dance step, and not pay attention to the strong hand in the small of her back where Harry's had been just thirty seconds before. *Keep moving.* Jack fell into step and soon they were back in the dance. She had an urge to wave the compliment away, to tell him he was being absurd, to whack him on the arm, say something wittily self-deprecating . . .

Hang on, though. What was it Mum used to say about what to do if someone pays you a compliment? Oh, yes, just two words are all you need . . .

'Thank you.'

'You are welcome. I meant it.' Almost imperceptibly, he tightened his hold of her. His closeness was devastating. And he smelled gorgeous – clean and scrubbed, yet still with that faint tang of sea breeze, this time mixed with something like sandalwood, or was it citrus? Lime, maybe?

Mum, wherever you are, I owe you . . . Don't let me lick his neck . . .

'Thank you, ladies and gentlemen,' the band leader crooned into the microphone as the dance came to an end – far too soon.

'Oh, that was a quick one.' Pulling back from Jack's grip to join in the smattering of applause, Amy found herself still breathless, even a little dizzy.

'OK, let's slow things down a bit here,' the band leader went on, and immediately the sultry sounds of a slow, smoochy number struck up. All around, couples were moving closer together, beginning to sway to the moody sound. Amy was rooted to the spot. She wondered whether she ought to return to her seat until she realised that Jack was still holding her hand. He stood very still for a moment. And then with one single, urgent movement he pulled her close, wrapping his arms around her, as, wordlessly, they began to dance together again.

With her head resting on Jack's chest as they danced, Amy found herself unable to process normal thoughts. It was as though, in pulling her towards him, Jack had stripped her of all her defences, and yet on another level she had never felt so safe in her life. So safe, and yet . . . so dangerously alive. Jack felt amazing, and as her hands moved a little way down the hard contours of his back she knew that she'd better not look up at him or . . . or what?

She wanted him to say something. No, she didn't. She wanted him to say nothing. His body was moulded to hers and the sensation was so wonderful that words, any words, would have got in the way. Luckily the dance floor was crowded. There was no need for self-consciousness; she could lose herself in the moment, dancing with Jack, feeling him warm against her, knowing, though she didn't know how – the tautness of his muscles, maybe – that he was feeling powerful emotions as well.

Just being held. Amy closed her eyes. She felt as if she had been on the road for ever – certainly the last couple of weeks had been a bumpy, strange and unforgiving journey. And she'd stood up, faced everything, on her own. Moving out, crossing oceans, facing strangers – suddenly it was all so complicated. And such hard work. Alone. Oh, yeah, well, thank heavens for friends, for Debs and Jes. Obviously they meant the world to her but where were they now? On the other side of the world.

But Jack Devlin was here, holding her, and they were dancing together to music that worked its magic into Amy's soul. Slowly, the icy shard of loneliness in her heart, the one whose presence she'd refused to acknowledge until right now, began to melt.

Shyly, she lifted her head and looked at him in gratitude. He gazed right back at her, a soft smile playing on his lips, lips that Amy knew she wanted, more than anything, to kiss.

Not here, though, not right now. The music was coming to an end and out of the corner of her eye Amy could see that Alice Hewitt sat by herself, enjoying a temporary reprieve from the stream of well-wishers, who had been queuing up to proffer their congratulations and weigh her down with flowers and gifts.

'Thank you,' Jack said, his voice husky, as the music came to an end and they drew reluctantly apart.

'That was . . . nice,' Amy stuttered, pressing her cool palms to her cheeks.

'Nice?' Jack repeated, looking cheekily down at her with his head tilted slightly. '*Nice?*'

Amy giggled. The tension popped like a bubble. 'OK, it was *very* nice. I'm English, remember we don't do exuberance as well as you Americans do!'

'Is that so? Well, thanks for the dance and the sweeping generalisation, Miss English Rose! Want me to jump on a table and punch the air? Shout "You Ess Ay" a few times?'

'Be my guest,' Amy replied as coolly as she could, 'if you feel the urge.'

'Yeah, well, maybe later. Come say hi to the birthday girl.'

While the band leader announced an interval, Amy and Jack walked over to where Alice sat, radiant in a sea of tissue paper and bouquets.

'Happy birthday, Mrs Hewitt,' Amy said, bending to embrace the old lady.

'Thank you, dear – and call me Alice.' She gestured towards all of the flowers. 'See all this? My, but have you ever seen so many flowers outside of a funeral home? Do you think I should get that microphone back and tell everyone I'm not dead yet?'

'Yes, Grandma, I definitely think you should,' Jack replied with mock solemnity. 'Now, can I get you two ladies something to drink? Some of Anya's curious fruit punch. She says she was up all night peeling lychees for it!'

'Well, what's this evening for if not taking risks?' Alice replied. 'Count me in.'

'Me too,' said Amy.

Jack bounded off purposefully, the very picture of a gentleman with duties to perform in the noble cause of chivalry, and joined the back of a rather long queue.

'Pull up a chair, Amy, we've got some talking to do.' Alice tapped the arm of her wheelchair, and Amy obliged. Alice sat back, sighed deeply, and suddenly looked solemn. Older too.

'What's the matter?' Amy asked, nudging her chair closer as Alice closed her eyes for a moment.

'Amy, dear, why did you come to Patchogue?'

The question hit Amy like a cannonball. Suddenly all her lies from the day before thundered back to haunt her: Mr Smith, Wendy – Mandy, the photograph, the coincidences . . . What on earth could she say? She couldn't keep fibbing, that was for sure.

'Alice . . . I . . .'

'Don't worry, dear, I'm not angry with you.' Alice leaned forward and put her hand on Amy's knee. 'There wasn't a Mr Smith being moved into Pleasant Shores yesterday, was there?'

Amy shook her head, dropping her eyes to her white sandals, which now seemed treacherously frivolous. *Strappy dancing shoes for the party for the old lady I fibbed to.*

'And Claudine, the reception nurse, came over and told me that a young English woman had asked directly for me. You did that, didn't you?'

Amy nodded. Still the floor and her sandals were terribly interesting.

'It didn't take a genius to work out that you were there because of the ballet shoe.'

A stab of defiance poked its way into Amy's psyche and she looked up for Jack. He should be here too, explaining himself to his grandmother. But he was still inching his way up the drinks queue, talking animatedly to the man in front and not giving Amy or his grandmother so much as a glance.

'I mean, the London stamp on the package, your reaction when I lifted the shoe out of the box – well, I'm sorry, but not even I could recognise one of

Margot Fonteyn's shoes from the sort of distance you were at.'

'Alice, I owe you an—'

'Not that it is one of Margot's shoes, of course,' Alice went on, ignoring Amy's interruption.

Amy gasped. 'What? You *know* it isn't hers?'

'Oh, sure I know,' Alice laughed. 'I knew before I even touched it.'

'But how?'

Alice was sitting up tall in her wheelchair. 'Amy, I stitched Margot's shoes for years. Let me tell you – you think that the dancer has a special relationship with her shoes, don't you?'

Amy's head was reeling.

'What was it your mother said: "The shoe is an extension of the dancer's body"?'

Amy nodded.

'Well, let me tell you, those shoes are an extension of the shoemaker's body too, by the time she's finished making them. I know every inch – no, every *fraction* of an inch – of every shoe I ever sewed. Each dancer's shoes are completely different. They might as well be different colours. There are no similarities whatsoever, to the experienced shoemaker, between one dancer's shoes and another's.'

'Is that so?' Amy breathed.

'Absolutely. Say, if a big mama pig had sixteen piglets, don't you think she'd be able to tell every one of her darlings apart, even though you and I would struggle?'

'Um, I guess,' Amy said, frowning.

'Margot's shoes had a far stiffer toe box, and the

256

pleats on the shoe I held yesterday would have cut off the circulation to her second toe – it was a little long, you see – and the whole feel was wrong. Plus, it was too small.'

At last, Amy allowed herself to smile. 'Apart from that, it was a dead ringer?' she said with pretend innocence.

'Precisely so! A real trip back down memory lane!' Alice smiled back. 'No, that shoe was made in England, I could tell by the satin. And it was never Margot's.'

They lapsed into silence for a few moments. Amy twisted her hands awkwardly, her head full of questions for Alice, yet there was another, darker side of her that was also wondering whether there may never be a better time to seize her chance to somehow get the shoe back. Was she not in the United States of America specifically for this purpose? But then, wouldn't that somehow make Jack's kind gesture in getting hold of the shoes somehow look cheap?

'Poor, dear Jack,' Alice murmured, looking fondly at her grandson, who was still inching up the queue. 'He's so thrilled that he managed to get a pair of Margot's shoes – well, only one shoe, as it turned out, but that's by the by – for my birthday. Such a thoughtful boy!'

Amy chewed her lip. It was hardly her place to blurt out that Jack knew, that she'd had a showdown with him and that he was keeping quiet too, for her sake, was it? Hadn't she meddled enough in Alice's family business? Plenty of families are built up and thrive upon little white lies, small deceptions, don't-tells and keep-it-to-yourselves, at least, so she'd been led to believe.

She looked out of the open side of the tent, out at

the night sky, where the lights on the masts of the little boats had finally come into their own. The scene was breathtaking, colourful and yet somehow light and natural, as though the whole night sky was picked out in jewels for Alice's eightieth birthday. She glanced at Jack, who was looking at the display as well, pride and happiness written all over his face. His lovely, sexy face. Then he glanced over to her. Although brief, the look said it all; there was no point pretending. A delighted shiver ran right through her body, chasing the spectral images away. Amy knew then that she would never betray Jack's secret. She would never tell Alice that Jack knew it wasn't Margot's shoe. And she would never tell Jack that Alice knew the same thing. This would be her privilege, her consolation prize, and the decision bathed her in a warm rush of satisfaction.

'Amy?'

'Yes, Alice?'

'The shoe belonged to your mother, didn't it?'

'Yes, Alice, it did.' As Amy replied she felt strangely, wonderfully calm. Of course Alice had twigged that it must be Hannah Powell's shoe – how else would the pieces of the jigsaw fit into place?

'I thought so, my dear.'

'They . . . they were sold by accident. I came to find them.'

'Quite right, quite right.' Another pause.

'I . . . I . . .'

'You don't need to tell me the story, Amy dear. Your pain is in your eyes.'

'Thank you,' Amy mumbled gratefully, though nothing

would have made her happier than to have blurted out the whole sorry tale from start to finish. Well, maybe missing out a detail or two, like her Oscar-worthy speech at Nuala McCarthy's wake, or her mad dash from the Polish girls at the gym, but that would have taken all night, and this was Alice's party, and Amy was about to cry. Not that she felt sad, she just felt . . . *accepted*. For the first time in, well, *ages*. In fact, since Jesminder had lobbed that cushion at her when she decided to make the trip in the first place.

'I . . . I should go back to my table,' Amy went on. 'I'm monopolising the hostess, and that's bad form.'

'Is that right?' Alice said with a twinkling smile. 'Do I have to be the hostess at my surprise party?'

'Good point,' Amy replied, 'but there are loads of people who want to talk to you.'

'Then let them stop by Pleasant Shores once in a while. Heaven knows, the days can be long enough in that place. Just how many baskets can a person weave before wanting to throw them at the wall?' Alice had never seemed so animated. 'No, you stay right there, Amy. I've . . . well, I've got a confession to make.'

'You? A confession?' Amy asked.

What now? Don't tell me you called the police and I'm going to be arrested for . . . for impersonating a friend of an imaginary daughter of a non-existent new resident of an old people's home in order to fraudulently gain entry . . . Oh, what the heck. Bring it on.

CHAPTER TWENTY-THREE

Alice cleared her throat. 'You know, Amy, I got a little curious about you after you left Pleasant Shores yesterday.'

'You did?' said Amy, slowly.

'Uh-huh. Like I said, there's occasionally a little too much free time at Pleasant Shores; some of us can be guilty of thinking too much. Anyhow, I'd been looking around for something else to concentrate on, take my mind off getting overexcited about my so-called "surprise" party.'

'What? You mean you knew about tonight?' Amy gasped.

'Are you kidding me? Honey, there's no such thing as a secret round these parts! You won't tell Jack, will you?'

Amy shook her head.

Alice smiled. 'Actually, I've been thinking about you a lot. You seemed so curious yesterday, yet so lonely . . .'

'Alice . . .'

'Don't worry, I told you I'm not going to pry. It's just that I wondered what would take a girl across the world to try to find her mother's shoes – and then it came to me!'

'Alice,' Amy persisted, 'I'm sorry, but it's complicated ...'

'Women travel alone for two reasons. Either they're looking for something, or they're running away from something. Wouldn't you agree?'

Amy said nothing. What could she say? What would be the truth, anyhow?

Both. If I'm honest, I'm doing both.

'I admire you, Amy. It took guts for you to come all this way to find your mother's shoes.'

'Thank you.' There was more coming. Amy held her breath.

'I had to do a little investigation.'

'I completely understand.' Amy pressed her hand onto Alice's knee. 'I was trespassing, I had no right . . .'

'No, dear, I meant the shoe. I had to see exactly what it was you came to find, don't you understand?'

What? Is she talking in riddles?

'No, Alice, I'm not sure I do. I came for Mum's shoes, that's all, I promise you.'

'Truly?' Alice looked perplexed. Leaning forward in her chair, she took Amy by the hand. 'You weren't looking for a message?'

'I'm sorry? A message? What message?'

A shade of doubt crossed Alice's lightly rouged and powdered face. She took a breath as though about to speak, then let it go, paused, and looked around her uncertainly. The packed marquee was shrouded in a noisy blanket of chatter, old friends were greeting one another, jokes and stories were being exchanged, shrieks of laughter, shouts of greeting – the place was abuzz with chatter, which leaked out of the open side of the marquee and carried over the bay. Not for the first time, Amy felt like a very small part of something far, far larger. A *community*.

'Alice?' Amy's heart had begun to pound. She couldn't explain it. Something was wrong here. Alice reached down and picked up the oyster-coloured beaded evening bag that lay at her feet. The effort made her wince.

'I could have got that for you,' Amy said, in a voice that didn't sound like her own.

'Well, Amy, that does put a bit of a different slant on things, but I've gone this far now, I guess I'm going to have to go all the way with this. You see, in my day, it was very common for ballerinas to conceal notes from their lovers, or from admirers in the audience, in the shanks of their ballet shoes – did your mother never tell you that?'

Amy, her throat tight, shook her head, not trusting herself to speak. 'You found something inside the shoe, didn't you?'

Alice stilled her hand and looked into Amy's eyes. Then she said, 'No, dear, but I wouldn't be surprised if there was something in there, that's all. It feels like there is. You truly never suspected there might be something in the shoe?'

'No!' Amy cried. 'The only reason they're so precious to me is because they're the only pair of Mum's that I own. They were the ones she wore on her very last performance, before she retired from ballet. I treasure them – I treasure all my shoes, it's a bit of a thing of mine – but these are extra special. I'd certainly never go poking about under the shank – the very thought! In fact, when I was a little girl, Mum always told me that they were just for looking at, that I wasn't to go pulling them apart ... oh ...'

'Did she now?' Alice whispered.

Alice drew Amy's mother's dancing slipper from her bag. The sight of it nearly finished Amy off; she wanted to lunge for it and rip it apart with her teeth, but she sat still, looking from it to Alice.

Then Alice lifted a fork from the table.

'I was planning on talking to Jack this evening, explaining the mix-up and getting him to pass the slipper back too. But now we're together, and I wouldn't trust a job like this to an amateur. May I?'

Amy hesitated.

Alice picked up on her uncertainty. 'I won't damage the shoes, Amy.'

So she nodded.

Alice carefully prised out the shank, and, with a sigh of satisfaction, gently eased out a tightly rolled piece of paper.

'Aha!'

Amy was stunned. 'Is that ... ?'

'It looks like a letter, Amy. I'm so sorry to spring this on you. I genuinely thought you must have known that something was there. I've been jumping to conclusions all over the place, haven't I?'

'No,' Amy murmured, taking herself by surprise at the hard edge in her own voice. 'I knew nothing, obviously. I thought they were ... just ... shoes.'

'Oh, my dear!' Alice handed the piece of paper – and the shoe – to Amy. 'Why don't you slip outside for a few minutes, to read it in peace? It's stuffy in this corner, isn't it? I need to go over and talk to Hank, there – his sister's been unwell these past few weeks. You take a little time to yourself, dear. I'll come back and see you later.' And with that, Alice wheeled herself across the empty dance floor, waving away the several people who leaped up to offer help.

Outside, Amy stumbled over the shingle and perched on a coil of thick rope, oblivious to the stiff breeze, which had been imperceptible inside the marquee. The paper was tightly rolled; it took several careful attempts for Amy's shaking hands to unfold it. In the soft glow from the stars and the festive lights, she read the irregular handwriting.

My darling Hannah,

Do you remember the last night we spent in Paris? It still burns in my soul. So much fire, so much passion! I know you're here with your husband and your little girl, and I don't want to cause a scene but . . . meet me at our place after the party . . .

Sergei

Dully, Amy looked up. For a few moments she was calm. Calm and lucid, as the words settled into her mind. Through the entrance flap of the marquee she glimpsed Jack, standing still in the centre of the dance floor, a tall glass of lurid pink liquid in each hand, topped off by extravagant umbrellas. Slowly he turned full circle then, presumably catching sight of his grandmother, shot off out of view. A whiff of cigarette smoke passed under Amy's nostrils.

Fire? Passion? Don't want to cause a scene? Sergei!

Mum – what's going on here? You and Sergei? No! And when I was a little girl? What about Dad? No, no. I can't believe it. I won't believe it.

The date on the letter confirmed Amy's worst fears. It was written when she was five years old. In fact, it would have been right around the time of Dame Margot Fonteyn's party. There was no hiding from it. Now, thinking back to the picture, there was an intimacy in their body language she had denied at the time. *Ohmigod, my mum was having an affair with Sergei. She cheated on my dad . . .*

Suddenly it wasn't so nice, being all alone in America. Only minutes ago Amy hadn't wanted to think about London. Now she couldn't think of anything else. *I need to run, run away from this place – Sergei? How could he? How could he pretend to be my friend when he had an affair with my mother when I was little? Or – hang on – it could have lasted for years. Right up until she . . .*

For all she knew, Jack was still circling the dance floor, holding a glass of punch, looking for her. Or maybe he'd have given up by now and handed it over to someone else? Whatever, she was leaving. Her chest felt tight, as though her heart was being compressed by a huge elastic band of deceit. All those years, thinking she had the perfect parents, the perfect family! Had it all been a sham? She didn't know, couldn't think. But she had to get away; she was in no fit state to be seen back inside the marquee.

'No!' she yelled at nobody. 'How could she?'

She stood up, and began to stumble over the shingle, away from the marquee. A sob escaped from deep within her, then another.

It was very dark, with no floodlights, no fairy lights, and no streetlights for another fifty yards or so.

As though in a visitation, her father's face swam before her eyes. 'Dad! Dad!' She didn't know if she shouted the words aloud, whether any sound had come out or not.

'Hey, you OK?'

Harry was perched on a bollard, trying to hide a lit cigarette behind his back.

'I'm fine, Harry. Oh, *please* don't do that, life is too short, OK?'

'You're crying . . .'

'No, I'm not . . . Ouch!'

Not looking where she was going, Amy's foot slipped on a patch of mud and she twisted her ankle awkwardly beneath her. 'Ouch! Ouch! Ouch!'

Amy's sobs had been dry, desperate and primitive up until then, but the sudden pain in her ankle pierced right through her, and tears began to stream down her cheeks.

'Want me to go get Jack for you?' Harry asked, flicking the cigarette away, jumping off the bollard and dusting ash from his bow tie.

Jack?

'No! I mean, no thank you, I have to go.' Heaving herself up, Amy tested the sore foot on the ground. It was agony. But she was almost at the road – she could hop from there . . .

I'm going to get back to Ser— to that man's house, pack up my things and get the heck out of there as fast as I can.

Oblivious to how she looked, wiping tears from her face, Amy began to hop. Her calf burned, everything hurt, but she hopped all the way back to her car. She located the key in her tiny bag and opened the door.

'Thank goodness for automatic cars!' She patted the dashboard as she heaved herself painfully into the driver's seat and switched on the engine. Pausing for a moment to take a few deep breaths, she pulled out of the parking lot, rolling down the window and calling out to Harry, who was watching her departure: 'And please, *please* don't smoke, Harry, OK?'

Back at the house, sitting in the dark, the glow from the laptop created an eerie blue illumination. *I must not worry Jes and Deb. I must not worry Jes and Deb. I must not worry Jes and Deb* . . .

From: Amy Marsh
To: Jesminder; Debbie
Subject: Howdy from the U S of A!
I'm still alive (just) and having a fantastic time. It has been – how will I put this? – a voyage of discovery, and I'm knackered. Just had a thought, any chance u

cud look into cashing in my ticket and getting me back home early? I think it's mission accomplished over here, and anyhow, I miss not having anyone 2 call me Slagheap. Has aclickaway.com folded without me? V. sorry if so. Hey, let's set up a sandwich bar instead. Anyway this pumpkin's going 2 turn into a slipper if I don't get some sleep so c u soon.

Luv Amy ☺

PS. No worries or anything but if u cud find out about these flights asap that'd be ace ☺

Amy read over the message, sighed sadly, and hit 'send'.

That ought to do it.

CHAPTER TWENTY-FOUR

New York was a very different beast on Amy's return. The summer sky had clouded over and threatened stormy weather as she queued in the taxi line outside Penn Station. It seemed everyone else in New York had had the same idea and so, one hour later, bedraggled and bruised from all the people elbowing her, Amy stumbled into the back of a yellow cab. However, there was not even time to lean back into her seat before the cab shot off into the traffic, her driver yelling abuse the whole way at any driver who got in his way. Foolishly, an exhausted Amy confided she was a tourist. At one point, she thought he was going to drive off the island when he started driving towards Brooklyn Bridge but was savvy enough to question it. At last, they made it to her hotel.

Terrifying. And yet, if she got a grip of herself and looked at it differently, perhaps not? *I am an adult. Nobody can make me feel inferior without my consent. Come on, Marsh!*

Still, it took an effort to check in and haul herself up to her room in the sprawling, red-brick hotel building but finally, gratefully, she sank onto the double bed in her economy room, having remembered to tip the porter for heaving her luggage all the way up from the foyer.

It was amazing to think that only this morning she'd been sitting at Sergei's kitchen table, furiously writing the hardest note of her life – harder even than the one she'd written to Justin, what seemed lifetimes ago – telling Sergei that she'd found out everything about the affair he'd had with her mother, how she couldn't believe he'd been guilty of such betrayal and how she didn't want to have anything more to do with him, ever again.

Then she winced as she recalled the little postscript that good manners just wouldn't allow her to omit: 'PS. Thank you for letting me use your house.'

After that she'd made contact with Maria, who would be back the following day anyway; watered Sergei's precious white flower border for the last time, resentfully picked up his mail, turned on his pool filter and burglar alarm, returned the hire car to the depot downtown and limped onto the New York-bound Jitney.

One of the first bus stops en route was Patchogue. Her heart had leaped as the bus pulled into town and she'd scanned the streets desperately for signs of anything – or anyone – familiar. But, needless to say, she hadn't caught sight of Jack – she assumed he'd be busy taking the marquee down today. Would he spare her a thought, the English girl who crashed the party, then disappeared at the stroke of midnight? The idea was too depressing on an already depressing day, so she'd stuffed it down and tried to concentrate on her book.

We didn't even exchange phone numbers . . .

From: Jes
To: Amy
Subject: Changing flights
Date: Saturday 7 July

You know something, Amy, text-speak in emails is incredibly annoying – there are fewer lines to read between, for a start. Is anything up? What happened to the 'give it time' thing we agreed on before you left? It's Saturday here, but things sounded quite urgent so I logged in at home and was able to call in a few favours.

Bad news is flights are completely full tomorrow, I'm afraid. Fourth of July vacation season, remember? There'd be nothing stopping you doing what we usually tell everyone NOT to do and just showing up at the airport in the hope of getting a cancellation, but I wouldn't fancy your chances much at this time of year. Sunday should be a lot easier – get yourself to a computer terminal at JFK and sort the ticket switch out online. Do I take it that you've managed to track down all of the shoes, given that you're planning an early homecoming? Nice work!

Phone me.

Peace,

Jes

From: Debbie
To: Amy
Subject: Come home early my arse!
Date: Saturday 7 July

Listen, Slagheap, Jes and I pulled more strings than a team of bell-ringers to get you these cheap fares – why the heck do you want to come home early? If you've found all the shoes, can't you go and do some sightseeing? Like, seeing the sight of wotsisname – Jake, was it? – horizontal, on some boat deck? You OK, missus? Has anything happened?

Anyhow, Jes is looking into it for you. Give us a shout to let us know what your plans are, otherwise we'll have to make stuff up.

Take care,

D

Amy smiled ruefully but silently thanked her friends as she headed back upstairs to her room.

'What a day,' she murmured, flicking through a million TV channels on the big screen at the end of her bed, then reaching for the 'off' switch with a heavy sigh. Outside, the heavens opened and rain drove furiously against the window. 'What a big, bad, busy day.'

And then her thoughts strayed back to Sergei and her mother. It was hard work, staying furious with her mother. Amy's thoughts spun into turmoil whenever she thought about her. *What on earth was she playing at, cheating on Dad? He was gorgeous! He thought the world of me and Mum, devoted his life to us! We were the Three Musketeers, the Three Amigos, the Three Bears – he used to say I was a little mini-mummy, because I look so much like her . . .*

She had to get out. Although her body was weary from travelling and from nursing her aching ankle, she knew perfectly well that sleep would be in short supply if she just gave up and went to bed.

Anyhow, don't they call this 'the city that never sleeps'? When in Rome, I guess . . .

One of the shoe addresses was a piano bar in Greenwich Village, New York City. She'd take a cab there, try at least to score one complete pair of shoes from the American leg of her trip, then head for JFK the next morning, switch her tickets, and fly home.

Or at least, fly back to Jesminder's.

Good plan. Decisive, easy to execute, and mercifully quick. She'd be on that plane back to London by this time tomorrow, after one last, valiant stand. Quickly, before the decision ran away, she whipped out her phone and sent Jesminder a text:

Defo cmng home 2moro. Will txt 2 let u no wht time. Amy ☺ x

Amy made quite an impression, entering Oliver's Piano Bar in downtown Greenwich Village a short time later. Showered, made-up and zipped back into the Audrey Hepburn dress that had made her feel so pretty – *was it really only the night before?* – she did her utmost to embody the epitome of English cool, managing to attract the attention of just about everyone in the place in the process. Oh, it could have been the cute dress, or the swingy, freshly washed hair – and maybe they *did* have something to do with it. But mostly, it was the fact that she wore a white strappy wedge sandal on one foot, and a fat, un-laced sneaker on the other, bandaged one. As she limped and hobbled over to the bar, the effort, and the pain, must have been written all over her face.

'Lost a shoe, Cinderella?'

'Been in a fight?'

And the place was busy, as well. Easing herself onto a barstool, she took a few moments for her eyes to accustom themselves to the gloom.

Low-ceilinged, muggy and just a touch claustrophobic, with black-and-white posters plastered on every wall advertising smash Broadway shows of the fifties, the bar had a settled, laid-back vibe, a kind of 'if you don't like it, you know what to do' assurance that Amy, despite her low spirits, really liked. It was refreshing – *bracing* – to walk into a take-it-or-leave-it place where nobody knew her name, emboldening rather than frightening. The room was furnished with small wooden tables and round-backed chairs, the kind of chairs that dancers straddled, back-to-front, in dance routines in the movies. Wax-encrusted bottles in the middle of each table held stubs of burning red candle, illuminating the customers with a softly decadent glow. Couples, mostly, some gorgeously made-up, heads close together, talking intimately, kissing now and then. A beautiful, Oriental-looking woman was in the middle of her stage act, just about to begin her next number. Behind her, a musician with a beard was tuning a double bass and a smiling man with a spherical stomach perched behind a drum kit, twirling brush-ended drumsticks. Completing the line-up, an earnest young black man in a tuxedo sat behind a baby grand piano, which was tucked away to one side of the stage. Amy caught his eye for a moment and he smiled at her before turning his attention back to his piano keys, and beginning to play.

'Can I get you something to drink?'

The barman had leaned over the counter, his mouth about two inches from Amy's ear.

'Oh!' She jumped. Then, realising that a stiff drink was exactly what she needed after the day she'd had, she asked, 'Do you have any vodka?'

The barman put his head on one side. 'Vodka? In a *bar*? Are you crazy?' He teased her as he reached for the bottle. 'Like anything in it?'

Amy smiled back. 'Some tonic, please.'

The singer's dress was a high-necked, shimmering column of silver sequins, which hugged her tall, lean figure. A slash from ankle to thigh revealed endless legs encased in sheer black tights, and on her feet, silver strappy sandals (far too big to ever have belonged to Amy), with heels that Amy knew she would insist were at least seven inches high until her dying day.

Wow, respect! New York, I think I love you!

Four other equally glamorous women – obviously performers as well – sat around the table closest to the stage, each of them black, elaborately coiffed and wearing sequined dresses similar to the one worn by the lady on stage. One was touching up her lip gloss, a second was inspecting her long nails; all had cocktail glasses in front of them, cool, languid creatures of the night. Amy, on the other hand, was still working hard to make sure that her confident side kept the upper hand over a niggling urge to turn and hobble for her life. But the bar had a warm feel to it, so she did her best to relax, took some deep breaths, tried to lose herself in the occasion, to enjoy the show for a while, then maybe hunt down the shoes, leg it, and tell Jes and Debs all about it when she got home.

The woman on stage leaned down slightly and spoke into her microphone, her voice sultry and melodic. 'OK, ladies and gentlemen, I think you'll know this one. Join in, if you're in that kinda mood, and if not, well, just enjoy . . .'

As she began to sing 'Moon River', her rich, soulful voice filled the room and a smattering of applause tickled the walls, kicked off by the sequined women at the front.

'Thank you, you're too kind,' she purred, inclining her head slightly before continuing with the song.

That's Phyllis's favourite song!

Thinking of Justin's mum gave Amy a strange feeling, an unwelcome reality check, together with a creeping realisation that no matter what happened when she got back to London, things would never be the same again. Something had been lost for ever, whether she and Justin sorted themselves out or not. Phyllis no longer trusted her, and that really, really sucked. There would be no more five-a-day phone calls, no more dawn raids on the Next sale. Amy was going to miss all that.

She raised her glass to her lips and downed the drink in one, something she wasn't in the habit of doing. The alcohol rush sent a hot surge right through her; she caught the barman's eye and he began to pour her another.

What the heck. I'm twenty-four, not fourteen, I'll never see these people again, my foot hurts, and I don't have to drive anywhere, or answer to anyone, or keep

*up appearances. I can just sit here and drown my
sorrows.*

'Drowning your sorrows?' The barman smiled,
pushing the fresh glass across the counter at her. 'You're
much too pretty to be looking so sad!' He pulled a sad-
clown face, forcing Amy reluctantly to smile for a
second time. 'Are you waiting for somebody?'

Amy's mission came crashing back to the front of
her mind. 'Well, sort of – Jamaica,' she replied. 'Do you
have somebody working here called Jamaica? I need to
speak to her.'

'Ah.' The barman stood up straight, biting his lip.
His face hardened. 'I'm sorry, but Jamaica's moved on.'

'Moved on?' Amy echoed. 'Moved on where?'

He shrugged. 'Who knows? Left no forwarding
address – not that any of us expected her to. You want
something from her? Because let me tell you, you
wouldn't be the only one!'

'So, she's just . . . gone?' Amy didn't know what else
to say.

'Yup, 'fraid so. Vanished into the ether. And good
luck to her.' He moved off to serve another customer.
Amy stared deep into her glass, focusing on the olive
at the bottom, as though hoping it would jump out of
the glass and offer some advice as to just what the heck
she was supposed to do now. The vodka was hitting
home, but not in a good way. Her spirits were plummeting even lower. What now? Was she destined to fail
to track down every single pair of shoes from now until
the end of time? Who, what, was trying to teach her
some sort of lesson?

Downing the second drink in three gulps, then sliding off the barstool, Amy knew she wasn't going to hold her composure together much longer. She stumbled painfully into the toilets, to the bizarre accompaniment of a round of applause. 'Moon River' had come to an end and the singer was curtsying and blowing extravagant kisses all around the bar, while the band flowed into the opening bars of 'Somewhere Over the Rainbow'.

Moments later, safely installed in a cubicle, Amy put her head in her hands and wept.

She wept hot, drunk, miserable tears. She was crying for love and loss and foolishness; for sore ankles, disappointments and betrayals; for loneliness, homesickness and homelessness; and for sheer, white anger. She cried for her dad, for her mum, and for herself. For Sergei, everything she thought he was and everything he now appeared to be, for Justin, for Phyllis, for Jack, for her shoes, for missing Debbie and Jes, and for not knowing what the hell she was going to do next.

I've come all the way here for nothing – apart from the discovery that my own mother wasn't who she made out she was . . .

'Come on, honey, no guy's worth so many tears!' A slender black hand, beautifully manicured with long, ruby nails and an enormous, heart-shaped diamanté ring, was reaching under the wall of her cubicle, holding out a clutch of tissues.

Amy, shocked into ceasing her sobs, stared down at it for a moment. The hand wiggled impatiently.

'Honey? This position ain't exactly all that comfortable for me, y'know?'

'Th-thank you,' Amy spluttered, leaning down and taking the tissues from the elegant hand. 'I'm sorry.'

'What? You don't want to start apologising to me, honey. Sounds like you've got more than enough trouble of your own to be getting along with! Now dry your eyes this instant or you're gonna look terrible tomorrow morning, and that's another thing you don't want – trust me!'

''K then,' Amy mumbled, scrubbing at her eyes and giving her nose a huge blow.

'That's my girl.'

Amy took some deep breaths, but a final, dry sob escaped from her lips before she could stop it.

'You want me to call somebody for you?' came the voice.

'No, thank you, I'll be fine.' *And there's nobody you can call, anyhow.* 'You're very kind.'

'So I keep hearin,' the voice said ruefully. 'So, do you need a contract taken out on whatever guy's made you feel this bad?'

Amy froze, a fresh tissue halfway to her nose.

A loud sigh came from the next cubicle. 'I was kidding.'

'I know!' Amy replied, far too quickly.

'You take care of yourself, y'hear? Don't let the world do this to you, OK?'

'I will. I mean, I won't – I mean – thank you . . .' but the next-door cubicle door had opened, and banged shut.

A few minutes later, and Amy's equilibrium was sufficiently restored for her to unlock the cubicle door and hobble to the washbasin. She stood side by side with one of the performers from the table in front of the stage – long, silver column dress, gorgeous black skin, a perfect manicure . . . and a huge diamanté heart ring.

'I'm Amy,' she said simply. 'Thank you.'

The woman, who was peeling off the longest, flutteriest false eyelash Amy had ever seen, turned and smiled, revealing gorgeous, even white teeth and kind, coal-black eyes. She leaned across and kissed Amy on one hot cheek.

'I'm Sparkle.'

CHAPTER TWENTY-FIVE

'My goodness, we need to do a little work here and there, don't we?' Sparkle rummaged in her make-up bag, which lay open beside the basin, pulled out a tub of cleanser and a cotton wool pad, and handed them to Amy. 'You want to make a start? You won't be able to see in the morning either, if you leave that mess to set looking like that.' She glanced at Amy's bandaged foot. 'And you've got enough to worry about, already, dontcha?'

Amy risked a glance in the mirror, gasped in dismay at the panda-eyed reflection, and shook her head. 'Crying's so inconvenient, isn't it?' she murmured, squirming at how English and prim she sounded.

But Sparkle was nodding, getting to work on her own lashes. 'And overrated. Don't forget overrated!'

The cleanser was icy-cold, stinging Amy's sore eyes as she dabbed it gingerly all around the swollen rims.

'What brings you here all alone, Amy?'

Amy was looking straight ahead, into the mirror. 'I'm looking for Jamaica. Do you know her?'

'*Do I know her?*' Sparkle exploded, hurling her false

eyelash into the basin. 'Does the devil know trouble?' Then she picked up the lash, shook droplets of water from the basin off it, and stuffed it furiously into her make-up bag. 'That bitch broke my heart!'

Amy shrank back a little, giving Sparkle a bit more space. She thought it best not to say anything else, for safety's sake.

Jamaica sounds like quite a woman – leaving in a hurry, no forwarding address, breaking Sparkle's heart – Sparkle, who's got 'I-can-take-care-of myself' written all over that beautiful face . . .

'Y'know,' Sparkle went on, 'for such a small person, Jamaica sure knew how to cause trouble. Bitch! Bitch! Bitch!'

They must have argued over a guy. I bet Jamaica took Sparkle's lover with her when she bolted!

'And . . . breathe,' Amy soothed, touching Sparkle's arm. 'I'm sorry, I didn't want to open up old wounds. I just wanted to ask about a pair of shoes she bought on eBay, actually. Nothing important.'

Sparkle glanced down at Amy's mismatched feet for a second time and raised an expertly pencilled eyebrow. 'Honey, I think we both know that the phrase "nothing important" should never be used within a hundred miles of the word "shoes", don't we?'

Amy giggled.

'That's better! Now, shoes, you say – not those killer Jourdans Jamaica was parading round the other day?'

Amy's heart began to pound. She had owned only one pair of vintage Jourdans. 'Blue, with a silver strap?'

''Bout this high?' Sparkle asked, holding out a slender thumb and forefinger four inches apart.

Amy nodded, robbed of speech.

'So cute! Jamaica had the smallest feet in showbiz – smallest *everything*, actually – otherwise I'd have borrowed them in a second!'

Sparkle turned back to the mirror, and Amy cautiously resumed dabbing cold water on her face.

'Tell me what happened, why don't you?' Sparkle's question was muffled by the thick pad of cotton wool she was using to clean off her lip-liner.

So Amy once again found herself telling a virtual stranger the whole story, beginning with her phone call to Justin, when he'd dumped her.

'. . . didn't give me a chance to explain . . .'

'Terrible!' Sparkle unclipped her giant teardrop earrings.

'. . . I just didn't see the *need* to tell him about the ballet trips . . .'

'We all need our secrets, honey!' The silver lamé shawl was folded neatly away.

'. . . every last pair . . .'

'He *didn't*!' Off came the stick-on beauty spot.

'. . . posted out all over the world . . .' *Oh! A wig!*

'The dumb-ass schmucko!'

'. . . he should have known I'd never do that sort of thing . . .'

'Well, I certainly wouldn't have you down as a tramp, honey.' The last of the make-up came off with just a few deft strokes.

'. . . couldn't just sit around doing nothing so I flew over here . . .' *What great skin!*

'Of course you did, sweetheart! Could you unzip me, please?'

'. . . bit of a rollercoaster – oh, sure, no problem – so I'm going to fly home in the morning . . .'

'You are? That's such a shame . . . ah! That's better! Catch these babies for me, please, honey?' Amy was handed two large silicone false breasts as Sparkle reached into the holdall which was lying on the floor and pulled out a pair of Calvin Klein briefs, jeans, a black shirt and – gloriously – an astoundingly delicious pair of tan snakeskin Gucci cowboy boots. 'Won't be a minute. I'll change in there.'

'Em, OK then.' As soon as the cubicle door closed, Amy looked up at the ceiling, closed her eyes and shook her head slowly.

I cannot believe I'm so dim sometimes. Sparkle's a drag queen! Duh! And quadruple duh!

'What would you like me to do with your breasts?' she called through the door, to the amusement of the person who had just walked in to use the bathroom.

'There's a little red purse inside my suitcase – see it? I call it my titty-bag. Would you be so kind?'

'Sure.' Amy eased the breasts gently into the bag and closed the zip. *Well, here's another first for my memoirs.*

Sparkle re-emerged from the cubicle as a ridiculously handsome young black man, reintroduced himself as Assante, embraced Amy for a second time, and together they walked – or at least, Assante walked and supported Amy who hobbled – back into the bar for another drink.

'So, you want to know about Jamaica?' he asked, as they toasted their new friendship in more vodka.

'Yes, please,' Amy replied. 'Do you know, I'm starting to discover that the next best thing to actually getting the shoes back is finding out about the person who bought them so that I can imagine the new life they have now, even though they're not with me any more.'

She hadn't realised this before. The vodka was making her mouth move a lot faster than her brain but, so far, her mouth seemed to be doing a pretty good job.

Assante shook his head bitterly. 'Well, you'll be organising a rescue mission if I tell you too much about Jamaica, if that's the way you feel. Maybe I'd better keep shtum.'

He gripped the glass tightly, mouth hardened, obviously reliving something pretty intense.

'Go on,' Amy urged. 'Your turn. Tell me.'

Assante didn't need further prompting. 'OK, here goes. He and I were dating . . .'

Amy hurtled up to speed. *OK, so Jamaica is a drag queen also. Ri-ight.*

'. . . but we had – how can I put it? – *conflicting* professional issues.'

'Oh?'

'He's an actor as well, same as me, and sometimes we find ourselves competing for the same parts – not often, as we have such different physiques, but it can be . . . problematical . . . when there's a clash.'

'I can imagine.'

'So last week, you'll never believe it, but my agent

rang me up to give me a heads-up on my absolute dream part – auditions by invitation only, and they wanted me to try out!' Assante's eyes were shining as he spoke. 'Remember the movie *Tootsie*?'

Amy, no mean film buff back in her university days, nodded enthusiastically. 'Loved it!'

'You did? So did I, obviously! Well, it's going to be put on Broadway – can you even *begin* to imagine the fabulousness?' Assante's eyes were brimming with excitement.

'Trying!' Amy squeaked back, scrunching her eyes shut.

'Attagirl! And they need an understudy for the Dustin Hoffman role, you know, Michael Dorsey/Dorothy Michaels?'

'But that'll be amazing!' Amy cried. 'Remember how he stood up to "the Tongue"?'

Assante clapped his hands. 'You diva, of course I do! My favourite role of all time!' Then, just as suddenly, his face fell, as if a light had been flicked off.

'What happened?' Amy prompted.

'Jamaica rang his agent without telling me, and got himself called to audition as well! I was furious! He knew I'd waited my whole life for a chance to do this. And I was certain he'd get the part. Being so much smaller, he'd be a more convincing Dorothy . . . so I, erm, I . . .'

'What? What did you do?' Amy leaned forward.

'Assante, sweetie, you gonna introduce us?' The other sequined performers had stood up and were heading for the restrooms, carrying holdalls. They all paused to look Amy up and down, crowding round the little table like a flock of exotic birds.

'Oh, sure! Lay-dees, meet my wonderful new friend, Miss Amy from London town! Amy, say hi, if you would, to Miss Precious Stone . . .'

'Hi!' Amy laughed, as Precious curtsied and fluttered her eyelashes.

'Ms Daisy Meadows!'

'Darling!' Daisy pouted, kissing Amy on each cheek.

'Miss Shanghai Noon!'

'Well, hello, you gorgeous little morsel!' The Oriental singer gave Amy a raunchy wink.

'And last, but never ever least – Madam Butterfly!'

'Why, how do you indeed do, pray tell?' Madam Butterfly kissed Amy's hand. 'But alas, we can't stop, darlings. First we must change! Don't go anywhere!' They drifted gorgeously towards the restrooms, as everyone in the place turned to watch them go.

'And when they come back I'll introduce you to George, Raymond, Lemar and Isaac, OK?'

'Great, twice the fun!' Amy smiled.

'Where were we?'

'You were about to tell me what you did when Jamaica sneaked himself an audition for *Tootsie*.' Amy tried not to giggle at her own words. *This is definitely not the sort of conversation I have every day . . .*

'Oh, yes, I was, wasn't I? Well, I kind of locked him in my apartment. Which, well, kind of made him miss the audition.'

'Ah,' Amy breathed, searching her head for an appropriate response. Assante was looking slightly ashamed of himself, but really, only very slightly. 'Well, I guess you had some justification, didn't you? He only got himself the audition by breaching your trust, didn't he?'

'Exactly! Diva, I am *so* liking the way your mind works!' They high-fived each other, before a look of pained puzzlement flashed across Assante's face. 'So why the hell did he have to cut up all my clothes?'

'No!'

'Uh-huh.'

'He didn't!'

'He surely did. Every stitch. Even my hats. We sort of broke up after that.'

Amy covered Assante's hand with her own, and nodded. 'I'm not surprised. There can't be too many other routes for a relationship to take after something like that, can there?'

'Amen to that,' Assante agreed.

There was a pause. Assante was looking at her strangely.

'What? What did I say?'

'You don't see the connection?' he asked gently.

'No, Assante.' Amy smiled. 'I have never had a jealous lover destroy my . . . ah.' She nodded. Wryly, they clinked glasses. 'I kind of have, haven't I?'

Then Assante moved his hand so that it was covering Amy's, and gave it a squeeze. 'Justin, did you say his name is?'

'Justin Campbell.'

'Well, honey, you tell me you never cheated on Justin Campbell, and Justin Campbell says you did?'

'Basically.'

'Basically?'

Amy nodded. 'Yeah. I was seeing another man, but only at the ballet . . .'

'I'm liking that style of yours more and more, diva!'

'It's true! Justin wouldn't have understood, he didn't much like Sergei . . .'

'Sergei, hmm? Foxy name.'

'. . . so I didn't tell him.'

'So he stole your shoes and sold every pair? Honey, no matter how big or small a bitch you've been, no diva deserves a dog like that!'

'Excellent point, thoughtfully put,' Amy said, swaying slightly in her seat as the third vodka found its target. Her ankle twinged. 'Though it's hard to be fabulous in sneakers.'

'Well, honey, I'll be the judge of that for tonight, OK? Diva, the man trashed your shoes! What a total dog! Tell you what, you find your tallest stilettos and use them to dig that dog a grave!'

Amy laughed loudly. Her laugh sounded strange, alien, just a little bit dirty – she liked it.

They raised their glasses again and toasted each other for the umpteenth time as the band, minus its singer, played a jazz number. Amy found herself closing her eyes and swaying to the tinkling melody.

'You like jazz?' Assante asked.

'I've never really understood it,' Amy admitted, 'but I like this, that's for sure!'

'That's because jazz needs context,' Assante explained. 'You wouldn't like this so much if it were playing in a supermarket, now, would you?'

'That's true – and something like rock or hip-hop would sound all wrong in a place like this, wouldn't it?'

'Mightn't that depend on what mood you were in?' Assante asked. 'Or what time of day it was, or what you'd had for dinner? Or who you were with?'

'Hmm, possibly,' Amy mused, 'but all I know is that I can't imagine anything more right than listening to this, here in the middle of New York, with you.'

'Why, thank you, Miss Diva, I'll take that as a compliment.' He inclined his head a little.

'You should. I meant it as a compliment. Thank you for brightening up a day that had potential to be an absolute stinker!'

'Hey, diva, life's a disco! Remember that, won't you? Don't you go sitting the dance out, y'hear?'

'I'll try!' Amy laughed, as Assante's friends emerged from the restroom, metamorphosed from exotic birds into lithe, sharply dressed young men.

'Diva, as I said, allow me to introduce you to Raymond, George, Lemar and Isaac! Guys, Amy here has been enduring a bit of a Jamaica-style situation of her own back home in London – what do you say we take her out and cheer her up?'

George, the tallest of the group, was looking her closely up and down, until she began to squirm in faint discomfort.

'Don't tell me,' he began, leaning over and touching her knee.

'What? What have I done?' she asked, tugging self-consciously at the hem of her dress.

George's hand began to travel slowly down her calf,

292

towards her ankle. He crouched down, staring at her undamaged foot intently, then, abruptly, he looked up into her eyes. 'I bet you're the person who sold Jamaica those heels from England, aren't you?'

Amy nodded, grinning, as Assante burst out laughing. The others crowded rapturously round Amy.

'Those babies were yours? You *diva*!'

'The blue Jourdans? So sublime!'

'Why'd you go selling a pair of killer heels like those? Or did they make you twist that ankle, is that why you got rid of them?'

'No!' Amy laughed. 'It's a long story – I've already bored Assante with it!'

'Well,' Isaac said thoughtfully, glancing round the others, 'you can bore us with it over falafel and a bit of belly dancing, if you're not doing anything for the next few hours? The restaurant's right around the corner.'

Amy looked up at Assante, who had draped a fringed white silk scarf around his neck and was placing a black fedora hat on his head at a daring angle. He stood up and reached out his hand.

'Nobody puts Baby in the corner!' he purred, beckoning flamboyantly.

'*Dirty Dancing*! My second favourite movie of all time!'

'And your first?' Lemar, standing behind her, crouched down and laid his chin on her shoulder.

'Why, *Strictly Ballroom*, of course!' She laughed. 'What else would it be?'

'*Paso doble!*' they called out in unison, snapping

upright, and adopting devastating bullfighter stances. Amy whooped with delight.

Several snappy dance steps later, Lemar and George broke off and stood on either side of Amy's chair, each proffering an arm to help her to her feet.

Laughing, she caught both arms and stood, tiny between the two tall men, the combination of vodka and sprained ankle making her wobble unsteadily.

'I feel like Kylie!' she announced, as they began their procession to the door.

'We know!' the others chorused, as they hit the muggy New York streets singing.

Life's a disco, Amy reminded herself, smiling broadly at Assante. Don't sit the dance out . . .

CHAPTER TWENTY-SIX

It was the first morning Amy could ever remember not minding having a hangover. The previous evening had been one of the best of her life.

Laughing, singing and chatting in the easy company of Assante and his friends, Amy, lost in the moment, had managed to relax and have real fun, against all the odds – the throbbing ankle and broken heart – and when her companions treated her to what was effectively a group belly-lap-dance to the accompaniment of Tom Jones's 'You Can Leave Your Hat On', the little tears of laughter that escaped from the corners of her eyes were mixed with other tears of raw gratitude towards Assante and his timely reminder about the importance of participating in life and everything it brought along. So, raising her arms above her head, she swayed to the music, singing and applauding her new friends' raunchy performance.

Now, as she stood in the departure lounge at JFK Airport, rubbing her aching temples and trying to make sense of the information screen in front of her, a buzzing sensation against her hip proclaimed that somebody was trying to reach her on the phone.

Pressing her hand against her other ear to block out the airport noise, she glanced at the unfamiliar number flashing up on her screen, frowned, and answered.

'Hi, Abe, how've you been?'

The voice at the other end was confident and familiar. So familiar that it took a few moments for it to sink in who it actually was.

'*Justin?*' Amy nearly fell over.

'Yup, that would be me. You still in New York?'

'I'm at the airport. H-how on earth did you know I was in New York?' Amy had no idea where the words came from. The shock of hearing Justin's voice, coupled with her headache, almost made her pass out. She swayed a little, then sat down unsteadily on her suitcase.

'Jesminder told me. You're a dark horse, Abe. New York!'

'Why *not* New York?' Amy shot back, stung by his incredulous tone.

'I thought you were staying at Jes's.'

'I was,' she replied tartly.

'So have you had a good trip?' Still the voice was chatty. Justin could almost have been talking to his mother about a Sunday walk in the park. Meanwhile Amy could scarcely breathe.

'Justin, I tried to phone you so many times, why didn't you answer?'

She heard Justin exhale loudly. 'Oh, Abe, because I was mad at you, that's why. I thought you'd been shagging around.'

'I *wasn't* sodding shagging around!' Amy cried, startling the man who was standing in front of her, trying to read the departure information. 'I don't shag around. You should have known that.'

'I'm sorry, OK? But things didn't look too pretty when I first got a handle on them. Surely you must admit that.'

Amy's blood began to boil. Was that the best apology she was going to get? She could feel her cheeks burning. 'You never gave me a chance to talk to you, to explain. How could you not have?'

'Abe, hang on . . .'

'We've been together a year and a half, Justin. A year and a half! And then all of a sudden you turn into a brick wall. I didn't deserve that. Nobody deserves that.'

'Fair enough, Abe, fair enough,' Justin's voice soothed.

Closing her eyes, she could almost feel his hands stroking her hair, his breath on the top of her head, the crinkles in the corners of his eyes when he looked at her with that half-amused expression on his face – the expression he always wore when she went off on one. 'I was a bit previous, I guess. And I'm sorry. Sheez, Abe, you're making me work for it, aren't you?'

Amy said nothing, just sat on her suitcase, trying to stay calm. *Work for it? Work for what? What's coming next?*

'You still there, Abe?'

'I'm still here. So, when did you finally get round to reading my letter, then?'

'Letter?' he echoed.

'The letter I left on your desk?'

'Oh, the letter! Sheez, no, I tore *that* up, obviously.'

'Y-you did?'

'I wasn't in any mood to read what I thought would be a whole bunch of excuses back then, Abe. I was far too mad. Remember Natasha—'

'Of *course* I remember Natasha!' Amy cut in, rubbing her aching head and scrunching her eyes. 'She's been a hard act to follow, Justin. So are you phoning because you're finally ready to listen to what actually happened?'

'I told you, Abe, I know what actually happened. At least, I know now.'

'You do? So, did Jesminder tell you?'

There was a pause. A sigh. Amy held her breath. 'No, Abe, Sergei called me. Yesterday.'

Amy was stunned. 'Sergei?' she spluttered. 'Why on earth . . . ? How on earth did he get your new number when I couldn't?'

Justin laughed. 'He got hold of Mum's number from Directory Enquiries and managed to sweet-talk her into letting him have it. Quite the silver-tongued devil, isn't he?'

'Oh, stop it,' Amy snapped. She really, really didn't want to think about Sergei any more than was absolutely necessary. Then, more softly: 'How is Phyllis, by the way?'

'Oh, she's fine, thanks, much the same as usual,' he replied, his voice far softer. 'She misses you, I think.'

'I miss her too.' Amy fought down the lump that was forming, rather inconveniently, in her throat.

Justin didn't seem to notice the emotion in her voice. 'So anyhow, this Sergei bloke caught me on the hop a bit. I thought the call was going to be from one of my tour organisers – I don't think I'd have answered it if I knew it was going to be *Sergei* – but anyway, once we started talking he seemed OK.'

'That's what my letter tried to explain. That's the *truth*, Justin.' Amy found herself shivering, though the terminal building, with its acres of glass, was stiflingly hot. 'I should have told you from the start, but it just became too difficult!'

'Yeah, well, whatever, it was nice to get the full story, Abe.'

Why the heck did you listen to Sergei, of all people, and not to me? Justin Campbell, why?

'I could have told you all that, Justin. But then, you wouldn't have believed me, would you?'

Another pause. Amy picked at the studs on the front pocket of her jeans, waiting.

'Probably not.' Justin's voice was a mask she couldn't get behind. Amy hadn't a clue what he was thinking. 'But, hey,' he went on, far more cheerfully, 'what's all this about you going on a mission to get your shoes back? You rock, Abe! What a thing to do!'

'Well, like you say, Justin, whatever.'

There was silence on the other end of the line. Around Amy, the terminal building was getting busier, yet there seemed to be a small exclusion zone invisibly cordoned off around her, as though the world was giving her a wide berth while she negotiated her way through the very conversation she'd been praying for ever since Justin had jumped to the wrong conclusion and dumped her, two weeks before.

'Have you found them?'

'Some.'

'Ah.'

'Not as many as I'd hoped.'

'Ah.'

Another pause.

'Justin?'

'Yup?'

'You do realise that you sold Mum's dancing shoes, don't you?' Amy closed her eyes.

'Well, I have been feeling really bad about that one, to be honest,' he replied, his voice much softer. 'It wasn't until after they'd gone in the post that I started dealing with how much they meant to you.'

'They meant the world to me.'

'I know, Abe. And if I'd been thinking straight I would have kept them back. I promise you. But, well, I was just so mad at you! I thought—'

'I know! I know what you thought!' Amy burst out. 'You thought I'd cheated on you, like Natasha!' She rubbed her head. Now it was really pounding. 'Let's not go over that again.'

'OK.' He sounded relieved. 'Sorry, Abe. Bygones?'

'Bygones.'

Can it really be that easy? Can so much hurt be brushed away with one little word?

'Did you manage to get them back? The dancing shoes?'

Amy could hear the tension in his voice, could

almost feel him hold his breath after he spoke. It was comforting. At last he was betraying an emotional reaction. It was *something*. Evocative too: it spoke to Amy of the good times they'd shared – and there had been loads of those – the gigs, the walks in the park, the movie trips, the snuggly nights in . . . for a moment she was reminded of the old Justin.

'Well, I got one of them back.'

'Only one? Why's that, then?'

'You tell me. You put only one in the box before posting it to Patchogue.'

'Patch-og? Is that how you pronounce it? I'd assumed it rhymed with Minogue, as in Kylie. Odd, that. You'd think with words there'd be some sort of standardisation . . .'

'Justin? The shoe?'

'Oh yes, sorry, Abe. Was there really only one in the box?'

'Yes. I saw it being unwrapped.' The memory brought a vision of Jack to the front of her mind, his thigh pressed against hers on that little bench at Pleasant Shores, his arms around her as they danced. It made her head swim even more. She didn't know whether to feel guilty or not. And she didn't have space in her overworked, aching head to decide.

'Ah, yes! I know what must have happened. Sheez, what a nightmare! Going all the way to the States and only finding one!'

'Tell me what happened, Justin.'

'Well, I did drop a couple of shoe boxes when I was taking them out of the boxes and stuffing them into jiffy bags. Maybe I got a pair mixed up. I was kind of mad.'

Amy was nodding. It was strange, discovering such a mundane explanation. No code, no secret meaning – no 'omen', as Jack had put it. It had just been Justin, in the height of his anger, being a careless git.

'Sheez, that won't do my eBay seller's rating any good. It'd be just typical if the sodding buyer posted a stinking rating on my board. Damn! I'm just about to put up that old vinyl collection. Nobody will bid for it now.'

Amy's ear and brain were going numb, listening to his rant. Listening to him describe Jack as the 'sodding buyer', thinking of Jack buying the shoes as a gift for Alice . . .

How dare you?

But above all, she was thinking of the shoes themselves, her mother's dancing shoes, being talked about as mere inconveniences, imagining one of the shoes being hurled angrily into the wrong box . . .

'Poor you, Justin, it would be dreadful if all this hurt your eBay seller's rating.' Her voice was freighted with sarcasm. She was too strung out to shout at him.

'Um, yeah, sorry,' Justin replied.

Amy sighed. She had slept badly and now she felt desperately tired.

Life may be a disco, Assante, but everyone needs the occasional slow dance. Who is this man I'm talking to? And is it his fault or mine that I don't really know? Come on, Marsh, it's as though you've been away for a year.

So much has happened. It's almost as though I'm not the same person any more.

'Still, never mind about that right now. We can sort it out when you get home.'

I've learned so much about myself, about human nature, kindness, and trust, and letting go . . .

'Sorry? Did I just hear you right?'

She definitely heard the smile in Justin's voice as he replied. 'Yup, you certainly did. What time does your flight get in, Abe? I'll meet you.'

Amy said nothing.

'But you'll probably be wiped out after the flight,' he went on, 'so maybe we'll just have a cosy night in?'

Still nothing.

'Abe?'

'I'm still here, Justin.'

'You OK?'

NO!

'Well—' she began, but Justin cut in.

'Duh, stupid me – it's the shoes, isn't it? Listen, don't worry, soon as you're back we'll hit the shops and score some replacements, OK?'

'No, really, Justin.'

'I insist. Got a bit of a bonus off the last tour I organised, so what do you say we blow it on restocking that big old shoe cupboard of yours? It'll be like nothing happened – only better!'

Please, please don't let that have just happened.

'Justin, stop, OK? Just stop!'

'Why – what have I said?'

'These shoes were irreplaceable! Why, please tell me,

303

do you think I am here, in America, trying to track them down again, rather than on the King's Road buying new ones myself? Because they are – or at least they were – *irreplaceable*!'

She must have raised her voice. Some people were looking at her strangely, but she didn't care.

'What?' Now Justin raised his voice too. 'Nothing's irreplaceable, Amy – come on!'

A heavy silence thundered down the line.

'OK,' he went on, 'sorry, that came out wrong. Obviously, *people* are irreplaceable, but shoes?'

'I'm not coming back to you, Justin.'

Amy wasn't sure exactly where or when she made that decision. It just arrived, landed, like a butterfly on her nose. It was over.

'Abe . . .'

'I'm sorry, Justin, but we're finished.' As Amy spoke the words, a wave of sadness washed over her as she realised that, subconsciously, she had made the decision a long time ago.

'Abe, don't say that. I've told you, everything's going to be fine. Listen, I'll meet you off the plane . . .'

'But, Justin, I'm not flying to London today. I'm flying to Miami.'

'What?'

Amy glanced up at the departure information and gasped. 'Oh! And my flight's just been called. I have to go, I'm afraid.'

'But Jesminder said you were coming home today.'

'I changed my mind. Haven't told Jes or Debs yet. I'm just about to ring them.'

304

'What? Come on, Abe! When did you change your mind?'

'Last night.' Despite herself, Amy found herself smiling softly at the memory of the evening before. 'When I was disco dancing.'

CHAPTER TWENTY-SEVEN

The hot wind, which chased Amy as she stepped out of her motel onto the streets of Miami, was in a funny way as bracing as the stiff sea air of Ballyvaughan. Warming, enlivening, it seemed to coax and reassure her as she picked her way through the busy afternoon streets.

It was only after she had been walking for ten minutes or so in the sunshine that she noticed her limp was scarcely perceptible; the ankle hardly ached, even though the aspirin must have worn off hours ago. Almost overwhelmed by a sense of lightness, of purpose, of doing the right thing, Amy walked from block to block, squinting at the map leading her to Madeleine Hayes at 8363 Carson. Whoever, wherever and whatever that was.

Something strange had happened to her during the flight from JFK down to Miami, after she had been last to board following her conversation with Justin. She couldn't quite put her finger on it. She'd strapped herself in, pulled out a packet of tissues, apologised in advance to her neighbour, telling her to pay her no heed, swallowed two aspirin and a bottle of water, and settled down to cry for the duration of the flight.

Only it didn't happen. As the plane took off, she unwrapped a tissue, looked down at it, and waited. Nothing. Well, her headache began to dissipate, and the throbbing in her ankle lessened as the aspirin kicked in, but not a single tear escaped from her hot, tired eyes, however hard common sense told her that they ought.

She'd felt like the heroine at the end of one of her beloved movies, gazing out of the aeroplane window with a dreamy I-have-loved-and-lost-and-survived expression on her face, poised to face an uncertain future and all that it might hold, whilst the camera faded to soft focus and the credits began to roll. She'd tried to chill out and just enjoy the flight but instead, crashed out and slept, only to be woken by the stewardess telling her to buckle up for landing.

This, for Amy, was an unexpected reaction, to say the least. Perhaps there would be a delayed grief response in the days or weeks or months to come but meanwhile, her inability to coax out a full-on meltdown was like being handed a chunk of new energy on a silver tray. She felt great.

As she walked, a combination of good guesswork and, unlike in Ireland, a decent map, brought her at last to Carson Street, a wide boulevard of mixed houses and shops, flanked by palm trees and enormous dusty cars. Number 8363 turned out to be a large, white, flat-roofed wooden house, situated next to what looked like a small art studio, with steps leading up to the front door from the pavement.

A pounding heart was becoming familiar to Amy now, as she climbed the steps and rang the doorbell.

Please, please, don't be a lunatic. Or a psychopath. Or a gorgeous surfer dude with board shorts and streaked hair and come-to-bed eyes. I am so not in the mood for any of that.

An outer mosquito-screen door made of wood and mesh protected the main, glass-panelled front door, making it hard for Amy to peer inside, but she could dimly make out a wide, tranquil entrance hall with a polished wooden floor. Beyond that, a broad staircase divided in two halfway up and gave onto a galleried landing that appeared to be hung with large works of modern art.

'Whaddayawant?' A shrill, grumpy voice called out from upstairs. Amy shrank back a little, then immediately relaxed as she saw the owner of the voice begin to slouch downstairs.

It was a teenage girl – at least Amy's best guess was that it was a girl, dressed head to toe in black, with long hair dyed so black it was almost blue, a chalk-white face, black lipstick and fingerless gloves adorned with studs.

Didn't realise there are Goths in Florida. I thought it's just old people. Wouldn't they overheat in all those black layers? And what have they got to be miserable about, with all the beaches and sunshine?

The girl, aged around fourteen, slouched across the hall, slack-jawed, head tilted to one side, as though the effort of balancing it upright on her neck was just, like, *way* too taxing. She pulled open the front door and spoke to Amy through the mesh of the mosquito screen.

'Yeah? What?'

'I'm sorry to trouble you,' Amy began, feeling about a hundred years older than the girl who stood in front of her, 'but I'm looking for Madeleine Hayes?'

The girl's eyes narrowed for a moment, then she sighed and shook her head in exasperation. 'Studio's next door. You not able to read or something?'

The girl then banged the door shut and made for the stairs at a dead-slow lope, shoulders hunched, and obviously muttering to herself.

Mum would've killed me if I'd spoken to strangers like that!

However, the girl did have a bit of a point because when Amy stepped back onto the pavement and looked at the art studio adjoining the house there was a large sign above the door proclaiming 'The Art of Madeleine Hayes', and a smaller sign that simply said 'Open'.

Gingerly, she pushed open the door, poked her head inside – and gasped. There, right in the centre of the spartan, brightly lit space, was a large, shining sculpture in the shape of . . . a stiletto shoe!

Amy blinked. She did a double take and blinked again. Yup, it was, indeed, a giant stiletto – she wasn't hallucinating.

Off to the side, a woman stood with her back to Amy, in front of a heavy-duty workbench, banging a piece of metal furiously with a hammer.

Still reeling with bewilderment at stumbling across

a shoe sculpture, now Amy had to contend with the sight of a pair of bright orange dungarees worn over a baggy purple T-shirt, black Doc Marten boots despite the searing heat outside, and muscular arms, tattooed from bicep to wrist, intent on hammering some blameless object into submission.

Amy eased herself fully into the studio and quietly shut the door behind her, wincing as each hammer blow assaulted her eardrums.

'Yes! You beauty!' The woman held aloft the piece of metal she'd been hammering, stroked it, blew on it, and smiled broadly, clearly satisfied with the result. Still without noticing Amy, she then pulled on what looked like a pair of First World War flying goggles, picked up an industrial-sized blowtorch, twisted the handle on top of the gas bottle that stood by her side, and lit it. Instantly, a spear of blue flame roared into life.

'Woo-hoo!' The woman cried, 'OK, bring it home, baby! Come on!'

She looks more like a mad scientist than a mad artist. A blowtorch! I wouldn't want to get on the wrong side of this one, that's for sure. If it wasn't for the fact that I've just crossed an entire continent to speak to this person, I'd be out that door before you could say . . .

Just then, the woman glanced round and caught sight of Amy.

'Be right with ya!' she called out, through sparks from the blowtorch and a cloud of frizzy, salt-and-pepper hair that poked out from above and below the goggles, making her appearance almost cartoon-like. And definitely less intimidating.

The blowtorch was switched off as abruptly as it had come on and immediately the room was plunged into a silence that was almost as shocking as the hammering noise had been a few moments before. The woman pulled off the charcoal-coloured gauntlets she'd been wearing, lifted the goggles up so that now they perched comically on the top of her head, and walked towards Amy, hand outstretched, smiling broadly to reveal small, slightly crooked, very un-American teeth.

'Madeleine Hayes, glad to see you!'

'Amy Maa-aaargh!-sh! That's quite a handshake!'

'So people keep telling me – sorry about that! Twenty years of working with metal does that to a girl!'

'Looks like fun,' Amy remarked. 'That shoe is amazing.' A single spotlight illuminated the sweeping curves of the sculpture.

'Thank you, I appreciate that.'

'Does it have a name?' Amy was unsure whether that might be a stupid question or not; her knowledge of modern art could be written on the back of a postage stamp.

'Not yet,' Madeleine replied. 'I started out calling it *The Foot Soldier* because I wanted to explore the machinery that drives our perceptions of beauty, but then, after I finished, it took on a whole new personality, a new confidence . . .'

'Yes! I can see that!' Amy said excitedly. 'It's telling me, "If you want to find out what's driving me, you're going to have to beg for it."' She clasped her hands together, caught up in the beauty of the sculpture, then just as suddenly she remembered that she knew nothing about modern art and had just announced to its creator that her sculpture was telling the world to beg for it.

Yikes.

'I'm sorry,' she mumbled, 'did that sound a bit deranged?'

But Madeleine was looking at her and smiling. 'Absolutely! I liked it. But I kind of agree with you. It's funny, you know, when I started that piece I hated stiletto heels.'

'You did?' Amy sneaked another glance at the Doc Marten boots, acknowledging that when it came to footwear, they were almost certainly singing from opposite ends of the spectrum.

'I did. But you know, the more I worked on it, the more the shape got to me – you know, the feel, the smoothness, the arch of the sole, the elongation of the front of the foot, the pointy toe. I had to admit I was dealing with something pretty darned sexy.'

'I wear stilettos a lot, I'm afraid.' Amy giggled apologetically. 'I like what they do for me.'

Madeleine nodded. 'Well, thanks to the sculpture, I can understand that, though you'd better watch out. When you're seventy, with bunions, corns, hammer toes and arthritis . . .'

'I shall sit in my hospital bed and raise a glass of smuggled-in whisky to the wise sculptress of South Beach.'

'I'll drink to her too. She sounds great.'

They stood side by side in easy silence, contemplating the sculpture. Amy was curious about how much it cost, but the question seemed impertinent, particularly as it was almost certain to be way, way out of her price range, which, when it came to souvenir shopping, was usually confined to postcards and quirky sandals from market stalls.

Instead, she spoke of the next thing that came into her head. 'It must be wonderful, having the freedom to create whatever you want. I do a desk job.'

Madeleine nodded. 'Well, yes, I do have freedom, but y'know, freedom doesn't put food on the table. I do a lot of commissioned pieces to earn a living – but the trick with those is to put in a little bit of yourself, a piece of your own personal freedom, in everything you do, even if it's buried under mountains of instructions from other people.'

'I like that idea,' Amy said. 'It's kind of . . .'

'Subversive?' Madeleine suggested.

'Yes! It's subversive. Very rock 'n' roll. It's not easy to be subversive when you work in Internet travel, I have to say.'

'Hey, I'm sure you can work on that! So, are you here to discuss a commission? Or just to look around? Either way, you are most welcome.'

Once again Amy had allowed herself to forget the purpose of her visit. Madeleine's polite reminder jolted her out of her new-found artistic slant on life and back to her mission.

'Well, Madeleine . . .'

'Maddy, please.'

'Thanks, well, Maddy, I'm actually here about a mix-up over a pair of shoes that were accidentally sold on eBay.' She jerked her head towards the giant stiletto. 'Weird, huh?'

'Oh, yes?' Maddy looked interested. 'Shoes, you say?'

'Well . . .' Amy started, and then stopped. She felt like she'd told the story so many times, in so many places, so many different ways, that the thought of embarking on it all over again was almost over-whelming. One thing she did know, though, was that the more often she told it, the closer to the actual whole truth she came.

I am never, ever going to spin a pack of lies to anyone, ever again, as long as I live.

'OK,' she resumed, 'here's where I'm at . . .'

It felt as though it had all happened to somebody else. Had she really been through all that, and in such a short space of time?

Maddy listened to every word, clearly concentrating hard to keep up. Amy was careful to keep the conver-sation shoe- and Justin-related, rather than touching on the complications of the ballet slippers and a certain Jack Devlin, but still, it was a heck of a tale, even without those not-insignificant embellishments.

'Wha-a-ogh!' Maddy exclaimed when Amy finished. 'So, have you managed to get many back?'

'No, I most definitely have not. That's another thing,' Amy cried, jolted back into hyperanimation by the question. 'I've been useless! One and a half pairs!'

'A half.'

'That's right.'

'Come and take a closer look at my sculpture, sweet-heart.'

Amy felt Maddy's strong arm around her shoulders, gently moving her forward, towards the stiletto in the centre of the room. As they approached, the components of the piece came into sharper focus, and Amy's eyes grew huge.

'Wow,' was all she could say.

Up close, she could plainly see that the entire, beautiful piece was made up of hundreds upon hundreds of stiletto heels, all brought together with wires, glue and a bit of welding, to form one single, magnificent shoe, and encased in a mould of Perspex so that the individual heels shone, smooth and trapped within the piece, for ever. *Wow indeed*.

Together, they gazed at the sculpture, until Maddy broke the silence.

'I think we need to head on outside.'

A wall of bone-dry heat assailed them as they left the air-conditioned comfort of the studio and stepped out into the untamed garden beyond. Right there, slap-bang in the centre, was one very strange, very random thing: a massive heap of shoes.

Discarded, heel-less shoes.

As though in a trance, Amy walked towards the pile. Maddy stood still and watched. Amy walked right up to it and stopped, wide-eyed. Then, starting at the very top, on automatic pilot, she began to scan the heap, searching for familiarity.

It took her about five minutes to pinpoint one of her own pairs of shoes. Hard to miss, they were the silver Gina mules – or, at least, the remains of the silver Gina mules. They lay near the top of the pile, heel-less and ruined. For Amy, it was a scene of almost biblical destruction.

And there! Pink Manolos – bought for a song because of the smudge on the toe that had come off with a single dab of surgical spirit . . .

Oh – there! Louboutins, bought by Amy on eBay, sold by Justin on eBay two months later . . .

It went on and on. The more she looked, the more of her shoes she saw. Grey suede Pierre Cardins, those prim, schoolmistressy courts from Russell & Bromley that Justin had so appreciated, the Carvela sequined flimsy sandals that reminded her of sipping cocktails by the beach in Greece . . . they were all right there in front of her.

Her search was over.

CHAPTER TWENTY-EIGHT

Amy took a step or two back from the pile of dead shoes. Behind her, Maddy spoke.

'I don't need to ask if your shoes are in there,' she said. 'I bought in a big consignment from England not long ago. All of them were tiny, just like you. And they're all in there, somewhere.'

'So I see.'

'I'm sorry, sweetheart, this must be a real shock for you.'

'No kidding.'

Amy continued walking backwards across the lawn, retracing her steps. Then, turning abruptly, she looked at Maddy and covered her face with her hands. She was trying to stop her face splitting into a huge smile. But it was impossible.

'Amy? Are you OK?'

'Oh, I'm fine!' Amy spluttered. 'It's just so insane, so . . . so . . . *funny*!' And she began to laugh. The whole escapade suddenly seemed so unreal that there was simply no other response to be had. Maddy looked on, leaving her to it.

'You're amazing!' Amy squealed. 'Most people would call security if they had someone like me in their back garden!'

Maddy folded her arms and, grinning slightly, said, 'Don't think I'm not thinking about it, sweetheart. You go on, let it out.'

'No! Well, yes! OK! I just can't believe it – my shoes, sacrificed in the name of Art.'

'I'm truly sorry about that.'

The sight of Maddy's crestfallen face brought Amy crashing back to some semblance of normality. 'No. Don't be.' She wiped her tears of laughter away with her sleeve and walked over to Maddy, grabbing her hands. She was still out of breath. 'I've hounded down enough buyers by now to realise that they are the innocent parties in all this. It's . . . fine, really.'

'You sure?' Maddy squinted into Amy's eyes.

'No,' Amy replied truthfully, 'I'm not sure, but I'm working on it.'

'Way to go!' Maddy slapped Amy on the back, in similar style to the handshake earlier on. Before, Amy would have been sent sprawling, but she'd seen it coming, and braced with milliseconds to spare. 'Sounds like you've come a long way, haven't you?'

'Uh-huh, more than you know,' Amy answered, reaching round to rub her stinging back. 'More than you know.'

'I think this calls for a drink, don't you?'

'Are you sure you can spare the time?' Amy was

parched; dehydrated from the flight and the heat and the emotions of the day. She would have sold the shoes on her feet for a drink.

'Sure I'm sure. Come on, let's go inside the house. I'll introduce you to Charlotte; fix you some dinner, if you like. You hungry?'

She was ravenous. 'Well, kind of. Thank you so much! But, erm, I think I've already met Charlotte.'

The cool, airy hall that Amy had glimpsed earlier on gave a thoroughly misleading impression of the rest of the house, but as Amy sank onto a giant floor cushion in a sitting room so crammed with squishy chairs, throws, cushions, wall hangings, small sculptures, books on art, incense-burners, rugs, tribal masks and knobbly candles that it was impossible to see the floor, she was very glad of it. It couldn't be more of a contrast with the minimalist haven she'd shared with Justin, but it was a hundred times more homely – despite the scowling totem pole that glared disapprovingly at her from the far corner. Kicking off her shoes, she snuggled down with a bottle of beer, having been rebuffed by Maddy when she'd offered to help with dinner.

Pounding thrash metal music was coming from upstairs, causing the fringing on Amy's floor cushion to vibrate, but when Maddy had stepped into the hall and yelled upstairs for Charlotte to turn it down, the house suddenly became deafeningly quiet. The unspoken 'There, you happy now?' was loud and clear, though.

'That girl!' Maddy sighed, as she brought in a tray laden with three steaming bowls of thick fish chowder, and a plate of crusty rolls. She set the tray down on the huge Indian coffee table that dominated the middle of the room.

'That looks delicious,' said Amy, restraining herself from lunging at a bowl and sinking her face straight into it.

Maddy went back out to the hall. 'Charlotte!' she yelled. 'Dinner's on the table!'

Whatever the shouted response was, and Amy couldn't quite make it out, it definitely wasn't 'Great, Mom, just coming!' or anything vaguely close (plus the final three words were along the lines of 'ruining', 'my', and 'life') because Maddy came back into the room shaking her head.

'Well, all the more for us, I guess. Charlotte is going out.' Her face was unreadable.

'Is Charlotte all right?' Amy asked tentatively.

'Oh, sure. She's just being fourteen, with all that that entails.' Maddy sat cross-legged on a cushion, a bowl of chowder balanced on her lap. She picked up a spoon and tasted the soup, then wrinkled her nose and reached for the pepper mill.

'She had such pretty manners when she was a kid, but they'll come back, sure as anything.'

'She still is a kid,' Amy couldn't help pointing out. 'I knew nothing when I was fourteen.'

'She's a kid, yes, but she's a young woman also,' Maddy replied. 'Can you remember how confusing that was?'

'Mmm, yes, I guess. This is gorgeous, by the way.' The soup was delicious, thick and comforting and creamy. Amy savoured the first mouthful and shut her eyes for a second.

A sudden flashback hit her. 'When I was around fourteen I decided to go on strike and not speak to my mother. It was a pretty major protest, I seem to recall.'

'What were you protesting about?'

Amy giggled. 'I can't remember, but I know I felt very strongly about it at the time.'

'Really? So how long did you hold out?'

'Oh, I don't know – perhaps nearly a whole . . . day.'

'A woman of principle!' Maddy laughed, and Amy joined in. 'Well, just think of Charlotte as a younger version of yourself – only with a bit more resolve! What are you, twenty-two? Twenty-three?'

'I'll be twenty-five in three days,' Amy admitted. 'The big quarter-century's looming.' She grimaced, slathering butter on a roll and tucking in.

'Huh,' Maddy snorted, 'you wait until your next biggie's the big five-oh, then you'll have something to worry about. That's only four years away for me.'

'You're looking good on it,' Amy said. Which was true – Maddy wasn't conventionally beautiful, but she was so lively, so warm and yet strong, with her cloud of frizzy hair, mad clothes, twinkly eyes and expressive, artistic hands, that Amy loved being near her. She was a real Earth Mother.

Lucky, ungrateful Charlotte . . .

'Shall I go up and say hi to her? See if she wants to come down?' Whilst not exactly relishing the idea, none the less Amy felt compelled to try to make herself useful, and tackling Charlotte was the noblest thing she could come up with.

'That's a cute idea but, believe me, it wouldn't get you anywhere. Just leave her, she'll be all right.'

'Is she like this all the time?'

Maddy shrugged. 'Pretty much, these days. But I don't see all that much of her so I'm not a hundred per cent sure. She lives most of the year with her father in San Francisco – which was her own choice, by the way – I'm not an unfit mother or anything like that.'

'Obviously,' Amy replied emphatically, rolling her eyes. 'But you said that it was *Charlotte's* choice? You mean you actually let her choose who she wanted to live with? Why?'

'Why not?' Maddy countered. 'Charlotte's an intelligent girl, knows her own mind, and even though Vance – that's her father – and I couldn't manage to live together doesn't make him a bad person or an unfit parent either. She's just here with me for a three-week vacation right now.'

'When did she make the choice?'

'Two years ago. It was traumatic at the time – OK, let me rephrase that – it was *profoundly* traumatic and horrible at the time. I felt like I was having an arm ripped off. But, well, we got through it. Besides, San Francisco's a terrific city for souls like Charlotte – free spirits, you know? And she'll come back to me, I know that, so long as I play it right just now.'

Amy gazed into the bottom of her empty soup bowl. *Two years ago . . . traumatic at the time . . . she must have*

*been giving up her daughter around the same time my
mum died . . . a whole continent away. How many small
tragedies are played out in homes all around the world,
every single day?*

A sudden clumping of boots on stairs was accompanied by a very, very angry young voice yelling into the living room.

'Will you *ever* remember that I can't stand the stink of fish? It's disgusting! And don't you dare come to the door when you come and get me tonight or I swear I will *never* speak to you again!'

'Bye, Muffin. Take care, and have a magical evening,' Maddy called back to the black-clad vision that had appeared at the door, scowled, then slammed out within the space of about four seconds.

Maddy looked over at Amy and smiled ruefully. 'She'll be ready and waiting for me when I go to pick her up at eleven-thirty. She always is.'

'You're amazing,' Amy said, 'being so lenient with her.'

'Oh, it's not lenient,' Maddy insisted, 'but it is, I believe, appropriate, for now.'

'Fair enough,' Amy conceded. '*Appropriate* it is. You don't let me get away with much, do you?'

'Nor Charlotte either, but don't tell her that! She thinks she's in charge, and that everything I say is wrong, that I don't understand her, that I'm out of touch – all good, healthy, teenage stuff. I just get to process it all and roll with the punches, I guess.'

'Sounds exhausting.'

'It can be, but then I don't have her all year round

so I try to live in the moment when she's here, give her a good, long leash, but most of all, to be there, be there, *be there*. I think if you get that last bit right, you're doing OK. More soup?'

It was getting late. Amy washed up while Maddy went out to tidy up the studio for the evening. Amy had been blown away by Maddy's knowledge and passion about the world of sculpture, a subject that was a total mystery to her. And how she'd treated Amy's questions so kindly – *did I really ask her if her hands got sore sometimes?* And how Maddy had asked about London, and her work, deflecting Amy's mumbled embarrassment about her uncreative job with an emphatic, 'Hey, sweetheart, work is what we *do*, but it isn't necessarily who we *are*.'

Later, as they settled down with steaming mugs of coffee, Maddy turned the conversation back to shoes.

'Did you say you managed to get back only, what was it, one and a half pairs?'

'Yup, I'm a failure. It's official.'

'So what's with the half-pair?'

Amy sighed and sipped her coffee. 'How long have you got? Ballet slippers. I only got half a pair of ballet slippers.'

Maddy jolted a little.

'Not much use to your sculpture,' Amy joked, 'but they belonged to my mother. She was a ballerina, did I say? And they were the shoes she wore for her last ever professional performance. They were my most precious possessions. At least, they *were* until a couple of days ago.'

'Is that so?' said Maddy in a low voice.

'Yeah. I tracked them down to a lovely old lady called Alice in an old people's home in New York State, only when she opened the box, there was only one shoe.' She paused. Thinking of Alice made her think of Jack, and a surge of butterflies whooshed through her body.

'So the old lady gave the shoe back to you?' Maddy pressed. 'That was good of her.'

Finally letting go, Amy told Maddy everything. About Sergei, Jack and Alice, the love notes traditionally concealed in pairs of pointe shoes, the prising open of the shoe and the revelation within. When she'd finished, Maddy fell back against the plump cushions and stared at her thoughtfully.

Amy shrugged. 'I know, it's messy. But I'm over it. Well, over ever seeing that liar again.'

Maddy drained the last of her coffee. '*Au contraire*, sweetheart, sounds to me like you're a long way from being over it.'

Unused to being contradicted when it came to reminiscences about her mother, Amy shot Maddy a look, scowled, and shrugged again.

'That's definitely a Charlotte face!' Maddy laughed. 'How old did you say you were again, Amy?'

'Cheek!'

'Anyhow,' Maddy went on, her face more sombre, 'about those ballet slippers . . .'

Amy yawned. 'Can't we change the subject? Actually, I'd better think about getting back to my motel.'

'No, I'm afraid we can't. Would you mind coming back over to the studio with me?'

'Sure, of course.' Puzzled, Amy heaved herself to her feet. Her injured ankle was beginning to throb again. She was tired, but obediently she followed Maddy next door to the studio, where the halogen lights hurt her eyes when Maddy switched them on, a jarring contrast to Maddy's soothing sitting-room candles. There, in the centre, was the stiletto sculpture again, almost rude now, by night, in its thrusting sexiness, out and proud, seeming to own the entire space. Amy loved it even more second time around.

'Over here.' Maddy led her over to the workbench. 'I didn't think to mention it before, but I got rather more than I bargained for in one of the shoe boxes that arrived in the English consignment.'

No, surely not . . .

But Amy knew even before Maddy kneeled to open the bottom drawer of her workbench what she would find inside. The slipper was wrapped in the same ivory tissue paper that had protected it since the day Amy's mother had given them to her. Maddy drew the little parcel out of the drawer and handed it carefully to Amy as if it were spun from cobweb and gossamer.

'I'm so happy to be able to return this to its owner, Amy. I thought I might use it for sketching practice, actually. But there you are, now you've safely recovered *two* complete pairs of shoes on your travels!'

'Thank you.' Amy faltered. She stepped towards Maddy and gave her an awkward hug. Maddy stiffened. Plainly when it came to hugs she was out of practice these days.

'You're welcome.'

They stood for a moment, Amy unsure what to do

next. She couldn't just make her excuses and leave now, not when Maddy had been so kind, and yet . . .

'Well?' Maddy was looking at her strangely.

'Well, what?'

'Don't you want to see if there's a message in this one too? You did say that ballerinas hid letters in *pairs* of ballet shoes, didn't you?'

'Did I? I did, didn't I? Or did I?'

'You did, Amy, you did.' Maddy crossed back to the workbench and pulled a pair of pliers from a selection that was carefully hooked up above the outsized welding lamp in the corner. 'These oughta do it. Come on, let's go back into the house and you can check it out . . . Amy?'

'Yes?' The voice seemed to be coming from someone else. Amy's mind was, for the umpteenth time, in turmoil.

'Do you want to do this?'

Amy's response was as wholehearted as it was unexpected.

'Yes!'

CHAPTER TWENTY-NINE

Maddy left to pick Charlotte up, leaving Amy on the floor cushion in her sitting room, clutching the letter, with Maddy's parting words, 'I think you could use some time on your own,' echoing from the airy front hall.

Of course there had been another letter, hidden in the toe box of this shoe as well. How could there not have been? She'd already read it twice, then she'd let Maddy read it, she'd put it down, picked it up again, folded it up, unfolded it and thought long and hard about tearing it up into tiny little pieces and pretending it didn't exist.

But that would have been impossible.

And the first thing she'd said was: 'Who'd have thought that such a little shoe could contain such a lot of secrets?' Maddy had not replied.

Now, in the stillness of her sitting room, with the totem pole still glowering down at her and giving nothing away, Amy gazed around and wondered why she had had to travel halfway around the world in order to learn such a momentous fact.

Although dated October twenty-five years ago, the language, the turn of phrase, were still unmistakably Sergei's.

My darling Hannah,

Thank you, thank you, for Paris. At times when I think that I can no longer bear to leave things like this, I think of Paris, and of you, and our night there together and I feel strong, like a lion, and then weak again, because I know that it is impossible for us to be together always. I wonder if it will break me. I worry about you also, my darling. When we are not together the only thing that keeps me alive is my work, yet is it not wrong that this is also the thing that tears us apart? But this tour, South America, it will be the best one ever. The company is ready, they are magnificent, and they are performing from their hearts, which fills me with a different joy. At least, as they say, we will always have Paris, but I love you, my Hannah, I always have and I always will, and whatever life brings to us, I will always miss you. You will be in my heart for ever.

Your Sergei

Even though Amy had suspected it for days, now there could be no possible room for doubt. Her mother and Sergei had been in love – passionately in love. But now there was more.

Paris again! I wonder whether both notes refer to the same night?

As though on autopilot, Amy reached for her bag and fished out the first note, the one Alice had found in the other shoe. Then she glanced at the dates and frowned. October, twenty-five years ago. That would mean that her mother and Sergei had their night of grand Parisian passion around six years before the night of Margot Fonteyn's party, when they'd looked so cosy . . . no, correction, it must only have been five years and . . . nine months . . . before Margot Fonteyn's party, when Amy was exactly five years old . . .

'What did I TELL you about not coming to the door? Honestly, what has happened to your brain, Mom? What did you think I'd been doing in there? Huh? Jeez, I can't stand it here – I'm going upstairs! Do NOT wake me up in the morning, OK? I swear, I'm outa here if you do that!'

Amy lifted her head from the letter and listened to the thundering bootsteps on the stairs, and then waited for the inevitable slam of a bedroom door.

Good work, Charlotte. See if you can get it right off its hinges next time. Why not just enjoy the fact that you've got a mother? Trust me; you'd miss her if she wasn't around.

'You OK?' Maddy entered the sitting room and eased herself down onto a cushion with a heavy sigh. 'Charlotte appears to have had a pleasant evening.'

'Maddy, you know the guy who wrote the notes?' Too shocked for embellishment, Amy simply added, 'He's my real father.'

Maddy looked at her, opened her mouth as though to speak, but said nothing.

'I've just worked it out. I thought at first it was only an affair, but now . . .'

'Oh, Amy . . .'

'The dates match up perfectly. I'm going to be twenty-five this week, and Mum and Sergei were together in Paris twenty-five years and nine months ago!'

Maddy frowned. 'Is that so? But that's not conclusive, though, is it? Dates are never completely precise when it comes to—'

'I'm certain of it, Maddy. The more I think about it, the more pennies keep dropping. My dad's not my dad!'

Amy's face crumpled. Maddy leaped to her feet and dived for the box of tissues on the floor beside the totem pole. 'Here, quick.'

Carefully, Maddy nudged her cushion over to beside Amy's and laid a tentative, tattooed arm around her shoulders.

'I wonder whether he knew? My dad – Patrick, I mean – I wonder if he knew that I wasn't . . . you know, *his*? Oh, Maddy, you have no idea how weird that sounds. He was my dad! He brought me up, he put sticking plasters on my knees, he made chicken soup when I had a cold, he took me to the pictures, he tucked me up at night – how on earth can he not be my real dad?'

'Sounds to me like he was a pretty good father, whether he was your so-called "real" dad or not,' Maddy pointed out.

Amy was scarcely listening. 'But . . . of course! It

explains why Sergei's always gone out of his way to catch up with me whenever he's in London, why he took me to the ballet, why he takes such an interest in everything I tell him. I thought it was just because he knew my mum . . . Eeuw, but of course, he knew her a whole lot better than I . . .'

'Steady on, girl,' Maddy soothed, as a strange, dry sob escaped from Amy's lips. 'Let's try and keep this real, OK?'

Amy took a few gasping breaths. 'OK, fair enough. But I can't stop thinking about my dad! How could Mum behave like that? How could she have had an affair?'

'Things are rarely black and white, Amy,' Maddy soothed. 'I thought Vance was having an affair once. Turned out he was just working overtime so he could put a down-payment on the studio next door as a gift for me.'

Amy looked up and forced a smile. 'Really? So why on earth did you let a man like that go?'

'We decided together,' Maddy replied, her small eyes miles away. 'We saw that we had different needs, that's all. We'll always love each other, though. You know, Amy, it's pretty clear from what you've told me that your mother loved you very much indeed, didn't she?'

Amy nodded, biting her lip.

'And she and your dad . . .'

'Patrick, you mean? Or Sergei?' That little note of bitterness was still there, for both to hear.

'Patrick, of course – they were happy together?'

Amy sighed. 'Yes, I truly think they were. We were, all three of us.'

'She sounds like an amazing woman, not to have allowed what looks to me like the great love of her life to disrupt your happy childhood, and most of all . . . no, Amy!' She held her hand up sternly, as Amy tried to interrupt. 'She made Patrick happy too – how do you think she managed that?'

'By being amazing,' Amy replied without hesitation. '*Voilà!*'

'As they would say in Paris,' Amy frowned.

Maddy picked up the ballet slipper, which lay on the floor between the two cushions, turning it over and over, looking at every detail, as Amy watched.

'See,' Maddy said after a while, 'your mother hid those letters in – correct me if I'm wrong here – a place where she could be pretty certain your dad wouldn't stumble across them, didn't she? So she'd be sure he'd never be hurt by the fact that she'd kept them?'

'S'pose,' Amy agreed.

Maddy gave a little laugh. 'It's kind of cute, in a way, you know, the love letters and the ballet slippers, like two grand passions combined, isn't it?'

'Maddy, I don't think I'm quite ready to think of Mum's "grand passion" with Sergei in any sort of grown-up way. And definitely not as "cute" either. I'm sorry. It still seems sneaky. And unfair. I still can't really take it in.'

'And the only person who can tell you what actually happened is Sergei, isn't it?'

Amy winced at the thought. 'Well, I burned my boats there, that's for sure. I wrote him a note telling him I didn't want to see him ever again – that was when I just thought he'd been sleeping with my mother, you know, on a casual . . . eeek! Get these pictures out of my head, someone! But, well, whatever. It didn't cross my mind then that he might have been my . . . father.'

Maddy was silent.

'You know something?' Amy said, after a few moments.

'Not yet, sweetheart.'

'I've got his eyes.'

'You do?'

'Yes. I've got Sergei's eyes. Huh, Justin used to say I must have been fathered by a barn owl because of my big dark eyes. Mum's were green, Patrick's blue. I thought I was a throwback to a previous generation but, in fact, my eyes were staring right back at me every time I went to the Royal Opera House with Sergei.'

'Phone him, Amy.'

'Don't be daft.'

'You can't run away from this one.'

'I already have.'

'You've run away from a situation that you don't fully understand! If I were you I'd want to speak to the one person who's still alive to give you the whole story. The other two are dead!'

As soon as she'd finished her outburst an expression of sheer horror crossed Maddy's face. Amy could only stare, as Maddy clapped her hands to her cheeks and let her jaw drop open.

'I cannot believe I've just said such an insensitive thing,' she mumbled. 'Amy, forgive me, I'm so terribly sorry . . .'

'It's fine,' Amy insisted, though fresh tears were misting her eyes. 'Dead' was such a hard, cold word. 'And you're right. I need to call Sergei. I mean, I need to ring . . . my father.'

Apart from anything else, I think I need to hear him say it . . . say, 'Yes, Amy, you are my daughter.'

'Do it now,' Maddy whispered.

'Now? It's the middle of the night and my brain's spinning as though it's starring in its own horror movie! He'll only just have got back from his latest tour today. I'll ring him in the morning. I've going to have a list of questions a mile long for that man so I'll need to be fresh. Anyhow, I'll need to be getting back to the motel before they lock me out for the night.' She made to get up from the cushion.

Maddy held an arm out, preventing her. 'You'll do no such thing, Amy. You can stay here – you can borrow some of Charlotte's pyjamas. Go on, I insist. I have an underused spare room, and I just will not stand the thought of you going back to a lonely motel room after the night you've had!'

'But—'

'No buts. You're staying put. Now, I'm going to go heat some milk and take it up to Charlotte. It's a bit of a thing of ours. I call it the Neutral Zone. Most nights, right around midnight, I sit on the end of Charlotte's bed, we drink hot milk together and I find out about her day. Then the next morning it's back to the same old teenage standoff.'

'You're a great mum, Maddy,' Amy said.

'Well, believe it or not, I've got great raw material

up there to work with. So long as we keep talking. Phone him, Amy. Phone him *now*.'

Maddy slid away to the kitchen, leaving Amy alone. Sighing, she pulled her notebook and a pen out of her bag, and got to work.

She thought for a very long time.

QUESTIONS FOR SERGEI
1. What happened?
2. Why didn't you tell me?

Much later, Amy stared at the piece of paper and sighed again. It looked as though her list of questions to ask Sergei, should she ever pluck up the courage to phone him, wasn't going to be a mile long after all.

She peered blearily up at the totem pole. 'What do you think, then? Phone him now or later?'

Nothing. The four stacked faces glared impassively back at her.

'Or not at all?' she went on, hopefully.

Still nothing.

'Was that a wink? You there, number three . . .'

Sighing and rubbing her eyes, she poked a finger at the third face down on the pole. 'Come on then, give me a sign! Anything, do anything, and if you do, I'll phone him now!'

Nothing.

'OK then. I don't believe in signs anyway. Listen, you, you're not going to trick me into not phoning him just because you don't give a sign when I ask for a sign – huh, where's that phone?'

'Here, sweetheart.'

Maddy's voice from behind her almost made Amy jump out of her skin.

'You been looking for advice from the Beatles? Quite right. I do it all the time.'

'Pardon?' Amy looked quizzically at Maddy, then back at the totem pole, only more closely this time. Suddenly it was obvious. Each of the four faces, even though abstractly carved and decked out in carved feathers, long hair and warpaint, was indeed one of the Fab Four.

'That's genius,' she breathed. 'Should have guessed from the round glasses on the top one. And yes, I have been asking for advice, but only from Ringo.'

'I hope he didn't tell you to Let it Be?' Maddy smiled. She leaned over and pressed the phone into Amy's hand. 'Do it, Amy, do it now.'

'You think?' Amy was still giddy. 'OK, I will!' She punched in a number or two and then stopped. 'Hang on, what if he's mad at me?' The phone fell from her hands onto the rug.

'What if he isn't?' Maddy retorted, picking it up and handing it firmly back.

CHAPTER THIRTY

'Sergei?'

Amy's voice came out small, like a child's.

'What? Who is this? *Amy?* Is that you, Amy?'

'Yes, it's me. Did I wake you up?'

'No, not really, I have not been really asleep. Amy, it is so good to hear your voice!' There was a micro-pause; Sergei was obviously still getting his head together. 'What is the matter? Are you OK? Are you safe? Where are you?'

'No, I'm fine, Sergei.'

Relieved, Amy turned towards Maddy and gave her a thumbs-up. Thank goodness, Sergei hadn't shouted at her, or banged the phone down as soon as he'd heard her voice. It was odd, hearing Sergei asking if she was all right and knowing that his need to know was so much more than just as a concerned friend of her mum's. Maddy smiled back, before retreating towards the kitchen.

'Where are you, Amy?' he repeated.

'I'm in Miami, with a friend.'

'Ah, I am glad you are not on your own. Amy, your letter, I just got back tonight and Maria gave it to me – I was so worried.'

'Well, things have happened . . . and I've been thinking a lot since then. Sergei, you know what I have to ask, don't you?'

There was a heavy silence from the other end of the line.

'Yes, Amy, I believe I do.'

'You're my father, aren't you?'

It was almost a release, asking the question. And yet, despite the wave of calmness that engulfed her as soon as the words were out, suddenly it also felt like a betrayal of Patrick; as though with one small question she was negating his devoted years of being her parent.

No! Dad, wherever you are, it's not like that! It can't be!

'Amy,' Sergei spoke almost in a whisper, his voice full of emotion, 'I am proud to say that I am. Yes.'

Earlier, when in turbulent private moments she allowed herself to anticipate his response, she had thought she might burst into tears, or swoon like an Austen heroine, perhaps even leap to her feet and start shouting accusations, but instead she leaned back against the wall and closed her eyes.

'Wow,' she whispered.

It was all she could think of to say.

She could hear him breathing on the other end of the line, hundreds of miles away. Maddy had returned from the kitchen and stood in the doorway watching over her, poised with the box of tissues in one hand and a pan of warm milk in the other. When Amy caught her eye she raised the pan slightly and mouthed, 'You want some?' Amy nodded and Maddy melted away.

'Don't go anywhere,' Sergei said thickly. A muffled exchange of words followed. He was obviously in bed, with Lisa, his wife, explaining who was on the line.

An appalling thought struck her like a sledgehammer. *What if he hasn't told Lisa? What was I thinking, crashing into his bedroom in the middle of the night?*

She was taken aback by how much the thought troubled her. She'd always liked the sound of Lisa. Sergei's face had always glowed when he spoke of her and Amy had wondered in the past whether they might ever get a chance to meet. Now the ground rules had just been ripped up and thrown away. Lisa had gone from being the wife of her friend, to the wife of her father . . .

I've got a stepmother!

Opposite, scowling John, Paul, George and Ringo seemed unimpressed by the bombshell.

I don't want a stepmother! They're never good news in fairy tales.

'OK, Amy, I am sitting up, and Lisa has gone to make some tea.'

'Why didn't you tell me?' The question came out in a rush.

Sergei sighed. 'I wanted to, every second I was with you, but I could not.'

'Were you ashamed?' Once again, Amy's voice didn't sound like her own. The questions weren't coming out the way she expected them to either.

'Ashamed?' Sergei echoed. 'What, how could I be ashamed of you?'

'Not of me!' Amy practically shouted. 'I meant you! You, Sergei, weren't you ashamed about having an affair with my mother behind . . . behind my father's back?'

'Amy, you have got to listen to this very carefully.' It was clear that Sergei was doing his utmost to remain calm. His tone was measured, but she could hear his breathing; it was shallow, panicked, even. 'I did not deceive Patrick. Patrick was a good man.'

'But—'

'And your mother, Amy, she did not deceive Patrick either.'

'Yes she did. She . . . slept with you!' Amy was holding the phone so tightly that her fingers were beginning to throb.

'Listen, can I come to you?' Sergei asked. 'There is a long story to tell and it is time you heard it. I can be with you in the morning. I can leave now . . .'

'I should have heard it years ago!' Amy cried, torn between anger and bewilderment at what Sergei was saying.

'Perhaps,' Sergei admitted. 'But we thought it would be for the best that you were not told. Trust me, Amy, Patrick was never deceived.'

'But . . .' Amy began, but then it hit her. *Patrick was never deceived.* Her father knew! Or rather, *Patrick* knew. Patrick, who taught her to ride a bike, who made her pancakes on Sunday mornings and who painted stars on her bedroom ceiling, knew the whole time that he was not her father. A tear stung her eye. She blinked it away.

But then she found herself asking a question that had been gnawing at her from the moment she had made the discovery. 'Sergei, not being told when my parents were alive is one thing, but why didn't you tell me the truth, you know . . . recently? Now that they're both, well, not here any more?' She wanted to add, 'It's been kinda lonely, you know,' but stopped herself in time. A germ of self-preservation, born of two years of thinking herself alone in the world, was telling her that it would be a bad idea to come across as needy. She didn't want to appear as though she felt Sergei had some sort of obligation towards her.

I should have thought this through a whole lot more before picking up the phone . . .

'My dear, that is when I wanted to tell you so much! But I could not.'

'Why?'

She heard him sigh. 'Because telling you would have been an act of selfishness on my part. I grieved for you so much, knowing how lonely you must have been, having lost both of your parents, but what right did I have to come in and stir up the memories that would in all probability be the most precious things that you had left? What if you'd rejected me? Then I'd have had nothing, and your childhood memories would have been destroyed! Can you understand that?'

'Well . . .' Reluctantly, Amy had to acknowledge that he had a point. What if he had indeed steamed in after the death of her mother and announced that he was her real father? It would have been like staking a claim on her, and she knew for certain that in the rawness of her early grief, he was right: she would have rejected him. But still . . . 'Were you ever planning to tell me?'

'I hoped to, one day, although I could not imagine when the right time was going to come.'

'And you say you didn't sleep with Mum behind my father . . . Patrick's back?'

'No. I did not.'

Amy, despite her confusion, despite the seeming impossibility of his words, found, first to her surprise and then to her immense relief, that she believed him. She wanted it to be true, for one thing, but more urgently, having spent the past weeks surrounding herself with little fibs, little embellishments and little stories, she just knew that the man on the other end of the line was telling her the truth. It couldn't have been clearer if he'd been standing in front of her, strapped to a lie detector.

She knew immediately that she had to see him. Not so that she could strap him to a lie detector, but just so that she could be face to face with him, the man who, against all her expectations, had just become the point of her whole trip.

No more chasing, no more running, no more hiding behind phone wires . . .

'Can I come to you, instead?'

'Pardon?'

'You said you could come to me, but can I come to you? Could you make time tomorrow to tell me what happened?' She held her breath for his reply.

'Of course.'

Charlotte looked different the next morning, dressed in a long purple nightshirt, with her blue-black hair scraped back in a wide hairband and her face scrubbed clean. She sat blearily at the table, blinking like a baby owl at the morning light.

'Mom tells me you had a big night last night,' she said, avoiding Amy's eyes and pouring juice into a tall glass.

'Mmm, slightly,' Amy replied. 'She was very kind to me. Oh, and thanks for lending me your pyjamas.'

Charlotte shrugged, picked up the glass, and headed for the door.

'Bye, then,' Amy called after her.

'Good luck,' came the almost inaudible reply, as Charlotte made for her room.

Amy was drinking a mug of jasmine tea. Maddy, who didn't do coffee, had been working in her studio since six. She gazed around the kitchen, thinking yet again how strange life was. The path that had taken her to Miami, to Maddy's kitchen and to the discovery that Sergei was her father, had been a journey unlike any other she had ever taken before, probably unlike any she would ever take again in her lifetime. She would have to savour it, to remember it, the details: the old man at the wake; Debs and Gabriel; pregnant Sophie's swollen toes; little Harry, smoking outside the marquee; Assante; the funny clock on the wall over there with the hands going round the wrong way, the shoe sculpture . . . dumping Justin . . . Jack Devlin . . . She cupped the mug of tea in her hands and smiled slowly, shaking her head.

It's been some trip. And it's not over yet.

*   *   *

The shoe sculpture knocked her for six when she entered the studio a few minutes later. This time it was poised, aloof, like a cat stretching after a long sleep in front of a fire, with a similar hint of feline menace.

Maddy had her back to Amy. She was staring down at her workbench, contemplating a piece of barbed wire.

'I'm not very good at goodbyes,' she mumbled. 'You ready?'

'Yes,' Amy replied. 'Maddy . . . I don't know how to thank you . . .'

'Save it!' Maddy held a hand up. 'There's no need.'

Her awkwardness made Amy smile. 'Yes, there flipping well is a need! Maddy, thank you, for taking me in, for listening, for encouraging me to ring Sergei . . . my father . . .'

'I'm sure you woulda done it anyhow,' Maddy replied, twisting the barbed wire between her hands.

Amy wanted to rush over and hug the older woman but, remembering her stiffness when she'd tried the day before, she allowed her British reserve to kick in, and stayed put.

'I don't know about that. Whatever, it was really . . . great for me to be part of your family home for a night. I don't get many chances to do that sort of thing.'

Maddy glanced round, her face brightening despite herself. 'It's only a part-time family home, really.'

'Don't knock it!' Amy laughed. 'Trust me on this one, Maddy, you have created a wonderful family home. I'll never forget it. Charlotte's a lucky girl.'

Maddy stopped twisting the wire, and grinned. 'Well then, that's a nice thought for me too.'

'And thank you for putting my shoes to such good use,' Amy went on.

'You don't mean that,' Maddy countered.

'Like I said, I'm working on it.'

'You know what? I came in here last night, after you'd gone to bed. Took a long, hard look at that piece.' She jerked her head towards the stiletto sculpture. 'And I realised that I'd found a new title for it.'

'Oh?'

'Ever since you arrived, it's taken on a new identity. Like I said, I started off intending to make one very definite sort of statement, but gradually I began to see it in a different light, although still, only as an object. And then you came along and your story has given it life, the sort of life that artists dream about when they contemplate their work, so I'm going to call it *Amy's Quest*. Would that be OK?'

CHAPTER THIRTY-ONE

I'm not going to stop I'm not going to stop I'm not going to stop.

Amy had flown to JFK, picked up another hire car, and was driving past Patchogue.

With the sunroof fully open to welcome in the early evening rays, she could smell the coastal air as she drove from the airport back towards Sergei's house.

Back to my father's house. What's Russian for 'Dad'? Amy shook her head. The concept of having a new family was just a bit too fresh to sit neatly in her vocabulary.

The country-and-western music station was playing an oldie called 'I've Got Friends in Low Places' and Amy sang along, drumming her fingers on the steering wheel and wondering why on earth her spirits should be so sky-high.

Maybe I could just pop in for a moment, have a quick look down at the harbour?

But delays to her flight had robbed her of most of the day. Soon it would be dark, and Sergei was expecting her.

It was only as she turned the car into his driveway, caught sight of the house, and a gardener standing on the front lawn watering the white flower beds with a hose, a huge, shiny 4x4 Jeep parked in the driveway beside a hot little red sports car, that reality bit and her tummy flipped over. Suddenly it wasn't just 'Sergei's house' any more, the place she'd taken sanctuary in, the place from which she'd fled only a day or so before when she'd learned about his relationship with her mother. Now it was Sergei and Lisa's *home*, the place where they brought up Anna and Katya, half-sisters she was about to meet. Sisters! She was no longer an only child. The thought made her stomach somersault.

Crammed with nervous uncertainty, she reversed the car back out onto the road and parked by the kerb. Driving straight in felt far too pushy.

I have no right to be here. This isn't fair on Lisa . . .

'Amy!' the gardener called out when he spotted her. *That must be Antonio, Maria's husband.* He whipped round and waved furiously, taking the hosepipe with him and spraying water into the open top of the little sports car.

She giggled at the scene, and waved back.

After a short struggle, Antonio managed to turn the hosepipe off. He bounded down the drive towards her. 'Amy, are you well? It is lovely to meet you. Maria didn't think we would see you again!'

He opened the door and stood expectantly. Amy took a deep breath, climbed out and pecked him on the cheek. 'Hello, Antonio, how's your mother?'

'She is doing great, thank you! Maria and I are so grateful to you for helping us out.'

Amy waved the thanks away. 'It was nothing, really. I'm glad she's doing well.'

'Do you have a bag? Can I—'

'No!' she said, alarmed. 'I'll leave it in the car for the—'

'Amy!'

She whipped round. Sergei stood at the front door, stock-still. Dressed all in black, the glint of his watch on his tanned wrist, hair smoothed back – he was like a fifties' movie star. His arms lay by his sides, palms outwards, mouth slightly open. Handsome, dashing, kindly . . . yet Amy could tell in an instant he'd had little sleep over the past twenty-four hours.

She smiled at him nervously as she approached. 'You look tired.'

He walked down the steps and came towards her. 'Not any more.'

Amy had expected to cry when he hugged her, but she didn't. It was all so curious, and so interesting; a dispassionate part of her brain was in analysis over-drive, trying to absorb every single detail, as they embraced.

I'm hugging my father. Sergei Mishkov – my dad! Oh, Dad – Patrick – if you're watching, is this OK? Because it feels . . . nice . . .

Sergei pulled back and clutched her hands, looking closely at her, dark circles under his shining eyes.

They really are like mine, those eyes! If ever I had a second's doubt, well, I don't any more.

He turned to Antonio, who was standing awkwardly beside the boot of Amy's car.

'Antonio, may I introduce you properly to my daughter Amy?'

Antonio looked at her for a few moments, then nodded, half-smiling. 'Maria said it was so. Welcome, Amy.'

'Lisa and the girls are inside, waiting to meet you. Shall we?' He offered his arm, and she took it, clutching him tightly.

'Sergei, did Lisa know? Did I get you into trouble last night?'

He patted her hand. 'Yes, Lisa knew. I told Lisa about you a long time ago. She is looking forward to meeting you.'

Lisa was exactly as Amy had imagined her to be: tall, beautiful, warm, with a huge smile that even the beaming photographs around the house hadn't captured in its full glory. Her thick blonde hair tumbled over her shoulders and she moved with such grace, she could have been a dancer herself, although Sergei had once told Amy that Lisa had abandoned ballet in her teens to go to university to study modern languages. That was how they had met, eight years earlier. Lisa had been hired as an interpreter for one of Sergei's Russian ballet companies when it came to perform at the famous Carnegie Hall, and, according to Sergei, the moment she walked into the theatre he knew that he would marry her. If Lisa was struggling, she didn't show it.

'This must be strange for you,' Amy faltered, 'I'm sorry—'

'Amy,' Lisa cut in, 'I've known about you for as long as I've known Sergei, and often imagined how it would be when we eventually met. Sergei's family, as far as I was concerned, has always included you, and his happiness makes me happy too.'

Amy found it hard to take in that this poised, elegant woman could be only a few years older than herself, but as Lisa led her into the sitting room, almost unrecognisable from when Amy had last occupied it as it was now strewn with teddy bears, storybooks and a large pink model castle, she had a few moments to regain some composure. Amidst all the rubble, two small girls were fighting over a stuffed turtle.

'Anna! Katya! Poor Speedy! Put him down before he loses his head!'

The two girls ignored their mother and carried on their tug-of-war over poor Speedy.

'He's mine!'

'But I want to play with him!'

'Girls, we have a guest!'

Amy smiled ruefully to herself. *We have a guest.* Obviously Lisa was having more difficulty than she was letting on about the reality of welcoming her husband's daughter into their home. *A guest. But then, what else could she have said? 'Girls, your big half-sister's arrived!' I don't think so . . .*

But there was an honesty about Lisa that made Amy warm to her. She hadn't said she was excited about Amy's visit, or that she'd been looking forward to this day for years, or anything gushy and false that would undoubtedly just have stored up trouble for the future. She was just getting on with it.

Sergei followed them into the sitting room just as the girls' row over the turtle was drawing to a natural conclusion. There was a new person in the room. Speedy was forgotten.

Lisa stood aside to allow Sergei to make the introductions. 'Anna, Katya, this is Amy. Remember we told you about her?'

'H-hello,' Amy stammered.

The girls stood side by side and recited, 'We're-very-pleased-to-meet-you-Amy,' then stood awkwardly, glaring at their father, waiting for further instruction.

She had expected to find little moppets wearing ballet tutus, or at least snow-white broderie anglaise frocks, with ribbons in their adorable ringlets and bows on their adorable socks. She'd imagined polished red shoes, strings of beads, and award-winning levels of charm and delightful behaviour – in fact, did she even wonder, during a moment of delirium on the plane, whether they might step forward in turn and offer an adorable hand for an adorable handshake, or an adorable cheek for a little kiss?

Instead, the two little blonde girls who stood nudging each other aggressively wore dungarees, sneakers and expressions of pure mischief. Anna, aged six, was a full head taller than her sister and the image of her mother. Same enormous blue eyes, same easy, loose-limbed grace, it was hard to see any connection with Sergei – but there! The child muttered something to her sister and jerked her arm towards the castle – a movement that was him all over. Amy had to stop herself from laughing out loud.

But the little one, Katya, had the same eyes as Amy. Shocking, big dark hazel eyes set in a sweet little round face, with curly blonde hair tied in a ponytail on top of her head. Amy looked at her and thought, Yes, you two funny little things are my sisters, no doubt. Whatever comes of this, my life will never be the same again.

CHAPTER THIRTY-TWO

'Your mother was six years older than me,' Sergei began, with the first of what were to be many faraway looks in his eyes. 'I meant it when I told you a few weeks ago at the Opera House that she looked after me, that she mothered me – she was like that with everyone, always fussing around, thinking of everyone else before herself.'

Lisa was putting Anna and Katya to bed, after a raucous late supper where neither child had heeded a word their parents had said to them, preferring instead to have food fights and then noisily blame each other for the ensuing mayhem. Sergei Mishkov – adored, revered, respected world-famous choreographer – was a doting lump of putty in the company of his little girls, beaming and shrugging in turn, leaving control (such as it was) in the hands of Lisa, who battled gamely to ensure that her girls consumed more food than they ended up wearing down the fronts of their dungarees.

'Yes, I remember you telling me that,' Amy replied, curling her bare feet underneath her on the sofa and sipping the brandy Sergei had poured for her. She hadn't quite mustered up the courage to ask for a splash of Coca-cola to make it more palatable.

I hope to goodness I don't get hiccups. Now that would be embarrassing.

'I was just starting out on my ballet career; the great Hannah Powell was already a legend. I idolised her even before I met her, though I never dreamed that she would be interested in me, a Russian upstart boy, newly arrived in London with – what is the word – a *crush*? An infatuation?'

'Crushes can be fun,' Amy said absently. A picture of Jack Devlin had just flashed shamelessly across the front of her brain, making her colour a little.

'This was not fun – not at the start.' Sergei, on the opposite sofa, leaned forward and looked earnestly at Amy. 'She *consumed* me. I spent every moment of every day thinking of her.'

Amy dropped her eyes. She definitely knew what that felt like, that glorious, all-encompassing, blissful agony . . . it made her heart twang, just thinking about it.

'Mmm,' was all she said in response.

'You can perhaps imagine how I felt when, after a few months, I was chosen to partner her. I was the happiest man alive. And the luckiest. She was approaching the peak of her career then, and I felt the responsibility of what was being asked of me very keenly. I was determined that I would not let anyone down, that I would not let her down.'

'And you didn't!' Amy smiled. 'Didn't the *Daily Telegraph* once give you six stars in a review, when the maximum was meant to be five?'

He nodded. Modesty was not required. 'She made it so. She gave me wings. I would have done anything for her, Amy, anything.'

'Well . . .' Amy faltered, 'she thought the world of you . . .' The phrase sounded redundant in the face of Sergei's impassioned tribute, so she tailed off.

'Artistically, we were soul mates,' Sergei went on. 'And when we . . . became lovers . . .'

Sergei stopped and looked sideways at the flickering log fire, then, guiltily, back towards Amy, as though seeking guidance from her as to just how much she was ready to hear.

'Go on,' she breathed. 'Please.'

'Well, for me, and for your mother as well, it was the most natural, the most obvious, the simplest and yet the most complicated thing that could have happened. We could not help ourselves. It was an inevitable extension of our dancing. The intimacy between us was far, far too great, too intense for it not to have been so.'

Amy stared into the giant schooner glass that held her swirling amber puddle of brandy. She nearly said, 'So you two really loved each other, didn't you?' but the question was as unnecessary as the tissue that she had stashed up her sleeve in anticipation of a meltdown. She looked at Sergei, who was gazing into the flames. Questions came and went in her mind, formed and then evaporated.

'But it was difficult,' he said, exhaling loudly, snapping back to the present and cupping his brandy glass, swirling it as Amy had done hers. 'We could not be together so often, not least because my visas to leave the Soviet Union were strictly controlled. Our careers were beginning to take different paths and although we still partnered each other on stage whenever we were requested to do so, well, I had been noticed, Amy. People were beginning to make me offers – solo performances, lead roles, all over the world. Then I was offered the biggest dream of all – to dance with the New York City Ballet – and I had decided to defect to the USA. And all the while your mother was still wonderful, still luminous on stage . . .' He tailed off, clearly lost for the right expression.

'Your career was taking off and hers was beginning to pass its peak?' Amy offered, gently.

'Mad, isn't it?' Sergei frowned. 'The career of most dancers is so pitifully short. Of course there are exceptions, but in general, yes, what you say is so. How I raged about it!' His eyes narrowed as he remembered. 'To me your mother's dancing got better and better, so much depth, such insight, such understanding of each role, but hey, new faces, new names in lights, always a new face to draw the crowds and the headlines . . . it was so wrong!' He placed his glass on the carpet, punched the palm of his left hand with the fist of his right.

'Sergei, Mum always told me that she was ready to retire when she did, that she knew her best days were behind her and that she was ready to move on.'

But then . . . she would say that to me, wouldn't she?

Sergei shrugged, unsure. Now he looked just like Katya.

'Anyway, our last . . . night together, our last *real*

night together, was in Paris, twenty-five years ago. I remember every detail. It was only autumn, yet we could taste the early frost in the air. Still, we ate outside, warmed by love, if you will, at a pavement café behind the Champs-Elysées. Your mother wore the Russian fur Cossack hat I gave her . . .'

'I know that hat!' Amy cried. She had used it as a nest for Fluffy, her toy rabbit.

Perhaps I won't mention that to Sergei.

He smiled. 'Best to say, well, it was not so long after that night that she told me that she was . . .'

'Pregnant?'

'Quite so. Pregnant, yes.'

'Ah.'

He sighed a deep, long sigh. 'Now comes the part where I am not so proud of my history, not so sure if I did the correct thing.'

Amy tensed, wondering what was coming. She gulped some brandy – too much brandy – and coughed. It made her eyes water.

'I asked Hannah to marry me.'

'What?' Amy was stunned. The glug of brandy was still scorching a path down her throat as she stared at Sergei. 'You *proposed*?'

He nodded. 'It is true. But she turned me down. She said it was because she did not want to come to live in America, but there were other reasons, I know. In many ways she knew me better than I knew myself. You see, I was still very young and my career was – apart from Hannah – everything to me. Your mother recognised that, Amy. In fact she laughed when I asked her . . .'

'She what?'

'Well, in her eyes it was out of the question that I should begin a family life, as a husband and a father, when I still had so much dancing to do, so much to achieve. She said she would be fine, that deep down a baby was what she wanted more than anything at that time, and that distracting me from my career would break her heart.'

'And do you think that was true?' Amy coaxed the words out. Now it was she who was staring at the fire.

'Yes, Amy, I truly believe it was true. Otherwise, how could I have lived with myself for all these years? It was the right thing to do *at the time*. And yes, I would have died if I had not been able to devote myself to dancing. Hannah knew that, so she refused to marry me. Perhaps she was afraid of what I might turn into if I was not able to pursue my career. Perhaps I was too . . . but anyway, somehow we thought that we would be able to work things out, that this way we would all, including the child, be happier.'

'I see.' She didn't. Not really.

'And I asked myself almost every day whether I should have insisted, *made* her marry me. Things were different twenty-five years ago, Amy.'

Something was missing. Amy furrowed her brow at the fire. A huge, vital, beloved part of the jigsaw hadn't even been mentioned. She leaned forward, laid her empty glass on the coffee table, and looked hard at Sergei.

'Where exactly does Patrick – my dad – fit into all this?'

Sergei sighed, and shook his head. 'Patrick? He fits in at the beginning, in the middle, and at the end.'

'Ah.' His voice was so gentle; Amy gulped down another inconvenient tear. 'Go on.'

'I knew Patrick from almost the first day I met your mother. He was her best friend.'

'Best friend,' Amy echoed. 'Yes, that's what she told me too. All the time.'

'I could see he was completely in love with her – anyone could – and who could blame him? He used to make sure he travelled to the same theatres that she was performing in, would get himself a place on the set design team for almost every performance. They had a very special relationship, right from the start. You see, Patrick was *funny*; that's what he had that I didn't.'

'He had a lot of special qualities,' Amy said, a touch defensively.

'Oh, yes, of course he did! But you know, living life in a language that is not your own is tough on the personality, Amy. It flattens it. You are always thinking, thinking, thinking, and so I wave my arms about, I act the clown a little, but I never had what Patrick had. He could tell the little jokes, make her smile sometimes when I could not, or when I was too caught up in the performance that I was going to give. He was a good guy. I was jealous of that.'

'You were?'

'Sure I was! Hey, Amy, your mother and I had a wonderful love affair – *wonderful* – but I do not want you to think that in choosing Patrick she was taking second best. If there were to be any losers in all this, at that time, then it would be me.'

Amy was thinking, furiously. Thinking about dates, trying to piece it all together.

'Hannah and Patrick grew closer as her pregnancy progressed. Every day I fought with my jealousy about this. Sometimes I wanted to punch Patrick, other times I was weak with gratitude that he was there to take care of her. It was confusing for me. I was young and selfish. Yes, perhaps she turned to him in her hour of need, perhaps it was a rebound thing, but no matter, he was there. He would have gone to the end of the world for her. The fact that she was carrying my child was of no matter to him, he accepted the situation for what it was. The woman he loved – the woman *we* loved – was going to have a child and he was willing to raise that child – *you*, Amy – as his own, so that he could be with her. And I was always grateful for that. No, grateful is too small a word ... I do not have one that is big enough.'

Sergei paused, unsure of himself, and Amy inclined her head, encouraging him to go on.

'Hannah had retired from professional ballet by this time. It was becoming harder and harder to see her and then when we did see each other it was too painful, too difficult, plus she told me that – oh, how did she put it? That she wanted to free up her whole heart for Patrick and for her child. So we decided that it would be best if we did not see each other any more. She told me she wanted to set me free, that her reward would be to follow my dancing, to think of my success, and to make a new life for herself and her child.'

'I never knew the date of their wedding,' Amy cut in. It had just struck her. 'They never celebrated their anniversary. At least, I don't think they did – I was only twelve when Da— Patrick died – maybe they did, but they never told me.'

Sergei was silent.

'Did they get married before I was born?'

He nodded. 'A month or two before. A small wedding, only two neighbours as witnesses.'

'Mum used to tell me that she didn't like big weddings. She said she'd had enough of fuss and frills when she was a ballerina . . .'

. . . but she never told me that she was pregnant at her own.

'I was not invited to the wedding, for obvious reasons. In fact I did not see you at all until . . . much, much later.'

'Why not?' Again that small, child-like voice.

It took a while for Sergei to gather his thoughts. Upstairs, Lisa could be heard calling 'night-night' to Anna and Katya, the lamp in the hall was switched off, replaced by the comforting glow of tiny night lights.

'I could say that I was thinking of Hannah, or of you, or even of Patrick. But as I told you, I was selfish back then. I did not have any free time at all – I filled my world with my career at the New York City Ballet, every moment. Part of me did it to show Hannah that her faith in my dancing was not misplaced when she set me free, if you will, to pursue my dream, but if I am honest, I needed to do it for me as well. I needed to see how far I could go.'

Amy nodded. Now she was wrestling with conflicting emotions – her relief to be at last finding out the truth, and a rogue, passionate urge to plunge into an almighty sulk.

After all, whichever way we dress it up, I was still rejected . . .

Sergei fell silent. They could hear Lisa coming down the stairs. Amy was going to have to phrase her next question carefully.

'So,' she began with a jarring false brightness, 'that was it, then? I mean, you didn't have any contact until after Mum died and we started going to the ballet together? My word! You really must have been busy, Sergei!'

He seemed startled by the question.

'Oh, but I did, Amy, I did.'

CHAPTER THIRTY-THREE

'You guys OK?' Lisa had slipped in to join them. She crossed to where Sergei sat, took hold of one of his hands and gave it a squeeze, then went over to the armchair by the fire, so that the three of them formed a triangle around the thick cream rug in the middle of the room, now cleared of toys and looking more like it had done when Amy had stayed in the house alone, just two days ago. Amy could see that Lisa's first instinct would have been to curl up beside her husband on the sofa and was quietly grateful for her sensitivity in leaving a little space between the two of them.

Sergei smiled at his wife. 'I have been telling Amy about my time with her mother, and the point we parted, before the child . . . before *Amy* . . . was born.'

Lisa nodded. 'That was a tough time, wasn't it?' Then she turned to Amy. 'And you didn't know any of this at all? You poor thing!'

Amy pondered this, and frowned. 'Well, yes, maybe, but I didn't grow up thinking I needed anyone to feel sorry for me! My father – Patrick – was just that, my *father*, and I had a wonderful childhood.'

'I don't doubt that for a moment . . . oh, goodness, that wasn't what I meant!' Lisa looked flustered, glancing towards Sergei for help.

'It's OK, we know what you meant,' Sergei soothed.

'Totally,' Amy agreed, more brightly. 'And actually, it *is* nice to get some sympathy for the last few days. You can call me a poor thing all you like about those. I feel like my brain's been trapped in a high-speed blender most of the time. When I set out on this trip, I thought the purpose of it was to take some time out, track down some precious possessions that were stolen from me, and make a point to a boyfriend – now an ex-boyfriend – who needed a wake-up call.'

'A worthy quest in its own right,' Sergei pointed out.

'Especially the last part.' Lisa smiled. She made an exaggerated show of stretching, and stood up. 'You know what? I think I may just go up and have a nice long soak in the bathtub before bed. Those girls have worn me out today. Will you two be OK down here?'

Sergei caught her hand as she passed on her way to the stairs. 'There is no need for you to leave us, is there Amy?'

'Of course not!' Amy nodded furiously. But secretly she was glad, all the same. Sergei had more to tell her, there were still things that didn't add up, and try as she might to be generous, she knew she wanted to hear them alone.

*   *   *

'I did not see Hannah for five years,' Sergei admitted, after Lisa had kissed them both and retired upstairs. 'I thought that it would be best if we had no contact at all. Hannah married Patrick; she was busy making a family life with him. I did not come to see you when you were born, and for a long while I made myself believe that what I was doing was honourable: stepping aside, denying myself the chance to play a part in my daughter's life, giving you all space.'

'I think I can understand that,' Amy admitted. 'How did it make you feel?'

'Truthfully?'

She nodded.

'Truthfully, Amy, it was tough at first, but after a while it was not so bad. My life was so exciting. I was surrounded all day by creative, busy people, I was being the big star, you know, the jet-set life, the parties, the endless rehearsals and performances. Like I said to you, I threw myself into it twice as hard after Hannah and I parted. I knew when you were born, knew that I had a daughter, but . . .' Amy could tell he was wrestling with himself. Was he wondering just how much truth she could take? 'I had never seen you, Amy, never met you. It was sometimes not too hard to make myself . . . not be sad . . .'

It hurt to hear Sergei's words. But still, Amy found that her need for the truth made her ache for him to keep talking.

'I see, Sergei, I really do. Go on, please.'

'But then I met Hannah again, and everything changed.' He was staring into the fire again, his face miles away, far back in time. 'It was in New York. There was a party in honour of Margot Fonteyn, to celebrate her contribution to ballet over so many years. I knew that Hannah would be there and I was excited about that. Hannah and Margot had met on many occasions, they had a lot of respect for one another. Hannah made the trip specially for the party.'

'Was Patrick there?' Amy asked.

Sergei hesitated, and then nodded. 'Yes, he was. And so were you.'

'Me?' Amy was taken aback. 'They took me with them? I have no recollection of that whatsoever!'

'They did indeed. I . . . um . . . went to some lengths to find out whether Hannah was to be travelling alone to New York, or if she would have Patrick and you with her. I rang all of the hotels that the ballet companies use in New York and used my influence, such as I have, to try to find out where Hannah was staying and who she was staying with.'

'Crafty,' Amy murmured. 'Now, why would you do that?'

'So much time had passed. And now, here was an opportunity to spend some time with her, to catch up with her, but I knew that if Patrick was there I would have to take care not to appear pushy. This is why, when I discovered that he was in New York as well, I wrote a note which I hoped I would be able to pass to her.'

'That sounds a bit—'

'I know how it sounds!' Sergei cut in hastily. 'But I was nervous, excited, I did not want to spend an evening in the same room as Hannah and just exchange the time of day, you understand?'

'So what happened at the party?' Amy asked in a low voice.

'I was late.' Sergei got up from the sofa and crossed to the drinks cupboard, which lay along the back wall of the sitting room. He pulled out the brandy decanter and refilled Amy's glass, followed by his own. Amy did not object. 'I had to first attend a press reception for the opening of a new dance studio in Greenwich Village, which was to be given my name, and of course it ran hopelessly over its allotted time. I am afraid I got a little agitated. I was worried that I would miss Hannah. So I got a cab across town to Margot's party . . . and there she was – my Hannah!' His face shone at the recollection. 'More beautiful than ever, if that were possible.'

Amy studied his face. 'Was she with Patrick and me?'

'No, Amy. It was late. Patrick had taken you back to your hotel to put you to bed. Hannah told me that I'd missed you by about ten minutes.'

Amy reached for her glass and took another sip. The taste wasn't doing much for her, but still, she was enjoying its loosening effects.

'But she told me she had a photograph of you in her purse, if I wanted to see it.'

'And did you?'

'Of course I did! I may have been doing a good job trying to put you out of my mind for five years, but I was curious. I did not know anything about children, did not expect to feel anything much when I saw the picture but . . . well, as soon as I saw it, I saw my own eyes looking back at me.'

Amy smiled. 'I can imagine. They are similar, aren't they?'

'And your face, it was my own mother's! It was at that moment I realised that you were a part of me. It was the most amazing moment of my entire life, I promise you that, Amy. And apart from Anna and Katya, nothing else has come close since.'

'So what did you do?'

Sergei's face hardened slightly as he thought about his reply. 'I realised straight away that I wanted to see you. I was furious that I had missed you by such a small amount of time, and you were to be flying back to England early the next morning.'

'Quite the jet-setter, at five years old, wasn't I?'

'Indeed. So I asked Hannah if I could arrange to meet you properly, and Hannah was not so sure, she said that a party was no place to be discussing such things, that we had to go and – what's the expression? – work the room. Talk to other people. So I slipped her the note I had written. In it I asked her to meet me alone after the party . . .'

'Yes, I know the note,' Amy whispered.

'When I wrote it, it was just in the hope that I could have some private time with Hannah, just to talk, to catch up on old times.'

'Oh?' Amy experienced a twinge of suspicion; something about his anxiousness to explain. She studied his face.

'Amy, I promised you that Hannah was never unfaithful to Patrick, didn't I? And she was not.'

'OK. Sorry.'

Sergei raised the palms of his hands upwards. 'Apologies not necessary. I only wanted to talk to her. But as soon as I saw the photograph of you, I knew that I had a whole new reason for meeting her alone. To learn about my daughter.'

'So you met, then? After the party?'

He nodded. 'We did.'

'And what happened?' Amy's brandy glass was nearly empty again. She stared at it incredulously.

This glass must have a hole in it . . .

'At first, I was – how can I say it? – a bit of an ass. I got myself wound up and went to her with my demands, telling her that I had rights, as your father, to see you.'

'What, you *shouted* at her?'

He sighed. 'No, I did not shout. I would never shout at Hannah. But suddenly I felt that I was the one who had missed out, and that I should be allowed back in . . .' he snapped his fingers '. . . just like that!'

'Wh-what did Mum say?'

'She was very gentle with me, as usual, went into her mothering mode, you know. She told me that if I really wanted to play a part in your life, then I would have to make a commitment to you that I would visit *regularly*, so that she could make sense of my presence to you. You were so young . . .'

'Five,' Amy whispered. 'I was five.'

Sergei nodded. 'She said if I made that promise then she would not stand in my way, and she would try to make Patrick understand.'

Amy's head spun at the idea of Patrick, the man she'd always called Dad, being told to budge up and make room for Sergei's involvement. It seemed unreal, and somehow unfair. And yet . . .

'I knew straight away that I would not be able to keep such a promise.'

'You did?' Try as she might, she couldn't keep her disappointment out of her voice.

Why on earth not?

'By this time I had begun choreographing, and was about to embark on an international tour of Europe and the East. I would be travelling constantly and could not, in all honesty, commit to any schedule.'

'So you told Mum straight away, that night, that you couldn't commit to visiting regularly?'

He nodded. 'Like I said, I was selfish. I guess I thought back then that I had years and years in front of me in which to get to know you, but not to establish my repu-tation in the world of dance. So Hannah said that if that were the case, then it would be best for all of you – for all of us – if things stayed as they were.'

'With no contact?'

'No physical contact, precisely so,' Sergei concurred. 'Although from then on she kept in touch, sending me photographs, school reports, your little drawings, letters . . .'

'She did that?' Amy gasped.

'She did. With Patrick's consent, of course.'

'You had my *school reports*?'

'I did. I still do.' He smiled warmly. 'And what was with the forty-three per cent in mathematics when you were fourteen, madam? Chasing too many boys that year, were you?'

Amy grinned back. 'Probably.'

'Aha, that is what I thought. But anyway, the envelopes from Hannah kept arriving for the next seventeen years, until they suddenly stopped.'

'Two years ago,' Amy breathed.

'Precisely so.' He looked from the fire to her face, smiled weakly, then turned back to face the flames again. 'That is the main reason why I came to find you. I needed to be close to you, and not just because I was worried about you, but also because you were my link to her.' He shrugged. 'Like I said, I am selfish sometimes.'

Amy shook her head. 'Call it selfish if you like, but I loved our ballet evenings . . .'

Sergei held up a hand. 'Please, no past tense allowed! We shall have many, many more, shall we not?'

'I hope so.'

The silence that followed was long, yet companionable. So much to take in!

I wonder where I was, what I was doing, when Mum sat down and wrote to Sergei, sending photos and drawings. Was I beside her, obliviously watching TV? Or did she do it at night, when Patrick and I were asleep?

'I think that now you know the whole story, Amy.'

'Thank you for being honest, Sergei, but I do have a couple more questions.'

'Yes?'

Amy paused before asking the question that had haunted her ever since discovering the letter. 'Was my mum still in love with you? She did keep your letters. Why? Did she ever truly love my dad?'

Sergei took a deep breath. 'Amy, I have come to

understand over the course of a lifetime that Hannah and I were each other's grand passion but you and Patrick were the loves of her life.'

'Thank you,' Amy whispered. She hadn't known how much she needed to hear that.

Collecting herself, she still had one more question. 'But I still don't understand one thing. How would Mum have known that you received the letters and school reports and stuff? If you weren't in touch, I mean?'

He seemed taken aback by the question. 'Oh, but I was! Do you not remember the presents?'

'Sorry?' Amy was mystified.

'The Snow White costume, the scooter, the big teddy bear, the Russian dolls?'

Of course I remember them! Those parcels from 'overseas'!

'These were from you?'

He nodded.

'Sergei, I don't believe it! Mum told me they were from my Great-Uncle Stan, who was a sailor and travelled all over the world!'

Oh. My. Goodness. And those birthday cards . . .

'The cards were from you too, weren't they? The ones that said "Love always to Amy, from S" – that was you! There is no Great-Uncle Stan!' It was all falling into place. 'Of course! Mum always just handed me the card, never in an envelope . . .'

'Always I wrote a letter to Hannah and placed a card for you alongside.'

Suddenly Amy had a thought that made her snort with laughter.

'What is it?'

She clapped a hand over her mouth. 'Do you know what, Sergei, I'm feeling a bit sad for poor old Great-Uncle Stan all of a sudden! I'd invented quite an impressive picture of an old salty dog, battling the high seas, having adventures . . . and to think he never existed!' She chuckled. 'I think I've had too much brandy!'

Sergei laughed. He looked younger, visibly more relaxed now that his tale was told. His shoulders were less hunched, his forehead less furrowed. 'Well, I will spend the rest of my days filling the void in your life that the loss of Great-Uncle Stan has made. Will that be all right?'

'It will be better than all right, Sergei. After all, I've lost a great-uncle, and gained . . .'

Yet she couldn't say it. Thoughts of Patrick came crowding back in, and to say she had gained a father seemed like the ultimate betrayal of him. But she didn't want to hurt Sergei's feelings either.

As though reading her mind, Sergei spoke. 'Amy, I could never replace Patrick. He was more of a father to you than I ever could be. But I want you to know that I will always be here for you, and that this is your home.'

'Absolutely.' Lisa, dressed in a long, silken Oriental bathrobe, had tiptoed in and was leaning against the doorframe, listening. 'Welcome to the family, Amy.'

CHAPTER THIRTY-FOUR

From: Debs
To: Amy

Listen, Shoe-girl, it's all going tits-up at aclickaway.com without you. Flights are grounded, computers are crashing, holidaymakers are stranded but most importantly, not one single person is wearing wellington boots to work. So Jes went to the boss, batted those eyelashes and suggested a transatlantic rescue attempt and guess what? The man from Del Monte, he said yes!!!! So, babe, we're coming to get ya! See you in New York tomorrow!

   Luv

   Debs ☺

   PS. We'll stay just long enough to help you celebrate your birthday – can't have you turning THAT old without a bit of a splash, can we? Know any decent cocktail bars in the Big Apple? ☺ And does New York have any shoe shops????????

   xxxx

Amy had sat up late the previous evening, long after Sergei and Lisa had gone to bed, emailing Debbie and

Jesminder a detailed account of her adventures since she'd last been in touch, all about Maddy, and Assante, but most of all, about her talk with Sergei. She reassured them that she was fine, and that she'd see them tomorrow in New York, kind of a reward to herself for all the upheavals of the last two weeks. Writing it all down had been cathartic, it somehow made sense of everything, and when Debbie's email announcing her and Jes's surprise trip came through shortly afterwards, she'd whooped with delight, dissolved into grateful tears and slept the deepest sleep of her life.

The next morning, Amy said an emotional farewell to Sergei, Lisa, Anna, Katya, Antonio and Maria, before climbing into her hire car and heading back to New York, promising to return in the autumn for a longer stay, perhaps even for Christmas too. But she found she couldn't just ride right on by Patchogue without stopping in. That simply wasn't an option.

'I thought I'd never see you again.'

It was a sparkling Patchogue morning. Pale, clear sunshine washed over the harbour, illuminating the two people who sat side by side, dangling their legs over the harbour wall.

'I thought that too,' Amy responded.

'You left in such a hurry.'

'I had no choice. I was upset. I didn't want to spoil Alice's party.'

'That's OK. You're here now.'

Amy smiled gratefully.

'You know something, Amy?'

'Tell me.'

'I've decided I'm not going to smoke any more.'

Amy placed her arm around the boy's shoulders and gave him a squeeze.

'Good choice, Harry. Well done.'

They sat in silence for a few moments, Harry tossing pieces of shingle into the water between the smaller boats that bobbed around the edges of the clear harbour. Off to her left, Amy gazed at the shingle beach where, only days earlier, the marquee had stood, and she had danced with Jack, his arms wrapped around her body, eyes closed, safe from the world.

'You won't forget to visit Jack as well, before you leave?'

'Jack?' Amy, with a huge dramatic effort, faked a careful, pondering face. 'What, Jack Devlin? Do you think I should?'

'Sure I think so! He was trying to find out where you'd got to for a long time after you left, you know. I think he must have wanted to dance with you again, or something.'

Amy scratched her chin. 'Is that so? But, Harry, surely Jack would have found lots of nice girls to dance with after I'd gone? *Did* he?'

Amy Marsh, you are going straight to hell for this.

Harry was thinking hard. 'I'm not sure about that. Oh, wait . . . yes! You're right! He did!'

She froze.

'He danced with Miss Hallyburton.'

She unfroze.

'Did he indeed?'

Result!

'So who are you going to visit first?'

Amy thought. 'Well, as I don't know where Jack works, I'd better go and get directions from his grandmother, hadn't I?'

'You don't?' Harry seemed surprised. 'But it's just over there!' He stood up and pointed into the distance, on their right. 'See that big boatyard by the water? Painted blue? That's the place!'

Amy wanted to squeal with glee, to grab Harry's hands and dance around in jumpy, playground circles. But with superhuman effort she smothered the urge, stood up, dusted herself down and planted her hands on her hips, saying primly, 'Well, maybe I'll go there first, then. Just to be polite.'

Oh. My. Word.

The boats in the boatshed were all made of wood. She could have been in any century she chose. All around, timeless, gorgeous shapes – hulls and keels, masts and prows – were being hewn by hand, crafted into sinuous, elegant vessels that Amy knew would grace the waves for lifetimes to come.

Harry had gone back to find his mother, so Amy had walked to the boatyard alone, nerves giving way to fear, giving way to terror, the nearer she got. She'd had to pause for a while, take some deep breaths, get a grip.

Amy Marsh, come on! What would you do if you weren't afraid?

It was only around a ten-minute walk.

He'll despise me for legging it from the party without telling him.

Yet strangely, the prospect of a frosty reception emboldened her. She took a huge gulp of air, letting it out in a long, ponderous whistle.

Well then, I suppose I'll just say sorry for my behaviour, and leave.

The blue boatshed was big. Inside, she could hear people hammering things, hard, as she approached.

And then I can cry all the way back to New York.

Freshly sawn wood, that resinous, outdoorsy, evocative scent, hit her like a steamroller as she stepped further inside. It was delicious. It transported her back to days long ago, in Patrick's shed at the bottom of their little garden. He'd had a passion for carpentry, often using his skills in his set designs, and some days he practically lived out there, making boxes and shelves, bowls and candlesticks. Amy would sit on the floor and play amongst the pretty, curly wood shavings as they fell from his workbench. Happy, simple times.

But back to the present. Where was Jack? The huge shed with its enormous, sliding double doors was almost windowless, artificially lit by large, hot lamps on the ceiling. All around, men were at work. Up ladders, prone beneath hulls, kneeling against workbenches, sawing, hammering, planing, measuring, shouting instructions to one another: the clamour was intense. Amy stepped forwards, stealthily studying each man. None was him.

She was beginning to attract attention. She didn't

need to be a psychic to sense that interested glances were being shot in her direction as she moved around the shed. The heat grew more and more intense the further in she ventured; men were perspiring freely, some wore shorts, some overalls, many paused to check her out as she passed. She wished she was wearing more than just a little pink vest top, white shorts and the white sandals, as her skin prickled under the heat of the lamps and the overt scrutiny.

And then, at last, she saw him. Halfway up a ladder, facing away from her, he was planing a rail at the top edge of a graceful hull that seemed to her inexperienced eyes to be almost complete. About thirty feet long, the boat was raised on a stand and already looked as though it couldn't wait to get on the water . . .

But never mind all that. There's Jack, up a ladder, in long khaki shorts . . . with sturdy workmen's boots . . . and . . . no top on!

The muscles on his back tensed and flexed as he worked the plane back and forth across the fresh, curved wood. A glistening sheen of sweat covered his tanned skin and when she caught sight of his face in profile, she saw sheer, concentrated effort, a man at one with his craft.

She checked her watch and smiled naughtily. It was eleven-thirty.

'Diet Coke break?' she purred in her sexiest voice. '*Amy!*'

Jack whipped round, steadying himself on the ladder as the plane dropped from his grip and fell into the boat.

'Careful!' Amy cried in alarm, her hands rushing to her face. 'Sorry!'

He climbed down the ladder and stood facing her. His face was a mixture of shock, confusion and – dare she hope? – delight at the sight of her. Meanwhile his half-naked body, shiny with sweat, chest heaving with exertion, was . . . well, *distracting*, to say the least. He opened his mouth to say something, checked himself, and closed it again. Weeks passed, or maybe it was only ten seconds or so. Amy couldn't be sure.

'Wait there.'

He had to do a little sidestep to get past her, then he shot off to a locker room set off to one side, where Amy watched him towel himself down and pull on a dark grey T-shirt. When he returned he looked a lot more composed, walking purposefully towards her and shouting up at one of his workmates.

'Ed? I'm taking my break now. That all right with you?'

A bearded man who looked to be in his fifties peered down from halfway up the mast of one of the other boats, regarding Amy closely, then directing his reply at Jack: 'Sure. You kids have fun now, OK? Have him back before sundown, lady!'

They departed the shed to a growing fanfare of wolf whistles. Ignoring them, Jack took Amy's elbow and practically marched her outside. It felt nice.

'Sorry about those guys,' Jack mumbled.

'It's OK. Maybe it was you they were whistling at?'

'Funny. This way.'

They began to walk back in the direction Amy had

just come, towards the pretty part of the harbour. Amy searched her head for conversation.

'Was your America's Cup boat built in that shed?'

He seemed thrown by the question. 'What? Not a chance! That boat was, well, a little more . . . detailed. Made from fibreglass, bigger, crew of thirty-five, that kind of thing. The boats I build in there are more traditional.'

'Ah.'

He doesn't seem to be in the mood for chitchat. Can't say I blame him.

'Jack, I'm really sorry I disappeared. I found something out at your grandmother's party that upset me quite a lot, so I ran away.' It was a relief to get the apology out as early as possible, even though she hadn't meant to blurt it out quite so soon.

Jack was staring straight ahead. 'Grandma told me you'd made a discovery in the dancing shoe – which didn't make much sense to me – and that you'd seemed upset and gone outside. Then Harry told me you'd driven away. Why didn't you come in and tell me you were leaving?'

His hurt tone was one that Amy had never heard before. It made her regret her hasty departure all the more. Then, even more than that, she regretted her glib, jaunty reappearance in the boatshed, her bad attempt at small talk.

He must think I'm some sort of heartless cow! That it's all a big joke for me . . .

'There was a love letter hidden in the shoe. I discovered from it that my mother had been having an affair.

388

At least, that's what I thought I'd discovered. I have been subsequently proved wrong.'

'Ah. I see.' He scratched his head. 'Actually, no I don't. Could you run it by me again?'

'It was a love letter from Sergei, the man I'd thought was just an old friend of my mother's – remember I told you about him? He let me borrow his house? Anyhow, I put two and two together, made five, and got a bit upset. So I ran outside, fell over, twisted my ankle, hopped to the car and drove away in tears.'

'Well, I have to say that's a better explanation than some of the ones I'd been coming up with.' Now there was a definite note of sympathy in his voice.

She looked him in the eyes. 'Such as?'

'I began to figure that you must have been looking for an opportunity to get away from me, and that you saw a window of opportunity when I was in the drinks queue, made up an unusual cover story for Grandma, and went for it.'

'Jack!' Amy exclaimed. 'You can't have believed that? Not after . . . our dance, and . . . everything?'

He shrugged, but his face had definitely softened. 'Sometimes yes, sometimes no. But since I never heard from you these last couple of days, I came to the conclusion that I couldn't be too high up in your thoughts.'

They'd reached the spot where Amy and Harry had sat shooting the breeze not long before. Amy sat down in the same spot and, after a pause, Jack followed suit.

'Jack, it's been awful. Awful, and weird, and wonderful, and back to awful again, with a bit of wonderful thrown in. I have just had the most unbelievable few days.'

'Well, lucky you,' he replied, a touch reproachfully.

'Please!' She held her hands up in a gesture of surrender. 'It's a long story. Can I explain?'

'I think you'd better. And it had better be good – you heard Ed, we've got till sundown to fill! Although . . .' Then he checked himself, glancing down at his dishevelled workwear. 'Amy, do you see that building over there?' He pointed to a smart, glass-fronted brick building on the water's edge, resplendent with the Stars and Stripes flying from a tall white flagpole above its eaves.

'I see it.'

'Good. That's a boat club. Of which I have membership.'

'Oh, do you now?'

'What if I were to take you to said boat club, settle you down in the bar and provide you with a cold drink while I take a shower and change my clothes? Would you be able to give me your word of honour that you wouldn't seize the opportunity to execute another of your trademark daring escapes?'

'Hmm.' Amy pretended to ponder the suggestion, trying not to laugh, but on seeing the earnest expression on his face, she sobered up and touched his arm gently. 'Seriously, Jack, I'm done running.'

And with that, they swung themselves to their feet and walked towards the boat club.

Comfortably ensconced in the deserted boat club bar while Jack showered, Amy smiled at her two text messages:

So happy u hv a whole new family. Can't wait 2
c u & give u a hug. Times Square @ 1 pm 2moro?
Peace. Jes. ☺

Yo Sl@g. Just thinking just as well u never
jumped Sergei ☺☺☺ Hope u ok. c u 2moro.
Luv ya b@be. Deb xxxxx

Laughing, Amy was about to begin composing cheeky
replies to the texts when Jack re-emerged, scrubbed
clean, dressed in an open-necked white shirt, dark blue
jeans and his leather deck shoes. His hair was still damp
and he was rolling his sleeves up as he strode over to
her table by the big window that overlooked the harbour.
He smelled of soap and fresh cotton. Amy squirmed as
he sat down close by her side.

Hubba, and again, hubba . . .

'Now it's me who feels scruffy,' she said, tugging at
the hem of her shorts.

He looked her up and down with exaggerated concentration, his tanned brow furrowed. 'Nah, you'll do.'

She raised an eyebrow. 'Careful, a girl can get too
much flattery, you know.'

'I'll try and remember. OK, so, well, over to you, if
you don't mind?'

It was easier, opening up to Jack, since writing the
long email to Jes and Debs the night before. She found
as she spoke that she was able to explain herself far
more clearly and sensibly than the jumble of facts that
had tumbled out of her mouth when she'd given her
story to Maddy in her studio. Besides, Jack was easy to

talk to. Amy had the feeling that she was really being *listened* to; that he cared about what she said but, more importantly, that he was on her side.

'Phew,' was all he said, after she'd finished. 'You've had quite a time of it.'

'Well, it's been challenging, that's for sure,' she replied. 'I'm sorry I didn't get in touch, Jack—'

'Forget it,' he cut in. 'You were busy having your whole life turned upside down. I see that now.'

'But I thought about you such a lot!' The statement sounded odd, tinny and false, as she spoke it. But she plunged on, none the less, staring down at her white sandals, not daring to check the expression on Jack's face in case she didn't like what she found. 'I was shattered, for a while, and then I was so caught up in all the stuff that was happening, and it all seemed to happen so fast, and I knew that if I wanted to get in touch with you I'd have to ring Pleasant Shores and ask to speak to your grandmother to get your number and what on earth would I have said to her?'

Jack smiled. 'Well, from my point of view, "Tell Jack it had nothing to do with his lousy dancing" would have been a good start . . . ouch!'

Amy whacked him playfully on the leg. 'Silly me! Of course! No, but you see, I thought I'd never be coming back this way again, so I guess a subconscious part of me must have decided that it'd be better if you just thought I was some sort of vanishing nutcase, though I can't say I was thrilled with that thought.'

'Can't imagine why,' Jack mused.

'You know, it's been immense, all this. After I ran

away from the party I honestly thought that life couldn't get any worse. I had no home, no parents, no faith in Sergei, no shoes, no direction, no time to explain to you, and, and a very sore ankle . . .'

'In that order?' Jack asked tenderly, 'or did the shoes come first?'

Whoa there, big feller, sarcastic you may be, but have I just stumbled across my perfect man?

'Very good, Jack, very good.'

'And now?'

'Now?' she echoed. 'Everything's changed.' She looked at Jack. 'Absolutely everything.' He was staring at her, deep into her eyes. There was to be no running away from him this time.

CHAPTER THIRTY-FIVE

'Hold this.'

'I can't!'

'It's OK, just stay with it.'

'No! You do it, Jack. Have your . . . your steering stick back.'

'*Steering stick*? It's called a tiller, actually. Here, allow me . . .'

'I knew that. Woo-hoo! This is great!'

Amy hadn't needed much persuasion to accept Jack's offer of a sailing trip in one of his boats. Warm sunshine, a light, non-threatening breeze and slack water meant – apparently – that conditions couldn't be more perfect for messing about on the water.

She'd grabbed a sweater, baseball cap and sneakers from the car, buckled herself into a lifejacket that Jack had looked out for her, and, as he held her carefully by the hand, climbed aboard what at first viewing seemed to be no more and no less than a cute little white-painted wooden boat called *Lazybones*.

By the end of the trip, however, she had discovered

that she had in fact been crewing a Corliss 15 Daysailer, which was a hand-built sloop, mahogany-trimmed with a fir and plywood deck, a hollow Sitka spruce mast and boom for lightness and strength, stainless-steel standing rigging and a Marconi sail rig. Jack knew every inch of the elegant little faintly Italian-looking craft – he became one with it instantly – whilst Amy sat listening and trying to make herself useful.

If this boat was a shoe it'd be a white, open-toed Bruno Magli Summer Collection slingback with a three-and-a-half-inch heel, no doubt about it.

She learned how to adjust the sails, and tried hard to understand how you can move in one direction when the wind seemed to be blowing the boat in the other. Jack was a patient teacher. Amy could tell that he was making an effort to keep the nautical terms to a minimum and her heart warmed to him even more.

I may have told him my life story, but I think I'll keep the shoe references to myself for now.

'Tightening this rope will make her heel a little – that means tip over slightly. But don't worry, you won't fall out.'

He pulled some ropes and immediately the little boat tipped sideways and began to go faster in the quickening breeze. Amy held on for dear life, exhilarated, and slightly terrified, feeling more alive than she had done in ages.

'This is amazing!' she shouted. 'Won't it tip right over?'

'Never,' Jack called back stoutly. 'Impossible – keel's too heavy. That's the fin-shaped thing underneath.'

'Thank you, professor!' Amy laughed. 'Ellen MacArthur I may not be but I do know what a keel is!'

'Glad to hear it! You had me a bit worried after the "steering stick" thing!'

'I just forgot the word! I was concentrating!'

It was fabulous. The wind and the spray and the sunshine, seabirds wheeling and calling as the little boat powered along the coastline. Jack's expertise was evident even to a novice like Amy; whenever the boat's progress began to falter, or if a sail started flapping, he instinctively made little adjustments to the ropes here and there and within seconds the boat was tight as a drum again, powering confidently through the clear waters of South Bay. Yet he wore his knowledge so lightly, not making a big issue out of anything, just getting on with the business of sailing, a vision of contented concentration. Now and then he'd catch her eye and smile. And she'd smile back, and inside, she'd want to burst with happiness.

'Thank you, Jack. That was just brilliant. I'm definitely going to learn how to do that properly!'

'Really?' His face lit up. 'I can teach you, if you like?' Then it clouded over again. 'I mean . . . you did say you'd be back this way more often . . . now.'

They were walking from the harbour back to the boat club, Amy struggling unsteadily with sea legs, feeling the ground come up to meet each footstep a fraction of a second before she was ready for it, like crossing a swing bridge. She held her arms out to steady herself. Jack caught her hand. And held on to it.

'Now that I've got a home here? Yes, for sure.' It was lovely, having her hand held. Jack's hand was warm. Strong. His presence at her side was so natural and yet so exciting. Amy felt proud, and just a little bit bold.

'Good.'

'Jack?' There was something she had to do. She had to do it right now or else her whole world would come to an end.

'Yes?' They stopped walking. The boat club was only a few yards away; they were practically standing in its shadow.

'You know when I ran away from the party?'

A pause. She could hear his breathing. 'I do seem to have a vague memory of you not being around to help out at clearing-up time, yes, Amy.'

She smiled. 'Well, there was something we . . . that is, you and I . . . nearly did back then, but didn't do, in the end, wasn't there?'

They were still standing side by side, facing the entrance to the boat club. Jack kept hold of Amy's hand.

She heard his breathing stop. Her skin was prickling from head to toe.

'I believe there was, yes,' he replied eventually. His voice was taut, somehow, *waiting*.

Then they turned, as one, to face each other. Amy's nerves disappeared. She looked into Jack's eyes. Then, thinking for only the tiniest, subconscious millisecond how useful a decent pair of stilettos would be right at this moment, she stood on tiptoe, closed her eyes, and they kissed.

A long, long time later, they drew apart. Jack was

smiling. Amy felt dizzy. For a few moments she felt robbed of reason, of thought, even of balance as she swayed slightly on her first-time sailor's legs. She clutched Jack's forearms to steady herself.

'Mmm, that was nice,' she said, blushing slightly.

'Nice?' Jack echoed. 'That word again! It's going to take me quite a while to get used to this British understatement of yours!'

'Sorry!' she giggled.

'You know what?'

'Tell me.'

'It *was* nice. You were right. It was *very* nice. And I'm looking forward to doing it again, only next time without lifejackets.'

The sun was already setting over the prows and masts in the harbour as, later on, they stood close together beside Amy's little hire car, to say their farewells before Amy's long drive back to New York City.

'You're going to get into trouble,' Amy said. 'Ed told you to be back by sundown, didn't he?'

Jack shrugged. 'Ed knows I don't cut school without good reason, don't you worry. I do way more than my allocated time in that place. I get caught up in whatever it is I'm doing, lose track of time. Most of the time I'm the last man out of there.'

'I can imagine that. But you know how the saying goes: "All work and no play . . ."'

'". . . makes Jack a dull boy?" Do you know, Amy, I haven't heard that one in, oh, let's see . . . a couple of days now!'

'Sorry,' she giggled.

'Anyhow, I enjoyed . . . playing today, Amy. Will you make sure you come out to play again soon?'

'Definitely!'

They kissed again. They were getting good at it already. Reluctantly, Amy began reaching for her car keys. Part of her desperately wanted to spend the next day – positively her last one of the trip before flying home – right here with Jack in Patchogue. They'd had such a good time, he was so gorgeous, and fun, and sexy, and such a good kisser . . .

But her friends were coming to New York to meet her, and she wasn't going to miss out on seeing them for anything.

They'd stay in touch – it was up to her when she chose to come back. She knew she held all the cards, and now she had to get on with her journey. And Jack had to go back to work. But even so, knowing that it would be several months before she could even contemplate coming back to the States seemed an uncompromisingly bleak prospect.

Real life was so tedious sometimes! Aclickaway.com required her to get back to work and, distant and just a little bit empty though it seemed right now, she had to get back and pick up her London life from scratch.

Solemnly, they exchanged phone and email details.

'Oh, Amy?'

'Yes?' Amy finished tapping his details into her phone and looked up.

'If I were to say the words "Bristol pilot cutter" to you, would you have any idea what I was talking about?'

Mystified, she shook her head. 'Nope, none whatsoever. And I'm not going to embarrass myself by hazarding a guess, either, like I did with the America's Cup the other day!'

'Mmm, good call. It's a type of wooden boat – fast, light and beautiful. They were made in England for taking pilots out to larger boats so that they could steer them into harbour safely.'

'Really?' Amy frowned. She didn't exactly want another lesson about boats – not right now.

Hello? Jack? Isn't this fond farewell time? Hello?

'Yup. In those days piloting boats was a free market – whoever got to the big boat first got paid to pilot it into port, so the little boats were designed to be as fast as possible. Every outing was like an Olympic sprint.' He was getting lost in boatdom again, his eyes were miles away. 'So they designed this long keel and gaff-cutter rig, you know what?'

'Amaze me.' *And get to the point!*

'Some people say that there has never been a better sailing boat, before or since.'

'Unbelievable.' She raked her hair impatiently with her fingers.

And what has this got to do with my goodbye kiss, precisely?

Jack nodded earnestly. 'Yes, I know. Well, in September there's going to be a week-long course on how to make 'em.'

'How . . . *marvellous!*' The hint of sarcasm she'd been trying to keep out of her voice squeezed itself out at the last moment.

'It's taking place in England.'

In England? What, like, England where I'm going back to?

'No way!' Amy's eyes grew huge. 'Are you going to go? I mean, to come?'

'Well, it would be a pity to pass up an opportunity for such a unique learning experience, wouldn't you say?'

Amy threw her arms around his neck and hugged him tightly. 'And we can go out!'

Woo-hoo! Code red for new shoes! Code red for new shoes!

EPILOGUE

August, mid-morning, and Amy Marsh, who had been twenty-five for just under a month, was running through her checklist, keeping careful track of time as she didn't want to keep her friend waiting.

OK – purse, phone, Oyster Card – check.

Tube map – check.

A crisp unseasonable wind buffeted outside and droplets of rain began to patter against the window of the small North London flat she had rented all by herself, dipping for the first time ever into the small trust fund left for her by her mother and Patrick.

Umbrella – check.

Over on her coffee table, her new, second-hand laptop still displayed the email from the HR department at Debenhams. Closing the program down, and clicking the laptop shut, Amy couldn't stop from smiling. She'd been invited to interview the following week for the position of Assistant Shoe Buyer. Hardly the most glamorous of starts but Amy would learn a lot and she could be patient! Whatever happened, she was heading in the right direction and would give it her all.

Bottle of water – check.

She surveyed her reflection one last time. Her hair was growing longer; the below-the-shoulder look seemed far more grown-up than the old swingy bob she'd worn for years. She liked it.

Comb – check.

Glancing down, she caught sight of the greetings card that had accompanied Jack's five-page letter. She beamed. In the letter, he told her all about his plans to come over in two weeks' time, how much he was looking forward to seeing her, news about Alice, about his work and his sailing, finishing up with five kisses. *Five.*

Book on sailing for beginners, to read on the tube – check.

She wore jeans, tucked in to her high black Prada boots – last week's Internet find of the *century* – a cream long-sleeved cotton top and a down-filled showerproof gilet that veered defiantly more towards the functional than the sexy.

After all, she smiled to herself, *I'm not exactly on the pull.*

Fifty minutes later, she was standing in Next in Oxford Street, browsing the very last few items on the dwindling sale rail with Phyllis, Justin's mum.

'You know, Amy, I think we've missed the best of the bargains – oh, hang on!' She pulled a swirly orange, loosely crocheted giant polo neck from the far end of the rail, holding it out in triumph. 'What about this?

It's down from forty pounds to thirty-six to twenty to eleven ninety-nine – to just *three*!' She began to rummage on the underside of the garment as Amy cast around frantically for something tactful to say. The jumper was ghastly. 'Yes! It's pure new wool! Look, Amy, pure new wool for three pounds!'

'Em, Phyllis, do you know, I'm sure I've got something a bit like it at home already.'

Phyllis looked aghast. 'You have? You poor thing! It's hideous! I was going to buy it and use it as a new bed for Mrs Tompkiss. That cat's getting fussy in her old age, you know. If it's not natural fibres, she's not interested.' Shaking her head, Phyllis stuffed the evil-looking jumper under her arm and continued rummaging.

The selection was dismal. Amy knew from one sweep of the rail with her eyes that there wasn't anything there to interest her. She sighed heavily.

Phyllis broke off from her rummaging and turned to face her. 'You know, Amy, it's lovely of you to ask me out today. I've missed having you around and if you ask me, that boy of mine's got his head in the wrong place.'

'But, Phyllis, I really wanted—'

'You didn't need to do it, you know,' Phyllis went on. 'Just because we didn't make it to this silly old sale on the opening day because of . . . because of what happened, doesn't mean you had any obligation towards me, you know – much as I love seeing you again, of course. But a phone call now and again – that would have been enough. We treated you badly, Justin and I.'

'Phyllis, I *wanted* to see you. Truly!' Then Amy paused, selecting her words carefully. She didn't want

Phyllis to know that she was happier now than she had been for most of the time she'd been with Justin, but she didn't want to lie either. 'So much has changed over the last couple of months, but one thing's been brought home to me more strongly than anything else. Friends are to be cherished. That's all.'

Phyllis smiled. 'Well, I'd have to agree with you on that one, dear.'

She took Phyllis's arm. 'So, what do you say we head off to the main part of the store and check out the new season's stuff? The sale rail's a bit, well, *tired*-looking, isn't it?'

'Shall we?' Amy could tell Phyllis was tempted.

'New season, new beginnings.' Amy laughed.

'But wait!' Phyllis stopped dead in her tracks. 'You'll want to go to the shoe department, won't you? Check out the stilettos? Am I correct? Amy?'

'Well . . .' She could feel the beginnings of a blush at the base of her neck. 'Not today, no thanks.'

'Oh?' Phyllis's eyes narrowed. 'And why would that be? Mmm?'

The blush deepened with Amy's reply. 'Actually, Phyllis, I'm saving up for a pair of sailing wellies.'

SHOES AND YOU QUIZ

Shoeholics, why not take our fun quiz to see which of these shoe styles best suits your personality?

QUESTIONS:
1. On a typical night out, where do you go?
2. What kind of film do you most like to watch?
3. Where's your favourite place to go on holiday?
4. What's your favourite shop?
5. What's your favourite type of music?

Q1
A) Latest celebrity hangout where you blag your way into the VIP area and spend the night pressed up against Prince William and the blonde one out of Girls Aloud.
B) Down the local pub with your friends for a few pints and some good conversation.
C) Your favourite local restaurant for a candlelit meal washed down by a nice bottle of Pouilly-Fumé.

Q2
A) A glossy rom-com with killer outfits like *The Devil Wears Prada*.

B) Latest three-hour arthouse movie described as 'challenging' . . .

C) Classic Hollywood fare, such as *Breakfast at Tiffany's* or *High Society*.

Q3

A) Miami or Los Angeles, anywhere you can top up your tan and go shopping!

B) You love to go to far-flung places to experience the 'real' culture and hang out with the natives. Your idea of hell is a package holiday to Magaluf . . .

C) Barcelona and Paris, stylish cities with funky nightlife and beautiful architecture.

Q4

A) Exclusive shops on Bond Street or your favourite little boutique where the owner keeps the best pieces especially for you.

B) Farmer's market, stocking up on organic vegetables and home-made cakes.

C) Vintage stores or hitting the high street for the latest Marc Jacobs-inspired garments.

Q5

A) R&B. You love shaking your booty on the dance floor, and have perfected the Beyoncé wiggle!

B) Anything relaxed and chilled out like Zero 7 and Groove Armada.

C) You love the modern soul-sisters like Norah Jones or Corrine Bailey Rae, or classic Motown tracks.

MOSTLY A'S - CHRISTIAN LOUBOUTIN STILETTO

You are glam, sexy, and a little bit dangerous. Your style icon is Sarah Jessica Parker, who reportedly trained herself to walk comfortably in those killer Manolos by wearing them in her apartment with ankle weights. When she took them off she could trip down the New York sidewalks as if walking in her slippers!

MOSTLY B'S - BIRKENSTOCK SANDAL

Chilled and easy going, you take comfort and a relaxed vibe over high fashion. You like travelling and embrace new cultures and experiences (you're always the one to order the most exotic meal on the menu and drag your friends to the latest art exhibition).

MOSTLY C'S - SATIN BALLET SHOE

You like clothes that are pretty and girly, and always accessorise perfectly. Individual and trendy (you secretly like the comfort of the flattie but would never admit that's why you wear them!), you like to look good but would never dream of blindly following a trend, and prefer timeless classics to high fashion.

L243, 537/

LEABHARLANN CHONTAE LONGFOIRT
Longford County Library & Arts Services

AFP